NO ONE ELSE

The Ladies Who Brunch Book Two

HARLOW JAMES

Paperback ISBN: 9798813188039
IS Paperback: 979-8-9898908-1-1
Special Edition Paperback ISBN: 9798369605578

Cover Designer: Abigail Davies, Pink Elephant Designs
Editor: Jeanine Harrell, Indie Edits with Jeanine

To any woman who has sacrificed a part of who you are or what you
want for a man...
The problem isn't you.
It's him.
Because the right man would never expect you to sacrifice who you
are and what you want to be with him.
So he's the not the one for you.
And the one who is will love you like no one else.

*"Love has to be two people coming together and saying I want this,
even when it gets messy and hard."*

Unknown

Contents

Prologue

Amelia

Age Sixteen

"So, what do you think Mom and Dad want to talk to us about tonight?" My big brother, Nick, bounces on the edge of my bed while I sit at my desk, filling out my new planner for school.

We still have two weeks left until the beginning of my junior year, but I'm always excited for the start of the new school year. My backpack is full of brand-new notebooks, my planner is color coordinated for each subject, and I already have my outfit picked out for the first day. Plus, my braces are finally off after five painstakingly long years, my boobs decided to arrive fashionably late to the party as well but better late than never, and I finally found a mousse that can tame these wild blond curls of mine.

I feel like I've reached the other side of puberty with an air of confidence, so I'm optimistic that this year will be a turning point for me in the awkwardness I've felt most of my life growing up.

To anyone on the outside, it would appear that I have everything —parents who are still happily married, a big brother that I genuinely get along with and am close to, and good grades with high hopes of attending UCLA in two years.

But inside, I struggle with finding my purpose. I know I want to do something with my life that will make a difference, something that can help people and make the world a better place, but I haven't pinpointed what that is just yet.

My mother tells me to give it time, that I don't need to have all of the answers about my life right this second. But internally, I'm freaking out. Being a planner by nature forces me to think ahead, contemplate my future, and when I can't decide on what happens next, my anxiety flares.

Thank God I have constants in my life that I can rely on because if my foundation started to crumble, I honestly don't know what I might do.

"Maybe they want to do one more mini vacation before we go back to school," I suggest, spinning around in my seat to face him.

Nick and I are only thirteen months apart, so we've always been close. While my brother has established himself as a popular jock in school, captain of the football team, and all-around cool guy, I've struggled to fit into this world. However, he always makes sure I'm included with his friends, that people know not to mess with me, and if anyone treats me wrong, they'll hear from him. I'm sad this will be the last year we attend school together since Nick will be a senior and leave for college next summer, but that just gives us even more of a reason to enjoy more family time together while we can.

"That would be sweet. We only went camping once. Maybe they found another place with last-minute availability."

"Or maybe they're going to ditch us and take a trip just the two of them. They haven't done that in a while."

Nick and I know that our parents are not typical, especially after being married for almost twenty years. They still act like they fell in love just yesterday and could be the poster couple for what a marriage should look like. Sometimes they are too sickeningly happy, but I try to remind myself it's better if they can't keep their hands off each other than hate each other's guts.

Plenty of my friends and other kids we go to school with have parents that are divorced, and I count my blessings each night that Nick and I aren't in that same boat.

"Nick! Amelia!" my mom calls from downstairs.

"Let's go get this over with so we can eat. I'm starving." Nick leaps from my bed and races downstairs.

"When are you not hungry?" I call after him, laughing as we enter the living room, finding our parents sitting on opposite ends of the couch. Huh, that's weird. They're usually right next to each other.

"Hey, you two. Have a seat." My father directs us to sit on the loveseat opposite them, his facial expression hard to read.

"Is everything okay?" I ask as we sit down, anxiety flaring up the longer I take in their body language. My father is leaning forward, resting his forearms on his knees, and my mother is curled up into her corner of the couch, her legs tucked up under her with a box of tissues sitting on the table beside her.

"Did someone die?" my brother echoes my next thought, and then my heart begins to race even faster.

"No. No one died," my mother replies calmly, almost eerily. "But your father and I need to talk to you about something."

My father clears his throat. "We have always tried to be honest with you two," he starts, looking over at my mom.

"We know."

"Well, this is one of those moments where honesty isn't going to be easy, but it's important," my mother continues for him.

"What the heck is going on?" Nicks asks impatiently.

My parents share a look, and then my mother speaks. "Your father and I are separating."

Suddenly, the floor feels like it's giving out underneath me. "What?"

"Seriously?" Nick asks.

"Yes. For a while, anyway," my dad replies.

"Are you...are you two getting a divorce?" I whisper, not wanting to know the answer but fearful that the reality is there.

They share a look again. "We...we don't know," my mother says.

Nick shakes his head. "I'm sorry. I'm confused. You two love each other. Heck, most of the time, I have to shield my eyes when I walk into a room because you're playing tonsil hockey."

My mother begins to cry, a few tears running down her cheeks. "We do love each other, son..."

"This just doesn't make sense," I say, looking back and forth between us. "Was it all just an act then? Were you two pretending so we wouldn't suspect anything?"

"Um, well..."

"Look, it was my idea," my mother cuts my dad off. "I'm not proud of it, but we've come to a point where we can't hide it anymore. Your father is going to stay in a hotel for a while..."

Nick launches himself from the couch. "And then he'll move out for good, right? That's how it always starts."

"Nick," my mother speaks, but my brother just shakes his head and walks away, pounding his feet on the stairs as he marches up to his room and slams the door. She then looks over at me. "I'm sorry, Amelia…truly."

"I don't get it, and I know there are probably things you can't really discuss with me, but have you guys considered counseling?"

My dad nods. "Yes, but…"

"But what?" I interrupt him. "Do it. Fight for our family, damn it!" I stand up now, raising my voice at my parents, which I've rarely done before.

"Amelia, there's just things you can't possibly understand…"

"What I don't understand is why you're both willing to throw almost twenty years of your lives away, that you're willing to rip apart our family, over what?"

They remain silent.

And I can't even begin to form any other words to say.

So I spin on my heels and march up the stairs as well, feeling broken, rattled, and even more unsettled than I ever have in my entire life.

My parents might be getting a divorce, my family is being torn apart, and all I can wonder is, does anyone ever really get a happily ever after? Is it even possible to repair something that's broken?

Or are we all naive to think that love really can conquer all…

Chapter 1

Amelia

Present Day

"**G**reat. Now I want you to tell John what you want him to do to you." With a nod of my head, I encourage Melissa to voice her desires to her husband.

She takes a deep breath and then speaks. "I want him to fuck me hard with his big, thick cock, so hard that he makes me scream. I want rough sex, sweaty sex, the kind of sex that makes you melt into a puddle afterward." John's eyes go wide. "I want him to spank me, blindfold me, tie me up, and treat me like a woman he can't get enough of. And I want us to both lose control together."

Swallowing after that admission, I fight to stay in therapist mode. "That was good, but I want you to say that to him. Turn to face him." I watch her twist in place as John remains facing forward. "John, turn to your wife. Listen to her. She's trying to tell you what she needs, what she wants. How often do men wish women would just tell them what they want?" I gesture to her with my hand. "She's telling you this right now. Really listen to her." He inhales and then turns to face her, but then his eyes drop to his lap. "Look at her, John." His eyes lift reluctantly.

"John, I want you to fuck me so hard with your huge dick that I can't walk the next day. I want it so hard that I scream and wake up the neighbors. I want you to fuck me like you did before we had kids when it was just us and all we'd do is lie in bed all day and go at it like rabbits. I need it, John. I need to feel like you still want me."

He sighs. "First of all, where on earth did you learn to talk like that, Melissa? And second, that was different. We didn't have kids. We didn't work full-time jobs. We didn't have this life now, and I'm freaking exhausted by the end of the day."

Melissa slumps in her seat as her eyes shift in my direction again. "See? This is what I get in response." Then she turns back to her husband. "I'm not saying every night. And I know that having sex all day is unrealistic now." She places her hands over her chest. "I just want to feel like you want me, that you desire me, that you think about me all day and can't wait until the kids go to bed so we can be alone and you can show me that I still make you horny. Lately, I don't even know if you find me attractive anymore."

"Of course, I find you attractive," he argues. "But by the time we get in bed, I can barely keep my eyes open. Work is crazy, and the kids have so much energy I feel like I can't keep up with them and you. And please don't take this the wrong way, but you never used to want sex as much as you do now. The past few years, we've been lucky to do it once a week, sometimes once a month."

"The kids were babies. I was exhausted and felt like a stranger in this new body. But now I want it, I need it. My body is craving it,

John. I can't explain it, but the important thing is that I want it with you, my husband."

"Melissa has entered her thirties in the last few years as well, John," I interrupt to clarify something. "And it's very common for a woman's sexual desires to peak when she reaches her thirties."

"But that's where mine were in my twenties," he replies. "Now I feel like I'm a shitty husband that can't give her what she wants because my libido has sailed." He hangs his head as I see Melissa's lips tremble, so I try to defuse the situation.

"You two are in a very exhausting phase of your lives right now —raising kids, working each day, managing a house—it's a lot. And sometimes, sex can feel like just another thing you have to do. But maintaining that physical relationship is what will keep your marriage together. Remember that your children will leave one day, and the person that will still be there is your partner. Sex will help you feel connected as husband and wife and not just glorified room-mates, or this person that you share a bed with." Melissa wipes a tear from her eye. "You guys are making great progress, and I think we can get you where you want to be."

"I love you, John. You are the man I want to be with, but I need sex. And I don't want to see everything we've built together come apart because of this." Melissa reaches out for her husband's hand, and I watch his eyes well with tears as well.

Turning to her, he speaks. "I love you too. I just don't know how to muster up any more energy. I don't want our marriage to unravel either, but knowing that you're unhappy makes me feel like less of a man."

A thought occurs to me, and I'm grateful for this contact I've made in recent years. "You know, John, I have a colleague I'd like for you to speak with if you would be willing. He owns a men's health clinic, and I think you would benefit from getting your testosterone levels checked."

"What? Why would he need that?" Melissa asks.

"Well, one of John's major complaints is exhaustion, and you'd be surprised how many men have lower than normal testosterone levels and how that affects their overall energy level as well as their sex drive. I have many former clients who had their levels checked, especially after a vasectomy, started doing weekly injections, and many areas of their health, including their sex lives, changed drastically. It may be something we can look into."

Melissa turns back to her husband. "Would you be willing to do that?"

John shrugs. "At this point, it's worth a shot."

"Excellent." The timer on my phone to my left goes off, signaling the end of our session. "Okay, well, that sound means our time is up, you two. I'm very proud of what you were able to voice today. Melissa, especially. You were very honest about your feelings, and that takes a lot of courage. Shall we schedule another visit for next week? Same time?"

"Yes, Dr. St. Clair. Please," Melissa replies with a hint of desperation in her voice. The poor woman. All she wants is her husband to fuck her sideways, and she can't get what she needs. And I know John loves her—that's not the problem. I'm almost positive there's something going on internally with him that we can fix relatively quickly, and if it's not that, then I will do my best to help them figure this out.

It's the part of my job that I love because I know I can make a difference in their lives—come hell or high water, I will help them. I will help them achieve the best sex of their lives and keep their marriage together.

"Perfect. Just remember, next time we will be in my new office off Westchester." I jot down their names in my planner and then rise to see them out. As we walk to the door, I grab a card for the clinic, handing it to John. "Here you go, John. I promise these guys will help you and make you feel very comfortable talking about how you're feeling. This is individualized care, and at least with a few tests, we will have a starting point to figure out if there is something physically going on that's preventing you from being intimate with Melissa."

"I appreciate it," he says with a sigh. "This is all just overwhelming."

Resting a hand on his shoulder, I look between him and his wife. "I know, but you two took a huge leap to solve the issues going on in your marriage just by being here. A lot of couples don't have the courage to do that. That action alone tells me you want this, and my job is to help you achieve the marriage you both need and want, the kind that lasts a lifetime."

With a parting smile and a hug from Melissa, I watch my last couple of the evening leave my front yard, closing the door behind them.

"That went well," I mumble to myself before returning to their chart and making a few last-minute notes before packing up my notebooks and planners for the day so I can now shift into resting at home for the rest of the evening.

I can't wait until next week when I will no longer be holding my client sessions out of my house but finally in an office of my own. Working from home has been convenient, but now I'm itching to separate my personal and professional life. And the space I found is perfect, centrally located in LA so my clients don't have to drive out of their way for their sessions.

It's crazy to think I've been a practicing sex therapist for almost five years now since I worked my butt off in college to finish early and do my mandated internship hours, all before I turned twenty-six. But building a brand and name for myself as a licensed marriage and sex counselor has been extremely gratifying—and I love that I get to help people achieve the greatest sex of their lives with their partners.

Now if only I could find my own.

Before I continue, let me set the record straight—I, Amelia St. Clair, am no nun. I am not a virgin, nor have I had nothing but mediocre sexual experiences in my life. On the contrary, I have had some incredible sexual partners. But here's the thing—once these men learn about what I do for a living, a lot of them can't handle it. They feel like I'll be judging their every move, psychoanalyzing them during every conversation, or judging them sexually. That's why I tend to drop my specialty after we've slept together, if it ever gets that far.

It makes dating difficult. My friends say I'm quirky, and my job makes me interesting, but sadly, most men just can't handle a sexually confident, open and honest female. So, with the exception of partners back in college and a few first or second date hook-ups in the last five years, I'm still searching for my partner—the person that I can be open and honest with, that will fight for the intimacy that can only be experienced between two people with open lines of communication.

It's what I strive to give to my patients—and hopefully, one day, I'll have it myself.

I walk into my kitchen as the rumbling of my stomach leads me to the fridge. As I grab some leftovers to heat up for dinner, I open up my calendar on my phone and check to make sure that my schedule is intact for the next few days before me and my closest girlfriends leave for our trip to Hawaii.

Charlotte, one-quarter of our foursome, invited us to her parents' thirtieth-anniversary celebration in Hawaii this weekend, so we all decided to make a trip out of it. Usually, we try to do a girls' trip once a year anyway. This doesn't necessarily count as that, but Charlotte has been dreading this reunion with her parents for months, especially because of the toxic relationship she has with her mother, so all of us decided to tag along for emotional support.

Speaking as a therapist, there is no better example than those two for a mother-daughter duo that could benefit from a little couch session. Luckily, that's not my area of expertise, and I would never volunteer to do that, given our friendship, but I soon hope that Charlotte learns to put up some boundaries when it comes to her mother. No one should have to put up with negative treatment from anyone, even if they're related to you.

As the microwave dings, I grab my dinner and take a seat at the table, digging into the chicken teriyaki, brown rice, and broccoli I made last night as I keep scrolling through my calendar.

Tomorrow is my bikini wax appointment so I'm swimsuit ready, Wednesday is my next pole class, then Thursday night, the night before we leave, is my final opportunity to perfect my new office before leaving for Hawaii. The furniture is in place, and the walls have been painted. But I still have a few pictures to hang, some decor to add to the bathroom, and I want to make sure that the internet is up and running since I was having issues with it the other night after it was installed.

All of the stress will be worth it once everything's done. I just need to keep reminding myself of that to prevent an imminent panic attack from coming on.

"That's it, Amelia. Now lengthen your legs more. Cross your ankles and point your toes." Fiona, the instructor of my class, directs me to move as I spin with both legs straight but crossed around the pole, one arm beneath me gripping the pole to keep me upright, and the other outstretched above my head as I spin. "Good. Now drop your head back and breathe."

I follow her instructions, inhaling as my body struggles to stay in position, but in a good way, the way strength feels when you know it comes from within.

A few years ago, I was searching for something new and exciting to break up my monotonous life and fitness routine when Penelope, another part of our foursome, made a joke about learning how to do pole dancing like a stripper as a form of exercise. Much to her delight, I did my research and found that pole dancing is a great way to incorporate strength and cardio, so I signed up for classes and haven't stopped going since. She loves reminding me that if my therapy gig ever fails, I could now strip as a backup. Not that I'd ever do that, but as I've worked through the class, I've actually gotten pretty good—and it's made me feel more sexually confident. I guess it's just nice to know I have options if the need arises.

"Excellent. You're doing it. You're in Reverse Superman. Well done." She slow claps as she walks around me, making pride swell in my chest as a few of the other girls join her in applause. "Now, dismount when you're ready." I slow myself down and gently release my body from the pole, finding my balance again as I stand upright on my feet, while still holding onto the pole just in case. "You did great, Amelia. I know we've been working on that move for a while and you nailed it."

"Thank you. It felt amazing to finally perfect that one. I think I want to start trying the more advanced moves soon."

Fiona smiles back at me. "I think you're ready for that. That's the point of pole. It's not just about being sexy and stripping, even though a pleasant result from taking this class is that you could if you wanted to." She winks at me. "It's about making your body do things you never thought possible because you never really tried. Pushing through those doubts and fears, trusting the strength that we possess both mentally and physically is what makes this exercise so empowering."

"I agree one-hundred percent."

"We won't see you on Wednesday, right?"

I shake my head while reaching down to fetch my water bottle and black-rimmed glasses from the floor, pushing them back up my nose. "No. I'll be returning from Hawaii the night before so I know I'll be exhausted, but I'll be back the week after." I push my curly hair from my face with my towel as I wipe the sweat from my brow.

"Sounds good. Have a great time. I'm jealous. Maybe one of these days I'll make it to Hawaii."

"I've never been so I'm definitely looking forward to it."

I gather my things and walk out to my car, still dressed in my tiny, black bike shorts and green, open-neck sweater over my sports bra that I wear during class. Driving home, I think about my checklist that I need to complete before I leave for Hawaii tomorrow and the load of laundry I want to make sure is finished. Our flight doesn't leave until early in the afternoon, but I hate feeling stressed because something was left to the last minute, so making a list always helps me feel more at ease.

Cruising through my neighborhood, I soak in the family feel as I drive by houses that look similar to mine. When I decided to buy a house, I knew I wanted something I could see myself in long-term, somewhere I could raise children in the future, perhaps convince my future husband to move into one day, something that felt like the home I grew up in, full of warmth and comfort. I wanted someplace where I could build my own family like the one I grew up in.

Families stroll along the sidewalks, pushing babies in strollers or pulling children in wagons as my car whizzes past. A few are out for evening bike rides now that the sun has begun to set on this hot Southern California night, and it's finally comfortable enough to escape the air conditioning in their houses. Others are headed toward the park on the corner, where the kids can burn off some of the energy they've been storing up all day inside.

But it's not just their presence that has my chest feeling heavy, that familiar pain of longing resting there. It's their faces—smiles, obvious laughter, love, and commitment so blatantly clear that it only reminds me I haven't found my own family yet, let alone a husband.

Shaking my head, I bring myself back to the present, rerouting my mind to the tasks I must complete this evening. It's what I do when I feel myself going back to that place of failure because I haven't found my person yet—I focus on what's in front of me now, what I have to look forward to, and remind myself that the best is yet to come.

It has to be.

"Welcome back!" The high-school-aged girl behind the counter greets me as I walk into the gelato shop just a few doors down from my new office. The complex my new office is in has a row of shops, then a courtyard shaped like an upside-down U, and then another row of shops, all attached to one building—and this little gelato shop is right at the end of one of the rows on the corner.

And I'll tell you what—I was not thinking about the daily temptation I would face having gelato available to me like this when I was looking at this building for my practice. Now, based on the employee's greeting, apparently, I've been in here far too many times in the past two weeks, and they're beginning to recognize the unhealthy pattern as well.

"Hi there." I step up to the glass display case and look to see if there are any other flavors I want to try. Peering over the black frames of my glasses, I settle for the lemon flavor today, in the mood for something bright and fruity instead of decadent and chocolate. "I'll have one scoop of the lemon, please."

"Sure thing." As I wait for the girl to finish scooping my treat, a voice behind me catches my attention.

"So, I can't tell Daddy?"

A female voice responds. "Nope. This has to be our little secret."

The little boy giggles. "Okay, Grandma. I like secrets." Twisting around, I see a small boy, no older than five or six, holding the hand of the older woman beside him, the one I'm assuming is his grandma. "And I love ice cream." Suddenly, he sees me looking over at him and then takes a step toward me in line. "Do you love ice cream?"

"I do," I answer with a smile on my lips, admiring the excitement in his voice and the joy in his bright-green eyes that stand out against his jet-black hair. "But this is gelato, so it's a little different from regular ice cream, but I actually think it's better."

"What kind did you get? I'm getting the green one."

"I'm not sure you're going to like that one," the grandmother replies before I can answer. "It's pistachio."

"What's a pistachio?"

"It's a nut."

"Like peanuts?"

"Kind of, but not really."

He turns to me again, his nose scrunched up. "I don't want that then. What flavor are you getting?" he asks me again as the employee hands me my scoop of lemon gelato.

"Lemon."

His eyes light up. "Oh, lemon! I want that too!"

"Are you sure? It's kind of sour," I clarify.

"Like sour gummy worms?"

I chuckle and reply, "Yes."

"Then, yes, I want that."

I pay for my scoop and step out of the way, admiring the boy and his grandma as they order. Little kids are always a pleasure to watch. They have so much optimism in their eyes, their view of the world is less jaded than those of adults, and most of them have yet to experience disappointment and hurt that affects them through the rest of their lives. They simply find joy in the little things, exist without thinking about consequences, and know how to make everything fun.

I can't wait to have kids of my own someday and give them a childhood like I had—well, until it felt like my world stopped spinning.

"Well, I hope you enjoy your gelato," I say to the boy and his grandma as I pass them on the way out the door.

"You too!" He waves at me, and with a smile on my face, I exit the shop and head back down the sidewalk to my office.

Walking up to the mahogany framed door with frosted glass, I feel a sense of accomplishment come over me. The green curtains I hung to cover the glass on the inside only serve to provide the much-needed privacy that my office requires, and the small flower beds on the sides of the door give an even more welcoming feel with the bright-yellow and pink blooms catching your eye the moment you turn the corner. The tan stucco makes the door pop, and once my sign is in place above the door on the eaves of the building, the entire look will come together, offering a comfortable and welcoming place where people can feel free to be honest, and work on their relationships and intimacy.

"Oh, this is just perfect."

A deep, masculine voice with a hint of amusement catches me off guard from behind, causing me to twist to find the owner. And when I do, I almost drop my container of gelato on the floor, which is just as well because with how hot this man is, he could melt it on the spot anyway.

"Um, hello. Can I help you?"

He crosses his arms over his broad chest as a smirk plays on his lips. Sandy-blond hair sticks up on his head, and dark-green eyes stare back at me as I struggle to find words in his proximity. "Nope. Just you being here will help me."

My brow furrows. "I'm sorry. I don't understand…"

"I take it this is your office?" he asks, pointing to the door I'm standing in front of. My keys are in my hand since I was juggling my purse and gelato to try to open the door.

"Yes. It is. And you are?"

"Ethan Fuller, your new neighbor." He juts his thumb over his shoulder, and the outline of his muscular arms becomes apparent under the fabric of his suit jacket. The man can definitely wear a suit, no doubt about that. But I'd have to say it's that smirk of his that's the real killer.

"Oh!" I bend down to set my purse on the ground, rising just in time to see him checking out my ass. Hesitantly, I take a step toward him and extend my hand. "It's so nice to meet you. I'm Amelia St. Clair."

"Dr. St. Clair," he replies as if he's correcting me, still grinning from ear to ear.

I turn back around to face my door, realizing he must have read the name of my practice from there. "Oh, yes. I'm a licensed therapist specializing in marriage and relationship counseling."

"I know. As I said, this couldn't be more perfect." He releases my hand and runs a hand along his jaw, scratching through the scruff there, creating a sound that might as well be like a guitar pick strumming my clit, because I instantly feel a bolt of arousal between my legs.

Where the hell did this man come from? I mean, it's been a long time since I've physically had a reaction like this to a man at first sight. He's tall, handsome, and confident, which is apparent in his demeanor and his words, and right now, he's staring at me like he just won some sort of prize.

I don't know if I should be offended or count my lucky stars.

"Care to elaborate?" I finally ask. I mean, I guess we would have met eventually when I returned from Hawaii next week, but it's nice to at least know the person that purchased the other empty space in this complex. I remember the owner telling me she was grateful to fill both units within a short time of each other.

"Well, Dr. St. Clair," he starts mockingly, which has me retreating slightly. "While you seem to be someone who believes in the sanctity of marriage and repairing things that are most likely broken to begin with, I prefer ripping apart the pieces, dividing up things equally, and encouraging people to move on with their lives. And now that I know the very people who are looking for those services will literally be right across the complex from me, you've just made my job ten times easier."

"I'm sorry," I stutter as my heart races. "What the heck is that supposed to mean?"

He leans closer to me as a whiff of his cologne penetrates my senses. And instead of leaning back like I should, I close the gap between us even further, so close that I can see every fleck of gold in his eyes as I narrow my eyes back at him. And then my vagina really becomes feral as his proximity makes me wonder what the weight of his body would feel like on top of me, his solid frame pushing me down into a bed…

Jesus, Amelia. I know it's been six months since you've been laid, but this guy is acting like an ass, and you need to focus on figuring out why he's so damn pleased to be your new neighbor.

But he remains silent, so I push him further. "I believe I asked you a question, Ethan Fuller." He bites his bottom lip, holding back his pleasure at my flustered state, but still doesn't speak. "Who the heck do you think you are?"

And finally, his lips part, and he says the words that steal all of the oxygen from my lungs, deflating years of dreams becoming a reality in an instant. "I'm a divorce lawyer, and you just made me rich."

Chapter 2

Amelia

"You look like you stayed up all night partying," Penelope says to me as we walk through the airport after going through security.

"Gee, thanks." She's not wrong, though. While she looks like a walking doppelgänger for Cindy Crawford, I look like Weird Al's long-lost cousin who slept with their finger in a light socket. My hair is unruly today from how hard I tossed and turned on my pillow.

"Seriously? Everything okay?"

"I didn't sleep well," I reply, and it's the truth, just not the entire truth.

Running into Ethan last night kept replaying through my head all evening as I showered and finished packing for the trip. A mixture of dread and fear filtered through my mind along with what may happen now that he's opening up his practice across the courtyard from mine.

Why on earth would the owner of the building agree to have a marriage counselor and a divorce attorney that close to each other? That's like letting Walmart and Target build stores right across the street from each other.

Um, Amelia, are you stupid? Target and Walmart literally do that. It's good business.

Ugh, shut up, subconscious. You're supposed to be on my side.

But honestly, how on earth will this be a good thing? I've built a name for myself in Los Angeles by helping people save their marriages or heal after sexual trauma. I've waited years to finally open up my own office and build a practice that I can be proud of. And now, before I can officially open the doors, one of the worst possible scenarios has happened—the antithesis of what I stand for will be a mere few feet away from my door, inviting those looking for a way out instead of wanting to fight for love.

The possibilities are endless for how this might go.

My mind just kept spinning until almost two in the morning, and by the time my alarm went off at six, I felt like I had run a marathon in my sleep. I'm not going to lie; I was actually relieved this morning when I woke up to know that I wouldn't have to face him for a few days. It would give me time to get my head on straight.

"Okay. I have my snacks and my water, so now I feel like I can relax." Noelle walks over to where Penelope and I found seats outside of our gate as we wait to board our flight. She brushes her light-brown hair over her shoulder as she offers me a piece of her sour candy. "You want one?"

"No, thank you."

"Something is bothering Amelia Be Delia, but she's not talking," Penelope says as she leans forward in her seat, glancing up at Noelle.

Noelle takes the chair next to me. "What's going on?" Her eyes dip up and down my body. "On second thought, yeah, you don't look like you right now."

"And how do I normally look?"

"Honestly? A little uptight, always put together, confident but in a classy way," Penelope answers for her.

I'm so unsettled that I can't even act offended. "I don't disagree. I like feeling put together."

"But you look frazzled, especially your hair," Noelle says. "You sure you don't want to talk about it?"

I shake my head. "No. Not yet."

Penelope and Noelle share a look across me, but I continue to stare straight forward, hoping that I can fall asleep on the flight and wake up more relaxed when we land in Hawaii.

"Well, as soon as we land, we'll get some drinks, and hopefully, that will loosen you up enough to spill the deets." Penelope rubs my shoulder.

"I can't wait to relax a bit by the pool. I loaded my Kindle with so many books to make sure I'd have something to read," Noelle adds.

Penelope's brows draw together. "Don't you ever get tired of having your nose stuck in a book?"

"Nope. Reading is such an escape, and with romance, you're guaranteed a happily ever after. The tension is so exciting, the build up to the moment where they give in makes your heart race, and then when the shit hits the fan, it's like you can't read fast enough to find out if they get back together."

Penelope and I scoff at the same time. "Nothing, even a happily ever after, is guaranteed in real life, Noelle. Sorry to break it to you."

Noelle sighs as she slumps in her chair. "That may be true, but I refuse to believe that will happen to us. I know the right men are out there for us. And heck, they may be in our lives at this very moment," she states assuringly.

I scoff again as I stand. "I need to use the restroom. Watch my bag?" I say as Noelle nods, and I walk away, wanting to possess the optimism my friend has. And normally, I do. But right now? I'm not sure of anything except how off-kilter and defeated I feel.

"Ah!" Charlotte power walks across the hotel lobby, screeching like a wild bird as she greets each of us with a hug. "You're here!"

"We made it. Barely," Penelope says as she takes off her sunglasses and rolls her eyes. "I had a child behind me on the plane that kept kicking my seat. If I didn't respect the sacrifice his mother made for him to be alive, I would have pulled his oxygen mask down from the ceiling and used it on him like a muzzle."

Noelle smacks her. "He wasn't that bad."

"Easy for you to say. You were too engrossed in a book with your earplugs in to notice."

"New author?" Charlotte asks Noelle, whose day job is a literary agent specializing in the romance genre. The girl is always reading a new book, and I think it's where her romantic nature comes from. As soon as we boarded the plane, she popped her earbuds in and ignored us for the rest of the almost six-hour flight.

"Yes. And a very promising one at that. I haven't had a book capture me like this one in a long time. I'll tell you about it later."

"You and your dirty books," Penelope snickers with a teasing grin.

"Hey. As Rachel from *Friends* would say, I am not ashamed of my books. There is nothing wrong with a woman enjoying a little erotica."

"Oh, I'm not arguing with you. I just think it's impressive that you can read that smut and keep a straight face on the plane."

Noelle smiles proudly. "Years of practice, my friend."

As I slide up behind them, Charlotte takes in my appearance and starts asking the same questions I've been dodging since Noelle and Penelope picked me up on the way to the airport. "Hey, Amelia. You okay?"

"Oh, yes. I'm…fine," I stutter, trying to hold together my nerves. I thought arriving here would put me more at ease, but my social anxiety is starting to rear its ugly head.

"Something happened to our little Amelia Be Delia, but she insists everything is fine. Perhaps you can get her to speak up once we get some alcohol in her system," Penelope explains.

Charlotte shifts her sight back over to me with a furrow of her brow. "Okay, well, let's get you checked in first. I know you all must be hungry."

"Starving and in need of alcohol," Penelope replies as Charlotte leads us over to the concierge's desk to receive our keys.

After we all go to our rooms and get settled in, we meet down in one of the restaurants for a late dinner.

"So, how have things been going so far?" Noelle asks Charlotte after we place our orders and receive our first round of drinks. I take a large sip of mine and appreciate the burn of the alcohol as it slides down my throat. After unpacking and enjoying the view from my room, I instantly felt more at ease.

Ethan isn't here, and I don't have to worry about him popping up anywhere. This is exactly what I needed, so now I want to enjoy my mini vacation. How I'm going to handle him next week is something I don't need to concern myself with just yet.

"Um, interesting. My mother has been up to her usual shenanigans, and I've just been trying to let her comments roll off my back, although it's getting harder and harder to do when she keeps bringing Damien into the mix. The poor guy—he probably thinks my mother is going to try marrying us in our sleep."

Charlotte agreed to pretend to be in a relationship with her childhood enemy, Damien, to help appease her mother, who is always pressuring her to find a husband, as I mentioned earlier. Damien also needed her to help him impress his boss. Six weeks later, and they're both clearly struggling with their feelings, but I don't want to be the one to point that out unless necessary. Part of being a good therapist is getting the patient to realize things for themselves anyway.

Noelle continues questioning her. "Well, has he told you that it bothers him?"

Charlotte shakes her head. "No. He's actually been really great. It's crazy, but having him here makes me feel like I can handle all of this better, like I'm not handling it alone for once. In fact, he did something last weekend that really surprised me."

"What did he do?" Noelle asks.

"Well, I had something happen to me that's never happened before. I—I started my period in my sleep..."

"You've never started in your sleep?" Penelope asks incredulously.

"No, I have, but not while staying the night at a guy's place." We all cringe.

"Oh, God. How embarrassing," Noelle interjects.

Penelope chimes in too. "I mean, yes, that's unfortunate, but periods are a part of life. Please tell me he didn't freak out."

"No, I was the one who freaked out. I ruined his sheets and locked myself in the bathroom to shower. And then when I emerged, I ran off."

"So, what did Damien do?"

Charlotte smiles adoringly. "Well, he assured me it wasn't that big of a deal. But then I left in a hurry, and it kind of left things awkward between us. I was sure he'd want some space, that maybe what happened was a little too real for our fake relationship. But then he showed up later that afternoon with tampons, my favorite meal from Tony's, ice cream and Dove chocolates, and Matthew McConaughey rom-com movies."

"Oh my God," Noelle squeals, clutching her hands together under her chin. "That is totally something that one of the men in my books would do."

"Yeah, it sounds too good to be true," Penelope teases.

"I thought the same thing. But he was so sweet and just held me and fed me chocolates while we watched movies." She sighs, slinking back into her chair as I take another sip of my drink. "I'm so screwed."

I take this as my opportunity to speak up. "You finally experienced some intimacy with him," I say. "And how did it make you feel?"

"Uh oh, she's going into therapist mode," Penelope chides under her breath.

"Stop it," Noelle shoots across the table at Penelope before directing her eyes back to Charlotte. "Answer the question, Char."

Charlotte takes a deep breath. "It made me feel like I want this to be real. I was lying there with him in my old sweats, no makeup, and hair tossed up, and he stared at me like I was the most beautiful thing on the planet. He's nothing like I thought he would be, but I'm so scared that I'm the only one that feels this deeply. And last night, he shut down during dinner with everyone, like he became someone else for a little while—silent, retreating, barely saying two words to me. I wonder if all the pressure of playing this part is getting to him."

"His actions dictate that you're not the only one with feelings," I reply. "But you need to talk to him about it, Char."

"I know, but part of me just wants to wait until this weekend is over, when we can breathe a little. Besides, my aunt said something to me yesterday that still has my head spinning."

"What did she say?" I continue to question her. I try to avoid going into therapist mode with my friends for the same reason I avoid it with men, but these girls need a little pushing sometimes, and I'm hoping this trip will help Charlotte break through these boundary issues with her mother.

The fake relationship she started with Damien had disaster written all over it to begin with. But as her friend, I've tried to remain supportive, especially because it's clear as day that she's developing feelings for him, as she so eloquently admitted just a few moments ago.

Charlotte answers. "She said that the way my mother is with me is the same way their mother was with them—constantly making underhanded comments about their life choices and love lives, pressuring them to get married and watch their figures so they could snag a man. I never knew this. and I feel like it explains so much."

And all I can do is nod. "It does. But just because that's how your mother was raised does not mean that she has to perpetuate that cycle."

"Spoken like a true therapist," Penelope interjects before turning toward Charlotte. "Look, I know you don't want to make a big scene because it's your parents' anniversary and all that, but you need to stand up for yourself, Char. Your mother has beaten you up from the inside out long enough. And as your friend, I'm tired of seeing you put up with it, and it's getting harder to keep listening to it."

Charlotte grows defensive, and suddenly, the energy at the table shifts. "Well, I'm sorry if it's irritating for you, but this entire thing is complicated, Penelope."

"Hey, I'm sure she didn't mean it like that, Char," Noelle interrupts.

"No, I did," Penelope counters, holding a hand up to our friend. "This bullshit has gone on long enough. And it's obvious that you have feelings for Damien, so you need to man up and tell the man what you want before you chicken out about that too."

Standing from her chair, Charlotte stares down at our friend, confused, angry, and hurt. "You know, just because you don't have a relationship with your mother doesn't mean you get to pass judgment on mine, Penelope," she says. "And second, when's the last time you actually let a guy in longer than it took for him to give you an orgasm?" Penelope narrows her eyes at her. "Exactly. In fact, I know you avoid commitment because you're too fucking scared to let people in. You don't even let your parents into your life. So, don't judge me for how I'm dealing with mine." Charlotte looks over at Noelle and me, and I know my eyes are wide as I take in what's happening. "Sorry, girls, but I think I'm done for tonight," she says before draining the rest of her drink and walking away.

"Charlotte! Come back," Noelle calls after her, but she keeps retreating, leaving the three of us alone and silent.

"Fuck this." Penelope tips back the rest of her glass and stands. "Sorry, girls, but she needed to hear that."

"You could have been nicer about it," Noelle counters as she stands as well, so I follow suit.

"No. Charlotte doesn't need nice right now, she needs tough love. And I'm okay with being the friend who gives it to her. Sometimes that's what we have to do for each other—not just smile and nod along, but tell the truth. She needs to stand up for herself."

"She will," I interject. "She has to reach her breaking point."

"And have you reached yours, Amelia? What's going on with you?"

I take a deep breath and then stand up straighter. "I'll tell you when I'm ready, okay? But not right now. Not after what happened tonight and everything else going on this weekend, all right?"

Penelope and Noelle both nod. "Okay. That's fair," Penelope says calmly. "But I'm going to get another drink and then go back to my room and get some sleep. I'm exhausted."

"I think I'm going to check out the pool and read for a bit," Noelle says.

"I'm going for a walk and then pass out for the night as well. See you in the morning." We all part ways as I walk in the direction that Charlotte went, hoping to find her so I can check on her.

It's rare, but sometimes the four of us have our little tiffs, and we need some time to breathe before solving them. I love these women like the sisters I never had, but even sisters fight.

Sitting with her knees tucked into her chest on the beach, I slowly walk up to Charlotte so I don't frighten her. "Hey," I say as she looks up over her shoulder to find me standing behind her. "Mind if I sit?"

Turning back to stare out over the water, she shrugs. "I guess."

I take a seat in a similar position next to her on the cold sand and sigh. "Penelope and you will get past this."

"I don't know, Amelia. She was pretty clear about how she feels."

"Well, like you said, she has her own issues she hasn't dealt with and is most likely projecting them on you. We all have things we like to brush under the rug." Speaking from experience, Amelia?

She turns to me. "What's going on? The girls said you aren't yourself right now."

A heavy sigh leaves my lips again, but maybe talking to Charlotte about it will help me process. "I sort of ran into a problem with my new office this week."

"Oh shit." She reaches up to rub my shoulder. "What's going on? I thought everything was good to go when we return from here…"

I scoff. "Well, it was going well, swimmingly, really. But last night I met the guy who bought the other space in the same complex as my office."

"And?"

"And he's a divorce attorney."

Charlotte's eyes go wide. "Oh, shit."

"Yeah. How on earth am I supposed to keep couples focused on repairing their marriages when just around the corner will be a reminder of the other solution to their problems?"

Charlotte rubs my shoulder. "Maybe it won't be as bad as you think it is. Maybe you'll barely see him. Maybe you two could team up, and he might actually help you with clients. He might be working with a couple and recommend they seek counseling before going through with their divorce," she suggests optimistically.

"Ha. As much as I love you for trying to convince me of that, based on our first encounter, I'm going to say the chances of that happening are a big, fat no. He basically told me that I've already made him richer because my clients are going to walk right across the complex to him when they realize that what I do is pointless."

Charlotte's mouth drops open. "Oh, Jesus."

"All I want to do is help people, Charlotte. It's important to me given what I went through growing up."

"You do help people, Amelia. This guy being there isn't going to change that."

I sigh. "You know what the worst part about him is?"

"What?"

"He's hot as hell." Just thinking back to yesterday and that curl of his lips, his tousled hair, and those dark-green eyes has my heart racing again. He looked refined, professional, sexy, and dirty all at the same time.

Charlotte laughs. "Wow. So you really do have yourself a little problem to deal with back home, don't you?"

I nod. "See, Char? We all have things in our lives that cause us to make decisions we're not necessarily proud of, or react to situations that we don't know how to deal with, even me, the therapist." I point a finger to my chest.

"Well, if it makes you feel any better, you're a sex therapist, so as long as you didn't sleep with him, I think you get a free pass here."

Her comment makes me smile. "Yeah, there is no sex going on with Ethan, nor will there ever be, so that logic works for me." Then stop thinking about him fucking you over your desk, Amelia.

Yeah, that little scenario was one of the many going through my mind last night.

Charlotte sighs and then rests her head on my shoulder. "Thanks for coming to check on me."

"Of course. Everything will be okay."

"I'm just really mad at Penelope right now for being so blunt."

"That's valid. But when you're done being mad, make sure you two talk. Tell her how she made you feel. It will make you feel better and help you process why you got angry with one another."

"Man, what do other people who don't have therapists as friends do in crises like these?"

"Live the same way you do. Just because I'm a therapist doesn't mean everyone listens to me."

That makes her laugh. "Well, I think they should."

"I do too. But hey…I get paid either way."

Chapter 3

Amelia

Two Weeks Later

The last two weeks have been a whirlwind. The rest of the trip to Hawaii did not go well, except for the fact that Penelope and Charlotte made up a day later and apologized for snapping at one another. But that was the only good part.

Charlotte reached her breaking point during her parents' reception, going off on her mom and Damien's dad while revealing they were in a fake relationship. Someone recorded the entire thing and posted it on social media. Luckily for her, the feedback was actually positive when people related to what she was going through, but then she fought herself for the last two weeks over how to move on in her life, ultimately admitting that she's in love with Damien, which we already knew. Tonight she's supposed to meet up with him to apologize, so I made sure to send her a good luck text as soon as my last client left for the day.

Things are starting to go back to normal—at least as normal as they were before Ethan moved into the office across the courtyard. A part of me is wondering how long this little avoidance act I've been doing will last before I have to face the fact that the man opened his practice right next to me, completely negating what I'm trying to accomplish in my line of work.

I've made it my mission to dodge him as much as possible in the past two weeks, which wasn't too hard between my trip to Hawaii and then getting back to work. He also seemed to be MIA last week for the Fourth of July, making it even easier to avoid him. I heard him laughing with a client outside of his office a few nights this week, in which I spied on him from behind the curtain on my office door. But other than that, we haven't really crossed paths and I'm hoping that our interactions remain like this—limited or barely existent.

Now, it's a Friday night, and my last client left about an hour ago. Penelope, who works in P.R., didn't have any fancy restaurant or club opening for us to go to. So it's a rare evening when I can relax at home, enjoy the sunset on my patio with a mojito in my hand, probably go for a swim in my pool, and relish in the beautiful summer evening on this warm July night.

Sometimes those nights when I get to enjoy my own company are some of my favorite and the most peaceful.

After my last client leaves for the day, I like to unwind and finish up paperwork by putting music on in the background. As I take off my jacket and move to hang it on the hook behind my desk, "Hello" by Adele begins playing from my Bluetooth speaker, so I immediately start singing along. One of my secret fantasies is to be a famous singer. Even though that is not even close to how I want my life to end up, when a song comes on that I know I can belt out flawlessly, I do and pretend I'm performing at the Grammys after winning Best New Artist.

What can I say? We all have our unrealistic dreams, am I right?

I nail the first three words of the famous song, aiming to hit every note flawlessly as it continues to play.

"Hello?" I hear come from behind, making me jump.

"Ah!" Reaching forward, I press pause on my speaker and then look over my shoulder to find the last person I anticipated. "Ethan? What are you doing here?"

"Was that you singing?" he asks, ignoring my question.

"Um, yes." I can instantly feel my cheeks heat up, so I turn my face away from him. "You scared the crap out of me. How long were you listening?"

"Long enough to know that you shouldn't quit your day job."

Annoyance begins to build in my veins. "Well, I never asked for your opinion, so it's completely unwarranted." Crossing my arms over my chest, I twist to face him head-on. "Can I help you? Or were you just looking for some entertainment on your Friday night? If that's the case, there's a strip club down the street where I'm sure you could pick up plenty of married men looking to leave their wives instead of working on their problems."

Ethan's smile builds as he assesses me. "That's not a bad idea, actually, so thanks." His eyes move around the room, judging every inch of my office. "Your office looks like the inside of a house."

"Thank you. That's what I was going for."

"That wasn't a compliment," he says over his shoulder as he looks at the artwork on the walls.

"Again, is there a reason why you're here?"

"Haven't seen you in a while. Have you been avoiding me?"

"I didn't realize that it was required of us to cross paths."

He grins. "It's not, but I've also seen you run in the other direction once you see me across the courtyard, so I thought I'd come investigate for myself."

"Your detective skills are subpar then since there's nothing for you to discover. And not that I need to explain myself, but I'm a fast walker by nature. I pride myself on being efficient in multiple aspects of my life."

"Hmmm," he hums. "So sex with you must be on a schedule then, huh?"

My jaw drops open. "What?"

"I'm sure you have it penciled in your calendar too." He changes the octave of his voice. "Sex on Thursday at eight-thirty sharp. Five minutes for foreplay, ten minutes for penetration, and if my orgasm doesn't arrive within that fifteen minutes, then my boyfriend can finish, and I'll just roll over and go to sleep so it doesn't take time from that."

Seething, I can feel my nostrils flare as I stalk across the room to him. "You have a lot of nerve coming in here, judging my space, insinuating that you know me at all."

"You probably love the missionary position too, huh, Dr. St. Clair? It must be hard to convince people that sex can save their marriage when you don't even know how to have fun in the bedroom yourself."

I clench my teeth, seconds away from smacking him. But the way his eyes are bouncing back and forth between mine makes me think that perhaps he wants me to. He's looking for a reaction from me, and even though part of me wants nothing more than to put him in his place, I am a professional and will not give him that satisfaction. So instead, I pull a therapist move on him.

Calmly, I roll my shoulders back and take a few steps toward him. Reaching down, I pick up one of my business cards off the table by the entryway and hold it out to him.

"What is this?"

"What does it look like? It's my business card. Should you prefer to discuss your needs to ridicule my love life or contemplate just exactly how I behave in bed, I would prefer to do so in a setting where we can discuss just exactly why it is that you feel the need to wonder about those things in the first place."

"Is that so?"

"Yes. And then, at least that way, if I have to listen to your asshole remarks, I'll be handsomely paid while doing so." I flash him a tight-lipped smile, and all he does is grin back at me in return.

"I'm impressed, Amelia. Perhaps you're a little tougher than I pegged you to be."

"You can think whatever you'd like about me, Mr. Fuller. But until you can approach me respectfully, I would appreciate you staying the hell out of my office."

With a curt nod, he heads for the door. "Just promise me one thing, Amelia?" I don't entertain his question with a response. "When your clients realize that trying to save a troubled marriage is pointless, please point them in my direction across the hall. I can leave a map for them if need be."

"That won't be necessary. But if your clients ever feel the need to process what a disgusting human being their divorce attorney is, I would be more than glad to offer them my services to deal with trauma as well."

He laughs and then opens the door. "Have a good weekend, Amelia. You're going to need it."

Narrowing my eyes at him, I watch him walk out of my office, wondering what he meant by his final words. However, I don't dwell on it for too long, immediately moving to the door to lock it after him. Releasing the breath I was holding, I hold my hand out in front of me to assess how badly I'm shaking.

That man is an ass and an arrogant prick. After his idle promise, I'm wondering if I haven't seen the worst of him. The thing that irritates me more than anything, though, is that he's so damn attractive, my mind and my body are at war over what to do with him. Perhaps only time will tell what will be the best way to handle Ethan Fuller.

"Well, well, well. Look who's decided to join us looking freshly fucked and happier than a Cleveland Browns fan that's just been told their team is actually going to the Super Bowl." Penelope smirks up at Charlotte as she finally joins us at brunch, fashionably late.

It's a Sunday in the middle of July, and the weekly brunches I have with my three best friends have finally reconvened. The past few weeks have been insane, but I'm so excited to have the opportunity to share my good news and unfortunate circumstances with my girls. Venting with your girlfriends is its own special kind of therapy.

"You know I don't care about football, so that comment doesn't mean much to me. But the rest of what you said is true." With a pleased smile on her face, Charlotte reaches for her mimosa and leans back in her chair. Her dark hair is down in waves around her shoulders, and her smile is blinding.

"Shame you don't follow football, ladies. All that testosterone, muscular men in tight, shiny pants, grunting and yelling, and all that adrenaline you know they have to burn off somewhere…" Penelope trails off, licking her lips.

"Yeah, I think you have a problem," Charlotte mumbles before turning her attention to Noelle and me, smiling from ear to ear again.

"I take it your makeup with Damien went well?" Noelle prods further.

Her lips spread wider as happiness exudes from her. "Yes. Everything is good. We are happy, in love, and giving our relationship a real shot." She sighs wistfully. "I found my person, you guys, and only made a million mistakes to get there."

Charlotte reconciled with Damien Friday night as she planned, and we all knew that the vibe of today's brunch was going to depend on how that night went.

Noelle reaches across the table, grasping her hand. "Then it was worth it. And we are so happy for you, Charlotte."

"Thank you." Charlotte twists her head, looking around Frankie's Diner, the restaurant we go to for brunch each Sunday in a quaint neighborhood in Los Angeles. As soon as you step in the door, your eyes are hit with the nostalgic look that most diners from the 1950s have—teal booths, black and white checkered flooring, chrome details, and pops of red here and there. Frankie's Diner serves up classic American cuisine and bottomless mimosas too, which we always take full advantage of. "God, how long has it been since we've done brunch?"

"Almost three weeks," I answer her. "Between your parents'

anniversary celebration in Hawaii, the Fourth of July, and the past few weeks when you've been wallowing without Damien, it's been a while."

"Well, there will be no more wallowing," she says. "So what has everyone been up to while I was ruminating in my pit of despair?"

"Just work mostly. Spent some time with my parents over the Fourth," Noelle answers. "Avoided looking online for another date since I know nothing would come of it anyway. Read a few romance novels looking for my next book boyfriend since I can't find one in real life."

I guess after reading about fictional happily ever afters for a living, you become obsessed with finding your own. Out of all of us, she's the one that wants to find her soul mate and have a family more than anything.

"I have several events coming up in the next month and a half, so I've been swamped as well," Penelope adds. "And I'll let you know the dates of events that you bitches can attend before we leave. But I did manage to tan a bit yesterday, which was heavenly."

Penelope works for Edelman PR company, handling everything from businesses to celebrities since she works at the office based in L.A. I'm not even sure how she keeps track of everything and everyone she's involved with, but the woman is good at her job and always brings us along to take advantage of the perks.

"Nice. Damien and I spent all day inside yesterday." Charlotte grins over the rim of her glass.

"I don't think you need to elaborate on what you were doing," Penelope chides.

"Hey, I'm going to live in my blissful bubble right now until I have to go back to reality tomorrow at the magazine." Charlotte works as the senior advertising executive for Revision Magazine, one of the most profitable women's magazines in the country. "What about you, Amelia?"

I push my glasses up the bridge of my nose and take a deep breath, eager to share my news. "Well, I have officially been operating out of my new office for two weeks, girls, and it's perfect. My clients are happy with the setup, and I love having a separate space for work now. And yesterday, I received a phone call from the *Los Angeles Times*. I've been nominated for the Best of Los Angeles Award for Best Marriage Counselor."

"What?" they shout in unison.

"Amelia, that's amazing!" Charlotte declares. "We need to refill our mimosas and toast to that, for sure."

"How does that happen?" Noelle asks as she passes our glasses to Charlotte, who tops them off.

"It's all based on nominations, so that means that former clients must have filled out the survey."

"I might have seen your name on the list and emailed it out to everyone that I know, too," Penelope adds, giving me a wink across the table.

"Penelope! I haven't treated all of those people though."

She bats her hand at me. "Doesn't matter. I know that you take your job very seriously and deserve this honor, and this will help get your name out there even more, Amelia. You deserve this."

Noelle nods. "I agree. This will be great for business."

I can't hold back my smile. "Thank you, Pen. That really means a lot."

Specializing in female empowerment and sexual awakening, I've made it my mission to work with women looking for ways to learn about their bodies and what makes them happy in their sex lives, both with and without partners. However, in the past few years, my practice has gravitated more toward helping couples as a marriage and sex therapist, focusing on their physical and emotional relationships.

I've also partnered with a few companies I endorse that make sex toys. My clients can purchase them directly from me to aid them along their journey. Overall, I'd say I've used my sexual psychology degree and minor in business quite well since I graduated early from college. However, it always still shocks people when they learn how I make my living given how I can be perceived as the shy, quiet type.

Penelope raises her glass, and we all follow her cue. "To Amelia. To running a successful practice, being your own boss, and being the best of the best!"

"Hear, hear!" We clink our glasses together, and each take a sip of our mimosas.

"So when can we see your office? I know we didn't get a chance before Hawaii, and well afterward..." Charlotte shrugs, knowing how out of the loop we've all been with each other over the past few weeks.

"Well, how about after we're done here? It's not too far, and I did bring the keys with me," I say as I dig them out of my purse and jingle them in the air.

"Yes! That sounds perfect." Noelle looks to the other girls.

"I don't have any other plans today, so that works for me," Penelope agrees.

Charlotte nods. "I guess Damien can wait another hour or so to fuck me again."

Noelle smirks before she takes another sip of her drink. "Glad to know that you feel comfortable sharing that information with us."

Charlotte narrows her eyes at Noelle. "Like we've ever kept secrets from each other. I mean, if you can't discuss those types of things with your girlfriends and be candid about sex, then what's the point?"

Penelope nods. "Charlotte is right. So why don't I tell you guys about the guy I banged last night…"

Noelle holds her hand up. "Frankie! We're going to need more champagne!" Frankie acknowledges her from across the restaurant, beaming as he grabs us another bottle. "I especially need another drink if I'm going to have to listen to all of you discuss your sex lives while I'm not getting any."

"Hey, it's been a while for me too," I tell her, rubbing her arm for comfort.

"It happens. Lord knows I had cobwebs growing down there before Damien came around," Charlotte adds.

We all stare at Penelope. "Are you guys done wallowing so I can tell you my story now?"

Noelle rolls her eyes, I chuckle, and Charlotte urges her to continue. "Oh, please…tell us everything."

"All right. So this guy approached me at this event, and I swear, the outline of his dick in his pants was halfway down his thigh…"

"Oh my God, it's like walking up to someone's home," Noelle squeals as we approach the door of my office. "You even have flowers outside and…are those gnomes?"

I chuckle. "Yes. I saw them at the store and thought they were too cute. I had to have them and even bought a set for my house. I just wanted the front to feel welcoming because the idea of going to therapy can be daunting for some people."

"Well, you have definitely achieved that. Hell, I might just come by here to hang out since I'm digging the vibe so much."

Charlotte hugs me from the side. "I am so freaking happy for you, Amelia. This is incredible."

"Wait until you see the inside." I turn the key in the lock and welcome my friends into my office. A small table with a marble top and gold legs sits by the door to the left, full of business cards from other local businesses I support or recommend clients to, like the men's clinic I told my client John about. Next to that are a few chairs with olive-green cushions and a small coffee table full of magazines for people to read while they wait. To the right is my desk, which I'm hoping will serve as a receptionist's desk soon once I find the time to hire one. And then beyond that is the door to the small room where I actually speak with clients. I have a brown leather couch, two matching chairs, some plants, and my cushioned chair where I sit during each session, all in shades of tan, green, and white.

Noelle and Charlotte walk around, taking everything in. But then Penelope walks through the door a few minutes later.

"Where did you go?" Charlotte asks her.

"I was just scoping out the rest of the complex. Amelia," she says as she turns to me. "Did you know that there's a divorce attorney's office right across the courtyard from you?"

Noelle and Charlotte turn around so all three of my friends are facing me now with questioning looks on their faces.

"Ugh, yes." I move to sit in the chair behind my desk and begin to rub my temples.

Noelle furrows her brows at me. "I take it there's a story there." The three of them take a seat in the chairs in front of me.

Charlotte speaks up first. "You didn't tell them about Ethan?"

Penelope and Noelle spin their heads toward Charlotte. "Who the hell is Ethan?"

"Ethan is the divorce attorney."

"And Charlotte knew about him?" Noelle asks.

"I ran into him the night before we left for Hawaii. He was pompous and entirely too pleased that a marriage counselor was in an office right across from him. He kept alluding to the fact that I was going to make him rich because my clients would realize what a waste of money therapy is and just decide to divorce instead."

Penelope arches a brow at me. "Is this why you were acting weird at the airport?"

"Yeah. It messed with my head." I lean forward in my chair, resting my forearms on my desk. "I've waited so long to finally have this place." Waving my arm around the room, I let out a heavy sigh. "The last thing I ever imagined happening was having to worry about someone ruining it for me, making me walk on eggshells and wonder if his presence will affect my business and the mind frame of my clients."

"What do you mean?" Noelle leans forward in her chair.

"Well, it's like signing up for a gym, and then McDonald's builds a restaurant right next door. Now every time you walk into the gym, you're going to smell French fries and be tempted to drive through the drive-thru on your way home instead of waiting to make dinner for yourself, which you know is going to be so much better for you. But McDonald's is so much easier…"

"I don't know if people actually believe that divorce is easy," Charlotte challenges. "But I kind of see your point. However, you didn't mention the worst part about him." The corner of her lips tip up in a knowing grin.

"What's the worst part?" Noelle asks.

I slump back in my chair. "He's entirely too good-looking."

"I believe what you told me is that he's hot as hell." Charlotte laughs.

Penelope snickers. "Of course he is."

"Yup. So not only is the man the bane of my existence, but he's way too attractive, and my vagina took notice. And even the other night, he came into my office after my last client left, scared the crap out of me, insulted my singing, then basically told me to watch my back."

Noelle scrunches her nose up in disgust. "Ugh. He sounds appalling."

"What do you think he meant by watching your back?" Charlotte asks.

"I have no idea. But honestly, I'm sure he's capable of way more than I think he is."

Penelope stands up, tapping her finger to her chin. "I feel a war coming on."

"What?"

"Just be alert, Amelia. Don't let your guard down around him, and make sure that your clients know what a huge step they've taken by working with you—keep their eyes on the prize. But if Ethan starts messing with you, you let us know. We've got your back."

"I don't know what to expect, but I'm glad I have you girls to lean on."

Charlotte and Noelle both stand up. "Always, Amelia. That's what best friends are for."

I walk over to my girls and the four of us share a hug.

I love these women. They are my extended family. And no matter what happens, I know they'll be there to catch me if I fall.

"Look who decided to finally show. I was beginning to wonder if I was going to be stood up."

I take a seat across from my brother Nick in the booth of Tony's, a local Italian restaurant that is always busy. It's Monday night, and every so often, we get together to have dinner, just the two of us.

"You do realize this isn't a date," I fire back as I set down my purse next to me in the booth and unfold the napkin in front of me, placing it on my lap. "So check your ego right now, big brother."

He laughs. "Fair enough. Just glad I didn't have to explain to the waitress that I got stood up by my sister and not an actual date. I'm not sure if she would believe me."

Smiling, I shake my head at my brother before reaching out and grabbing his hand. "How are you? It's been a while since I've seen you."

He squeezes my hand back. "I'm good, Sis. I've actually been really busy." He bounces his eyebrows.

"Oh yeah? With what?"

"Not what, who. And her name is Elena," he says, rolling his tongue.

Laughing, I release his hand and lean back in my side of the booth. "And who is Elena?"

"The woman I started seeing. And fuck, Amelia…she's gorgeous and smart as hell. She's a Spanish teacher, and I know it's early to say this, but I feel really strongly about her."

"That's great, Nick. I'm so happy for you. So is that why you're in a good mood today?"

"Part of it, yes. But I'm also just happy to see you."

"I'm happy to see you too."

"So how's the new office?"

Nick is a realtor and the one who helped me find the place. Normally he deals with residential real estate, but if his client—like his sister—needs an office space, he'll dabble in commercial real estate from time to time. "I love it. It's exactly what I wanted, and my clients love it too."

"Glad to hear it."

"There is just one issue though…"

"What?"

"I have a new neighbor, and he's a divorce attorney."

Nick leans back in the booth with a frown on his face. "I know."

My mouth drops open. "What? You know?"

"Yeah, Ethan Fuller is a buddy of mine from college, and he recently moved back to L.A. He needed a new office too, and I knew there was another empty one in the complex where yours is, so I showed it to him."

"Nick! Why on earth would you do that?" I sincerely want to pinch my brother's nipple off right now. I reach across the table to attempt just that, but he bats my hand away and places both of his palms flat over his chest, protecting the goods.

"I didn't think it would be that big of a deal. It's not like he's your competition…"

"But he is! He's the person my clients will go to if they feel that I'm failing them. And now, you've made him readily available and within a few dozen feet!"

He runs a hand through his hair. "Fuck, Amelia. I'm sorry. I didn't realize this would upset you this much."

"I swear, sometimes I wonder if I got all of the brains in this family." He rolls his eyes at me. "This is bad, Nick."

"I agree it's not convenient, but unfortunately, these things happen, Amelia. And business is business."

"Oh, I could just strangle you, but at the same time, I guess I can't blame you for giving your client what he needed." Relenting to the fact that there's nothing I can do about the situation now, I decide to dig for information. "Well, what do you know about him?"

"Now? Not much. I know he moved back for personal reasons, but he wasn't too forthcoming with them, and I didn't pry. But back then? He was a decent guy, although you have to remember, most of my memories of him involve taking shots at frat parties."

"Well, he seems to be quite an ass now, just so you know."

Nicks laughs. "He's always been sort of cocky, but the guy could always back it up."

Great, now my mind is wondering how big his cock is.

Focus, Amelia.

"I'm just trying to help people so they don't end up like Mom and Dad, Nick." The energy between us shifts as we both go back to that night when our parents told us they were separating.

He reaches for my hand again. "I know, Amelia. And you are making a difference. I know that. But you do know that not all marriages can be saved, right?"

"I know, but I always want couples to know that they tried."

"And that's why I love you because your optimism always prevails."

"Optimism is great, but it's also kind of hard to sell the idea of a long-lasting marriage when you don't have one yourself."

He gives me an awkward smile. "You'll find your person. We both will one day. But dating in this day and age isn't easy. Hell, just finding Elena feels like I struck gold in a mine."

"But doesn't it scare you? The idea of finding that person and thinking you'll be happy forever, but then one day all of it falls apart?" I ask, knowing that if I'm being honest with myself, my fear of going through what my parents went through is part of why I'm still single. I know this about myself, and that relationships will go through waves, but I still have trouble voicing it out loud.

"It scares me every day. But then I look at Mom and Dad and what they overcame to save their marriage. You don't have to accept those low points as the end. If you find someone you truly love, fighting for the relationship is the only option. Sometimes it doesn't work, but sometimes it does. But you and I both know that what they went through wasn't easy even if they came out on the other side."

I nod. "I do. But I also know that both of them would tell you it was worth it. And I just don't want the option of divorce literally lurking around the corner for every couple I'm trying to help see that."

Thinking back to the night when our parents dropped that bomb on us, I can still feel the devastation. Nick and I cried together that night in his room, contemplating how different our lives were going to be from that moment forward. But the next day, our parents sat down with us again and told us they were planning on going to counseling as one last effort to save their relationship, partly because of my suggestion and reaction to the news. My father still moved out for a while, and things weren't great for a long time. There were dinners with just one of them, a lot of times I would hear my mother crying herself to sleep, and by the end of my junior year, I wasn't sure if they would make it. But then, one day, my father came back home. My parents acted like they did before, and part of me was skeptical to believe it. But in my heart, I knew they were going to be okay. And even though they never came out and said it, my mom made comments that alluded to their unsatisfactory love life having a lot to do with their separation.

Watching them go through a lull in their relationship, hitting rock bottom, bouncing back from it, and seeing them come out on the other side showed me the power of therapy. It showed me the power of love. And it was then that I realized what I wanted to do with my life—I wanted to help other people save their relationships too.

But when I got to college, I realized that sex wasn't something that just affected older, married adults. Fellow students and friends went through problems related to sex just as much, if not more. A classmate and friend of mine was raped at a party and struggled for years to overcome it. My girlfriends would complain about their lackluster sexual partners or a lack of confidence in the bedroom pertaining to their bodies or the ability to ask for what they wanted. And even through my own experiences, I realized that women shouldn't be ashamed of wanting, needing, or demanding more from sex.

So, I took my experiences and the experiences of others and worked toward a profession where I knew I could help couples and women achieve what they were looking for. And I haven't looked back since.

"Well, you and I both know that what Mom and Dad have is rare." My brother reaches for his glass and takes a sip of his water.

"Yes, but it doesn't have to be. Too many people give up because fighting for their relationship is work. It takes time, commitment, and a fear of failure. You have to remind yourself what a life without the other person in it would look like and ask yourself if that vision is scarier than working on repairing what's broken."

Nick sighs. "You're right, Sis. You always are." He winks at me. "So if you know this and believe it, then don't let Ethan's presence derail you from what you are setting out to achieve. What if I went over and talked to him, helped smooth things out?"

"This isn't high school, Nick. I don't need you to come to my rescue. And I honestly don't know that it would do much good. Besides, I'm a grown woman. I can handle myself. And I have Penelope in my corner. If need be, I can just snap my fingers, and she'll take care of him."

Nick throws his head back in laughter. "This is true. The girl is next-level crazy. Just let me know if you need any extra backup, okay? I don't see Ethan being that much of a problem for you."

"Oh, I'm not so sure about that. But I want you to be prepared to have to defend me if I need you."

"I will gladly punch that fucker in the face if he messes with my little sister."

Chuckling, I lean back again in my booth, eager to move on to the next topic. "Thank you. Now tell me more about Elena…"

"Hey, Charlie." The nurse practitioner behind the receptionist counter pops his head up once he hears my voice. It's a Tuesday afternoon and this place was my last errand to run before heading home.

Stepping into Ageless Men's Health Clinic always feels welcoming, from the clean and open space to the friendly people that work here, like Charlie.

"Amelia. What a pleasant surprise. What are you doing in here?"

"I ran out of business cards and needed to get some more. I was out running errands and figured I'd just pop in. Do you have a minute to help me?"

Charlie smiles, standing up and walking over to a filing cabinet where he pulls out a cardboard box and lifts out a sizable handful of cards for me. "Of course. No problem. And thanks again for sending people over. Business has been booming, and so many men are leaving as happy customers." He puts the cards in a plastic bag, sealing it shut, before walking back over to me and placing it in my hand.

"Of course. You guys are doing good work here. More often than not, women become the scapegoats for problems in the bedroom, when men have hormones and issues as well."

"That should be our new tagline." A voice to my right has me spinning in that direction as Dr. Anderson walks toward me. Brayden flashes his charming smile as he strides across the room in his white lab coat, his light-brown hair perfectly combed back, and his dark brown eyes trained on me. "Hello, Amelia."

"Brayden. So nice to see you."

"Likewise." His eyes eat me up as I stand there, my body coming alive from the attention. "What are you doing in here? I'd offer you a shot of testosterone, but I'm sure that's not what you're looking for," he jokes.

Charlie coughs behind him, stifling a laugh I presume, catching my attention momentarily before I look back at Brayden and hold up the plastic bag of business cards. "I just needed some more cards. I've been handing them out to a lot of clients lately."

He smiles with pleasure. "I'm aware. They all name you as their reference when they come in. I can't thank you enough."

"Well, the feeling is mutual. You're helping a lot of my clients."

"That's our goal. As you said, men's health is important too." Silence rests between us as I glance behind Brayden and find Charlie's eyes bouncing between the two of us.

"Okay then. Well, I best be going. This was all I needed."

Brayden clears his throat and then nods. "Let me walk you to your car?"

"Oh, that's not necessary."

"I want to." He turns back to Charlie. "Hold down the fort for a few moments, will you?"

"You got it, Doc. Nice to see you again, Amelia."

"Same to you, Charlie."

Brayden holds the door open for me, waiting to walk through before he accompanies me out to my car. I suddenly feel nervous. He's never done this before, even though we've always remained quite friendly with each other. We met at a conference last year, and when I learned about his clinic, I was eager to recommend his services to my clients. The venture has worked out well for both of us, but besides the casual conversations here or there, he's never alluded to anything else.

Flashing me that brilliant white smile of his, he waits for me to unlock my door and put my things inside before I turn around to face him. "So, Amelia…I don't want to seem too forward, but…"

"Is everything okay, Brayden?"

"Uh, yeah." He clears his throat before continuing. "I actually was wondering if you'd like to go to dinner with me sometime?"

My hand flies to my chest. "Really?"

He chuckles, shoving his hands in his pockets. "Yes. Jesus, I didn't think I'd be this nervous," he says before taking one hand out of his pocket and fiddling with his tie.

"You're asking me out?"

"Yes, I am. I think you're stunning, intelligent, and witty. Hell, I wanted to ask you out right after I met you, but I didn't want to seem too eager, and we had just agreed to work together, more or less, and I didn't want to cross those lines. Getting to know you a bit over the past year made me realize that I enjoyed your company and found you very attractive, but I couldn't get up the nerve to do something about it. However, I told myself that the next time I saw you I would take advantage of the opportunity and put myself out there. So, that's what I'm doing."

"I'm…speechless. I didn't know you felt that way." Nerves run through me, and some feel a little like excitement. Brayden is a great guy—attractive, successful, hardworking, and honest. And he just bared his true feelings for me, and I can't remember the last time I experienced that with a man.

But he's not Ethan.

Images of Ethan flash through my mind—his cockiness the other night when we were talking and my body's desire for him every time he gets close—and even though I know I shouldn't want him, the way he makes my body come alive is very different from the way I feel about Brayden at the moment.

But here is this guy, who is available and being vulnerable right in front of me, asking me out on a date. Maybe this is a sign that it's time to date again, to try to find my person. It's been a while since I've been on a date, and Brayden is the perfect guy to try to move forward with. Besides, it's not like Ethan is asking me out or that I would even entertain that idea.

Then why are you still thinking about it?

"So, what do you say? Would you let me take you to dinner next Friday?"

"Next weekend?"

"Yes, unless you already have plans. I'm free Saturday as well. Or the following week. Hell, give me a date, and I'll make it happen even if I do have plans."

My gut is telling me I'd be a fool to waste this opportunity, even though my heart is hesitant. But in a matter of a few moments, I know what the right decision is. "Yes, I'd love to. Next Friday night would be perfect."

His smile almost blinds me. "Really?"

I nod. "Yes. I would like to have dinner with you."

"Hell, that's great. Seriously, I can't wait, Amelia." He lifts my hand to his mouth and presses a kiss to the top. A flurry releases in my stomach, but I instantly catalog that it's not nearly as strong as the reaction I have to Ethan.

Stop it, Amelia. This man is interested and available. Focus on him.

"You have my number, so just call or text with the details." I smile up at him, pleasantly optimistic about this.

"Would you mind if I picked you up for our date?"

"That would be okay with me."

"Perfect. Talk to you soon, Amelia." He begins to walk backward with his eyes still on me.

"You too, Brayden."

On my drive home, I think about how I obviously never anticipated Brayden asking me out, but the idea of having a date this coming weekend has developed a little bubble of anticipation in me that I haven't felt in a while.

And even though the idea of adding dating again on top of

everything else in my life makes me feel anxious, I know this will help me push forward in all of the changes going on in my life.

Brayden is smart, kind, and supports my work. He's the antithesis of Ethan.

And that is why I need to pretend like Ethan Fuller doesn't even exist.

Easier said than done…

Chapter 4

Ethan

"Where are you going?" I chase down my wife as she walks down the hallway, locating her purse and slinging it over her shoulders.

"Out."

"What do you mean out? You've barely been home all day."

"Well, I'm meeting up with some friends, and we're going to grab some drinks."

"Monica, this has to stop."

She spins to face me. "No. Your nagging needs to stop. I'm allowed to go out. I'm allowed to have fun, Ethan."

"But what about our son? He needs his mom."

She shakes her head. "He's little. He'll never remember me being gone."

"Yeah, but I will. We're supposed to be a family."

"That's what you wanted, Ethan, when you begged me to have

this baby. But now…" She bites her lip. "I'm not sure I want to be a part of this family anymore. I'm too young, and there's too much life for me to live still."

"You mean you want to party." As I stare at the woman I've done nothing but try to do right by, I realize it may be time to admit defeat. This pattern has only progressed since Oliver was born, and she keeps pushing my limits. I barely feel like we're married anymore, like she doesn't care about being in my life or our son's.

"I want to live. All we do is stay home, take care of the baby, and fight. You don't even touch me anymore."

"It's hard to touch you when you're always gone!" I shout a little too loudly, glancing back down the hallway, hoping that I didn't just wake up our son. But honestly, I can't remember the last time Monica and I were intimate. It's been months, and Oliver is already two.

"Because this life isn't enough for me! I want more. I…I want a divorce." She heads for the door as her confession strikes me square in the chest, but I chase after her one more time.

Her admission only fuels my rage. "If you leave, Monica, I will fight you for custody. I'm not going to let you just walk in and out of our lives when you want or wait for you to change your mind. Make sure this is your decision, and you can stick to it…that this is really what you want."

She backs up in her steps as she steps out of our door. "I'm done, Ethan. You can have everything. I just want out." And then she hops in her car and drives away, leaving me alone to pick up the pieces of the life I thought she wanted.

"Ethan?" My secretary pulls me from my thoughts. "Are you okay?"

"Oh, uh, yeah. Sorry. Just lost in thought." I scramble to find my phone on my desk and see there are no notifications that need my attention right this minute.

"Okay." She smiles. "Well, the Nelsons are in the first conference room, ready when you are. Her lawyer is a pistol, just an FYI."

I stand, buttoning up my jacket as a wave of collectiveness comes over me again. "Well, so am I, so let the games begin."

As I walk into the conference room, ready to represent my client, I realize it's been almost three years since I was in this situation myself, and I can still remember how exhausting these proceedings can be. Luckily for me, my ex-wife didn't care to fight me in any aspect. But for those that do, I try hard to remind them to do what's best for all involved. The worst cases though are when one party was unfaithful. Those discussions always include elements of revenge, and usually, it's the kids that get used as pawns.

Well, not today. Today, we're going to act like civilized adults and get this divorce moving forward as quickly as possible so everyone can move on with their lives.

Sometimes that's the only part of my job that reminds me that what I do is worth it. I give people a fresh start, a chance to find happiness without someone that makes their lives a living hell.

I was given that opportunity, and I feel other people deserve the same.

Suddenly, a blur of blond curls catches my eye in the window, bouncing as she walks by casually on her way to her office, stopping me in my tracks and reminding me that thoughts of my ex aren't the only distraction plaguing me right now.

Amelia St. Clair has been an unwelcome wrench in my plan at this new location, a move that was not only necessary for my living situation but also to give me the chance to expand the practice I'm a part of. The partners at my firm were more than understanding when I explained my need to relocate to Los Angeles, and one of my associates decided to make the move with me as well.

But having a marriage counselor across the complex from us was not a detail I was considering as a possible obstacle we would face. Additionally, it doesn't help that the woman is beautiful, intelligent, well-spoken, fiery as fuck, and my old college friend's sister.

Making metaphorical flames shoot out of her ears has been one of the highlights of my day any time we cross paths. I feel like I'm back in high school, and the uptight girl that needs to be knocked down a peg or two is lurking around every corner, and I am more than eager to see how fast I can get under her skin. Even back then, I was impeccable at getting a reaction from girls, and now I feel the same challenge with Amelia.

And even as I explained to her, having her nearby might actually help my business in the long run.

But it certainly isn't helping my dick remember how long it's been since he's been taken care of by something other than my hand.

Being a single father hasn't afforded me much time to tend to my personal needs, if you catch my drift. But hopefully, having my mother nearby now will help alleviate some of those challenges and allow me to find someone to scratch my itch.

But why does my mind instantly conjure up the image of Amelia dragging her nails down my back when I think about that?

Shaking off the irritating attraction I feel for her, I watch her unlock her office door and go inside, making sure I take a few moments to appreciate the curves of her ass and hips before they disappear. She may have her heart in the right place when it comes to helping people, but I've seen too many instances in my line of work to know that most marriages are better off dissolving before someone ends up on *Snapped*. Some people just aren't meant to be together. Some people just aren't meant to be married.

And I sure as hell know after my experience, that's the last thing I fucking want again.

However, wondering what Amelia tastes like in other places than just her lips has me forgetting why I'm here. I'm moving on, progressing in my profession, and picking up the pieces of my life and putting them in place where I need them to be—and none of those pieces involve a curly-headed blonde with temptation written all over her.

Amelia needs to remain in the box of untouchable thoughts I like to keep somewhere far in the recesses of my mind, and even though I know I should leave her alone, the teenage boy in me is thoroughly enjoying watching her react to every little thing I say or do. Little does she know, the plan to get her next reaction has already been set in motion.

"Daddy!" My little boy runs out of the front door as soon as I vacate my car once I pull into my mother's driveway.

"Hey, bud." He slams into my legs, squeezing his tiny arms around me. I ruffle his dark hair, the hue he inherited from his mother, and hope that's the only thing he gets from her. "How was your day with Grandma?"

"It was fun! We went to the park, and I practiced kicking the soccer ball like you told me to."

"Nice. Did you score any goals?" I ask him as I lead him back up the path to my mother's front door. Her little house in the old neighborhood in L.A. holds many memories for me—a time when my mom was a single mother just trying to make ends meet and provide for us, and a time when I thought the reason my father abandoned us was because he didn't love me or want me anymore.

I swear I will do everything in my power to make sure my son never feels that way about Monica.

"I did. Grandma tried to block it, but I was too fast for her."

Chuckling, I walk through the worn front door as it squeaks, making a note to come by and tighten the hinges on it this weekend. "You are the fastest boy I know."

"The kid never stops moving," my mother says, coming around the corner from the kitchen to greet us, wiping her hands on a dish towel. Her dirty-blond hair, which was once the same hue as mine, has more gray in it now than blond, and her face shows laugh lines and years of hard work. But she's also the most beautiful and important woman in my life, and I don't take her help or presence for granted for one second.

I plant a kiss on her cheek as I move to meet her. "How was work?" she asks.

"Busy. The couple I met with today is actually compromising, so that makes my job a hell of a lot easier."

"Good to hear." She looks down at my son. "Go get your bag so your daddy can take you home, young man." Oliver rushes off, giving us a chance to talk alone. "You ready for next week?"

"No, but I know me not being ready won't change the fact that it's happening. I don't know what I would do without you, Mom." Pulling her into my arms, I hold on to the only woman I know I can count on.

"Ethan, you've done more for me by just moving back here. I get to be in Oliver's life more, and I get to see you every day." She peers up at me. "You boys are my world. And Oliver starting kindergarten is going to be a wonderful new chapter for you both."

"The past few years have been rocky, Mom, but I finally feel like we're on solid ground. Oliver starts school next week, soccer a few weeks after that, and I'm finally settling into my job. We're getting a routine down and I feel like I made the right decision leaving San Diego."

"This was a good move for you, son."

"I know. I'm seeing that now."

"So, the office is running smoothly?"

I nod, moving around her to get a glass of water from the fridge. "My assistant is competent, which definitely helps. Gary, the lawyer that came with me, knows his stuff, so I don't feel like I have to babysit him. And the location can't be beat."

"The little ice cream shop in the complex sure is tasty too."

I glance over at her after I shut the door. "Please tell me Oliver didn't have ice cream before dinner."

"Not today," she answers with a grin on her face.

I roll my eyes at her. "You know he gets crazy when he has too much sugar."

"I know. But he's my grandson and I will spoil him as I see fit." She pats my shoulder as she passes me.

"Just make sure he's eating a fruit or vegetable in there too, okay?"

"You act like this is my first rodeo raising a kid, young man. You turned out okay, if I do say so myself, and I know for a fact that you went through a period of time where all you survived on were Bagel Bites and Totino's Pizza Rolls."

Before I can reply, Oliver shouts as he runs up to us with his backpack on his shoulders. "I'm ready, Daddy!"

"Saved by the kid," I mutter out of the corner of my mouth to my mother, which causes her to laugh. "All right, bud, let's go. Are you ready to make pizza at home?"

"Yes!"

"Then let's do it." I lean over and plant another kiss on my mother's cheek. "We'll see you in the morning, Mom."

"Looking forward to it."

I lead Oliver back out to the car and head for our house, a newer build in a housing tract I was able to buy at an incredible price since the previous owners were foreclosed on.

When I was talking to my mother about how I was going to manage everything when Oliver started school this year, she convinced me to move closer to her so she could help me, although the last thing I wanted to do was have to depend on her. Like I said before, she busted her ass to raise me on her own. She paid her dues. But she also missed out on a lot of Oliver's first years since we lived a considerable distance away, and I was too busy trying to keep my marriage alive to think about visiting more often.

So after she insisted she wanted us around, I sold our house, convinced my firm to let me start my own office, and packed the two of us up and started our new adventure, just my son and me. My mom knew someone on the board of a charter school near my house and was able to get Oliver into their program for kindergarten, which starts next week, earlier than most of the public schools in the area. Nick, my buddy from college who is now a realtor, was able to find me an office and a house in just a few short months. And once everything was closed on, Oliver and I made the move from San Diego to Los Angeles a few weeks ago.

But I don't care. I just want him to have the best, to have better than I did, even though I wouldn't trade my childhood for a second and I don't dare knock how hard my mother worked to give me all she could. But I don't want him to feel like he's missing out on anything just because his mom isn't around, and I know there will come a point in time where he will question that.

Pulling up to our house, I feel satisfied with where I am now. I'm no longer concerned about making Monica happy. Every once in a while, Oliver will ask where his mom is, but he was only two when she took off, so he doesn't really remember her. After the night she asked me for a divorce, she only came back to the house once to collect her things. I tried to reason with her, offered to go to counseling or compromise on what she wanted, but she made her choice, so I vowed to protect my son from feeling like less than for the rest of his life.

It's Monica's loss not being here, watching him grow up and become the incredible boy he is. And I will never stop reminding him of that until I take my very last breath.

"Go take off your shoes, put your bag where it goes, then meet me in the kitchen." I direct Oliver to his room, hoping he'll follow my directions as I shuck my jacket and follow him down the hallway to change my clothes in my room.

Once I'm in a white shirt and black basketball shorts, I head toward the kitchen to find him sitting on his stool at the kitchen counter. "I'm hungry, Daddy." He bounces in his seat, and then in his next breath, he asks, "Is it time to make pizza yet?"

"Yes, it is. Do you need your chef's hat?" I spin around to locate the matching chef's hats I purchased for the two of us. Oliver is going through a phase of being picky with food, so my mom and I discussed allowing him to be involved in making the food so he could have some ownership over what he's eating. She read some article that suggested it, and it sounded like an easy way to help with the problem, so I obliged. Little did I know that trying to cook with a five-year-old would be one of the most chaotic things I've ever done. But Ollie loves it, and it's something that we get to do at night, just the two of us, so I try to enjoy every moment of it.

"Yes, Daddy!" He hops off his stool and takes his hat from my hand, placing it on his head. "Now, let's make the best pizza ever!"

I give him a high five after I place my hat on my head too. "Let's do it."

After we eat dinner and Oliver is clean, I tuck him in bed and sit on the couch, exhausted after a long day. I debate finding something new to watch on Netflix or seeing what's on television, but part of me is just too tired to care.

I decide to take a shower and pass out early tonight, hoping I'll wake up feeling rested and productive tomorrow. But as I lie down to go to sleep, the image of Amelia from today pushes itself forward in my mind.

I hate that I want her, that my body is all too curious about how her lips feel or what sounds she might make as I sink my cock into her. I hate that I wonder what her story is. I hate that no matter how much I know she's a nuisance to my job, I look forward to our inter-actions and catching glimpses of her throughout the day.

I know the last thing I need is to get involved with someone right now, but it's been a while since my dick had any female treatment, and right now he's focused on the newest option nearby. That's all it has to be, right?

Smirking, I place my hands behind my head and stare up at the ceiling. There isn't anything on television to keep me entertained right now, but perhaps irritating my new work neighbor can be my new source of entertainment.

I can't fuck her out of my system, so pissing her off will just have to be the next best thing. And perhaps tomorrow she'll find what I left for her in her office. Here's hoping.

"Good morning, Yvonne." I greet my secretary as I step through the doors of my office just after nine.

"Good morning, Ethan. Um, you have someone waiting for you in your office already."

That has me stopping in my tracks. My first appointment isn't until ten. "Really?"

She nods, biting her lip. "Yes. And I told her you weren't here yet, but she insisted on waiting for you there. I hope that's okay. She was very persuasive."

"Well, okay then. Please have my files for me when I'm through."

She lifts the folder. "They're already here."

"Thank you." I grab the folder from her, tucking it under my arm as I make my way down the hallway to my office, curious about who my impromptu visitor might be. But as soon as I step through the door and get a whiff of lemons and sugar, I know exactly who's here.

Spinning around from where she's standing along the wall, staring up at my degrees and awards framed there, is Amelia, wearing a fitted, sleeveless black dress that doesn't show much skin but definitely highlights her curvy figure. Her hair is down and wild around her face, and her eyes are glowing that honey brown I noticed the other day behind her black-rimmed glasses, but her scowl has me fighting my grin and delighted at pissing her off even more.

"Well, good morning, neighbor."

She narrows her eyes at me. "No, Mr. Fuller. This is not a good morning."

"Oh, Amelia, please call me Mr. Fuller again. I didn't know that was one of my kinks until you just said it." Chuckling to myself, I make my way around my desk to set down the folder, my briefcase, and my coffee. I mentally pat myself on the shoulder for perfecting that asshole remark.

Her mouth drops open. "God, you have no shame, do you?"

"What do you mean?" I ask coyly, slinking back in my chair and folding my arms over my chest as I watch her start to unravel.

"First, I sincerely hope you don't talk to your female clients like that because they could sue you for sexual harassment. And second, I believe you left something in my office the other day." She tosses the stack of business cards I left on her little side table by her door, and now I'm thoroughly pleased that she made this discovery at the exact time I was hoping.

"To answer your first question, don't worry about how I speak to my female clients. My crass comments are reserved just for you, I assure you. And second, I didn't know that leaving my cards there would be such an issue. There were plenty of other business cards on the table, so I figured it was a free opportunity for advertising." Grinning, I smile up at her as I watch her clench her jaw.

"Well, the opportunity was not extended to you. In case you've forgotten, you stand for everything that is the opposite of what I do."

"Oh, I haven't forgotten. I just wanted to make sure that your clients knew they had other options besides the kumbaya sessions you're holding across the way."

"God, my brother was right. You're cocky, and not in a good way."

And that morsel of information has me smiling even wider. "I see you finally made that connection as well."

"Oh, that you know my brother? That he sold you this office without thinking about how it would affect my business? Don't worry, he got an earful from me about it."

"Lucky him."

She takes a few steps over to my desk and leans over it, zeroing her gaze on me. And right about now, I'm wishing that her dress was cut low in the front so I could get a view of her cleavage and use that vision later when I'm alone.

Fuck, she's so hot, so voluptuous, so passionate—that has to translate to other things.

My dick instantly gets hard just watching her, and I can't remember the last time that happened. I'm a grown man, but I'm getting hard like a teenager.

This is not good, but damn, it feels good to misbehave—especially with her.

"Listen here, Ethan. You need to stay away from my office and away from my clients. My goal is to pretend that you don't even exist and go about my business, and I think you should do the same."

"Shame. I definitely know I can't pretend like you don't exist, Amelia. But please, do go on."

She points a finger at my desk. "Your business cards aren't welcome in my office, and neither are you. Stay on your side of the complex, and everything will be fine."

"And if I don't?" I ask, arching a brow at her.

She stands up tall again as a mischievous grin builds on her lips. "Then I'll have no choice but to retaliate."

"Is that so?"

"Don't test me, Ethan Fuller."

"Oh, Dr. St. Clair. Now I want nothing more than to know what you're capable of."

She turns around and heads for my door, and I watch her ass the entire way before she glances over her shoulder. "Don't say I didn't warn you." And then she leaves, and my dick twitches as I watch her walk away.

Chuckling, I reach for my cup of coffee and take a sip. "Fuck me," I mutter to myself, daydreaming about what I would have done with her alone in my office under any other circumstances.

This woman is getting under my skin now. She's ruffling my feathers and making me forget that I'm alone for a very important reason. I don't need a distraction, a fire to contain. But damn, she sure is the type that makes a man want to whip out his fire hose and douse a few flames.

And now I'm wondering, does Amelia have what it takes to go toe-to-toe with me? Does she have the balls (metaphorically speaking, of course) to retaliate?

Or will this little game we're playing just fizzle out as quickly as it started?

I genuinely don't want to hurt her business or my own, but it's too damn fun messing with her.

Perhaps I should go over and apologize, let her know that I didn't mean any harm and I don't really want to start a war. My immaturity was coming out, and I would honestly like us to remain civil. But would she even believe me?

Maybe I should just let this die down naturally, let her cool off and pretend like everything is as normal as it was before we crossed paths. Besides, I have more important things to focus on, like my son.

Remember your priorities, Ethan. Pissing off some woman is not something you should be concerned with right now.

Clearing my throat and reminding myself that I'm a grown-ass adult and professional, I shake off my impromptu meeting with Amelia and open up the folder on my desk, preparing for my meeting at ten and putting that sexually charged interaction out of my mind—at least until later, when I can take care of the steel rod in my pants as well.

"So, since I convinced you to come out, does that mean I have to pay?" Nick asks as the waitress walks away after taking our drink order. It's Friday night after a long week, and when he invited me out, I almost declined. But my mother insisted I take some time for myself and decided to keep Oliver overnight. Plus, he made friends with one of her neighbors' kids, so he was begging to stay to play with his new friend anyway.

"Yup. You initiated this date, so I'm going to order the lobster," I joke.

Nick licks his lips. "Make it two then. Calories don't count tonight."

I chuckle and then lean back in my chair, surveying the busy restaurant around us. The bar in the middle of the restaurant is packed as a baseball game plays on televisions hung along the ceiling. Booths and tables are filled with families and couples out for a Friday night meal, and the smell of fried food and beer fills the air.

"So how have you been, man? Sorry, I haven't checked in on you since we signed the papers for your office, but life's been busy, and I knew you had some settling in to do. Plus, I've been a little preoccupied myself," he says with a smirk on his lips.

"Busy with who?" I ask, knowing that the only reason for that remark would have to be his happiness over a woman.

"Elena," he says with a roll of his tongue.

"And who is Elena?"

"The woman I'm seeing. And fuck, Ethan…she's gorgeous. Olive skin, green eyes, and long dark hair. She's a Spanish teacher and last night, we role-played teacher and the naughty student…it was the best sex of my life."

I hold up my hand. "Dude, I didn't need to know that."

"I don't care. I'm going to tell anyone I fucking can because it was so fucking hot." He shivers from his memories. "Have you ever been spanked with a ruler? If not, you should try it, man."

A mental image appears, and I slap it away as fast as I can. "I feel like you're sharing too much this early in the evening."

He laughs. "Aw, come on, man. If we were still back in college, we'd be trading stories over the girls we hooked up with all night."

"That was a long time ago, Nick. Things have changed."

He grimaces. "You're right, dude. Sorry. But haven't you been sowing some wild oats since your divorce?"

"And when the fuck would I have time to do that? Up until recently, Oliver was with me 24-7 except for when I was at work." The reminder of how long it's been since I've been laid instantly brings up images of Amelia. I'm surely going to hell for lusting after my friend's sister, even if we're not exactly besties. But that was the point of going out tonight. Nick insisted we hang out, rekindle our bromance, and I'm definitely not in a position to decline the offer of a friend in a new place—well, new as in not where I was just living.

"Fair point. By the way, I didn't tell my sister about your divorce and stuff. I figured it wasn't my place to say."

My heart rate increases at the mention of her.

So Amelia doesn't know everything about me? I thought for sure her brother would have mentioned something when she found out he sold me my office space. "Well, I appreciate that. It's not something I like to go around advertising, but when people find out, it sort of explains why I do what I do."

"I know. But just so you know, I thought my sister was going to rip my nipple off when I told her I knew you. So, please don't be a dick to her."

I scratch the back of my neck. "Uh, well…"

"You already were, weren't you?"

I struggle to get comfortable in my chair. "We've had some not-so-pleasant run-ins, you could say."

Nick shakes his head at me. "Look, you're both adults, so I'm just going to say this—be careful messing with my sister, Ethan. She's a force to be reckoned with. And when she feels strongly about something, like what she does for a living, she will defend it wholeheartedly."

Yeah, I think I'm beginning to notice that. "Noted."

He wipes his hands against one another in the air. "All right, that's all I have to say, and now I'm washing my hands of this and not getting involved. Just don't make me regret helping you out, man. Otherwise, it won't just be her wrath you feel."

Fuck, now I feel like shit. "I won't."

Staring off into space, now I know I need to try to make things right with Amelia. Nick is one of the only friends I have in LA, and I don't want me acting like a pompous ass to his sister to jeopardize that friendship. I make a mental note to stop by her office on Monday and try to smooth things over.

The truth is, I'm not usually a dick, but her presence has rattled me, both professionally and personally. She's a threat to my business and my mind. I can't stop thinking about her and what she looks like naked—and that's a problem.

"What are you looking at?" Nick asks, pulling me back to our conversation.

"Oh, nothing. It's just weird being out without Oliver." Nice save, Ethan. Quick on your feet as always.

"I know." He clasps me on the shoulder. "But this is good for you. I promise, I'll make sure to keep you company when I can."

"You mean when Elena isn't spanking you with rulers?" I tease him.

A voice above me cuts me off before he can answer. "Um, not sure what conversation we walked into, but I feel like that comment needs explaining." I look to my right and find two men standing beside our table, grinning as Nick scoots his chair back to greet them.

"Jeffrey, my man. So good to see you." Nick and Jeffrey share an embrace and then Jeffrey reaches for my hand

"Jeffrey."

"Ethan."

"Nice to meet you."

"Likewise."

Then he greets the other guy. "Damien, long time no see."

Damien takes one of the empty chairs at the table. "I know. It's been like what, two hours?"

"Ethan, this is Damien, Jeffrey's colleague, best friend, and the boyfriend of one of Amelia's friends, Charlotte. I'm currently helping Damien find a house for him and Charlotte."

"Yeah, but she doesn't know about it, so don't say anything."

"Couldn't if I wanted to," I reply. "I have no idea who Charlotte is. But it's nice to meet you." Damien and I shake hands.

Jeffrey takes the seat next to Nick as the waitress comes by and delivers our beers. "Can I get you something?"

"I'll have what they're having," he says.

"Same for me," Damien replies.

She nods and retreats from the table. "So, Ethan. Nick tells me you two go way back?" Jeffrey asks as we all settle in again. I know Nick mentioned drinks with the guys, but I guess I didn't realize I'd have to make small talk with the guys. Jesus, it really has been that long since I've been out.

"Yeah, college. It's been years since we've seen each other though. I just moved to Los Angeles from San Diego about a month ago."

"Ethan has had some life changes happening recently…hence, why we needed a boy's night out."

Jeffrey leans forward. "Girl problems?"

I huff out a laugh. "Yeah, I guess you could say that. Recently divorced. Well, not super recently. A few years ago, but I moved here to be closer to my mom. She helps a lot with my son."

Jeffrey winces. "Man, I'm sorry."

"Nah, it's okay. It was for the best."

"Is your ex-wife okay with the move?"

"Well, she's not around or involved in my son's life, so I don't really give a shit what she thinks," I say a little too harshly.

Damien hisses. "Damn. I take it you're not a big fan of hers?"

"Nope," I say matter-of-factly, ready to move on from this topic.

The second I start discussing Monica, my blood pressure goes through the roof. "But enough about that. I'm just glad to be out with some adults for a change."

"Well, then maybe you can be my new wingman. Damien is practically engaged now, and since Nick is too busy getting hit in the ass with rulers, that means you're the next best thing." Jeffrey leans forward in his seat.

Nick purses his lips and speaks before I can reply. "Um, she's a teacher, man."

Jeffrey's eyes go wide. "Oh fuck. You landed yourself a TILF?"

"What's a TILF?" I ask, but I'm pretty sure I can figure out the definition.

"Teacher I'd like to fuck," Nick replies with a bounce of his eyebrows. "And believe me, she makes all of those fantasies come true."

Jeffrey practically drools on the table. "Does she have a hot friend? Maybe a math teacher that will spank me every time I miss one of my multiplication table problems? I might just get them wrong on purpose if that's the case…"

"I'll ask her the next time we talk," Nick replies arrogantly.

"Jesus Christ, what did I get myself into this evening?" I mumble loud enough for both of them to hear as I drain nearly half of my beer just as the waitress comes by with Damien and Jeffrey's. "I'll have another, please," I tell her, lifting my glass. She nods and walks away again.

"Oh lighten up, dude." Nick smacks my shoulder, almost making me choke. "See, this is why you need to start dating."

"Fuck no. Seriously, Nick, dating is the last thing on my mind."

"Why? I'm not saying get married again to the first girl you talk to. But you need to let out some pent-up energy, sow some wild oats like I said."

"I'm not sowing any oats. I just moved away from the city I've been living in for years, started a new job, and my son is about to start school. I don't have time for women."

"Come on. You seriously don't even want to try dating again? I mean, not right this second, but you don't want to find a hot teacher to play out some fantasies with?" He waggles his eyebrows. "I'm telling you…life changing," he whispers with a cheesy grin on his lips.

"Nope. I'm done with that shit. From now on, it's just my hand and me." I hold up my hand just as one of the servers walks by, cringing. "Fuck."

The boys all chuckle. "Well, I feel sorry for your dick then."

"Don't be. I've invested in some very expensive lotion."

All of us share another good laugh, and the conversation moves on to other topics. I know my brain doesn't want the complications of a relationship, but my body can only focus on the one woman it seems to be craving to satisfy my growing itch. And no amount of lotion and jacking off seems to be helping the itch to go away. I sincerely hope that's not an omen to the stupid decisions I feel I'd be willing to make just to know what it is like to be with Amelia. But part of me doesn't think that will be an issue anyway. She doesn't happen to be a huge fan of mine currently, and I don't see that changing anytime soon unless I try to smooth things over.

And it looks like I need to—for my friendship with Nick, for my own sanity, and so I can feel better about my behavior. Maybe then too, once we stop fighting, I won't want her as much. That fire and tension will be gone. That's probably what's fueling my desire for her. And if I squash that, Amelia will no longer be a problem.

Sounds like a plan. And now I know exactly what I need to do come Monday morning.

"I'm scared, Daddy." Oliver wraps his arms around my legs as we stand in front of the school, waiting for the gates to open. It's his first day of kindergarten, and I'm feeling all kinds of mixed emotions.

"It's okay to be a little scared. This is new, but it's also exciting. And Grandma will be here at the end of the day to pick you up." I crouch down to his level, holding his hands in mine now. "Plus, I can't wait to hear all about your day later tonight. We'll make spaghetti for dinner too."

"Spaghetti is my favorite," he says with a slight smile on his lips now.

"I know." Winking at him, I stand once more just as the gates are unlocked. "This is going to be a new adventure for you, kid. You're going to learn so much."

"I like adventures."

I rub his shoulder. "Good, because life is full of them."

"Let me get a picture of you two before we go inside," my mother declares, motioning us over to a tree nearby.

Oliver starts to bounce and wiggle as we move. "But the gates are open, Grandma. I don't want to be late." Judging by his enthusiasm now, I guess Oliver isn't scared anymore.

"Just really quick, honey. You'll want to remember this day later."

I move toward the tree and stand proudly next to my son. For years I envisioned this moment a lot differently, mostly because I anticipated Monica being here. But now, I know things are better this way. Standing tall, I let my mom take as many pictures as she wants and immediately ask her to send them to my phone.

After pictures are done, and Oliver is practically chomping at the bit, my mother and I walk Oliver into his school and meet his teacher. His classroom is colorful and full of information ready for him to absorb. Tables with tiny chairs are spaced out inside the room, a large blue rug is situated in front of a rocking chair in the corner, and the walls are covered with posters and bulletin boards that span every color of the rainbow.

After Oliver chooses his seat, I bend down in front of him. "Be kind to your classmates and pay attention today, Ollie," I tell my son as I hug him goodbye.

"You too, Daddy. Go make money and pay bills." He releases me and then picks up his crayon to finish his coloring page.

A few years ago, when I would drop him off at daycare, he used to ask me why I had to leave, and I would always tell him that I had to go make money so I could pay our bills. After that, he would use that as our parting words when we said goodbye. It's been months since he's uttered those words, but hearing them today almost brings a tear to my eye. It's the perfect reminder of how fast he's growing and how all of the hard work and choices I'm making are ultimately for him.

As I drive to my office, knowing I would be arriving late today, I think about what a hypocrite I sounded like this morning though. I literally told my kid to be kind to others, and here I've been acting like a dick to Amelia. All weekend I stewed on how I've behaved toward her and how now her perception of me is skewed.

I don't like feeling threatened, and given all of the other changes going on in my life lately, I'm beginning to think I've been taking out my insecurities and frustrations on her. Don't get me wrong, I've had a little fun watching her reactions to me, too, but I know that is not the type of dynamic I want to maintain with her, so I need to smooth things over today.

My plan is to go over around lunchtime when I know she won't have a client. I just hope she lets me into her office after her threat last week.

When I exit my car, I pull up the photo of Oliver and me from this morning on my phone and study it as I walk up to the building, smiling from ear to ear as I look at my boy. Pride rushes through me at how resilient he is, how kind and energetic and loving he is despite Monica's absence. At least I know at the end of the day that I'm doing something right by him. I've made a lot of mistakes in my life and still manage to add to the list on a daily basis, but there's nothing I've done in my life that I have more pride in than raising him well up to this point.

"Well, there's a sight I've never seen before."

I lift my head to find Amelia walking toward me, carrying a few bags over her shoulder and pushing her glasses up her nose. She's wearing a light-blue dress that makes her hair appear brighter and does nothing to hide her perfect body, but her face shines with mischief.

I stop in my steps, waiting for her to arrive in front of me. "And what sight would that be?"

"A genuine smile on your lips. And with the way you were looking at your phone?" She shakes her head. "I'm guessing you either got a dirty text from your latest flavor of the week or the latest paycheck from the last marriage you dissolved."

The guy who had every intention of making things right with her ten minutes ago says that I should correct her and put her in her place. But that asshole guy that enjoys making her flustered? He steps in front at this moment and takes the lead. "I only smile like that when I feel my client gets what he or she deserves. And how do you know that I'm not tickled pink because one of your clients has already stopped by my office and asked for a consultation?"

The pleased smirk on her face instantly disappears. "What you deserve is a root canal and to step on a Lego for helping ruin the sanctity of marriage."

I throw my head back in laughter. "Believe me, stepping on a Lego is a horrible experience I wouldn't even wish on my worst enemy. But I'm honored that you feel I'm yours."

Taking a step toward me, she hikes her bags up higher on her shoulder. "You are the enemy, Ethan Fuller. And I'm going to love watching you get what you deserve." She arches her brow and then spins on her heels, heading right toward her office and leaving me lusting after her.

God, I want to fuck her and show her how crazy she makes me. Why does one of the most beautiful women I've seen in ages have to be someone that stands for the exact opposite of what I do for a living, and why does she have to be my friend's sister?

"Fuck my life," I mutter as I finish the walk to my office and step inside, shoving my phone in my pocket. "Good morning, Yvonne."

My secretary is sitting at her desk acting as our receptionist, and her head lifts with a bright smile on her lips when she hears me. "How was kindergarten drop-off?"

"Great. Oliver was a little scared, but once we got inside, he was eager for us to leave."

"That's great. My son held onto my leg and screamed for five minutes until the teacher finally bribed him with candy, and I snuck out the door."

"Yikes. Sounds like fun."

"Parenting always is." She winks.

"All right, are we all ready for the new clients in the conference room?"

"Yup. Paperwork is on the table, ready to go."

"Excellent." I head to my office, grab my things, and then proceed to the conference room just a few minutes later. But when I go to take a seat in my chair, the brochure sitting on top of our welcome package for clients freezes me in my tracks.

"Before you go through with the big D, please consider therapy."

A picture of Amelia's office, as well as her contact information, stares back at me as I pick up the tri-fold of paper and read through her welcome pamphlet.

My blood pressure spikes, my jaw tightens, and suddenly the apology that I had planned for later today flies right out of my head.

"Yvonne!" I rush from the conference room and watch my secretary jump in her seat.

"Yes, Mr. Fuller?"

"What the hell are these?" I hold up the brochure in question.

With wide eyes, she slinks back in her chair. "Those are the brochures that Dr. St. Clair dropped by earlier this morning."

"What?"

"She said you two spoke and decided to cross-promote. I figured that's why she was waiting for you in your office last week. I really thought the slogan was quite catchy," she continues, feeding my skyrocketing blood pressure even more. "And what a great idea to offer counseling to our clients. Sometimes divorce can be avoided if you just talk out your issues."

Is there steam coming out of my ears? I feel like there's steam.

"Fuck!" Spinning around with the brochure in hand, I slam the door of my office open and beeline right for Amelia's door. I don't care if she has a client right now. This conversation can't wait.

Knocking way more than politely on the glass on her door, I rock on my heels as I wait for her to answer. And when she does and sees what I assume can only be described as pure rage on my face, her beaming white smile holds me hostage for a moment until her extreme pleasure from the state I'm in becomes apparent.

"Yes, Mr. Fuller? Can I help you?"

"Care to explain these?" I hold the pamphlet up for the third time in less than five minutes.

"Oh, those. I figured if you were adamant about leaving your business cards in my office, it's the least I could do to give your clients some reading material as well."

"Before you go through with the big D, please consider therapy?" I mockingly read out loud in a feminine voice. "Really catchy."

"I thought so." Her grin is controlled, but I can tell that she's fucking loving this.

"You know, I had every intention of coming over here today to apologize to you, to admit that I've been an ass since we met and that my reaction to you has been unwarranted, that you haven't truly done anything to me that justifies my behavior. But now…"

She opens the door wider and crosses her arms over her chest, pushing her breasts together, and I fight like hell not to look down and appreciate them. "Yes?"

"Now this is war."

Narrowing her eyes at me, we stand there in silence until she finally speaks. "Are you sure you want that?"

"You're the one who entered into this battle."

"But you started it."

"I don't think this complex is big enough for the both of us, Dr. St. Clair."

"Are we in an old western film now, Mr. Fuller?"

Fuck, the woman is making me lose my concentration. The flecks of gold in her eyes are distracting, the purse of her lips has me wanting to smash my mouth to hers, and the crinkle between her brows is so damn sexy that I wonder if she wears that same expression when she comes.

What the hell, Ethan? You're fucking losing it, man.

Before I do something I can't take back and give in to the physical draw I feel toward her, I step back a few feet and continue moving backward while keeping our eyes locked. "Don't say I didn't warn you."

"I'm not scared of you, Ethan. On the contrary, I think you're scared of me." I freeze in my movements but then she drops her arms and moves forward, closing the distance I just put between us. "I think my job and my presence here derails you, makes you think about all of the demons you're keeping locked inside. Perhaps you yourself could benefit from a little therapy." She grabs the brochure from my hands, whips out a pen from God knows where, and presses the pamphlet to my chest as she scribbles something on the paper.

"Here," she says, leaving the paper pressed to me until I reach up and grab it before she starts to walk away but still watches me from over her shoulder. "First session is on me. I don't normally help men in their thirties process their problems unless it's with their partners. But for you," she continues as she drops her eyes up and down my body, "I guess I can make an exception. Have a good day, Mr. Fuller."

I look down at her writing, her signature with a *'20 percent off your first session'* voucher written in the ink. And then she enters her office once more, the click of her lock echoing as she leaves me standing in place, hard as stone, and knowing now more than ever—I am thoroughly fucked when it comes to this woman.

Chapter 5

Amelia

Closing the door to my office, I march over to my desk and place my palms on the surface, leaning forward as I catch my breath. "Holy shit."

As I stare at my reflection in the mirror on the wall, my heart threatens to burst from my ribcage. I'm so nervous that I think I might pass out, and my armpits are so sweaty I could give Mary Katherine Gallagher a run for her money.

But keeping my cool in front of Ethan just ranked in one of my top five moments of my life, hands down. The look on his face was priceless as I put him in his place and offered him a little therapy of his own.

The truth of the matter is, we all have shit in our pasts that we don't deal with, try to sweep under the rug, or perhaps just don't realize what an impact it had on us until later in our lives. But I can tell that Ethan's problem with me has far more to do with him. It's not just me being a threat to his business—and part of me hates that I want to know what it is.

Alas, I know he'll never take me up on my offer for a discounted session, but that wasn't the point. The point was that he has a lot of balls trying to cross over into my territory and stake a claim. So now I've turned the tables on him, and there's one person I want to tell about my triumphs more than anything.

"Talk to me, Amelia Be Delia." Penelope answers the phone sounding busy but cheery nonetheless.

"I dropped off the brochures this morning, and they got me just the reaction I was looking for."

Penelope cackles through the line. "Excellent. Did you show him your BDE?"

"I really hate that phrase, Pen. I don't have a dick."

"Big Dick Energy doesn't just apply to men, Amelia. Would you rather me say Big Vagina Energy?"

I contemplate her words in silence. "I see your point."

"Thank you. So I take it our little enemy wasn't pleased about the delivery?"

Smiling, I finally relax a bit and slink back into my chair. Glancing at the clock, I note that I have ten minutes until my client arrives. "Hardly. I dropped them off at his office this morning before he arrived, which he was late today by the way. Not sure how he's managing a business by starting work at ten a few days a week, but that doesn't matter."

"Focus, Amelia."

"Right. So I told his secretary that we had an agreement to cross-promote, and I would love for the pamphlets to be used in the welcome paperwork for their clients."

Penelope's laughter has me grinning even harder. "I love it."

"Needless to say, I imagine his secretary did as she was told, but he discovered it just a few moments ago."

"Is he fuming?"

I stand up and move to my door, peering around the curtains to see if he's still outside. "He was when he came over and gave me a piece of his mind a few moments ago. It seems he's gone back into his office for now, but the best part was when I wrote a 20 percent off voucher on the pamphlet he had in his hand. The look on his face was priceless, Pen."

"Good work, soldier. Now, let me know if you need me to drop the atomic bomb. You know he won't know what hit him if we do that."

Yesterday at brunch, as I was filling the girls in on the developments with Ethan, everyone started brainstorming ways to get under his skin and put him in his place after his business card stunt. Penelope's final move is pretty monumental, but I don't want to have to use it unless absolutely necessary.

"I'll keep you posted."

"Excellent. In the meantime, try not to sleep with him, okay?"

I nearly choke on my tongue. "Penelope, that is not going to happen."

She sighs knowingly, like this conversation is not stimulating enough for her, and she's getting bored. "Oh, Amelia. Do you not remember what we just went through with Charlotte?"

My confidence starts to retreat. "What do you mean?"

"All the sexual tension boiling over between Charlotte and Damien was bound to end with them fucking, and look what happened. I hate to break it to you, honey…but you're in a very similar predicament."

"No…I'm not…"

She cackles again. "I imagine it must be hard for you to hear this, given your profession and all, but Amelia? You're in denial, honey. You want the man's dick."

"Penelope!" I scoff, marching back to my desk and noting that I only have three minutes now before I absolutely have to get off the phone. "Look, I know I admitted that the man is hot, and there is no denying that. But after the way we've interacted with each other? I could never..."

"Never say never, girl."

"Ugh. Whose side are you on?" My resolve is wavering the longer this conversation goes on.

I'm not naive. I know I'm attracted to the man. And yes, perhaps I've fantasized about him a handful of times since we met, but it's harmless. There is no way in hell I would actually act on it.

"Yours, girl. And you should know by now that I always root for my friends partaking in some toe-curling, good ol' nasty fucking. Every woman needs to be fucked within an inch of her life once in a while, and sex with the enemy? That's the best kind, my dear."

I see my cheeks blush right before my eyes as I look up in the mirror, staring back at the woman I barely recognize at this moment.

I'm usually so cool, calm, and collected. But Ethan makes me irrational, crazy, and impulsive. Never in a million years would I say things to a man as I have to him, even if he crossed me. I have no problem defending myself when the situation warrants it, but Ethan makes my talons come out, and my words have been far sharper than I normally would allow them to be. There's more to this attraction I feel toward him, and that's forcing me to show my not-so-nice sides.

"I have to go."

"The truth hurts sometimes, doesn't it, Amelia Be Delia?"

"My client is coming. We'll talk later."

"Use protection!" she shouts into the phone before I end the call and slam it on my desk, as if hurting the phone will undo the truth of that conversation.

But I barely have time to think about the can of worms Penelope opened up and the lasting ramifications of my discussion with Ethan this morning before there's a polite knock on my door.

Smoothing down the front of my dress, I greet my first client with a smile on my face and slip into therapist mode, hoping that underneath my put-together shell, she can't see that I'm just as much of a mess as the next person.

After my run-in with Ethan on Monday, I thought for sure I would have heard from him the next day in some shape, form, or fashion. But I was greeted with nothing but silence, which is even more unsettling in a way. However, by Wednesday, I now know why he didn't retaliate yesterday because his next move required some preparation.

As I pull up to the office, I see a sign spinner standing on the corner of the street, holding up a giant arrow advertising his firm. "Fuller & Grant will get you what you want in your divorce!" the sign says in big, bold lettering as the man head bobs to his music playing in his headphones.

I roll my eyes as I park my car and hustle up to my office, not at all prepared that there was more to his scheme. A sign spinner is eye-catching, although I don't know that they really do much from an advertising perspective. However, it's not just the sign spinner that he's added to his move.

A standing chalkboard sign is stationed right at the opening of the courtyard that separates our offices, and the message on the board has me biting my tongue in an instant.

"20% off lawyers' fees if Dr. St. Clair didn't help you. Come in and ask us how we can help you move on with your life."

A giant, double-sided green arrow points toward his office and mine, and by this point, all I can see is red, and I'm not even color-blind.

It's one thing to innocently leave business cards or fib a small white lie about handing out brochures to clients. But this? This is borderline slander. He could ruin my reputation if people start giving up on therapy before they actually make their breakthroughs or if people assume I don't know what I'm doing because he's insinuating that I can't help them.

I drop my bags off in my office and march across to his, ready for a fight. My palms are sweaty, my pulse is racing, and my feet are pounding the pavement beneath them.

But then I stop before I ever open the door.

This is what he wants. He wants this reaction from me. He wants to see me pissed and angry, fueling the fire and war between us.

And even though I want to tell him what I think and how his little move makes me feel, I also know that sometimes you have to be the bigger person and say nothing at all. But that doesn't mean I can't fight back. He'll just have to get the message through my actions and not my words.

I take a deep breath, plaster a fake smile on my lips, and retreat to my office to retaliate in private instead, knowing there's only one person who can help me put an end to this.

I hit Penelope's name and wait for her to answer.

"Hello, my friend. How can I help you this morning?"

"Do it."

She pauses. "Are you asking me to do what I think you are?"

"Yes." I nod, even though she can't see me. "It's time to drop the atomic bomb."

An evil laugh fills the line. "How atomic do you want me to be?"

"Money is no object. Hit him hard, Pen. I want this man to wish he'd never messed with me."

I hear her click a few buttons and then declare, "It's done. I already had the order in my cart, ready to go. I knew this call was coming."

"How many did you order?"

Her evil laugh rings out again. "Don't worry. Let it be a surprise."

"Thank you."

"You're welcome. And you can thank me again once you two screw. This is the most dire game of foreplay I've ever been a part of, and I'm not even the one in the running for an orgasm."

Thursday starts off the same as Wednesday, the chalkboard sign and sign spinner taunting me as I make my way to my office. But I'm not going to let Ethan and his shenanigans get me down today. Brayden called me last night, and we finalized plans for our date on Friday evening.

I'm not going to lie—between work and ruminating on how to make Ethan's life a living hell within legal means—this week made me forget about our date. But after talking to him briefly, I remembered how excited I was when he asked me out. The thought of dating again after a long time is scary, but I also know that it's necessary. And besides, it has to be a hell of a lot healthier than wanting to hate fuck the divorce attorney across the courtyard.

My first two sessions of the day are couples, one of which is John and Melissa. It's been a little over a week since I saw them last, and I know he's since been to the men's clinic that Brayden owns.

"Well, John. How did the appointment at the men's clinic go?" I ask as I settle into my seat and look across at the two of them sitting on the couch. Daylight fills the room, the bright hue almost like a ray of hope.

"Um, it was eye-opening," he replies, throwing his body back into the couch.

"How so?"

"He learned he has the testosterone level of a fifty-five-year-old man!" Melissa exclaims with a smile on her face.

"Jesus, honey. You don't have to shout it for the entire neighborhood to hear."

She turns to her husband and places her hand on his knee. "I'm not. I'm just excited."

"Why on earth are you excited?" John asks his wife incredulously.

"Because this provides us with a very logical explanation for your lack of a sex drive, John," I answer for Melissa as she nods in agreement. "This means we have something to consider when it comes to helping you and Melissa move forward."

John sighs. "Yeah, I guess."

Melissa turns to her husband. "They can help us, John. The shots they told you about at the clinic can get your levels back up, and Amelia can help us with what we need to do in the bedroom." She turns to me. "When can we start?"

I smile, loving her excitement. The woman clearly wants to get laid, and soon.

Yeah, I feel you on that one, sister.

"You can start tonight, Melissa."

"Okay. How?"

"I want you to talk about having sex with each other but not actually complete the physical act," I answer blatantly. John and Melissa just stare at me. "Look, the reason you're here is because sex is what you both feel is missing, so you need to start by talking about it. Tell each other what you want to do to one another. Remind each other about the things that you do that you both enjoy, or recall a memory of a particularly hot time that you never forget. You can compare it to phone sex if you want. Lie on your sides, face one another, and voice all of your ideas and thoughts out loud while staring into each other's eyes."

"But don't touch each other?" Melissa clarifies.

"No, unless you both decide to go there."

"How is that supposed to help?" John challenges me.

"Because our minds are so much more powerful than we care to admit." Yeah, just how yours can't stop thinking about Ethan, huh, Amelia? "By talking about it, remembering a time when you couldn't keep your hands off each other, and recalling sexual moments between you two, you're going to reactivate that part of your brain. And it will give you time to think about it."

"What if we get so turned on that we want to have sex?" Melissa asks now, hope in her voice.

"Then give in to that need, like I said, as long as you're both in that space. Believe me, I want you to have sex, but only if it feels organic. If not, just talk, and experience intimacy without being intimate. Sometimes we forget that all the things that come before sex are just as important as the act itself."

Like business wars as an act of foreplay.

John nods reluctantly. "Talking…about sex?"

"Yes. And I know it can feel awkward at first, but being able to talk about it makes the act that much more enjoyable. And John? Please get those shots regularly as soon as possible. I promise you will feel a difference in your energy and libido."

"I got one dose the other day, but the doctor said it can take a few weeks for things to kick in."

"That's correct, but I'm so glad you're open to trying this."

"Thank you, Dr. St. Clair." Melissa rushes across the room to hug me.

"You're welcome."

We spend the rest of the time working on other issues, and by the end of the session, both John and Melissa look more at ease.

That's why I do what I do. Being able to help people feel lighter, feel normal—it's the power of therapy. To know that you're not crazy, that your thoughts are validated, that the emotions that feel insurmountable at times can be named and have a purpose, and can be used in a healthy way.

And helping people achieve that with their partners is the icing on the cake.

After lunch, a client that I've been seeing for almost a year now comes in.

"Georgiana. It's so good to see you."

"You too, Dr. St. Clair."

I wait for her to settle into the couch and then read her energy before speaking. Her shoulders aren't drawn up, her skin looks clear, and I can almost see a smile on her face. "You look happy, Georgiana."

That hint of a smile builds. "I am. I…I met someone."

Georgiana attends UCLA, my alma mater, and came to see me shortly after she was raped by the boyfriend of one of her close friends. Not only did her friend not believe her after the fact, but the guy and girl proceeded to tell everyone that she came onto him. It has been a rollercoaster helping her work through the betrayal, intimacy issues, and trauma. But today it looks like we're making progress.

"I'm glad to hear that, although remember there is no timeline for how fast you need to move forward."

"I know, but he's in one of my upper division writing classes, so we bonded over our love of classic literature and have been spending a lot of time getting to know each other."

"Okay," I reply optimistically. "Continue…"

Georgiana proceeds to tell me about how much time they've been spending together, how he makes her feel safe, and how she feels he may be the guy she could move on with physically.

"That is a big step to take."

"I know. And I know I can change my mind at any time…"

"Yes, you can. Just because you feel ready one minute doesn't mean you can't have a change of heart in the next. And if he doesn't understand that, then he's not the right person."

"I told him what happened," she confesses, which is huge for her progress.

"And how did he react?"

"He hugged me, held me, and apologized that I ever had to go through something like that."

I smile, relieved that there are still good men out in the world. "He sounds like a genuinely good guy."

"He is. I know it's early, but I just wanted to say that I haven't felt this strong in almost a year, Dr. St. Clair. And that's all because of you."

Tears threaten to build, but I hold them back. It's not that I don't think I shouldn't be allowed to show emotion in front of my clients, but I like to keep the sessions about them. "No, that's because of you, Georgiana. You've put in the work. You're the one moving forward and working to overcome that experience. You're not letting the experience control you anymore, and that's the most powerful part of your strength."

When the session ends, I decide to walk with her outside to get some sunshine and fresh air.

"Thank you again." She wipes away a few tears from under her eyes. "I'll see you in two weeks." She pulls me in for a hug, and I have no problem giving that to her. Hell, I hug any client that needs it. The power of human touch is incredible and a highly underutilized antidepressant.

"See you then. Good luck, and remember to take things slow and make sure they feel right."

I watch her walk away, more than proud of how much she has grown since she walked into my office, scared, alone, and lacking confidence. But then a voice over my shoulder breaks through my moment.

"I didn't realize you made your clients pay for hugs."

I spin to face him. "Excuse me?"

"Is a hug part of the package deal? Something included with your fees so your clients can feel love since they aren't getting it from their partners?"

I'm floored. I didn't think Ethan's cockiness would allow him to stoop that low, but I guess I was wrong.

"For your information, and without breaking doctor-patient confidentiality, that young woman is not married. She's actually overcoming severe trauma from the past year. She isn't coming to me to save her marriage, and not that you deserve the right to know, but that's not the only thing I do, Ethan." I take a few steps toward him and poke a finger into his chest.

His eyes go wide as he realizes his mistake. "Oh." He clears his throat. "Fuck, Amelia, I'm…"

Holding my hand up in front of his face now, I cut him off, and thankfully he takes the hint. "Not every client I work with is married. Sometimes the point of therapy is about saving your own dignity, too, about trying to revive a healthy sexual relationship with yourself, or knowing that at least you tried everything in your power not to feel like you're walking around with the weight of the world on your shoulders."

He swallows. "I'm sorry. I…I shouldn't have said anything."

"No, you shouldn't have. And hopefully, this will remind you that you never know what someone else is going through. You may never know how hard someone has fought for their relationship with someone else or themselves, so you're better off saying nothing at all."

And then I leave, retreat back into my office, and let disappointment come over me.

Ethan and I have both acted immaturely and out of character since we met, but that little comment just now was crossing the line. And I don't want any more part in that.

Today was a reminder that what I do is far too important to worry about what he's doing. And so from now on, I'm going to protect my clients and my job from him. Ethan Fuller no longer exists as far as I'm concerned.

"Amelia St. Clair?" A masculine voice pulls my attention from the file I'm reviewing in front of me. I stand from my desk and greet the delivery man who just entered my office.

"Yes. That's me."

"These are for you." He sets two potted orchids down on the small coffee table in the front of my office, one yellow and one purple. "Can you sign here, please?"

I set the file on my desk and stride over to him, scribbling my name on his paper. "Thank you."

"No problem."

As soon as he exits, I turn to study the flowers, caught off guard by this unexpected gift.

I love orchids. In fact, they're my favorite flower. Back in college, Charlotte, Noelle, Penelope, and I went to get matching tattoos of our favorite flowers on our shoulders. It was a moment that solidified our friendship and reminded me that the bond we share is rare and delicate, just like orchids are.

However, I can't imagine any of the girls sending these to me. It's not my birthday, and there are two flowers here, not three. Usually, they will each send me something.

So who could these be from? I don't see a card anywhere, and the delivery guy didn't hand me anything.

But then it hits me—Brayden.

Tonight is our date, and he must have sent these to me in anticipation. But wouldn't he have left a message if that were the case?

I don't have much time to contemplate his intentions because my next client and her husband walk through the door just a few seconds later.

"Good morning, Dr. St. Clair." Kelly and her husband, Drew, waltz in just a few minutes before their appointment.

"Good morning."

Kelly instantly gravitates toward my delivery. "Aw, orchids. Such a beautiful flower."

"I agree." I move to grab their file from my desk, not wanting to waste any more time ruminating. "Are you two ready?"

Drew juts his thumb over his shoulder. "Are you aware there's a divorce attorney right across the courtyard from you?" he asks.

"Oh, I'm well aware, unfortunately."

"But you were here first, right?" He continues talking as we make our way back to the room where I hold my sessions.

"Yes."

"Damn, what a dick," he states bluntly.

And I can't help but chuckle. "This may sound unprofessional, but I have to agree."

Chapter 6

Ethan

You know when you step on a piece of gum, and it attaches itself to the bottom of your shoe, then you have to stand there and drag your shoe on the ground to try to wipe it off? But rather than it coming off cleanly, it makes an even bigger mess, the strings of stickiness stretching out between the ground and your shoe that are no longer recognizable as a whole?

Well, I feel like one of those pieces of gum right now—a sticky, stringy mess and borderline piece of shit.

Yesterday, I took things too far. I tried to be a smartass to Amelia again, teasing her about hugging her clients, and damn, did she make me wish I could burrow underground and not come out until winter was over.

And I can't even fault her for that. I was out of place. And it seems that no matter what I know in my head to be the right decision, my mouth is getting too far ahead of doing the right thing.

Like my sign spinner and chalkboard sign—a classic way to bring in business, but also a jab at her after her brochure stunt. But she hasn't said a word about it, which tells me that I'm the immature asshole in this situation, and I can't even fight the truth about that.

So this morning, I decided to take my chalkboard sign down and send her a peace offering—orchids. My mother always loved them, so I figured they were a safe bet. When I looked up online which ones to send, I decided on two. Yellow to symbolize friendship and new beginnings, and purple to represent admiration and respect.

The truth is I do respect her—I admire her determination, her strength, and her courage to stand up to me. And as much as I hate to admit it, she obviously takes her job very seriously, and I have to respect that as well.

But my actions and words have sent an entirely different message, and it's time I set the record straight.

I wanted to wait to approach her after I knew the flowers had been delivered, but she never came out of her office. And now it's almost five thirty, and I'm wondering if she slipped out without me catching her.

I've officially crossed the line into stalker territory, and as I peer through the blinds in my personal office that give me a view of the courtyard, a low, frustrated growl leaves my lips.

"Fuck this." I grab my briefcase and decide to stop waiting to innocently run into her on purpose. Time to man up, apologize for my behavior in person and make things right.

"Thank you again for agreeing to pick me up here." Amelia's voice has my head snapping up as I walk out the front door of my office and see her finally, standing outside her office door, talking to a man. He's tall, but not as tall as me, wearing a suit and a smile that

I can only read as pure excitement from just being in Amelia's presence.

"No problem. You were right. Battling traffic on a Friday night in Los Angeles would have taken too much time, and we wouldn't have made our reservation."

"Yes. My house is too far from here to keep up with the time-line." Amelia tucks one of her curls behind her ear, revealing silver drop earrings that glimmer as the sun catches them. She's wearing an olive-green dress that wraps around her body and cinches at her waist, highlighting her hourglass figure. It's something she could wear to work, but then again, it's offering a supple view of her cleavage that I'm sure she wouldn't deem professional.

And that's when it hits me—this man is here to pick her up for a date.

And that realization makes my stomach drop.

The man staring down at her like he just won first place at the science fair finally speaks again. "I'm just honored that you agreed to go out with me tonight." *Jesus, kissing her ass already?*

"Well, I'm honored that you asked," Amelia replies cheekily, and that's when I decide that it's time to make my presence known.

Clearing my throat a little louder than necessary, I catch Amelia's attention from across the courtyard, her eyes widening as she realizes I was encroaching on their moment. But then her eyes narrow into slits, and the hatred I know she probably feels for me right now becomes more than apparent.

"Good evening," I say, casually striding in their direction.

"Hello," the man standing next to her says.

Amelia looks between us as I arrive just a few feet from them, so we look more like three people having a conversation than me crashing their date. "Brayden Anderson, this is Ethan Fuller. Ethan, this is Dr. Brayden Anderson."

Throwing that doctor tag in there, huh?

I reach out to shake the man's hand, making sure to stand up tall and make a presence with the height advantage I have on the guy. "Nice to meet you."

Brayden intercepts my hand, a curious gleam in his eye. The man isn't stupid and obviously knows something is up. "Likewise. Do you two know each other? Work together?"

Amelia interjects before I can. "Oh God, no. Ethan works at the law firm just over there." She points with her finger behind me.

"Yup. I'm a divorce attorney. So while Amelia is stitching marriages back together, I'm ripping them apart. The circle of life, am I right?"

Brayden fakes a laugh. "Yeah, I guess. Well, we should really be going."

Amelia shoots me a glare. "Yes, we should."

"Daddy!" The pitter-patter of little feet pulls my attention to my left as Oliver runs toward me. And at that very moment, I realize that I had forgotten my mom had texted me a few hours ago saying they would be in the area, so she would just drop him off to me here.

Fuck. I was so distracted by Amelia and worrying about talking to her—which is pretty much a lost cause now that she's leaving for a date—that I completely spaced.

"Hey, buddy." I bend down and open my arms to catch him as he pummels into me. "How was your day?"

"I made three new friends, and I learned to read five new words, and now I'm really hungry."

I sniff, catching the scent of lemon. "Why do you smell like lemons?"

"Because Grandma took me to the ice cream shop just now, and I got the lemon kind, Daddy."

"Is that your new favorite flavor?" Amelia asks, pulling my sight up to her as she smiles down at my son. And at that moment, I realize she now knows my one and only weakness and a detail about my life that I always try to keep close to the chest.

"Yes! Hey, you're the lemon lady!"

"What?" I ask, thoroughly confused.

"Hi, there," my mother finally joins in on the conversation as I stand tall again while my knees crack from the pressure. "We saw you a couple of weeks ago at the gelato place. My grandson, Oliver here, has been obsessed with the lemon flavor ever since you recommended it to him," she says to Amelia. And now I'm even more caught off guard.

But Amelia doesn't miss a beat and continues talking to my son. "It's the best kind, huh, Oliver?"

"Yes. And when I eat it, I make this face 'cause it's so sour." Oliver scrunches up his face and puckers his lips.

Amelia laughs, and God, that sound is one I haven't been privy to from her just yet. Although I guess every time we've interacted so far has been less than amusing for her.

"That's the best part. And then your tongue gets kind of fuzzy too, huh?"

"Yes!" Oliver agrees enthusiastically.

Brayden clears his throat, much like I did earlier, to break up the moment. "Well, this has been fun, but we'd better get going if we're going to make our reservation."

"Oh, yes. Sorry." Amelia turns to Oliver once more. "It was nice to meet you, Oliver." And then she glances at me with a much softer look on her face than before. "Have a good night, Ethan."

But before I can reply, Brayden interjects while glaring in my direction. "You two have fun. I know we will." He places his hand on the small of her back and begins to lead her away.

"Don't have too much fun," I call after them like a petulant child, and once they're out of sight, my eyes drop down to my mother's, whose brow is arched so high, it's almost hitting her hairline.

"Care to explain that comment to me, son?"

"What?" I fake nonchalance, but I know my mother can see right through me.

"Who is that?"

"Yeah, who is the lemon lady, Daddy?" Oliver asks as he tugs on my coat.

I sigh, relenting to the fact that I know neither of them is going to let this slide. "Her name is Amelia St. Clair, and she's a marriage therapist whose office is also in this complex." I point to her door as my mother glances in that direction and then back to me.

"Oh, well, isn't that rich?" She chuckles.

"Uh, it's been interesting, to say the least."

"And that little comment you made to her date? That doesn't have to do with the fact that she's…"

"Pretty, Daddy. She's really pretty. Her hair is yellow like sunshine and lemons."

Smiling down at my son, I can see that he's already smitten with Amelia too. Welcome to the club, kid. "Yes, she is very pretty."

"We should be her friend. I like making new friends."

"Yes, Ethan. You should definitely try to be her friend," my mother suggests with a bounce of her eyebrows.

"All right, you two are high on sugar right now, it seems, so let's get some dinner and then get home, shall we?"

"Where are we going, Daddy?" Oliver asks as I grab his hand and walk out to the car with Oliver and my mom in tow.

"I was thinking John's Incredible Pizza so we can play lots of games and win prizes."

"Yes!" Oliver jumps across the asphalt until we arrive at my car. I open the door and help him inside, securing him in his booster chair before shutting the door.

"Now that your son can't hear, care to tell me what that was all about?" My mother crosses her arms over her chest and stares up at me.

"Amelia and I haven't exactly been cordial with one another, given what each of us does for a living, but I was eager to get things back on the right foot before I realized she was being picked up for a date tonight."

"And how did that make you feel?"

I glare in her direction. "I know what you're doing, and it isn't going to work. Amelia and I are adults, and she can date whomever she wants."

"It doesn't bother you?"

"Mom, I love you, but I don't have time for a woman, let alone a relationship. And truthfully, I don't know that I ever will again."

Her lips fall into a frown. "I met someone."

"What?" Her admission catches me by surprise.

She nods. "I have. I never thought I'd move on either after your father left, but life is too short to spend it alone. And you're a man... with needs..."

I hold my hand up. "Please don't finish that sentence. I can't talk about this with you."

She shrugs. "I'm just saying. If you like her, which it seems that you do even though I know you'll stand here and deny it until you're blue in the face, the least you can do is try, Ethan."

A heavy sigh leaves my lips. "I have tried before, Mom. And look where that got me."

"Not every woman is Monica."

"No, but any woman I bring around will impact Oliver even more. I don't want to risk him being left behind for a second time. And he's older now too. He'll remember it."

"You think he doesn't ask about his mom?" she counters. "Because he does."

"I know, and that's hard enough to explain. So what if someone comes in, someone who is around, and things don't work out, and he has to see her all the time? That's going to be ten times harder."

She holds her hands up in defeat. "Okay, I won't push anymore. I just know that you are far too young and handsome to be alone."

Pulling her in for a hug, I kiss her temple. "Well, I got my good looks from you."

"And your sarcasm."

"My best quality, in my opinion."

I say goodbye to my mother and then head for the restaurant where I plan to kick ass in as many arcade games as I can to win prizes for my kid. Let's be honest, though—I enjoy this place probably more than he does.

John's Incredible Pizza serves a pizza buffet and endless self-serve ice cream, and then you can purchase tokens to play arcade games and ride bumper cars in exchange for tickets. They also have this coin game where you have to time the drop of a coin to push others off the edge of a cliff. It's insanely addicting, and Oliver always whines when I get sucked into it.

"Just one more minute, Ollie."

"But Daddy...I wanna ride the motorcycle."

Three tokens slide into the abyss, and I pump my fist in the air as multiple tickets dispense from the machine. "Yes!"

"Yay, Daddy! More tickets!"

"That's right, bud."

We spend another hour or so playing games, and I take as many pictures as I can of me and my boy, sensing the lingering looks of multiple women throughout the night.

I'm no stranger to those glances, those smiles that allude to the pleasure they see in a man being a father to his kid. And if it were a different world, I'd take some of them up on the offer they're so blatantly putting on the table.

But one—like I told my mother—I'm not going to let just any woman into mine and my son's life. And two, these women aren't the curly-headed blonde that has my mind twisted up with thoughts of her.

By the time we leave, Oliver passes out within minutes of getting in the car, giving me time to drive in silence and think back over my day. I could barely concentrate at work with thoughts of talking to Amelia in the back of my head, so I didn't accomplish nearly what I wanted to. Knowing that if I just stopped by the office and grabbed my files from earlier, I could find some time this weekend to catch up on what I didn't finish, I decide to make a slight detour before heading home. If I have those papers, I'll feel much better come Monday and more prepared for my next mediation.

Although Oliver is asleep, this is LA, and I'd be stupid to leave him in the car, so I pluck him from his seat and hoist him over my shoulder, carrying him up to my office so I can slip in really quick. The kid definitely isn't as light as he used to be, and

I struggle to keep him up as I unlock the door and turn off the alarm.

As quickly as I can, I rush back to my personal office, grab the files, and then head back out, locking the door behind me. But that's when familiar voices have me freezing in place.

"I had a really nice time," Amelia says to who I can only assume is Brayden, or as I like to call him in my head now, fuckface.

"I did too, Amelia. It was perfect. Perfect food, perfect wine, and the perfect woman."

Sliding further into the shadows of the building, I hide so they don't see me, and I continue to eavesdrop as Oliver softly snores in my ear, his head still resting on my shoulder.

Amelia lets out a soft laugh as I roll my eyes, my back still turned to them. "I'm far from perfect, Brayden."

"Not to me. And I know this may seem forward, but I'd really like to kiss you goodnight."

I know I shouldn't, but I twist around so fast that I don't miss his lips touching hers, the sight only serving as a reminder that the attraction I feel toward the woman can't be more than that. But fuck, if it doesn't feel like someone is twisting a knife in my chest right now just watching this.

He's definitely more eager as their lips meet, but she also doesn't shy away from reciprocating the kiss. And all I pick up on is the lack of passion, the heat that I know without a doubt would be there if it were my lips on hers.

I look away just as I hear him speak up again. "Have a good night. I will definitely be calling you."

"Thank you again, Brayden."And then the sound of her key moving in her office door tells me that she's also grabbing something from her office before she calls it a night. Once I hear the sound of her door shut, I use that as my opportunity to rush back to my car so she doesn't know I was there. That's all I need is for her to catch me in the act of eavesdropping on their goodnight kiss.

But after I situate Oliver back in his seat and start the car to crank up the air conditioning, I wait for Amelia to walk out to her car like a gentleman should, just to make sure she's safe. I have no doubt the woman probably carries Mace or a gun if I'm being honest, but you can never be too careful in this day and age, and I would never forgive myself if something happened to her and I had left.

Watching her walk to her car is like watching someone dangle a steak in front of a bloodthirsty lion. You know it's a tease, and you know that the instinct is for the lion to attack, but patience is a virtue far too many animals don't possess—and I am a prime example of that.

I didn't get to speak with her today like I wanted, but come Monday, I'll make sure that I do. I just hope I have enough control by then to not act on the instincts I'm feeling toward her at this moment—the very R-rated and territorial inclinations to make Amelia mine.

Images of Amelia kissing Brayden haunted me all weekend on and off. I'd be doing something with Oliver or watching television, and the next thing I knew, I was seeing their lips connected.

It was like my subconscious was torturing me for being a dick and witnessing their moment. But also, all it did was remind me that regardless of how I feel, I shouldn't act on these feelings, these desires that are keeping me up at night and my hand well-lubricated.

Nevertheless, I know I still owe her an apology, so I don't even bother stopping by my office on the way into our complex Monday morning. I head right for her door and get ready to swallow my pride so we both can move forward.

The chime above her door rings out as I step through, entering her office that smells like her—lemons and sugar. I notice a candle lit in the corner and make a mental note to look at the brand, so perhaps I can order one for myself, you know, so I can torture myself some more.

Her back is toward me as she shuffles through a filing cabinet, whistling a tune and ignoring my presence. But I know she heard the bell—she had to have.

"Good morning," I finally say, forcing her to turn around to greet me.

Her fuchsia dress is sleeveless and form-fitting, much like the rest of her dresses, and her hair is down and wild around her face, as usual. She looks effortlessly beautiful, which instantly has my mind and body at war. "Well, it was until you showed up." And then she's turning her back again. "I believe I told you to stay the hell out of my office."

"I know, but I swear, I came here to make peace."

Slowly, she twists again and questions my sincerity with an arch of her brow and a push of her glasses up her nose. The move is so natural for her that she probably doesn't even realize she's doing it. But every time she does, all I see are sexy librarian fantasies involving her playing out in my mind.

Maybe Nick was on to something with the whole ruler thing.

"You're surrendering?"

"You make it sound like there was a battle to be won when you say it like that."

She scoffs. "Is that not what we were doing? Competing to see who could piss off the other person more?"

"We were, but I'm here to call a truce."

She crosses her arms over her body. "And why is that?"

Inhaling deeply, I blow out a harsh breath. "Because despite what you may think, I'm not the guy I've shown you I am, and I want to start over."

Her face softens, like she's almost sympathetic and starting to believe me. And then the next words out of her mouth catch me off guard. "You have a son."

I swallow hard as my pulse picks up. "I do."

"So let me ask you this? Would you be proud of Oliver if he acted the way you did when we first met, or said some of the things you've said to me?"

"Fuck no. I get it, okay? I was an ass."

"As long as you admit it, I can accept your behavior as an incorrect first impression and give you another shot."

"Damn. Your heart may just be made of gold."

"No, but it's my job to believe in the best in people." My mind instantly wonders if I even deserve that from her.

"Well, hopefully, I can redeem myself. And based on the other day, it seems you've already met my kid."

"I have. At the gelato shop a few weeks ago. I didn't know he was yours, obviously." She drops her arms. "His dark hair…"

"From his mom," I answer her question before she can finish the thought.

She nods in understanding. "And the woman with him?"

"My mom. She takes him to school and picks him up for me." My hands start to shake just offering this information to her, but I'm trying to get her to see that I'm not a complete ass, just a man who handled a situation poorly. "Look," I start, trying to steer this conversation back to the point of me being here, "like I said, I want to apologize."

"For…"

"For making an uncomfortable work situation for both of us. I may not agree with what you're doing over here, but that doesn't mean that I need to demean your profession or assume that what you're trying to accomplish isn't actually helping people either."

She tilts her head at me. "You don't have to agree with what I do for a living to respect me, Ethan."

"You're right."

Her lips curl up into a pleased grin. "Oh, my…how did those words taste?"

I can't help but smirk back at her. "Like acid, but I know you deserved them."

And her entire posture starts to soften. "Well, thank you. I hope you and I can both agree to stay on our separate sides of the courtyard."

"If that's what you want."

Her smile drops. "Uh, yes. I do." Her chin bounces up and down rapidly. "I think it's for the best." But her words don't sound too confident, and now, I'm seeing an opportunity to push for more information. I want to know just exactly why she sounds unsure.

"So, how was your date with Brenden?" I ask, kicking myself once the words leave my lips but admitting that part of me really wants to know. And that's why I got his name wrong on purpose— it's a classic man move.

"You mean Brayden?"

I shrug. "Sure."

"Um, it was nice. A very nice date." She returns to searching through her files, avoiding my eyes. I take that as an invitation to move closer to her.

"Nice?"

"Uh-huh."

"So I take it you're not seeing him again?"

That has her head popping up and facing me again. "No, I am. We're going out next weekend."

I'm confused. "Why, if the date was just nice?"

"Because it was nice," she emphasizes.

"You're gonna waste your time on nice?"

"It's not a waste of time. I like him. He's good-looking, a doctor, available, and interested. Why shouldn't I go out with him again?"

Her question lingers in the air between us that grows thick with tension. All we do is stare across the room at each other, waiting for someone to speak even though I'm dying to tell her that what I saw is not the promise of a relationship she should invest her time in.

But you aren't willing to offer her one, are you, Ethan? So why are you hell-bent on steering her away from him?

Angry with myself, I retaliate without thinking. "You know what? You should. You can do whatever you want, Amelia. You're a grown woman." With a tight-lipped smile, I head for the door, irritated again and disappointed that the calm energy I managed with my apology has completely gone away in just a few seconds because I decided to be an ass again.

"That's right. I am. And my dating life is none of your concern," she calls after me as I reach the door. "So much for burying the hatchet, huh, Ethan?"

I turn around, ready to fight with her some more, but then the orchids I sent Friday morning catch my eye on the coffee table. "Nice orchids."

Her face contorts with confusion about my change of subject. But she glances at the flowers and then replies, "Oh, thank you. They were from Brayden."

"No, they weren't."

"What?" She flicks her eyes up to me.

"Brayden didn't send you those."

"How do you know that?"

"Because I did."

Shaking her head, she crosses her arms again. "I'm sorry, I'm confused. Why did you do that?"

"I wanted to apologize on Friday after what I said to you about hugging your clients the day before. But admitting I am wrong is not my forte, if you haven't gathered that." I drag my hand through my hair, ruffling it more than it already was this morning. "So I opted for these."

"Oh."

"Oh?"

She throws her hands up in the air, a burst of irritation sparking from her eyes as she looks at me across her office. "What do you want me to say, Ethan? You're so damn hot and cold. I don't know what to think anymore. I've never dealt with a man like you. I have no idea what you're thinking, what your motives are. I don't know if…"

She doesn't get the opportunity to say anything else because I march across her office to where she's standing, weave my hands through her hair on the back of her head, and pull her into me, crushing my mouth to hers.

A small shriek leaves her lips before I'm smashing her to my chest, holding her head in place as I devour her mouth. Our tongues collide, her hands clench my waist and grip my jacket, drawing me closer to her, and the sounds of our pleasure echo in the room as I kiss the woman with every ounce of desire I possess.

Backing her up, I press her into the wall behind her desk, hitting a mirror hanging behind her but not stopping for one second to consider it falling. Thrusting my erection into her stomach, I hold nothing back, showing her what she's doing to me, what she's been doing to me since the first moment I met her.

I'm kissing Amelia, tangling my tongue against hers, nipping at her lips, and tasting her finally—and it's better than I ever imagined.

Our hands grip and grab for any part of one another, trying to get as close as possible while every nerve ending in my body lights up. Her soft curves press against me, spurring me on and making me consider how I ever thought I could resist her—and how I sure as fuck can't resist her now that I've tasted her lips.

"Fuck, Amelia," I mumble against her mouth, diving back into the kiss before she has a chance to answer.

But her hand on my chest, pushing me away from her, is the beginning of her reply. With wide eyes and one of her hands covering her mouth, she remains on the wall as I stand across from her with my chest heaving, trying to catch my breath.

"Ethan…" She pauses as we both breathe heavily. "Why did you do that?"

"Because that is the way you deserve to be kissed, Amelia."

"What are you talking about?" she asks breathlessly.

"I saw Brayden kiss you Friday night," I admit.

"What? How?"

"I had to come back to my office to pick something up, and I saw him drop you off." She remains shocked and still as I continue. "I could read your body language across the courtyard. He didn't make your knees buckle, he didn't have your chest heaving for air like it is now, and he sure as hell didn't make your pupils dilate like they are right now after my lips were just on you."

"You couldn't see my eyes that night. How do you know they weren't dilated?"

"Because that look in your eyes? That look is reserved for me. It's borderline wanting to knee me in the balls and borderline wanting to yank on my hair while my mouth is between your legs. Does that sound about right?"

"No."

"Liar."

Our ragged breaths continue to fill the room. "This isn't a good idea…"

"I think we both know that's the truth, but I've never been one to steer clear of things that I want just because it wasn't a good idea."

"You want me?"

"I think that kiss just now makes that pretty obvious."

The chime above the door rings again, breaking our moment as we both jump and pretend as if nothing was just happening. Obviously, we fail at that miserably.

I correct my coat and take a step back. "I look forward to talking more about this later," I declare, shooting her a look that lets her know I mean business before spinning around and plastering a smile on my face to greet her clients. "Good morning."

"Good morning," the woman of the couple replies, sliding out of my way so I can squeeze by her and her husband. And with one more glance at Amelia over my shoulder, I leave, adjusting my junk as I walk across the courtyard to my office, wondering what the hell I just started.

But the truth is, I couldn't regret that kiss even if I tried.

Chapter 7

Amelia

R attled from Ethan's appearance in my office this morning and that kiss, I do my best to focus on my clients for the day, but I know that my brain is elsewhere more times than I can count. By the end of the day, I'm so on edge from reliving that kiss that I contemplate grabbing one of the vibrators I have in stock in my storage closet and getting myself off before I drive home.

When my last client leaves for the day, I lock the door behind her and slink down into my chair at my desk, rubbing my temples while wishing I was rubbing something else. Ethan said we would talk later, but I don't know that I'm ready for that. I need to process what just happened, and I don't think I can do that if we're in the same room again so soon.

That kiss.

That was definitely different from the kiss with Brayden, weeks of tension boiling over as our mouths collided and our bodies touched everywhere.

I felt consumed by him—his height towering over me, his strength in the way he gripped my head and guided me against the wall, and his erection did nothing but confirm how much he wanted me.

I guess the good thing about the kiss is that I know the physical attraction I've been harboring for him isn't one-sided. But now that we've played tonsil hockey, the next question is, what does it mean?

My door jingles as someone tries to open it from the outside but realizes that it's locked.

"Amelia? Open up."

It's Ethan. I know that voice so well now, plus I was kind of expecting him.

"I know you're in there, Amelia. Your car is still in the parking lot."

"Shit," I mutter before standing and making my way toward the door. "I'm busy, Ethan. What do you want?" I ask through the door knowing I'm safe as long as I'm on the other side of it.

"We need to talk."

"I don't think we do."

He's silent for a minute. "So that's how you're going to behave after this morning?"

Closing my eyes, I take a deep breath and blow it out. "This morning was…"

"Incredible," I hear him admit through the door at a volume much lower than before, almost as if saying it out loud makes it more real.

And he's right. That kiss was incredible.

"Ethan, this is too much."

"Just open the door, Amelia. Please. I promise I won't do anything to make you uncomfortable. I just want to make sure you understand something."

Biting my lip, I contemplate remaining silent and answering him that way. But I also know that I'm an adult and need to face this head-on. Ethan makes me act out of character, so I should take the moments where I feel in control and use that to make sure he understands exactly who I am and what I'm willing to put up with.

Reluctantly, I unlock the door and pull it open slowly, revealing him in his suit but with the jacket missing and his sleeves rolled up to his elbows. The crisp white cotton looks phenomenal against his tan skin and green eyes, his dirty-blond hair sticking up in disarray as if he's been running his hands through it all day.

"What do you want to say?"

"Can I come in?" He peers behind me, searching for a client, I presume.

"Sure, but I can't talk long. I have somewhere to be." I don't really, but he doesn't need to know that.

"Okay." He steps past me, and I close the door behind him, watching him walk further into my office and using the moment to appreciate the outline of his ass in his black slacks. I wait for him to face me and say something first. "How was your day?"

"Um, well? I guess you could say I was a bit distracted."

He sighs. "Me too."

"Why did you kiss me, Ethan?"

He stands up straight. "Because I wanted to. I've wanted to know what your lips tasted like since the moment I saw you."

"You sure had a funny way of showing it."

"I know, and again, I'm sorry. But fuck, Amelia. You make me crazy." He weaves his hands through his hair, the gesture making his biceps pop underneath the fabric of his shirt. My God, I'm guessing Ethan is hiding a muscular work of art under that shirt, and now I really want to see it.

"Ha. Well, you don't exactly bring out the best in me either, Ethan."

He drops his hands and rushes toward me, forcing me to back up into the door. But he doesn't touch me. He just crowds my space. "You make me crazy, horny, and fucking pissed at myself."

"What? Why?"

"Because the last thing I wanted moving to L.A. was to become involved with someone."

"Oh."

"But no matter what I do, I can't get you out of my head. And I sure as hell want to kiss you again." He reaches up and drags his fingers down my cheek, stopping to pull my bottom lip down with his thumb. "Do you want that?"

"Ethan…" I practically pant, my body's response taking over as my brain begins to malfunction. I've been thinking about Ethan touching me like this for almost a month now, and suddenly it's happening, and my mind can't handle all of the sensations and thoughts slamming into me.

"I want to kiss you, Amelia. Again and again. And better than that," he says, stepping in closer, "I want to do other things to you too. Can I ask you a question?"

"What?"

"When's the last time you came?"

"You mean…"

"Had an orgasm, Amelia. By something other than your hand or your vibrator."

I swallow down the lump in my throat as my body begins to

overheat. I talk about sex every day, all day, but somehow Ethan asking me this question is making me feel like that sixteen-year-old girl again who lacked confidence in her body and in who she was. The mere mention of orgasms with Ethan is making me mute.

"It's been…a while."

"For me too."

"What are you saying?"

Now he's pressing his body up against mine again, and I know I should push him away—but again, brain malfunction is in full force. "What if we did that for each other? Made each other feel good and took out a month's worth of aggression on one another?"

"Like friends with benefits?"

"If you want to put a label on it," he replies honestly.

And then that malfunction starts flashing red sirens. This has disaster written all over it. This is exactly the type of relationship I would advise a client not to enter into because no one ever gets out unscathed.

"Can I think about it?" I ask, hoping that will give me the time I really need to process this all.

Lucky for me, Ethan accepts with a lift of the corner of his lips. "Yeah, that's probably a good idea. I know I'll be thinking about it." He backs away from me now, holding my gaze as the hue of his green eyes darkens even further. "Don't overthink this, though, Amelia. We're both adults. We can agree to scratch an itch and help one another out. Honestly, it sounds like a win-win to me."

"Um…"

He holds up a hand, cutting me off. "But I want to be clear. I meant what I said earlier today. I'm sorry, for everything. I don't want to fight with you anymore. I don't want to make each other's lives a living hell, especially not if we can actually enhance the other person's life in a much different way." He lifts one brow at me knowingly.

"Okay." My brain has been reduced to forming one-word answers at this point as I slide out of the way and hold the door open for him. "We'll talk soon." Good job, Amelia. That was three words. We're getting sharper by the second.

"I'm looking forward to it. Good night, Amelia."

"Good night, Ethan."

I shut the door after he leaves, locking it again and promising not to open it if he returns. My resistance against him began waning as soon as he touched me. My body came alive with a jolt of electricity that is unparalleled to anything else I've experienced.

Ethan is nothing but trouble, and his suggested arrangement reeks of it too. But I never was the girl who did things they weren't supposed to. Trouble was something I aspired to stay clear of in every facet. But now I wonder if this might be my one-way ticket to the other side…

"Damn it." I lose my grip and fall to the mat below me, huffing and puffing in frustration.

"It's okay, Amelia. You're not going to get this move right away. Broken Doll is fairly complex." Fiona comes over and stares down at me on the floor as I look up at her from my back on my mat. I needed to blow off some frustration, so I came to the Tuesday pole class this week.

"I know, but I at least thought I'd be making some progress," I reply, gathering control of my breathing.

"Progress takes time. You should know that better than anyone, given what you do for a living."

She's right. Hell, she's practically using my own words against me right now, the same words I tell my clients when they get frustrated that something isn't changing in their life as fast as they want it to.

Unfortunately, we live in an instant gratification society now, and no one has any patience anymore. We all want things to change at the drop of a hat or press of a button. And tonight, I'm the one who's getting impatient because I can't land a move after only trying it for thirty minutes.

I sigh, pinching the bridge of my nose before closing my eyes and taking a few deep breaths. I've felt off for the past two days and just wanted tonight to be a pleasant form of stress relief instead of yet another thing to frustrate me in my life right now.

I tried really hard to convince myself that entering into a physical relationship with Ethan would do nothing but throw me off-balance and that dating Brayden is the step in the right direction to leave these lingering feelings about Ethan behind. But it seems that I am naive about even that happening instantly. And the fact that he was radio silent today only made my uncertainty build.

Why would he approach me about a friends-with-benefits relationship and then leave me hanging the next day without any follow-up? I know I told him to give me time to think about it, but he's been so persistent so far that I was on high alert all day, thinking I would have to fight him off and then by the end of the day with no word from him, I felt nothing but disappointment.

And I think that's why I'm so on edge right now. Today did not go the way I thought it would. And for once in my life, I'm wishing that something could just be instant, that I could take a magic pill or click a button and these feelings would just go away.

"Let's try something else, and we'll come back to Broken Doll. What about Extended Butterfly? You talked about that one too."

I shake my head, not wanting to set myself up to feel like a failure again tonight. "No, I think I just want to freestyle for a while. Is that okay?"

Fiona smiles in understanding. "Of course. I'll turn the music up a bit more and go help someone else." She rests her hand on my shoulder. "Don't beat yourself up. Remember, enjoy the journey. Remember how strong you are and how far you've come. You'll get there."

"Thanks." I watch her walk toward the stereo, crank up the volume a little bit more on "Buttons" by The Pussy Cat Dolls, and then I turn back to the pole, mounting it as I climb toward the ceiling and begin to let my body do the talking.

I twirl, spin, hook my arms and legs around the pole, and attempt to shut off my mind as I dance and feel the beat of the music, pretending that I'm performing for someone else, until the vision of Ethan watching me flashes through my mind.

I try to push it out, try to picture Brayden instead, but light-brown hair turns sandy-blond in an instant, and blue eyes melt into green that penetrate me as he watches me move. Then suddenly, my heart rate increases as I feel his eyes track my every movement, my traitorous body igniting in a flurry of excitement at the fantasy I'm living out in my mind.

By the time I leave my pole class, my body is keyed up. Moving like that while imagining an audience watching me has my libido spiking and the need for release edging its way toward my clit with each second I'm driving to my house.

And when I arrive home, I storm through my door, up the stairs to my room, whip out my favorite vibrator from my box of toys, tear down my pants as fast as I can, and scream out through my orgasm that rips through my body in record time.

Yet another morning of radio silence on Wednesday actually gives me some relief. After I masturbated three times last night (yes, I was that keyed up), I finally passed out and woke up with renewed confidence in my decision. If and when Ethan approaches me, I know I'll have an answer for him.

But by lunchtime, my chest is tight, and I figure maybe I need to take back control. If I go over to his office and broach the subject, then I'm the one commanding the conversation. And the more I think about it, the more that sounds like the plan I want to carry out.

When I open my office door, though, what I see has my eyes bugging out and my stomach dropping.

Oh no!

"Fuck!" I rush back inside my office and locate my phone with unparalleled speed, hitting Penelope's name and cursing as it rings.

She finally answers right before it goes to voicemail. "Hello, Amelia Be Delia."

"Penelope! How many did you order?"

Her chuckles ring out, and all I can think about is the precious time that is being wasted as I listen. "Oh, about three hundred."

"Three hundred!" I shriek. "Why on earth?"

"You said money was no object, and I chipped in toward the cost myself. I wanted to show that fucker not to mess with you."

I slap my forehead as I pace around my office. At no point in the past two days did I think to call Penelope to cancel the order. Although, at this point, I don't know if there would have been enough time anyway to avoid the delivery. "This is not good."

"Why? What happened?"

But before I can answer her, there's a pounding knock on my office door, the force so brut that the glass shakes and the bell above the door rattles too. "Shit. I have to go."

"Amelia!" But I hang up the phone before she gets a chance to say another word. I'm just going to have to call her back after I deal with this.

Inhaling deeply, I march toward the door, unlock it, and open it to find a seething Ethan Fuller staring down at me. His jaw is tight, every muscle in his body is rigid under his suit, and in his hands is one of the many boxes that were delivered to his office just now. "Hi, Ethan."

"Amelia. Can I have a word, please?"

I momentarily debate slamming the door in his face, locking myself in my office, and never leaving, but it's time to face the music. Hopefully, we'll be able to laugh at this down the road. "Of course."

He hums as we walks through the door and I close and lock it behind him. It's my lunch hour, and I don't want to risk someone walking in here while we're discussing the items that are in that box.

But just as I turn around, I find Ethan holding up one of the giant, vibrating, pink dildos that Penelope ordered and had delivered to his office—one of three hundred of them.

"Care to explain why three hundred of these just showed up at my office?"

"Um, well…"

"I'm assuming they're yours," he continues. "Not sure who else in the complex would order this many dildos at one time."

"You never know what some people are into these days," I tease, trying to make light of the situation.

"Amelia, my secretary choked on her lunch when she opened this box. I had to perform the Heimlich maneuver on her so she wouldn't die."

Covering my mouth with my hands, I gasp. "Oh my God."

"Now, I'm going to give you one opportunity to explain to me how this happened and why, and then we're going to discuss what I approached you with the other day." His tone is commanding, and my panties are instantly wet. God, the man turns me on like no other. I'd be a fool not to take his offer and run with it.

I swallow. "Okay. First, that order was made when you and I were still fighting."

"And we're not anymore?"

"No. I thought about your apology, and I agree we need to move forward."

"Good. Now, why on earth were there three hundred?"

"For the added effect of embarrassment?" I suggest with a shrug of my shoulders. "My friend Penelope was the one that placed the order, not me."

"But you approved it?"

"It wasn't supposed to be that many. I only wanted to order fifty for the practice."

"Fifty dildos? Why on earth do you need that many?"

"I sell them to clients if needed. I have a partnership with the company. I buy wholesale and sell them for a profit. Don't get it twisted though. I'm not a dildo pusher. I'm just a woman who knows that sometimes a good sex toy can help you learn more about what you like…sexually, that is."

Dear God, my cheeks must be flaming red right now.

Ethan snickers. "Okay…so this was your next move in our little game?"

"Yes. That was the atomic bomb."

His brow lifts. "Quite the move, Dr. St. Clair. I'm impressed."

And his appreciation has me smiling. "Thank you."

"Now, here's the problem. I have three hundred vibrating dildos that need somewhere to go…"

"You can bring them here. I'll help you. I'm sorry," I say while shaking my head. "I didn't even think about canceling the order after Monday."

"Is that because you were thinking about something else you were supposed to consider from Monday?" he asks, moving closer to me after he drops the dildo back in the box he set on my desk.

"Yes…" I reply breathlessly, and eager to see his reaction to my answer.

"And what did you decide?"

You need boundaries, Amelia. Remember when you told Charlotte the same thing about her fake relationship with Damien? You need to know what to expect so you can handle this like an adult.

"If we're doing this, what does it entail?"

"What do you mean?"

"Well, for starters, are we exclusive?"

"I sure as hell won't be fucking anyone else."

Fucking. Oh my God, Ethan said fucking. He wants to fuck me. I think I might pass out. "Same." *Way to keep your cool, Amelia.* "Are we telling people?"

He chews on his bottom lip. "I think we should keep this

between us for right now. Not sure if your brother is going to be thrilled about me defiling his little sister, and I don't want to draw unnecessary attention if we can avoid it."

I swallow hard. "You're going to defile me?"

Ethan lowers his head to my ear, nuzzling my neck with his nose. "I want to do so many dirty things to you, Amelia, that even a shower won't restore your perfect image. I want to hear you scream my name, I want to see that mouth of yours wrapped around my dick, and I want to explore every inch of your body until I know it better than my own."

"Sounds like you've put a lot of thought into this," I reply, practically panting. I run my hands up his chest and wrap them around his neck, remembering how it felt to touch him the other day. This time it almost feels better. And it's crazy to me that we've gone from wanting to sabotage one another to talking about defiling—my, how things can change in an instant.

"I've been thinking about you like this since I moved in across the courtyard. I was just too damn stubborn to admit it."

"Is that what you're doing now, then?"

"Damn right. I want you so fucking bad. You've been nothing but a walking temptation, and I'm ready to give in."

"You have no idea how much I want you too, Ethan," I admit, letting the truth of my feelings out in the open. I know there's a risk I'm taking with him, but I also know that my mind and body are drawn to him, and the best way to relinquish that hold sometimes is to give in.

I want to give in with him.

"When I first saw you, the attraction was instant. But then you opened your mouth. Now, after seeing what an asshole you can be, I'm beginning to wonder if I have a thing for assholes..."

He laughs and then threads his hands into my hair, tilting my head to the side as he nibbles on my neck. "Show me."

"What?"

"Show me how much you want me, Amelia." He lifts his head before biting my bottom lip and dragging it between his teeth. "Tell me this, if I stuck my hands up your dress right now and brushed my knuckles against your panties, would they be soaked?"

"Uh-huh." *Oh God, please touch me.*

"You want me to find out for myself?"

"Yes…"

"Fuck." He crashes his mouth to mine, exploring with his tongue as I wrap my arms around his neck and pull him closer to me. We hit my door hard, rattling the bell again before Ethan lifts me in his arms and carries me over to my desk with my legs wrapped around his waist.

The feel of him is consuming—his hands, his kiss, his scent—he's manly and hard, but his touches are soft, edged with that little bit of roughness that's making my pussy drip with arousal.

"God, I want to see you come," he mumbles against my mouth.

"Then make me."

Rearing back, he holds me to him but stares down into my eyes. And I see when the lightbulb clicks on, and an idea pops into his head. "Take your panties off."

Without breaking our stare, he backs away, giving me room to slip my thong off and drop it on the floor. But Ethan reaches down, picks up my thong, and shoves it into his pocket before opening up the box he walked in with and extracting one of the vibrating dildos. He twists the bottom, turning it on and feeling the quaking of the rubber with his hand.

"Since I have so many of these now, I figured we should put one to good use."

I gulp down a hard swallow. "Okay. You should probably wash it first though."

"Good idea." He nods and then heads for the small bathroom just off to the side of my office. I continue to sit on my desk, waiting for him to return, but then decide to twist around and take a peek at myself in the mirror on the wall. My face is flushed, my mouth parted as I breathe heavily, and even though there's a sliver of doubt resting deep in my gut, my body is vibrating with need so hard that I can't turn back now.

Maybe we can fuck all the hate out of our connection and then just enjoy an endless supply of orgasms after that.

Just remember this is about sex, Amelia, and everything will be fine.

Ethan returns with the dildo, turning it on again as he approaches me at my desk, forcing me to turn toward him. "Put your feet on the desk." I do as I'm told, planting my feet flat against the wood but keeping my knees fairly close together. "Don't get shy on me now, Amelia. Let me see that pretty pussy of yours."

"God, your mouth is even dirtier when we're alone."

"I'm exercising control right now. Just wait until we get to know each other a bit better, then I'll really talk to you the way I want to."

Prickling need shoots down my spine to my core as I spread my knees and pull my dress up higher so he can see every inch of me. And the way his eyes darken makes me feel so powerful in this situation, even though he's the one standing over me and telling me what to do.

But that's the thing people, especially women, don't understand about sex. Power and control don't necessarily come from being rough and commanding—it comes from trust, giving yourself over to someone freely, and trusting them to bring you pleasure. That is powerful—and that is what I'm doing with Ethan right now.

"Fuck." Ethan moves forward and gently lowers the dildo to my slit, the vibrations low but powerful enough that I can feel them against my clit. "Does that feel good?"

"Yes." I throw my head back and close my eyes, drowning in the sensation.

"Look at me, Amelia. I want you to watch me pleasure you with this toy and then with my mouth."

After all the wicked things I've heard come from those lips, I'm dying to see if his tongue and mouth can back up his words.

Nodding, I lock eyes with him and feel him slide the toy through my slit, coating it in my wetness as I sharply inhale.

"You weren't kidding about your panties being soaked. You're fucking dripping right now."

"Don't stop." My body is primed and ready for an orgasm that isn't from my hands or me. Just when I think this is all he's going to do to me, Ethan drops to his knees and begins to slide the toy inside me. "Oh, God."

"Fuck, this is hot." His eyes are trained on the sight between my legs, and my eyes are trained on him, watching him fascinated by my body, welcoming the toy with ease. And then he moves forward, flicks his eyes up to me, and licks my clit with the flat part of his tongue.

"Jesus…" I toss my head back again, closing my eyes so I can savor this feeling, but Ethan stops.

"I told you to keep your eyes on me."

Coming back to reality, I focus on him again as he moves the toy while it's still vibrating, increasing the speed slightly while he flicks and sucks on my clit.

I keep one hand behind me to support my body, but then I reach forward with the other to grab his hair, pulling his face closer to my pussy. I have no shame about showing him what I want or need. I am typically a practice-what-I-preach type of therapist, especially when it comes to sex—but I don't know that entering into a friends-with-benefits relationship with a man you once couldn't stand is something I would advise my clients to do.

"Right there. Don't stop…Oh, fuck, I'm gonna come!" I shout, gasping before moaning out in pleasure, closing my eyes again to soak up the waves rolling through me.

I scream and moan and writhe as my orgasm rushes down my limbs and ebbs slowly. It's exquisite, intense, and almost borderline magical. God, it's been so long since I've felt that type of pleasure with another person, and this one certainly ranks among the best orgasms I've ever had.

Ethan doesn't let up until he begins to feel my body go lax, and then he stands up and removes the dildo from me, setting it to the side of my desk before unbuckling his belt. "God damn."

"That was amazing," I say through a heavy breath, my entire body feeling like Jell-O now.

"Oh, we're not done." I hear his zipper, and then Ethan lowers his slacks and moves his boxer briefs down just enough to pull his erection out—his very hard, thick erection framed by a sprinkle of hair that matches the hue on his head.

Oh my God, Ethan's dick puts that dildo to shame.

"You like what you see?" he asks me after several minutes have passed, and all I've done is stare down at his cock as he begins to stroke himself. Licking my lips, I simply nod in reply. "Good, now get on your knees."

"You're so bossy," I reply, even though I follow his directions. And here's the truth, I'm not one of those women who mind giving head. I actually enjoy it. But again, I think it's a power thing.

Sliding my dress back into place, I rest on my knees before him, watching his hand move up and down his length. Ethan is thick and long, a solid seven to eight inches that I know he can probably use very well. And I can't wait until I get to experience it myself.

"Damn right. Now open up."

Moving forward, I part my lips and watch Ethan move his cock to my lips, close enough that I dart my tongue out and lick all around his head.

"Fuck, Amelia. My cock looks so good next to that mouth."

I reach behind him, place my hand on one of his ass cheeks, and then pull him toward me, sliding his length further into my mouth, sucking him in as he goes as far back as he can.

"Jesus Christ. This…this is what I've been dreaming of. Every time you'd fire back at me with some sarcastic remark, every time I'd see you lick your lips in thought…" He weaves a hand through the thick curls on my head as I draw him in and out, circling my tongue, sucking him as far back as I can until I gag, but continuing to make him feel as good as he made me feel.

"Fuck, I'm getting close," he warns.

I look up at him beneath my lashes and nod, giving him permission to let go in my mouth. And right now, that's all I want—to watch him lose control just like he made me.

He grips my head and pulls me toward him a little harder but still gentle enough that I can manage his depth, speeding up his thrusts as he fucks my mouth. And I do everything in my power to bring him over the edge. I swirl my tongue around his head, I cradle his balls in my hand, and I swallow against him, waiting for him to detonate.

"I'm coming," he announces through clenched teeth as I feel the first hot spurt of him. And then it's a race to keep up with how much he floods my mouth. But his groans and harsh breaths are so sexy, and watching him come undone is even better than I imagined. He throws his head back, curses, and groans until he's spent.

"Fuck," he mutters and then reaches for my hand to help me up before pressing a chaste kiss to my lips. "Well, Dr. St. Clair, I think that was a very productive meeting." His smirk tells me he's trying to make light of the situation as he puts his semi-hard cock away and zips his slacks back up.

"And how often do you suggest we have these little meetings?" I know we both just came, but I'm already itching for round two. Ethan has unlocked my dormant sex drive, and now I'm ready and raring to go.

"There was nothing little about this meeting, Amelia," he counters with an arch of his brow. "But now that I know all the fantasies were trivial compared to the real thing, I don't see you actually being able to enjoy a meal during your lunch for some time."

"Ethan..."

He cups the side of my face, bringing his lips just millimeters from mine, but doesn't kiss me. "I meant what I said, Amelia. This is two adults enjoying each other's company and racking up as many orgasms as we can. I know I needed this just as much as you did." I nod, not sure what else to say. "And as long as we're on the same page, you can expect to see me quite frequently."

"Should I keep that dildo here just in case?" I ask him in a teasing lilt.

He chuckles but shakes his head. "Not unless you want to. That was more of a one-time thing for me. But next time, it will be my cock in your pussy, not some toy."

Oh God, do we have time for another round because I'm getting hot and bothered again...

"Oh."

"I didn't think fucking you right away was the gentlemanly thing to do, but rest assured—I will have you all over this office, especially on that little couch of yours. I feel like it's only right since you're a therapist."

Giggling, I try to lean back, but he pulls me forward this time and crushes his mouth to mine. Ethan kisses me like I'm a drug and he's an addict, like if he stops and goes up for air, I might evaporate before him.

And each time we kiss, I understand just how addicting this man could be as well. I know I'm entering into this arrangement knowing what it entails, but I also know I'm risking my heart too.

However, sometimes you just have to live in the moment, without contemplating the consequences, and focus on all the benefits instead—like orgasms. Those are pretty terrific, if I do say so myself.

"I'll see you around," he says when we part, turning slowly for the door and unlocking it.

"Yeah. See ya."

And then he's gone, and I'm rushing around my office to clean up and get rid of the smell of sex before my next client arrives, accepting that this may just become my new normal, all the while remembering that I'm not wearing any panties.

Chapter 8

Amelia

By lunchtime the next day, my body is buzzing with anticipation of Ethan showing up for our afternoon rendezvous. But sadly, my lunch hour remains silent. I momentarily debate walking over to his office to see what he's doing, but the risk of rejection keeps me inside my own office and safely behind my door.

I know that Ethan and I enjoyed each other yesterday, there's no doubt about that. But now I'm wondering if I said or did something to allude to the fact that I didn't want this to take off at rocket speed. Which, honestly, is probably a good thing. If we go too fast, we could crash and burn. But after that orgasm yesterday, I'm dying to feel that kind of pleasure again.

By four o'clock, I'm craving a cup of gelato, so I decide to break free from my office before I make the trip to the other end of the complex. But when I walk outside, I see the top of a black-haired little boy down by my feet in a crouched position, right next to my door.

"Oliver? Is that you?"

His head pops up, and I'm met with green eyes that look just like Ethan's, the color so vibrant it steals my focus. "Why do you have people in your flowers?" he asks me, curiosity etched in all of his features.

Confused, I take a few steps around him before I realize he's talking about my garden gnomes. And for a moment, I take note that he's here alone, so I know I need to stay with him. I'm sure Ethan or his grandma is nearby, but I'll wait here until I'm sure. "Oh, are you talking about my gnomes?"

"What's a gnome?" His face twists with confusion as he falls back on his butt on the sidewalk and continues to stare up at me, genuinely interested.

I close the distance between us and then crouch down to his level. "A gnome is a legendary creature, a small man or woman that is thought to live underground and guard the plants around them, so people put statues of them in their garden as a form of protection. There's also the thought that they have treasure underground they're protecting, so they can be very defensive if they feel threatened. Having them in your garden is a way to make sure your plants are safe. And they look cute."

"Treasure?" His eyes and smile widen with his question.

"That's what people say."

He looks back at the gnomes. "These don't look real though. They look like my Iron Man doll." He pulls a figure from the ground behind him, the classic superhero recognizable as soon as I take in the maroon-colored suit. And I'm going to be honest here—the only reason I know who Iron Man is, is because Penelope made us watch the movies because Robert Downey Jr. is the actor who plays him. And I mean, what self-respecting woman can resist Robert Downey Jr.?

"Well, they're just statues, but some people think they come alive at night when everyone is sleeping."

"Oh." His eyes light up again. "I wanna see!"

"I don't think they do if people are watching. That's part of the magic." Smiling down at this inquisitive little boy, I assume he can't be more than five or six. I didn't ask Ethan much about him the other day because our conversation derailed to other topics, and now that we're doing whatever it is that we're doing, I'm not sure if asking about his kid is allowed.

Nonetheless, I decide to do a little digging of my own.

"So, how old are you, Oliver?"

"Five. I'll be six in December. My birthday is December 24th."

"Oh, Christmas Eve? Does that mean you get double the presents?"

His eyes light up again. "Yes!"

Before I can ask another question, I hear a manly scream behind me, panic resonating in his voice. "Oliver!" And then heavy footsteps have me twisting to locate the owner of the voice, which almost makes me fall over and faceplant onto the ground.

God, he's so fucking handsome. And I am so screwed now that I've seen his dick.

"That's my dad." Oliver rises from the ground and rushes toward Ethan, who is speeding toward us.

"Oliver! There you are!" Ethan jerks to a stop in front of his son, sinking to his knees as he pulls him into his chest. "Why on earth did you take off? I was freaking out! You know better! Fuck, I had no idea where you were. You scared the shit out of me."

"I'm sorry, Daddy. I saw the pretty flowers and wanted to smell them," he says so earnestly that it melts my heart a little. "And you just said a bad word," he declares confidently, which has me fighting a smile. "But then I saw the gnomes, and Amelia said they come to life at night. One of them looks like you, Daddy."

Ethan releases his son and questions him with his gaze, his face relaxing a little now. "Is that right?"

"Yeah. He has a grumpy face like you do all the time." I catch the side of Oliver's face in what can only be described as a grimace. I stifle my laugh. Pretty sure I've seen that look a time or two in the past month.

Ethan gives him the same look back. "I don't look like that."

"You look like that right now, Daddy."

Ethan rolls his eyes and stands, then directs his attention to me. "Thanks for staying with him. My mother dropped him off to me earlier, and we're getting ready to leave for his first soccer practice today, but he ran out the door without telling me, and I was panicking."

Oh, so Oliver was here? That might explain why he didn't come over during lunch. My chest instantly deflates as all of the anxiousness I felt begins to dissipate. "No problem. It was lucky that I saw him anyway. I was going to go get a cup of gelato, and he was right outside my door."

"Are you gonna get the lemon kind?" Oliver asks, peering up at me with wide eyes.

"Probably. It is my favorite after all."

"Mine too." Then he turns to his dad. "Can we get some too, Daddy? Please?"

"Not before soccer, bud. If you eat that and then start running around, you'll probably puke."

"That's okay…"

"The answer is no, Oliver," he declares in a tone similar to the one he used with me in my office yesterday. And as soon as the words leave his lips, he flicks his eyes up to me, and I swear, he's thinking the same thing. My body comes alive again, heating up from the inside out. Now all I feel is need and regret that we couldn't meet up earlier.

We both remain in a stare down until Oliver breaks the silence.

"What is the girl gnome's name?" Oliver asks, pulling me from my more than obvious perusal of my nemesis turned fuck buddy.

Shaking off my embarrassment, I look back at Oliver. "What?"

"The girl gnome. Does she have a name? I think the boy should be Grumpy, like my dad."

"Thanks, Oliver." Ethan rolls his eyes.

Oliver's determination and teasing have the corner of my mouth lifting up in a smile again. "Okay. But no, she doesn't have a name."

"Can I name her too?"

"Sure. What do you think would be a good name?"

He runs back over to the gnomes as I feel Ethan's eyes on me. And sure enough, as I glance over my shoulder, I catch him checking out my legs—my very exposed legs under my dress. Realizing he was caught, he clears his throat and then moves after his son. "Oliver, we should leave Amelia alone. I'm sure she's busy, and you're in trouble, young man."

"She looks like you," Oliver says, disregarding Ethan's words. "Her name should be Sunshine since her hair is yellow like the sun."

"You think so?"

He nods. "Yes." Holding up Ironman against the female gnome, he smiles. "Iron Man thinks Sunshine is her name too."

"Well, who am I to object to Iron Man's wishes? Sunshine it is."

Ethan's phone ringing pulls our attention back to him. As he pulls his phone from his pocket and glances at the screen, he hisses in frustration. "Shit. I have to answer this. Come on, Oliver. It's time to go."

"Okay, Daddy." Oliver runs back to Ethan but looks back at me momentarily.

"It was nice to talk to you, Oliver."

"Let me know if the gnomes come to life, Amelia."

I chuckle. "I will."

Oliver runs back into Ethan's office as Ethan answers the call. "Ethan Fuller," he says into the phone as he walks away from me. "Yes, I have the contract ready to sign." But before he gets too far, he turns around, places his hand over the end of the phone, and speaks to me. "I'll be by your office tomorrow at noon sharp. Be ready for me." And with a wink, he continues on his way, leaving me trembling and even hotter, now in desperate need of that gelato to cool me down.

"**O**h, God, Ethan. Yes! Right there…" I stare down at Ethan's head buried between my legs as his fingers work in tandem with his tongue.

My God, does the man know his way around my pussy.

"Don't come until I tell you."

"But I'm close. God, please…"

"Don't fucking come, Amelia. I'm not done with you yet." He removes his fingers from me and then sucks my clit between his lips hard, pulling my entire body closer to him as I sit with my legs spread open on my desk.

Ethan came over just before noon as he promised and didn't give me a chance to greet him with words before his lips were on mine. We started on the couch making out like teenagers before he brought me back over to my desk and began feasting on me.

And boy, do I ever feel like his meal right about now.

He slides three of his fingers back inside of me, the stretch so exquisite and just the thing I needed to bring me right back to the edge again.

"Ethan…"

"Come for me now, Amelia." It takes a few more seconds of his fingers and tongue working together to make me explode, but I do, gripping his hair in my hand as I scream through my release. I sincerely hope someone isn't walking by right now wondering if I'm being murdered in here, or a client is being beaten or something. That wouldn't be good for my practice if someone called the cops and I had to explain the noise.

Luckily, Ethan must have been thinking the same thing because he reaches up to cover my mouth with his free hand.

"Jesus, woman." He wipes his mouth on his forearm as he stands and stares down at me, splayed across the surface of my desk, trying to gain my composure.

"It's unfair how good you are at that."

His smirk makes an appearance. "Glad you can appreciate my talents."

"Oh, I definitely do." Pushing myself up from my desk, I prepare to return the favor just as my phone rings.

Ethan's eyes dart to the screen at the same time mine do, where we see Brayden's name flash across it. He's probably returning my call from earlier, the one where I was going to cancel our next date and tell him I couldn't see him anymore, but I can't very well do that this second.

My pulse spikes as I wonder what to do, but Ethan's change in demeanor tells me it's too late to do anything. The damage has been done.

"You should get that." Ethan turns away from me, headed toward the door.

I flick my head back and forth between the phone and him, nervously moving toward Ethan as he stands by the door with his back to me, fixing the sleeves of his shirt. "Ethan…"

"Are you still seeing him?" he says, spinning around to face me, his face scrunched up, displaying his frustration.

"Well, no…

"Well, no? That doesn't sound very convincing, Amelia. I believe you were the one that asked if we were exclusive in this arrangement, but apparently, Brayden didn't factor into this."

Now my anger is starting to build. "What are you implying, Ethan?"

He shakes his head, staring down at the floor. "Fuck."

"What's going on?"

"Nothing. Look, I need to go."

"Ethan…"

He snaps his eyes back to mine. "End it. This doesn't continue until that's over." And then he walks out, leaving me standing there with my heart racing and my pulse spiking with fury.

Fuck. Well, that went sour quickly.

Frankie's Diner is bustling as I walk in Sunday morning, eager for a glass of champagne and some girl talk. But the calm, reserved person I usually am flies out the window as soon as I sit down.

"Ethan and I are fooling around," I blurt out as all of the girls stop what they're doing and focus their eyes on me. I'm not sure why I felt just laying that out there was the right thing to do, but I've been an analytical mess since Friday, and I need the opinions of my three best friends.

Noelle sets her fork down slowly, reaching for her mimosa next. "Okay, we can talk about that first, Amelia."

"Something tells me by the size of her eyes that there's more to this story," Charlotte adds, taking another bite of her food as she waits for me to answer.

I slouch back into my chair. "I don't even know how this happened, but honestly, I'm so damn attracted to the man that I can't think straight anymore," I answer.

"Told you it was only a matter of time before you two started fucking," Penelope says as she chews another bite of her waffle, smiling the entire time.

Charlotte puts her hand up. "Please start from the beginning, Amelia. I need to know how your little prank war turned into the two of you fucking."

"Technically, we haven't had penetrative sex yet, but okay." I spend the next several minutes explaining to the girls how after Ethan hired the sign spinner and put out his chalkboard sign, I told Penelope to order the dildos to be delivered to his office. Then I tell them about his comment about me hugging my clients and how

Ethan was there when Brayden picked me up for my date, and that's when I met his son.

"He has a kid?" Noelle echoes my admission. "That just makes him ten times hotter. Single dads are like kryptonite to a woman's ovaries."

"Right? And his son's so sweet. I actually talked with him a little more on Thursday when I found him outside of my office staring at my gnomes."

"Why does that sound dirty?" Penelope asks through a grin.

"Focus." Charlotte snaps her fingers in front of Penelope's face. "Back to the story."

"Okay, so the day of my date with Brayden, two orchids were delivered to my office. I thought they may have been from you girls at first but quickly ruled that out."

Noelle interrupts me. "You know, I think sending each other flowers regularly is something we should do. I mean, I know I love getting flowers randomly…"

"I swear, stop interrupting her," Charlotte seethes. "I want to know how the fooling around started!"

Chuckling, I wait for everyone to calm down before I continue. "I thought the flowers were from Brayden and mentally gave him kudos for sending my favorite ones without knowing. So Brayden picked me up for our date from my office since traffic is a nightmare on Friday nights in L.A…." The girls nod in agreement.

"Why do I feel like there's a but coming?" Penelope questions.

"Because there is." I sigh, sinking back into my chair. "When Brayden picked me up for our date, Ethan was outside with Oliver and his mom, and I introduced Brayden to them before we left."

"Okay…"

"Well, Ethan was acting…weird."

"How so?" Charlotte asks.

"Broody, irritated—he even made a comment to Brayden about how he hoped I didn't have too much fun on my date."

Penelope smirks in delight. "Oh, sounds like Mr. Grumpy neighbor was jealous."

"I thought maybe too, but tried to enjoy the evening nonetheless. And I did. It was what anyone would classify as a great first date, like I told you last weekend during brunch."

They nod in recollection. "But…" Noelle suggests.

"Apparently, Ethan saw me kiss Brayden goodnight when he dropped me back off at my office."

"How do you know that?" Charlotte asks, leaning forward in her seat, completely invested in the story as she bites on her nails.

"He told me Monday morning when he came by my office to apologize for his comment about me hugging my clients, which started off well until he admitted that he was the one that sent me the orchids."

All their eyes go wide.

"Wow," Noelle says as she takes a sip of her mimosa.

"Yeah, and then one thing led to another, and he was kissing me then asking me if I wanted to take out our aggression on each other in the form of orgasms."

Charlotte laughs. "Did he use those words exactly?"

"Basically."

"And what did you say?"

I bite my lip, nervous to tell my friends even though there's no going back on my decision now. "Well, he's performed oral sex on me twice since then and fucked me with a vibrating dildo, so what do you think?"

Charlotte spits her mimosa across the table, Noelle starts to choke on her pancakes, and Penelope throws her head back in laughter, holding her stomach as people around the restaurant glare at us.

Sputtering, Noelle fights to gain control of her breathing. "Jesus. Warn a person before saying something like that, will you? Why do the three of you always say shit like that while I have liquid or food in my mouth?"

"Penelope says stuff like that all the time," I argue, gesturing toward her with my hand.

"Yes, but we expect that from her, not from you, Amelia," Charlotte counters. "My God, Amelia? Who are you?"

"I honestly don't know, but this man is making me act insane like my conscience has fled my brain, and now my vagina is calling the shots." I throw my hands up in the air. "This isn't me. I'm not the girl that has oral sex in the middle of the day in my office!"

"Why not? I think every girl should be that girl at least once in her life," Penelope snickers. "And I knew it was coming to this. I'm just glad you finally gave in."

"Well, things were going well until Brayden called me on Friday and Ethan saw his name on my phone screen."

Charlotte winces. "Did you and Ethan agree to be exclusive?"

"Yes, and I had every intention of canceling on Brayden. In fact, I know he was returning my call so that I could do just that. And that moment would have been the perfect opportunity if Ethan hadn't been there."

"So, how did Ethan react?"

"He left. Told me to end it before things went further." I sigh, shaking my head. "Maybe I should just end this thing with Ethan too. It's uncharacteristic of me to do something like this in the first place, let alone with a man that I have to see every day." I stare across the restaurant in thought. "This can't end well, but there's something about him that makes me want to keep going, like he's a puzzle I want to figure out. Knowing he's a dad explains part of it, but I know there's more to him than that. He's so hot and cold, though, I feel like I'm experiencing whiplash, but I'm already attached to his dick and his tongue."

"Isn't it crazy that we can get attached to something so ugly?" Noelle interjects. "Like once we find one we like, it's suddenly the best dick we've ever seen?" Noelle chuckles.

"I think Damien's dick is beautiful," Charlotte says matter-of-factly.

"That's because you're sleeping with him. Once your heart connects, you're inclined to love the dick attached to the man. From there on out, his dick is perfect, his dick is beautiful, and all other dicks are still in the ugly category."

"The woman has a point," Charlotte concedes.

"Does the same thing apply to vaginas though?" Noelle asks. "I mean, vaginas aren't necessarily the most beautiful thing either."

"No. Vaginas are much better looking than penises," Penelope interjects. "Besides, I think men are so entranced once they look down there, the only thing going through their mind is, 'I wanna put my dick in there.'"

We all share a laugh. "Sounds about right. So what do I do, girls?"

"Well, did you call things off with Brayden?" Noelle asks.

"Yes. I spoke to him later that evening and told him that while I think he's a great guy, I didn't feel a strong enough connection."

"And have you spoken to Ethan since then?"

"No. I don't have his number. And besides, even if I did, I don't think this is the type of conversation to have over the phone."

Penelope is the first to offer her opinion. "I think the answer is clear. Your mind and body have already decided for you, Amelia. I think you're just looking for validation from us."

I sigh, swallowing down the truth. "I'm curious. I want to see where this goes, but part of me is scared too."

Charlotte reaches over and places her hand over mine. "I felt the same way with Damien, but all you can do is take it one day, or one orgasm, at a time." She winks at me. "But like you told me, make sure you have boundaries in place. Sometimes you just have to take the risk."

"Why can I give everyone else relationship advice and talk them through critical moments of their lives, but when it comes to my own, I feel lost?"

"Because you're human. And if you weren't, you wouldn't be so damn good at your job."

Chapter 9

Ethan

"Daddy?" Oliver's voice pulls me from my thoughts, thoughts that involve Amelia and the look in her eyes when I walked away from her on Friday for the thousandth time.

"Yeah, bud. Sorry, ask me your question again, please." I glance in the rearview mirror to find Oliver in the backseat, rolling his eyes at me but kicking his legs as we cruise down the road.

"Are her gnomes still in the same spot?" he asks, launching himself forward in his seat.

"I don't know. I didn't look, and you need to sit back in your chair, please."

"But I asked you to check, Daddy," he whines. "They are supposed to come alive at night, and I want to know if they moved. You said you would check on Friday, and you didn't. It made me sad."

"I know, bud. I'll check today, okay?"

"Don't forget, Daddy." He points a finger at me as he meets my eyes in the rearview mirror. And I can't help but smile at the determination in his voice, as if he thinks he's the one in charge here—which, let's face it, most of the time he is. The boy has me wrapped around his finger, and I'd do anything to see that smile of his never falter.

"I'll take a picture today, Oliver, just for you."

His eyes light up. "Yes!"

"But you have to promise to be a good boy at school for your teacher and be good for Grandma when she picks you up."

"I'm always good, Daddy. There are other kids who are bad every day, and I always tell them that they are, like Brayden. He never listens and throws things when we have to do work."

"Brayden, huh?" Figures a kid with that name would be a nuisance, but maybe that's just my own selfish disdain for anyone with that name.

Fucking Brayden.

I know I shouldn't care if she went on a date with him since I'm the one that's been up close and personal with the sweet haven between her legs and he hasn't—at least I'm assuming he hasn't after their lackluster date. But just seeing his name on her phone on Friday sent me over the edge, especially after she was the one that suggested we be exclusive. I know I acted irrationally, but my anger grew like a match being struck, quick and fast, before it died down later. But by then, I was knee-deep in a new client case and preparing for trial for another, and I figured having the weekend to cool off would be best.

And cooling off is exactly what I think needs to happen.

I can already feel myself becoming addicted to her, a detail I knew was inevitable. I tried desperately to convince myself I had control when I suggested our little arrangement. Now, I keep showing Amelia this side of me that is quick to erupt and hates a lack of control. I probably shouldn't be touching or thinking about her the way that I am, but I also can't stop.

Amelia St. Clair has dug her talons into me, and I don't want to push her away, even though subconsciously, I think that's what I'm trying to do.

I've never met a woman like her, independent, headstrong, vivacious, intelligent, and selfless—you have to be selfless to agree to listen to other people's problems and help them through them. I wouldn't last one day listening to other people bitch and moan about how their lives are unfair.

Life fucking sucks sometimes. It doesn't work out the way we think it will, but there's no time to sit there and fucking wallow. You have no choice but to stand up, dust off your hands and knees, and move on.

It's what I did, and look at me—I'm doing just fine.

Okay, Ethan... keep telling yourself that.

"Yeah, he's a bad kid, Daddy. He's mean to all the girls too," Oliver says, pulling me back to the conversation.

"Well, don't ever let me hear that you're acting like Brayden, Oliver, or you'll be grounded forever."

"What's grounded mean, Daddy?"

I blow out a breath. "Nothing good."

Ten seconds later, I'm pulling into my mother's driveway and shifting my car into park.

"Grandma said we're going to make blueberry muffins for breakfast today," Oliver declares as he unbuckles his seatbelt and races from the car.

"Sounds good." I follow him inside and find him already in the kitchen with my mother. "Morning, Mom."

She kisses me on the cheek, patting it for good measure. "Good morning. How was your weekend?"

"It was good. Watched some movies, played with some Legos, practiced soccer a bit."

"How was your first practice, my boy?" she asks my kid.

"I scored a goal, Grandma! My coach said I'm a natural."

We share a laugh. "He definitely has a knack for it, so we'll see how things progress as the season moves along."

"Good. I promise to be at all of your games so I can cheer you on."

"Yay! Is it time to bake muffins now?"

"Yes, sir." She reaches for his chef's hat like the one he has at home, placing it gently on his head. "Tell Daddy goodbye so we can get to work."

He spins around and runs into my legs, squeezing his tiny arms around them. "Bye, Daddy. Go make money and pay bills."

His standard parting words always make me laugh. "I will, bud. Love you." I press a kiss to the top of his head, ruffling his hair.

"Love you too, Daddy."

"See you this afternoon, Mom." I give her a kiss as well on the cheek.

"Have a good day, Ethan. Tell Amelia we said hello," she says with a wink.

"Yes! Tell Amelia I said hi, and don't forget about the picture of her gnomes, Daddy!" Oliver calls after me as I walk through the door and back to my car.

Hopefully, I can snap a picture on the way in and not draw any attention to myself until I'm ready to apologize for the second time to this woman. Fuck, I think I have a complex when it comes to her about being wrong—and she's one of the only people I've ever apologized to for it.

"**E**than, Dr. St. Clair is here to see you."

I look up from my desk to find my assistant, Yvonne, standing in my doorway, chewing on her thumbnail. She's probably nervous about letting Amelia in since the last time she was here was to drop off the brochures that she lied about us agreeing to give to my clients.

Glancing at the clock, I notice it's a quarter to twelve, so just before lunch. I planned on going over there in fifteen minutes, but it seems she's beat me to the punch—and I'm not sure that's a good thing.

"Bring her back, please."

Yvonne nods and scurries off, giving me just enough time to finish writing down my thoughts as the scent of lemons hits my nose. Looking up, I find Amelia standing tall with her shoulders back and her delectable body encased in a dark gray dress. The woman must own a dress in every color, but I'm not complaining. Dresses make for easy access.

"Mr. Fuller."

Her greeting makes me cautious. "Dr. St. Clair."

"Do you mind if I close the door?" She gestures behind her.

"Please do."

She shuts the door gently and then walks to one of the chairs on the other side of my desk, slowly taking a seat while keeping her eyes locked on mine. "How was your weekend?"

Her question catches me off guard, but I decide to roll with it. "Good. You?"

"It was good. Long." Silence descends between us before Amelia clears her throat and speaks up first. "So, I'd like to talk to you about Friday."

Leaning back in my chair, I clasp my hands over my knee and reply, "Okay."

She takes a deep breath and then delivers her statement. "I understand that you were caught off guard by Brayden's phone call, but I don't appreciate the way you spoke to me after, nor the way you stormed off. Your impulsive response made me upset because one, you didn't give me the chance to explain why he was calling, and two, you assumed something about me that isn't true."

"Which is?"

"That I would go back on my word. I don't do that."

"Well, I'm sorry that I made that error."

"And here's the thing," she says, crossing one of her legs over the other in her chair, drawing my attention to her tan and toned skin. "If you knew me better, perhaps you would understand that."

"What are you saying?"

"I'm saying that maybe we should get to know each other better before this physical thing escalates between us."

"That's not what I proposed." Panic begins to radiate from my chest. I'm not looking for dating; I'm looking for fucking. That's the only reason why I gave myself permission to enter into this arrangement with Amelia in the first place because I knew that doing anything more than that would send the wrong message—to her and to me.

I don't want a relationship. I don't have time for that in my life.

But hell if I can walk away from this woman now.

"I understand, but I'm requesting to make an amendment to our agreement."

As Amelia stares across the desk at me with determination and sincerity in her eyes, my original question pops up in my head. "Well, are you still dating Brayden?"

"No, and I wasn't. We only went on one date. He was returning my phone call from earlier, the one where I planned on telling him that I would no longer be dating him. And you would have known that if you had let me explain. I meant what I said—I want exclusivity with you."

I stand from my chair and begin to pace around my office. "I don't know if we can really put a label on what we're doing, Amelia. But if I have to see that guy put his hands or lips on you again, I'm going to chop off his hands myself."

Her lips lift. "Well, you don't have to worry about that. It's done."

I stare down at her and then slowly stride in her direction. "I'm sorry."

"Why do I get the feeling that you don't say those words very often?" she teases.

"Because I don't. But I do agree that perhaps this is moving too fast." *I need space from you, time away, to gain my bearings again.*

"Oh."

"I agree that maybe getting to know each other is a good idea, but this arrangement is primarily physical for me. I don't need the other stuff." *But does that mean you don't want it, Ethan?*

A flash of disappointment moves across her face, but she recovers quickly with a nod. "I understand, but I'm telling you that I do. So if this is a problem, perhaps we should part ways right now."

"Amelia…" I start, trying to find a way to explain to her why I can't give her more, even though deep down I know I don't want her to leave.

She stands from her seat in front of me with just a few inches of space between us. "Well, I'm glad that's settled then. Have a good day, Ethan." Twisting away from me, she begins to head for the door, but I grab her wrist and pull her back to me, framing her face in my hands.

"Where do you think you're going?"

"Back to my office," she repeats breathlessly. "I have work to do."

"Don't go." Debating on how to save this conversation from going completely south, I reach for a last-ditch effort. "Want to actually have lunch with me tomorrow? Not our usual lunch meetings, but…"

"You mean, share a meal?"

"Yes."

"I thought you didn't want more…"

"I want you," I answer honestly. "So if that means we need to talk instead of fuck, I guess I can be flexible."

She arches a brow at me but doesn't say anything for a while. The silence makes me uncomfortable, but finally, she simply says, "Okay."

I press my lips to hers, savoring just the feel of her mouth on mine as relief rushes through me. There's no tongue, just the soft caress of our lips, and it's just as addicting as when we're devouring one another.

When we part, I rest my forehead on hers and release her face, gripping her waist instead. My dick is rock hard, but after telling her that we need to slow things down, I probably shouldn't let my dick run the rest of this meeting. "I have one more question for you."

"Yes?"

"Do you mind if I take a picture of your gnomes?"

She rears back with a smile on her lips. "What?"

"It's for Oliver. He kept asking me all damn weekend if the darn things moved, and I told him I forgot to look, so I promised I would take a picture of them today for evidence."

Amelia's smile lights up the entire room. "That is the sweetest thing. And you know what? Let's move them, so it looks like it actually happened!"

"You don't have to do that."

"No. It will be fun!" She takes my hand in hers and leads me to my office door.

"Seriously, Amelia, you don't know what you're starting. I thought the same thing about that damn Elf on the Shelf, and now the entire month of December is pure fucking torture."

She releases my hand once we make our way out to the main part of my office, where Yvonne is eating her lunch, pausing in nervousness as we walk past her. And once we're outside, I follow the sight of Amelia's ass and hips swinging from side to side as she marches over to the flower bed outside of her office and crouches down to adjust the gnomes.

"Seriously, you don't have to do this."

She sets them in a different spot, somewhere clearly different from where they were before. "It's no problem. I think this is adorable. Oliver will love this."

My heart constricts a bit as I watch this woman who barely knows my kid go above and beyond to make him happy and believe in magic. I can't think about a time when Monica put that much thought into her own child. But Amelia is doing it without a second thought, and that's the kind of shit that tells me to watch how close we become. It's actions like these that had me putting up the walls I built three years ago and vowing never to take them down.

"There." She stands tall again, brushing the dust off her hands. "Get out your phone."

She points down to the gnomes with a shocked expression on her face, her mouth in the perfect little O. And even though I know she's being dramatic for the picture, all it's making me think about is how her mouth looks like that with my cock deep inside of it.

Jesus, Ethan, you have problems.

"Thank you, Amelia." I snap the picture and then place my phone back in my pocket and shove my hands in as well, not sure what to do with them. We're out in the open, so I can't really touch her. But after what she just did, I desperately want to.

"Please let me know how he reacts, okay?"

"I will. And lunch tomorrow?"

"Yes. Have a good day, Ethan." She turns and unlocks her office door, stepping inside with a small wave, leaving me standing out in the blinding sun lusting after her. And that's when I should have known right there that I was in trouble when it came to Amelia St. Clair.

"So what do you do when you're not trying to repair every broken marriage in Los Angeles?" I stare across Amelia's desk at her as she takes a bite of her chow mein. We decided on Chinese for lunch since there's a small shop across the street that a bunch of the other business owners in the complex rave about.

She pauses mid-chew. "I think for the sake of our arrangement, perhaps we shouldn't discuss work."

The woman might actually be on to something. "Not a bad idea, actually. But still, answer the question."

I know that getting to know each other better was her idea, but I have to admit, I'm having a little too much fun with this. I have permission to dig for information on this woman now, and I'm taking full advantage.

"Well, I have a group of girlfriends that I do pretty much everything with. We have brunch almost every Sunday together at Frankie's Diner. Have you heard of it?"

"Yes, but I haven't been yet."

"You should go. Take Oliver, he'll love it. They have amazing waffles with fresh strawberries and whipped cream."

"Sounds like something he'd be into." And there she goes again, thinking about my kid. "So what else?"

"Honestly, I like to get outside. Walking, hiking, going to the beach. Being stuck inside all day can make me go a little crazy. Oh, and I take pole dancing classes."

I nearly choke on a noodle. "Excuse me? What was that last one?"

She fights her grin but fails. "Pole dancing. You know? Like what a stripper does? Only I do it for the physical benefits, not to support myself financially."

"Fuck, Amelia. Why do you have to say shit like that?" I reach down and adjust my dick in my slacks.

She giggles as she wipes her mouth with a napkin. "You asked. So what about you?"

"I hang out with Oliver, primarily. We cook dinner together, play outside and practice soccer since he just started playing, and I love watching football. Pre-season has already started, but I'm a diehard Dallas fan, so I'm hoping we can make the playoffs this year."

"Football and Oliver, got it. No other friends you hang out with?"

"Besides your brother? Not really. Remember, I just moved back here from San Diego."

She moves her food around with her fork, avoiding my eyes. "And what about Oliver's mom?" Her eyes flick up to mine, waiting for my response.

The last thing I want to do is discuss Monica with her. I don't owe her those details, and it's not something I like discussing anyway. But I decide to at least appease her curiosity. "She's not in the picture."

Her face falls. "Oh. I'm sorry to hear that."

"It's her loss." I clear my throat, moving my own food around with my fork now.

See? This is why I don't bother getting to know women. I like to get in, get what I need, and get out, even though it's been months since I've done that before Amelia came along.

But the pity, the sadness in her eyes as she looks at me, is something I can't fucking stand.

"You sure orgasms aren't on the menu today?" I ask, trying to defuse the situation.

She rolls her eyes. "Men. And no, Ethan. You suggested lunch, so that's what we're having—lunch."

"Yeah, but you have a cookie that I'm dying to eat too."

"Did you just compare my vagina to a cookie?" She holds up one of the fortune cookies in the air.

"I did. And yours has the best fortune of them all—an orgasm. It's guaranteed to be true every time."

"Not every time," she mutters.

"It is if I'm down there."

I watch her rub her thighs together. I know just the talk about this is turning her on, but she clears her throat, closes the lid on her Styrofoam container, and stands from her chair. "Well, this lunch has been enlightening."

I follow her lead and stand as well. "Actually, it was kind of nice talking to another adult and one who wasn't complaining about their ex the entire time."

She laughs. "You signed up for that, remember?"

"Yeah, you're right."

"But don't worry. You won't hear about exes from me."

"Interesting. Why is that?"

"Because none of mine are worthy of talking shit about."

I scoff. "What do you mean?"

"I mean, all of my former relationships have either ended amicably, or they just weren't that meaningful to care about bashing the other person's feelings or reputation, or more importantly, venting to my girlfriends about."

"Wow. Sorry, I just figured you were one of those girls who's always had a boyfriend."

"And what makes you say that?" she asks, staring up at me from her side of her desk.

And for the first time in a while, I'm at a loss for words on how to explain my thoughts. Amelia has a heart. She cares about people and tries to see the best in everything and everyone. I just find it hard to believe that she's never been in love.

"Are you saying you've never been in love?"

"No. I have. I don't feel that it's ever been the earth-shattering type of love though. The kind that makes you swear off men for the rest of eternity or construct a voodoo doll to curse the one who broke your heart."

I arch a brow at her. "Have you had clients do that?"

She laughs. "Unfortunately, yes."

"Damn."

She looks to the side of the room as the conversation lulls. "Well, this has been fun, Ethan. We should do this again." Walking around her desk now, she stops in front of me.

"I think giving each other a few orgasms would be better than a meal, but I guess that's not a bad idea either." She swats me playfully in my chest, but I catch her hand and pull her into me before she can retract.

"Ethan…"

"Have a good day, Amelia." And before I release her, I press my mouth to hers, nipping and kissing her lips before teasing her with my tongue. Her moan spurs me on, and I draw her into my chest, wrapping my arm around her waist to hold her there as my other one finds her curls, and I bury my fingers deep inside them.

I love her hair—it's beautiful and golden but wild, hinting at the side of her that I know is untamed and adventurous as well. And even though I know I don't want more, my body is beginning to like the way being with her makes me feel.

She makes me laugh, can carry on a conversation, and isn't afraid to verbally spar with me. She's entertaining and different, and now I know that she fucking pole dances.

She's clearly not fighting fair.

When we part, I reach up and tug on her bottom lip. "See ya tomorrow."

"Bye, Ethan," she whispers breathlessly before unlocking the door and letting me leave, returning to my office that feels too far away from the woman pulling me in one kiss at a time.

And even though I keep telling myself that I'm completely in control, this little voice in the back of my head keeps reminding me that I'm so fucking screwed.

"So, where did you go to college again?" I ask after I finish chewing a bite of my Philly cheesesteak.

Even though we didn't plan on it, I showed up at her office today with sandwiches so we could have lunch again together—just lunch.

Last night as I was lying in bed, images from our earlier conversation kept flashing behind my eyelids, and details she shared with me kept echoing in my ears, particularly that little detail about her pole dancing. Fuck, do I want to be able to witness that for myself.

The way Amelia relaxed around me for the first time, how her eyebrows would draw together when I told her something that surprised her, and how she licked her lips each time she took a bite of her food—it all made me crave her company again, which is why I acted impulsively and decided to surprise her with lunch again today.

And judging by the smile on her face when she answered her office door, I'm gonna say she's not mad about my surprise.

"UCLA."

I snap my fingers. "That's right. I vaguely remember Nick mentioning his sister who went there now."

"You vaguely remember?"

"Hey, forgive me, but we were inebriated more often than not, and I sort of pushed away unnecessary details if they didn't matter to me."

"Understandable. I bet you have some juicy stories about my brother though," she teases as she pops a chip in her mouth.

"I do, but I can't tell you. That's like going against bro-code."

"Oh, but fooling around with me isn't?"

Fuck, she has a point. "That's different."

"How?"

"Because this is just sex."

Her face falls flat. "Right."

I feel like an ass saying it that starkly, but perhaps it will do good to remind her and myself of that fact. Nonetheless, I don't want our lunch to end just yet. My chest constricts with the thought of leaving. "What about you though? What was the UCLA experience like?" I ask, trying to sidestep that comment.

"Well, Penelope, Noelle, Charlotte, and I met our freshman year in English class. We clicked instantly, and our eternal bond was formed."

"Eternal?"

"Yes. We are very close. Those girls are the sisters I never had. I love Nick, don't get me wrong, but a female bond is just different. They understand everything that I think or feel, and we lean on each other for support in each phase of our lives. Nick tries to understand and be there for me too, but there will always be things he just won't get."

"Makes sense."

"So, anyway, they dragged me along to parties, mostly at Penelope's request. And believe me, if you meet her, you'll understand why you can't say no to the girl."

"She sounds like fun."

"She is, but she's also the one who ordered three hundred dildos and had them delivered to your office."

"Oh." I gulp loudly. "Don't mess with Penelope then, got it."

Amelia laughs. "Yup. They reminded me to have fun in between all the studying I did and the extra classes I took to graduate early so I could start working on my doctorate."

"How old are you?"

"Thirty-one."

"And you've been practicing for…?"

"Almost five years now."

"Damn. You did bust your ass then."

She smiles proudly, sitting up taller in her chair while taking a sip of her drink, mumbling around her straw. "That's right. When I put my mind to something, I can be quite determined." She bites her straw, smiling around it at me.

And my dick twitches.

"So, where were you practicing before?"

"Out of my house."

My brows pop up. "Really?"

"Yes." She sets her drink back down on her desk. "It was cost-effective, and clients actually enjoyed it. But once I had the money saved up for a deposit on this place and a strong client base and referrals, I bit the bullet and moved here."

"Just in time for me to move across the courtyard."

She rolls her eyes. "Unfortunately."

"Do you still feel that way now?" I ask, curious if her feelings toward me have changed since we started fooling around. "I mean, mad about me being here?"

"Well, the orgasms have definitely helped abate my disdain for you," she jokes. "But honestly, you still make me a little crazy, just in a different way now."

"I prefer making you so crazy that you scream out my name, but maybe that's just me."

"Ethan…" she breathes out. "We're supposed to be getting to know each other."

"I know. And I think that should include me getting to know your pussy some more. From what I've gathered already, I'm a big fan."

She scoffs and then stands to throw away her trash. "Thanks for lunch."

"Is that it?"

Turning to face me, she arches a brow. "Were you expecting more?"

"Don't you want dessert?"

"Did you bring cookies?"

"Ha. No. But there's a cookie I'd like to eat…"

"Between my legs," she finishes for me, rolling her eyes again. "I know. Jesus. You sound like a teenage boy. You realize that, right?"

I throw my hands up in defense. "What can I say? Once that door is unlocked after being shut for a while, my mind tends to focus on sex and sex alone."

"You're incorrigible."

"And you're beautiful," I reply as she freezes. "You should take it as a compliment that I'm craving you, Amelia. Trust me."

She smiles softly, tucking a strand of her curly hair behind her ears. "Then I will."

Drawing her into me, I circle my arms around her waist. "I'll leave you alone for today, but I'm dying to taste you again." Dragging my nose up her cheek, I find her ear and nibble lightly on the lobe.

"Is that so?"

"Yes. You're addictive, and I meant it when I said I wanted you from the first day I saw you. There's still so much for us to explore together."

"Uh-huh…"

"So don't overthink this, remember?"

Maybe you should take your own advice, Ethan, instead of wondering why on earth you're enjoying these little lunches when the physical relationship was your idea, to begin with?

"Okay." She leans back slightly so our eyes can meet. And the honey color of her brown eyes looks brighter behind the lens of her glasses, especially as a sliver of sunlight comes through the window and highlights them.

Amelia is gorgeous, sexy, and smart as hell. And I hate to admit it, but she's right—getting to know her better is making me see all the ways I misjudged her in the beginning, especially when it comes to sex. I mean, the woman let me fuck her with a vibrating dildo the first time we fooled around. I should have known I was in trouble from that moment on.

Our lips meet, and our kiss makes me dizzy by the time we part.

"I think we should exchange phone numbers," I suggest, knowing that being able to contact her that way would be easier.

"Oh. Yeah, that's a good idea." She walks over to her desk and takes her phone out of one of the drawers. We share our information, and then I'm headed for the door, debating how I plan to use her number now that I have it.

"Have a good rest of your day, Amelia."

"You too, Ethan."

The rest of the day crawls before I can leave and pick up my son, and I hope to God I get a chance to see her again tomorrow.

～

"Good to see you, man." Nick greets me as soon as he takes a seat in the booth across from me. We shake hands and settle in as the restaurant buzzes with conversation around us.

It's Friday night, and Oliver is staying the night at my mom's house again. His friend that lives on her street wanted to have a sleepover, and my mom offered to host it at her house. I told her she didn't have to, especially since she takes Oliver every day for me before and after school, but she insisted.

"It's not a big deal. Now that Oliver is in school, I miss our time together. And you deserve some adult time too. Maybe you should see what Amelia is up to?" she said with a suggestive lilt in her voice.

The truth is, I really contemplated it for a good hour, wondering if she would be available. But then my brain had me retreating and remembering not to send the wrong message. Taking her out to dinner would imply that we are dating, and we're not. We're just two friends who occasionally enjoy a meal or two together and partake in oral sex on our lunch breaks.

That's not dating—that's consensual fucking, and every person needs to eat to survive.

So what did I do instead of seeing if Amelia had plans tonight? I texted her brother.

I'm not gonna lie, sitting across from him now after knowing what I've done to his sister is making my stomach churn just slightly. But like I told Amelia, there's no sense in really telling anyone what's going on with us if it's just about pleasure.

And besides, I'm not really sure how Nick might react.

We're not best fucking friends, but our friendship does have a history, the kind that bonded us through shared experiences and mistakes early on in life.

Fooling around with his sister might have been something he could overlook when we were still in our twenties. But we're in our thirties now, and I'm not sure what the cut off is to qualify what Amelia and I are doing as inappropriate or boundary crossing.

"Thanks for coming out. I was sure you'd have plans with Elena tonight, so I was surprised you could come."

"Oh, I'm meeting up with her later. She had to chaperone some event at her school for her extra duty hours, so I figured I could have a couple beers with you in the meantime and then spend some time with my girl later on."

The waitress comes by, and we order a couple beers and two appetizers to share.

"Your girl? Are things getting serious then?"

Nick can't even hide his smile. "Yeah, they are. I'm actually going to introduce her to my parents in a few weeks. Amelia is coming over for dinner too, so it's kind of a big deal."

"Sounds like it."

"What about you? Still on the vagina ban?"

I look off to the other side of the restaurant, laughing but avoiding his eyes. "Well…"

"Since you're avoiding looking at me, can I assume that means no? Did you find a hot little piece of ass to help you loosen up?" I still don't answer him, but I can feel his eyes locked on me, waiting for a response. I don't give him one, so he keeps prodding. "Come to think of it, you do look a little more relaxed, not as uptight, like someone may have removed the stick from your ass. I bet it was like the Sword in the Stone, and only the right woman could remove it, right?"

"Jesus, Nick. Stop talking."

He bursts into laughter, slapping the table. "Then spill."

"I may have found a friend to help ease some aggression, but it's casual," I reply, hoping he accepts that and doesn't keep digging.

"You don't want to date her?"

"Ha, no." *Then why are you mad you didn't get to have lunch with Amelia for the rest of the week, huh, Ethan?*

After eating together on Monday and Tuesday, I was eager to continue our meals on Wednesday, but I got called into an emergency hearing that morning over a custody battle. From then, shit just spiraled. Luckily, since I finally had Amelia's phone number, I was able to text her and let her know I would have to work through lunch for the rest of the week to deal with everything. She understood, of course, but deep down, I was a little disappointed.

And I wonder if she was too.

"Why not? It's been years since Monica, man…"

"Look, you don't get it. It's not just me that stands to be disappointed, Nick. Oliver risks getting hurt too. He's already had one woman leave him, a woman who is supposed to love him unconditionally and be there throughout his entire life. She was supposed to be the only woman who would never let him down, but she did. I already know he's going to be screwed up in multiple ways from that, so the last thing I need is to introduce him to a multitude of women that all have the potential to do the same."

He nods slowly. "Okay, I get that. But you're telling me you don't ever plan on dating?"

Originally that was my mindset just after the divorce. But now, I'm not so sure. "Honestly, I don't know. I just know that it's complicated, and I'm trying to figure things out as I go."

"So does this friend of yours know that things are casual? I mean, in my experience, women tend to agree to casual at first and then expect more down the line."

Fuck, I hope Amelia doesn't get it twisted. I only gave myself permission to pursue her as long as it remained physical between us. But then she showed up in my office, put me in my place, and suggested we get to know each other better. And now, I can't seem to stop myself from doing and wanting the complete opposite—wanting and needing her, craving her company—and it's been a long fucking time since I've felt that way about a woman.

"Yes, she's aware. And I'm not saying it can't turn into something more, but I also don't want to give her false hope. So, for now, we're just getting to know each other and reaping the physical benefits."

Nick shrugs. "Can't argue with that. And hey, if things work out, perhaps you two can go on a double date with Elena and me sometime?"

I cringe internally. First, I'd have to admit that it's his sister I'm planning on fucking sideways all over her office. Once he finds that out, I'm not so sure that offer will still stand.

"Yeah, maybe," I reply, appeasing his suggestion and then turning the conversation to safer topics. "So how about them Cowboys?"

His head falls back, and boisterous laughter emanates from him. "Dude, why on earth do you insist on supporting a team that's only going to break your heart every year?"

Chuckling, I drain half of my beer. "It's about loyalty. I'd rather be loyal than a bandwagon fan."

"Hey, I'm not a bandwagon fan," he admonishes.

"The only reason you cheer for New Orleans is because Maddox Taylor is the quarterback."

"He's fucking awesome, Ethan. People are saying he's the next Tom Brady."

"Tom Brady is overrated too," I fire back, smiling around my beer. "And Maddox is also notorious for taking advantage of his fame. He's constantly in the press for partying and enjoying his stardom."

"Wouldn't you do the same?"

"Nah. If I got paid that kind of money to play football, I'd live and breathe it and wouldn't let anything derail my priorities. Are you saying you'd act like him?"

"Not at all. I like my quiet life too. I just want a good woman, a nice house, and a family. I think those are the things that make you truly rich."

"Damn. Well, when you put it like that, it sounds so simple."

"Yeah, because it is."

By the time I get home from the restaurant with Nick, it's just before nine. We had a few beers, shot the shit some more, filled each other in on the time since we've seen each other last, all the while avoiding the topic of his sister.

I felt relaxed after a hellish week, but I know one thing that could make it even better.

My thumb hovers over the call button for Amelia's number as I stare down at my phone in my hand. We never discussed seeing each other outside of work, but I'm horny and alone in my house, granting me the perfect opportunity to see her without my fatherly obligations or my job as an obstacle. Plus, I just really want to fucking see her or talk to her—any contact with her is what my body and mind are craving right now.

I decide to settle for a text message. That way, if she's busy, the blow off won't seem so harsh. My thumbs move over the screen, compiling a message that I hope will result in her coming over. I don't debate or talk myself out of it, and as soon as it's done, I press send and wait for a response.

Chapter 10

Amelia

Holding a glass of champagne, I use my free hand to dig my phone out of my small purse I brought for the evening after I feel the buzz of it on my hip.

It's Friday night, and I'm currently standing in a private exhibit at Night Gallery, an art gallery just east of the Fashion District in Los Angeles. Penelope's PR firm was in charge of publicity for the event, so naturally she scored us tickets to tag along.

"Do you need help?" Noelle asks, reaching for my glass of champagne as I struggle with the zipper on my purse one-handed.

"Yes, please. Thank you."

"No problem."

I hand her my glass and then use both hands finally to extract my phone, shocked by the text message that I see on the screen from Ethan.

"What?" Noelle observes my face and instantly questions what got that reaction out of me.

"It's Ethan."

"Oh! What did he have to say?"

I swipe across the screen and read the message at lightning speed.

Ethan: *Hey, beautiful. What are you up to?*

"What do I say to that?"

Noelle shrugs. "Is him texting you not normal?"

"Um, not at this hour. The last time we spoke was Wednesday when he had an emergency hearing and then he was buried in work for the rest of the week." Prior to arriving at the venue tonight, I filled all my girlfriends in on the developments that transpired with Ethan this week since brunch last Sunday.

Noelle points to my screen. "Then this is a booty call."

"You think?"

"Hun, it's after nine on a Friday night. You're not at work, which is when you usually see him or hook up. He's obviously horny and wants you. Why else would he be texting?"

"I…I don't know. Maybe I should ask him."

"Do it." She chuckles, taking a sip from her glass as I begin to type on my phone.

Me: *I haven't heard from you for two days, and now you text me at nine on a Friday night? Is this a booty call, Mr. Fuller?*

His response is almost immediate.

Ethan: *I mean, I wouldn't be opposed if you wanted to show me your booty. But honestly, I'm home alone, and you were on my mind.*

I show the text to Noelle, who fights a smile. "Smooth."

Me: *Really? And what exactly were you thinking about?"*

Ethan: *Your ass, your pussy, and your smile.*

Me: *Gosh, it's so nice to know what you think are my best qualities.*

Ethan: *You should be damn proud of all of them. In all seriousness, I debated texting you earlier, but I chickened out. I had dinner with your brother instead. And before you freak out, I steered clear of the topic of you and me in conversation. He does know I'm seeing someone, but not who.*

My pulse spikes as I read his message, but then it ebbs just as quickly.

Me: *Well, I'm actually at the Night Gallery for a private art exhibition right now, so I wasn't available anyway.*

Ethan: *Ah, no worries. Sorry to bother you. Have a good night, Amelia.*

Biting my lip, I debate whether I want this conversation to end. And within a few seconds, I decide that I don't.

Me: *Where's Oliver?*

Ethan: *At my mom's house for a sleepover with her neighbor. There's a little boy that lives just a few houses down from hers, and they've become really good friends since we moved back. So, I'm home alone in this house. It's unnerving.*

And before I can reply, he sends another message.

Ethan: *Is the event that boring that you'd rather talk to me instead?*

"Aw, he misses his kid," Noelle croons, reading the text message conversation over my shoulder.

"He's the sweetest little boy, Noelle. He named my gnomes for crying out loud."

She sighs dramatically. "God, I want kids, Amelia. Why on earth do you have to have a man to do that though?"

"Well, technically, you don't. You just need a few of his best swimmers."

"I just don't know if I could go through with that—picking some guy to be the father of my kid without knowing him."

"Yeah, but look at how disappointing potential men have been recently. I'm not telling you what to do, but I also know that you will be an incredible mother, and you don't need a man in your life to do that."

She stares at me, deep in thought. "You know what, you're right."

My phone pings again.

Ethan: *You still there?*

Me: *Yes, sorry. Actually, I was thinking about leaving soon anyway. I just need to finish this glass of champagne.*

Ethan: *How many glasses have you had?*

Me: *This is my third. Don't worry, Ethan, I'm not drinking and driving. We took an Uber, and I planned on calling one to take me home as well.*

I wait for his response as I see the dots dancing around on my screen.

Ethan: *You are not taking an Uber after you've been drinking, Amelia. Are you stupid? That's like asking to get assaulted.*

"Jesus. Someone has a temper," Noelle says over my shoulder as she continues to watch our text exchange.

"This is how he is, so hot and cold. One minute he's charming and relaxed, and the next, I want to punch him for trying to boss me around."

"Unless you're fooling around, right? I mean, then a little bossiness isn't the worst thing."

"Agreed." I turn back to my phone.

Ethan: *I'm coming to pick you up. I'd never forgive myself if something happened to you.*

"And then he says stuff like this."

Noelle arches a brow at me. "Sounds like he's a little more invested than you think he is."

"Really?"

She shrugs. "I could be wrong, but if you two are really just fooling around, why would he be texting you outside of work where you normally converse and also care to pick you up from here?"

"I don't know…but is it horrible that I really want to see him too?"

"No, Amelia." She places her hand on my shoulder. "You like the guy. And I'm beginning to think that maybe he likes you more than he's aware of too."

I glance down at my screen again.

Ethan: *You said you're at the Night Gallery, right?*

Me: *Ethan, it's really okay. You don't have to come get me. I can share a ride with Noelle or just wait for all of us to leave together.*

Ethan: *Too late. I'm already in the car. Stay put. I'll be there soon.*

Me: *You're not the boss of me, Ethan. I'm a grown woman and can handle myself.*

Ethan: *I know, Amelia. That's not what this is about. Just please…let me come get you for me, so I know you're safe.*

Well, how am I supposed to argue with that?

"Guess we all get to meet Ethan finally," Noelle teases beside me, handing me my glass of champagne back as I send a simple 'OK' text back to Ethan.

"Joy. This will be fun."

"There he is."

After I accepted that Ethan was on his way, Noelle and I went to find Charlotte and Penelope, letting them know that Ethan was coming to pick me up.

My three best friends and Damien, who Charlotte brought with her, twist to watch Ethan stride into the gallery, scanning the room for me. It doesn't take long before his eyes lock on mine, and then he starts heading in our direction.

"No wonder you want to screw the man," Penelope states as her eyes move up and down Ethan's body. And he does look incredible—dark blue jeans, a plain black T-shirt, and sneakers, his sandy-blond hair in disarray. I don't ever think I've seen the man out of a suit until now, and I can't say that I hate the sight. Apparently, Ethan Fuller looks good in anything.

"Hey, man." Damien reaches out to shake Ethan's hand as all of us girls stand by, confused as all hell at the casual way they're acting.

"Wait. You two know each other?" I ask.

Ethan turns to me. "I met him about a month ago when I went out with your brother. Jeffrey was there too."

"Oh, Jeffrey. If the man weren't so terrified of me, I'd show him what a real woman was like in the sack."

"You must be Penelope." Ethan reaches out to shake her hand.

"Heard a little about me, huh?"

"Just that you were the mastermind behind the three hundred dildos that were delivered to my office." Everyone laughs, including Damien.

"Don't fuck with my friend again, or else the next delivery will be much worse."

"Noted."

"I told you, man, these women can be a handful," Damien adds with a wink in our direction.

"But you like us—particularly me—that way, don't you, babe?" Charlotte says, staring up at her man. "Life would be boring with a woman who doesn't talk back or have an opinion."

"Oh, I agree. Doesn't mean you all aren't still a handful though."

"Perhaps Damien needs a little delivery to his office to show him how out of line we can act as well?" Penelope teases.

"Whatever you do, just please don't use my credit card this time," I mutter, which has everyone laughing again. "Ethan," I say, gesturing to my friends. "These are my girls, Noelle, Charlotte, and Penelope, of course." He takes turns greeting all of them.

"Nice to meet you, ladies. It's nice to put faces to the names."

"Has Amelia been talking about us?" Noelle prompts, sipping on her champagne.

"Just about how important you all are to her."

Noelle smiles, Charlotte casts me a curious glance, and Penelope purses her lips. "That's right, Ethan. So, if you do our friend dirty here, you'll have to answer to us. Just so you know, we're aware of how out of line you have been as well, so don't think you're not on our radar."

"I understand your reservations completely. Amelia and I didn't get off on the best foot, but now, honestly? I just want to do dirty things to Amelia, so if it's okay with you, I'd like to take her away for the rest of the evening."

My mouth falls open, as does Noelle and Charlotte's, but Penelope just smiles. "You'd better live up to the promises you just laid down because we will undoubtedly be discussing your prowess during brunch on Sunday."

"Penelope!" I admonish. "Don't listen to her, Ethan. Let's just go."

"I won't let you down," he says to Penelope with a wink and then reaches for my hand. "You guys have a good rest of your night."

"You too. Just remember to use protection." Penelope waves her fingers at us as Ethan pulls me away from my friends.

"See you Sunday!" I call out to them as he whisks me away. But then I almost fall as I attempt to follow his lead. "Ethan, I can't walk that fast in these heels."

"Sorry," he mutters, slowing down his gait as he holds the door open for me, leading me out into the crisp summer night with his hand on the small of my back now.

"You really didn't have to come get me." He holds open the passenger door to his car as I get situated inside, not bothering to answer me until he also climbs in and pulls out of the parking lot.

"I know I didn't, but like I said, all I kept thinking about was something happening to you if I hadn't. My alter ego did not approve."

"Alter ego?"

"Grumpy," he says, winking in my direction quickly before putting his eyes back on the road. "My grumpy side was not having it."

"Oh." I chuckle. "I see."

"By the way, Oliver loved the picture we took earlier this week. I forgot to tell you."

This information has me twisting to face him in my seat. "Really?"

"Oh yeah. He's been bugging me for another, but I told him the gnomes didn't move again."

"Remind me on Monday, and we'll take another."

He laughs. "I told you, we shouldn't have even started this. He won't let it go."

"He's a kid, Ethan. There's only a short amount of time where he will believe in magic, where thinking gnomes move at night to guard treasure will bring him excitement. Kids are so pure, and the world is so fascinating to them. Honestly, it brings me joy being able to do this for him, so don't worry about it."

He reaches over and grasps my hand, kissing the top of it. "You're incredible. And you look fucking amazing tonight, by the way."

I glance down at the silver dress I wore, the sequins glinting from the lights outside the window, reflecting off it as we cruise down the road. "Thank you."

"I wasn't lying to Penelope either. All I want is to do dirty things to you. I can't stop thinking about it. Not seeing you this week after Tuesday was torture."

His words resonate in my body, sending a thrill down my spine just like they did when I was standing in front of my friends and Damien. And then it hits me. "Oh fuck."

"What?"

"Damien was there. You said that in front of him, and he's friends with my brother. If he says something to Nick…"

"Jesus, I'm sorry." He runs a hand through his hair. "I wasn't thinking."

"Let me text Charlotte, tell her to talk to him."

"Good thinking."

I shoot off a text as quickly as I can, but Charlotte doesn't read it right away. I'm sure she's busy and will get it later. "Do you have Damien's number just in case he sees Nick before I see Charlotte on Sunday?"

"No. Like I said, I only met him the one time."

"Shit."

Ethan reaches over and grabs my hand, squeezing it in comfort. "Don't worry. Even if for some reason he sees your brother and says something, I'll handle Nick."

Shaking my head, I stare out the passenger window. "What are we thinking, Ethan? Being casual fuck buddies? I mean, are we crazy? It's not like we want the same things."

"The only thing I want right now is you, Amelia. All the other shit doesn't matter, in my opinion."

I sigh, knowing there's not much more I can do at this moment except doubt and debate whether continuing with this charade is really worth it. I already feel like I'm in too deep. This last week—well, at least the two days when we saw each other—gave me a glimpse at the man beside me that I've been dying to discover more about. And even though he has multiple sides that he's shown me so far, this side—the protective man that chose to drive out of his way to pick me up so I was safe—is my favorite one, with seeing him in the role of a single father at a close second.

"So, where is home?" Ethan asks before I rattle off my address and then verbally give him directions as we drive through the streets of Los Angeles, my nerves and uncertainty increasing with each passing second as we close in on my house. Luckily for me, Charlotte texts me back and eases my anxiety, assuring me she'll talk to Damien tonight.

When Ethan pulls into my driveway, he shuts off his car and turns to me. "Can I walk you to your door?"

"Sure."

My limbs shake from the chill in the air and the nervousness I feel. I want to invite Ethan inside, but part of me doesn't think that's a good idea either. My mind is all over the place, but before I can get a word out, Ethan crowds me against the door when I spin to face him.

"Ethan…"

He places his index finger over my lips, cutting me off. "Just hear me out. This thing between us is fuzzy, right?" I nod my head, grateful that I'm not the only one that feels this way. "But all I know for certain is that I crave you—your lips, your conversation, your laugh, and your wit. I think about you constantly, and I hate it."

"Why?"

"Because it's been a long time since I've given myself permission to think about a woman. Oliver has been my priority for years, but with you? I feel like I'm powerless over how entranced I am by you."

I trail my fingers down the side of his face, dancing the tips across the scruff on his jaw. "Entranced is a pretty powerful word."

"I'm just being honest with you. I thought maybe you would appreciate that." He leans forward and presses his lips to mine, and like a match being struck, my entire body ignites. I open my mouth to him, and Ethan wastes no time licking my tongue with his own. Our moans and collective sighs of pleasure echo around us on my porch as we make out like a couple of teenagers—hands groping, pelvises rubbing, lips and tongues touching as much as they can.

And that's when it hits me—I have to stop second-guessing myself and live in the moment. I want to know what it's like to be with this man. I want to let this pull I feel toward him take me under.

Does that mean I might drown? Yes. But it also means I might find something I've been searching for.

"Do you want to come in?" I whisper breathlessly against his lips before he nips at mine again.

"We don't have to, Amelia. I mean, fuck, I want to. But that's not why I picked you up."

Our lips meet once more. "I know, but I want you to come inside. I need you," I say, reaching down to cup his erection through his jeans, the steel rod achingly hard. My vagina clenches as I feel him, and a low growl leaves his throat as my hand moves up and down his length.

"Are you sure?"

"Yes."

He takes a step back, nods in agreement, and then I spin around to unlock my front door, flicking on the light switch on the wall as we step inside.

"Welcome to my home."

Ethan walks ahead of me, peering around my space. The living room sits off to our left, and the kitchen is behind that, visible thanks to the open concept floor plan. The staircase is to our right, leading up to the top floor where my room and two others are, one of which I use as a home office. Everything is decorated in soft browns, white, and touches of green. My home is my sanctuary, and I love it.

"This house is so…you."

"I'll take that as a compliment."

He twists to face me again, a soft smile on his lips. "You should. It feels homey in here, like every detail was chosen for a reason."

"It was."

"I get the feeling you don't do anything without a reason, do you?"

I swallow. "Not usually. I consider myself a fairly cautious and decisive person. I like rules and order, but…"

"But what?"

I take a deep breath before I let out my admission. "All that seems to go out of the window where you're concerned."

He swallows and stalks toward me, gripping the back of my neck and pulling me close to his mouth, where I feel the breath of his words hit my lips. "I know exactly how you feel."

And then his lips are on mine, and our bodies become intertwined, wrapped in each other as we stagger back and hit the nearest wall.

"Fuck, you're so sexy, Amelia."

"Ethan…"

He drags his tongue up the column of my throat. "And I fucking love hearing my name come from your lips."

"Ethan," I mewl again, desperate to feel him everywhere. I reach down and find the hem of his shirt, lifting it up his torso as he helps me remove it, tossing it to the side as he stares back down at me.

But my eyes are locked onto his chest, broad and sculpted, leading down to hard abs and a happy trail that disappears under the waist of his jeans. Ethan's arms are just as toned as his dress shirts hinted at, sculpted and lean.

His entire body is lean but defined—masculine and beautiful.

"You'd better stop staring at me like that, Amelia."

"Or what? What are you going to do about it?"

"Fuck," he curses. "This mouth of yours…" He pulls me into him again, kissing me deeply as his hands search the back of my dress for a zipper. But he ends up empty-handed and frustrated, making me laugh. "How the fuck do you get this thing off?"

"It's a side zipper," I reply, stepping away from him to watch his eyes as I take the zipper down and then carefully lift the entire dress over my head, tossing it to the floor. And the look of appreciation in his eyes is worth the battle it's taken for us to get here.

"Fuck me. Do you always go braless?"

"Only when the outfit doesn't allow for it." I reach up and tug on my nipples, teasing the already hard peaks.

"Jesus, you're perfect." Ethan steps up to me again, dipping his head down far enough to take one of my nipples into his mouth, sucking and gently biting on it. And considering our height difference, he doesn't last long until he releases my nipple and lifts me up from behind my thighs, walking me back over to the wall and keeping me in place with his hips as he lines up my breasts to his mouth and continues to lick and suck at them relentlessly, alternating between both.

"Oh God, Ethan…" I dig my hands into his hair, pulling on the short strands as he works over my breasts, building me up into a frenzy of need. My pussy is dripping for him, but he doesn't seem to want to let up anytime soon.

"You have amazing tits. I could do this all night."

"Seems like it. But there are far better things for us to do first, don't you think?"

His head pops up, and he locks eyes with me. "Where's your bed?"

"Upstairs."

Ethan carries me up the staircase as we kiss, and I rub my barely covered pussy against the button on his jeans, loving the friction but only wanting him more. As we turn the corner and enter my room, he stops dead in his tracks as his eyes veer off to the left. "Holy shit."

"What?"

"You weren't kidding about the pole dancing, were you?"

I turn my head over my shoulder to stare at the pole I had installed in my room so I could practice where the space allowed, right between my bed and the bathroom. "No, I was telling the truth."

"If I didn't need to be inside you so badly, I'd make you dance for me right now."

"Maybe next time," I tease, nibbling on his earlobe as he carries me over to the bed and tosses me on it, hovering over me as I stare up at him.

"I'm holding you to that." And then his lips are back on mine as his hand drifts between my legs, and he rubs his knuckles over the wet silk of my thong. "Fuck, you're soaked."

"I always am around you."

"You make me so fucking hard all the time, Amelia. You have no idea how out of control you make me feel." Ethan stands up and starts to unbutton his jeans, staring at me as he does it. It's erotic, intense, and I reach up to play with my nipples again as I spread my legs and watch him push his jeans and underwear down in one swift movement. He kicks off his socks, shoes, and pants and then stands before me, gloriously naked, stroking his length with need in his eyes.

The man is exquisite—intense, strong, and a little broken—but he's here with me, and that's all I'm choosing to focus on right now.

As he leans over me again, I feel his thumbs hook into the sides of my thong, pulling the fabric down and baring all of me to him. And it's not like he hasn't been between my legs before, but this is different. I'm completely exposed, and in some ways, I feel more nervous about this.

"You're shaking."

"I'm a little cold…and nervous."

He covers me with his body. "Is that better?"

"A little." He smiles down at me, and I reciprocate, but then our lips touch again, and sheer heat builds between us. I can feel his length against my thigh as Ethan's hands move all over my body, skimming over my curves, gripping my ass, pulling me into him as we begin to grind on one another.

"Why are you nervous? Are you second-guessing this?"

I shake my head, keeping my eyes on his. "No. It's just been a while. And it's you…"

"I get it." He nuzzles my cheek with his nose, forcing me to close my eyes and take a deep breath to relax. I want him, I want this, and I know he does too. "But I promise to make you feel good. Remember, I have to live up to my words for Penelope. I've got to give you something to tell the girls on Sunday."

Laughing, I find his mouth and kiss him with just a small bit of tongue, eager to feel him inside me. "Yes, you do. So, do you have a condom?" I whisper against his lips.

"I do. Hold on." He leaps from the bed, locates his pants, and pulls out his wallet to get a condom, ripping it open and covering himself as I wait for him. But he's back on me quickly, rubbing his cock between my legs, coating himself in my arousal. "You're so fucking wet."

"I know. Now fuck me, Ethan."

"Jesus. Say that again," he growls as he stares down at me.

I lift slightly from the bed and bite his lower lip, dragging it gently between my teeth before releasing it and smirking up at him. "Fuck me. Now."

He slams into me, making me scream, and begins to thrust with precision, rolling his hips as he slides in and out. Squeezing his shoulders, I shriek at the invasion and moan as he sets a punishing rhythm. "Is this what you wanted?"

My entire body breaks out in goosebumps as I claw at his shoulders and back, holding on for the ride. "Yes. Oh God, Ethan. Yes!"

"Fuck, Amelia." Our mouths connect again in a messy kiss as our bodies undulate together, and the mood shifts into carnal pleasure. My hips lift to meet all of his thrusts, one of his hands is buried deep in my curls, pulling my head back to grant him access to my neck as he licks and bites the skin there, and his other hand squeezes my hip for leverage as he slams into me over and over again.

The light through the window casts shadows all over my room, including shadows of our bodies moving together, and watching them dance against the wall is one of the most erotic sights I've ever seen.

Ethan turns to see where I'm looking and notices our shadows as well. "Fuck, that's hot. Look at us, Amelia."

"You feel so good, Ethan. Keep fucking me, please."

"I didn't plan on stopping any time soon." He lifts up onto his knees and spreads my thighs apart farther, pistoning his hips at the same delirious pace and staring down at where we're joined as he slides in and out of me.

"Ethan, touch me, please."

He wastes no time using his thumb to rub soft circles over my clit as my entire pussy begins to throb. I know the man knows his way around my body, but the fact that he can touch me in the perfect way to send me careening over a cliff in a matter of minutes is unparalleled.

"Don't stop."

"I won't, baby. You like that?"

"Yes."

"Are you gonna come all over my cock?"

His words do me in. "Oh, God. Yes, right there. Don't stop, please..."

"Fuck."

And then I'm gone, screaming and gasping as an orgasm tears through my body, leaving me fighting for air as the waves continue to roll through me. It's intense and powerful, and as soon as Ethan feels me start to relax, he pulls out of me, forcing me to prop myself up on my elbows to see where he went. "Ethan?"

But he doesn't respond because I feel his mouth on my pussy and his tongue diving deep into my core. "Oh fuck." My head falls back on the bed as he laps at my arousal and pins me to the blanket, drawing aftershocks from my body. I claw at the comforter, squeezing the fabric between my fingers before moving my hands to the top of his head. "Ethan, I can't..."

"God, you taste incredible," he mumbles against me, licking and sucking as I writhe and gasp for air.

"Please, Ethan."

He stands again and reaches for my hand, pulling me up to him as I rest on my knees on the bed. Holding my face in his hands, he kisses me, allowing me to taste myself before he backs up and demands, "On your knees, facing away from me."

I spin around, sticking my ass in the air for him and waiting with anticipation for his next move. I feel his hands travel over my ass and up my back, his fingers dancing along my skin before I feel his lips follow the trail he's painting with his hands. His mouth moves over my curves, kissing and licking my hips, my ribs, and my shoulder blades right over my tattoo before reaching my neck.

"You have an orchid tattoo..."

I glance over my shoulder at him, finding his face right near my ear. "I do..."

"Why didn't you tell me?" he asks, rubbing his cock between my legs but not entering me.

"It's not something I share with everyone, but I'd be willing to later after you make me come again."

He lets out a low growl. "You want more of my cock, Amelia?"

"God, yes," I moan.

"Tell me. Let me hear you say it."

"I want your cock, Ethan. Now." The feel of his head rubbing through my folds has me gasping for air before moaning out loud. "God, Ethan, stop teasing me."

"Now you know how it feels, how it's felt since the moment I saw you. You teased me and drew me in, Amelia. And now that I know what your pussy feels like wrapped around my cock, I don't know if you'll ever get rid of me."

His words drift off, and then he slowly fills me to the hilt, stretching me open and hitting me deep inside. And it's amazing; this position makes for such a tight fit and the perfect angle to hit my G-spot. "Jesus..."

"Fuck, you feel so good wrapped around me, Amelia. This pussy..." He smacks my ass, making me jump with surprise before the sting ebbs away and leaves behind a spark of desire. "You like that?"

"Yes."

Smack! He does it again, this time on the other cheek, as he slides in and out of me at a luxurious pace. He's not fast or furious this time—no, his thrusts are calculated, deep and hard, until I feel him start to swivel his hips and stretch me out with each circle.

"Oh fuck!" I bury my face in the blanket as his hips continue to swirl, and his cock reaches places inside of me that I haven't experienced before. "Ethan!"

"God, Amelia. I'm close."

"Me too. Touch me," I command as his hand moves between my legs, finding my clit again as he thrusts and circles, thrusts and circles, stretching me open and hitting me with sparks of pleasure that have me coming so hard I can barely breathe.

"That's it, baby. Take me with you." And then I hear his grunts and his hips still as he empties himself inside the condom, twitching inside of me and squeezing my ass until he exhales and slowly pulls out of me.

My body collapses on the bed, my mouth searches for lungfuls of oxygen, and then Ethan's arms wrap around me, pulling me into his chest.

"Fuck, Amelia." He presses open-mouthed kisses to the back of my neck. "I think you fucked the life out of me."

"Pretty sure you were doing the fucking."

Our breathing fills the room until we've both relaxed a bit. "That was incredible."

"It was." I turn on my side so I can face him. "Thanks again for picking me up tonight. I was not anticipating this happening at the end of my evening at all."

"The pleasure was all mine, I assure you." With a kiss to the tip of my nose, he stands from the bed, turning to find his pants on the floor and pulling them up slowly. "I should probably get going."

"Oh, yeah. Sure." I don't know why a wave of disappointment rolls through my heart as I watch him prepare to leave. It's not like I thought he would stay, but perhaps a part of me was hoping he would after sharing sex like that.

Remember, this is supposed to be a physical thing, Amelia.

But the things he says and does are very confusing for someone who's just in this for sex.

"I have to pick up Oliver early from my mom in the morning for his first soccer game," he says as he searches for his shirt.

"Your shirt is downstairs." Standing from the bed now, I walk over to my bathroom, where my robe is hanging on the back of the door, feeling Ethan's eyes on me as I walk by him. I need to shield myself from the disappointment I'm feeling, knowing he's about to leave. I need to protect myself before I let my heart fall even further than I want to admit I've already fallen.

But before I can reach my robe, Ethan's pulling me into his chest. "Amelia," he groans. "Fuck, how can I have just had you and already want you again?"

My body melts into his at his words as I feel his hand travel over my hip and down between my legs, circling my clit. "Ethan, you can't be serious," I giggle, instantly going from disappointed to optimistic.

"I am. I haven't even left yet, and I want you again."

"We can meet up this week."

"That's too far away."

He walks me forward until we're standing in front of my bathroom mirror, the sight before me astonishing.

Ethan towers over me from behind, his eyes darker than normal in the lack of light in the room. But he has one hand firmly planted on my left breast and the other moving slowly between my legs.

"I don't think I'll ever get enough of you."

I reach behind me to weave my hands in his hair. "You're pretty addicting yourself, you know."

"Fuck, you're still soaked," he mumbles in my ear, removing his hand from my breast to turn my chin toward him so he can kiss me.

My body hums with the promise of another orgasm as he continues to work me over. "Don't stop. Since you started this, you'd better finish it."

"Oh, I planned on it."

And then Ethan makes me come on his fingers, his mouth, and his cock again that night before he finally leaves, putting me into a deep sleep as a woman who's definitely in trouble when it comes to this man. Being in his arms makes me feel cherished, content, and safe, and the man definitely knows his way around my body.

But Ethan isn't safe. No, everything about Ethan screams mischief and heartbreak—but also indescribable pleasure. I can already see the writing on the wall, the way this will most likely all play out.

The optimist inside me is wondering, though, could there be more between us, especially after tonight? His words and actions tell me there is more going on between us under the surface, even if we're both trying to convince ourselves otherwise.

But the pessimist? She sees a man with baggage, a chip on his shoulder, and someone who doesn't know how to control his emotions. The way he's behaved from the beginning reminds me of a little boy experiencing his first crush but is so overcome with feelings that he doesn't know how to handle them.

And in that scenario, it's usually the girl who loses that fight, the one that ends up with the bruises and scars that never quite fade.

And yet, I couldn't walk away from him if I tried. Especially not now.

"Oh my God, is that a hickey?" Noelle shrieks as I take my seat at brunch Sunday morning.

"What?" I look down and pull up the neckline of my tank top, cursing myself for not changing my shirt when I knew it would ride down and expose the purple flesh mark Ethan left on the top of my left breast. "Shit."

"I take that as a yes, then?"

Slinking back in my chair, I take the mimosa that Charlotte hands to me and then drain half the glass. "Ethan fucked me three times Friday night."

Penelope smirks across the table. "And did he deliver on his promises?"

"Tenfold," I admit to cheers from my girls.

"Glad the man can back up his words then."

"It was incredible—so raw, passionate, and hot. God, the man is so fucking hot. He makes me forget to think."

"Those are the ones that are trouble." Noelle smiles knowingly around her glass.

"I know. He didn't stay the night though. He had to pick up his son from his mom's early on Saturday morning."

"That's understandable. Did you want him to stay the night?"

"Yes, but I also thought it would be against the rules of our arrangement."

Charlotte leans forward in her seat. "Like I said, I spoke to Damien and told him not to say anything to Nick."

"Thank you."

"But my follow-up question is, did you two ever have rules to begin with?"

"Just that we weren't telling anyone about us, but obviously that's out of the bag now. You girls know, and now Damien does too."

"That's not very many people, and people that would understandably be aware anyway."

"I know, but I want more with him. He agreed to my ultimatum of getting to know each other, but I don't know how he interpreted that exactly."

Noelle nods. "I get what you're saying. You guys are in that very fragile state after sex where you're definitely into one another, but it's too early to talk about what this means."

"Exactly."

"What would Dr. St. Clair say?" Penelope asks teasingly.

And I answer her without much contemplation. "She would tell her client to ask him and explain her feelings, to be direct, so she isn't wasting her time. But Amelia, the woman who still is figuring out her love life and how to navigate the fragile circumstances of this arrangement, isn't sure that's the best idea just yet."

"Why not?" Charlotte prods.

"Because he has a kid, which makes the stakes for him much more serious." The girls nod. "But all I know right now is that I've never had a man insist on picking me up from somewhere at night so I would get home safe, let alone a man that I feel this intensely about. When I'm with him, he consumes me."

"We all saw the way he looked at you the other night, the way he pulled you away from us to get you alone. I don't think you're crazy for feeling that way." Noelle says.

"His words say one thing, but his actions say something else entirely, you know? Like eating lunch together. Even though it was my idea for us to get to know each other more, he's the one that instigated it and surprised me with lunch the second time. And then,

Friday, he texted me outside of work. We never talked about meeting up outside of our offices.”

“I think you should definitely feel him out then and ask him how he feels when you see an opening. Otherwise, hang tight and enjoy the ride.” Penelope bounces her eyebrows.

“Oh, there’s plenty to enjoy, believe me.” I chuckle and feel myself blush as I take a drink of my mimosa.

Noelle clears her throat. “So, not to change the subject completely, but I have some news.” We all give her our attention as she takes a deep breath and speaks. “I’ve decided to look into getting a sperm donor so I can have a child.”

Penelope nearly chokes, and Charlotte and I sit there silently.

“Someone please say something,” Noelle requests, but the other two girls are at a loss for words, so I break the silence.

“Is this coming from our conversation the other night?” I ask.

Penelope finally speaks up. “You talked about sperm donors the other night? Where the hell was I?

“That’s not important, but yes, it did have to do with our conversation, Amelia,” Noelle replies. “I’m thirty and no closer to finding a man to marry and have children with than I was five years ago, during my optimal child-bearing years as society describes them. I’m tired of waiting on the right person for my life to begin when I’m the person that gets to make that decision. And my decision is, I want children, sooner rather than later.”

“That’s a big decision to make, Noelle,” Charlotte says cautiously. “You know we’ll support you no matter what you decide, but please promise us that you’ll think about it.”

Noelle reaches over and lays her hand on Charlotte’s. “I promise. Like I said, I’m just going to look into it now, do some research, and get an idea of all it entails. Then I'll know whether to move forward from there."

"Just let me know when it's time to go shopping," Penelope interjects.

"Shopping for baby clothes?" Charlotte asks. "That's not something I thought you'd be into, but I'm glad to see that you'll take your role as a future aunt seriously."

Penelope shakes her head as she chews. "No. Not shopping for clothes, shopping for sperm. I want to be involved in picking Noelle's potential baby daddy. I feel like my level of expertise with men will definitely come in handy there."

"Oh, Jesus." Noelle laughs, Charlotte leans back in her chair, and I drain the rest of the mimosa from my glass.

Thank God for champagne and good friends.

Chapter 11

Amelia

Thomas Lyle and his wife Anne arrive at their appointment Monday morning right on time. My mood is bubbly and energetic as I get ready to take on my day, especially after my more than pleasurable weekend.

Ethan left my house around three in the morning Saturday and then texted me last night, thanking me for our time together. His communication was unexpected, but ultimately it gave me another bout of hope that this thing between us could become more. And especially after having sex, I know our chemistry is too strong to let this be *just* casual.

I have never felt this way about a man, the type of connection that is overwhelming in multiple facets. And even though my feelings for him were not of the favorable kind in the beginning, the more I get to know him, the more I appreciate every side of him that he shows me. He's commanding and private but passionate and intense. But he's also hard to read, so I'm hoping with time, I'll be able to get a better feeling of where his mind is because I'm pretty sure I already know what his body is telling me.

You could just ask him, Amelia. That's what you would advise your clients to do.

I know, but I also don't want to scare him. What if I say something that has him running?

Then he doesn't deserve you.

I know you're right, subconscious, but since when does a woman actually listen to that voice in her head when it comes to a guy? No, she's got to second-guess every interaction and conversation until she's blue in the face.

"Good morning, you two." I hold the door open for my brand-new clients, pushing thoughts of Ethan to the recesses of my mind so that I can focus on my job until lunch.

"Good morning," Anne greets me with a soft shake of her hand.

"This office looks like the inside of a house," Mr. Lyle admonishes as he scopes out the room.

I shut the door behind him and walk further inside toward my desk. "I wanted it to feel welcoming since many people can have reservations about therapy."

He scoffs. "It's a bunch of nonsense, is what it is. Anne and I are fine, but she insisted this is something we need."

I'm beginning to think he's the one that needs it, but I don't say that out loud.

Anne looks over at me with an apologetic smile. At least she's aware of who she's married to.

"Attending therapy doesn't have to mean something is wrong. Sometimes it can just be preventive, like exercise. A lot of people exercise every day so their bodies remain strong and to reap the long-term health benefits instead of waiting until their doctor tells them they have to lose weight or move more."

All I get is a huff in return as his eyes land on me and begin to drift over my body. But when they land on my left hand, his eyebrows pop up. "Are you not married?"

"Uh, no. I'm not." I lift my left hand, waving my fingers in the air.

"Jesus, Anne. You really booked us an appointment with a marriage counselor that's not even married?" He turns to me, his face much angrier than before. "How the hell are you even supposed to offer any advice when you haven't been married yourself?" The venom in his voice is enough to make me retreat as I question his concern. "How old are you?"

I mean, the man has a point, but it's not something I've ever had a client blatantly ask before.

I don't entertain answering his questions before I speak. "With all due respect, I don't need to be married in order to counsel couples, and my age has nothing to do with my level of experience either. Relationships, both romantic and platonic, have many similarities, and yet, every couple is unique as well. So, my expertise lies in helping couples communicate, and you don't have to be married in order to do that. Now, if you'd like to begin, I can show you back to the room where I conduct my sessions. But if you feel uncomfortable with my personal relationship status, the door is right behind you."

"Wow. You have a lot of nerve telling me I can leave."

"No, I don't. This is my business, and I don't have to tolerate your lack of decorum."

"Thomas, please stop," Anne pleads, reaching for her husband's arm as he bats it away.

"No. I'm not going to stay here and listen to this woman tell me how to be a husband when she doesn't even have one of her own. We're leaving." He spins on his heel and heads for the door, pausing as he looks back to see if Anne will follow him. "Get over here, Anne."

She shoots me a sympathetic and almost pleading look and then marches over to him, walking through the door as he follows her. "This was a waste of time," he says as the door slams behind him, leaving me standing in place, wondering what on earth just happened.

I shake off the shock and then take a seat at my desk, staring off into space as I go over the last five minutes. I've never had a client react like that, but more importantly, I've never felt the need to go after one either. The look on Anne's face was so indicative of the type of marriage she's in—fearful, controlling, and demeaning. No wonder she was seeking counseling.

I make a note to call her later and follow-up with her, perhaps ask her to come in alone. But until then, there's nothing I can do but wait for my next client to arrive and hope the day doesn't progressively get worse.

"Hey, beautiful."

My head pops up from the paperwork I'm filling out on my desk as Ethan walks through the door. He seems just as happy as I did earlier before seeing his smile fall as he reads my face. "What's wrong?"

"Nothing." I close the folder on my desk and drop my pen down.

"Bullshit. It's like the light is gone from your eyes." I should be swooning at a statement like that from his lips, but all it does is remind me how much I let Mr. Lyle's words get to me this morning.

"I just had a rough morning."

"What happened?" He walks into the room and takes a seat in one of the chairs on the other side of my desk.

I blow out a harsh breath. "I had a new couple come in this morning, and the husband was less than polite."

Ethan sits up taller in his seat. "He didn't touch you, did he?" *Again, with the protectiveness. Ugh, he's something else.*

"No. Just disrespectful. Told me I had no business counseling married couples since I'm not married myself."

"Wow." Ethan runs his hand through his hair. "What a fucking prick. I'm sorry, Amelia." I shrug but look away from him, fighting back my tears. "You don't believe him, do you?"

"I mean, he has a point."

"Bullshit."

"Look, you don't have to do this, Ethan. You don't have to pretend to care about my job, especially since I know how you feel about it."

He stands from his chair and circles my desk, crouching down in front of me and grasping my hands in his. "How I feel about marriage has nothing to do with the fact that I can tell this man struck a chord with you, Amelia. And I hate to see you doubting yourself." He tips my chin up with his fingers, forcing me to look him in the eyes. "And trust me, even if someone were married, that doesn't mean they know anything about what it takes to make a marriage work. But you have helped hundreds of people, your success speaks volumes, and your credentials certainly outweigh his microscopic penis-sized opinion, okay?"

Moisture builds in my eyes as I stare at him. I know he doesn't believe that every relationship can be saved, but he's putting aside his own opinions to try and make me feel better. And I believe the words he's saying—he sees how passionate I am about my job, which just makes me fall even harder for him.

How can he not want more with me? And then the question lingering on my mind comes out before I can stop it.

"Ethan...what are we doing? You coming over here and saying something like that to me is far more involved than us just being fuck buddies."

His face contorts with uncertainty as he releases my chin and stands, turning his back to me. And my stomach drops instantly, regret filling me from saying anything. Apparently, it wasn't the right time, and now I can't take it back.

"Amelia..."

"Look, forget I asked," I say as I wave my hand nonchalantly and stand as well, pretending to fix things on my desk while I feel him watch me. "I'm just thrown off today. I get it. You're just being nice."

He reaches forward and grabs my wrist to stop me from moving, and then I slowly lift my gaze to meet his. I can tell he's struggling, that he has more to say, but all he does is stare at me, his dark-green eyes full of so many conflicting emotions.

I can hear my heart beating in my ears, my toes are going numb from the adrenaline racing through me, and even though I'm dying to hear what he might say next, part of me wishes we could just stay in this moment for a little while longer. Because the way he's looking at me right now has me questioning how I could ever feel the same way if another man looked at me like he is—like I am his and his alone.

"I...I don't...I can't..."

And then my heart shatters a bit. "It's fine."

"No, it's not fine, Amelia. Fuck. It's…" He sighs. "It's been a long time since I've felt like this about someone." He lets go of my wrist and then begins to pace.

"Felt like what?"

And then he's spinning to face me. "Like I want to be around you all the time. Like I want to know everything about you. Like you're the best part of my day besides my son."

"Oh."

"I told myself I wouldn't do this again, that I wouldn't allow myself to become involved with someone after Monica…"

"Who's Monica?"

"My ex-wife."

And like a key sliding into a lock, it all clicks into place.

"You're divorced?"

He nods once. "Yes."

I stand there, stunned, until I finally find a few words. "Now it all makes sense. How you were toward me in the beginning, why you have this hatred for what I do…but you said she's not involved in Oliver's life?"

"She's not. She didn't want to be a mom, Amelia. She left her son and me and started a new life without us, tossed us out like we were a meal she didn't feel like finishing. And believe me, I regret taking out my issues on you."

Oh God, no wonder the man is so condescending about my line of work and so guarded. "Ethan, I'm so sorry."

"No, don't be sorry for me." He shakes his head while clenching his jaw. "It was better this way, for Oliver and me. But fuck, Amelia, this is why I didn't want anything more with you."

"So, what are you saying?"

He stands still, time ticking by as he finds his words. "I'm saying I don't know what I want anymore, but all I know is I want you."

It's not clear-cut and defined, but his words offer me a glimmer of hope. Taking a few steps toward him slowly, I watch for his reaction until we're only inches apart. "I want you too…and Oliver." His eyes close. "We can go slow, Ethan. Figure things out as we go, but I don't want to avoid the possibility of what this could be because you're scared. The truth is, I'm scared too."

When his eyes pop open, there's almost a clarity to them. "Why are you scared?"

Reaching up, I cup the side of his face. "Because I feel like you have the potential to break me."

A huff of air leaves his lips as he pulls me into his chest. "I'm already broken, Amelia, and the last thing I want is to be responsible for making you feel like that."

Relief and optimism rush through me. "You are not broken, Ethan, but we owe it to ourselves to see where this goes."

Ethan doesn't say anything else before he kisses me, pulling me closer to his body and burying his hand deep into my hair at the base of my neck. I love when he does that; controlling me as our lips move over one another and our mouths do the talking.

"This was not the conversation I anticipated having with you when I walked in here just now," he says through a chuckle when we part.

"No? What did you want to talk about?"

"I wanted to make a list with you of all of the places in this office where I want to fuck you and then start checking it off one by one."

Tossing my head back in laughter, he takes advantage of my

exposed neck, bringing me back to his mercy very quickly as his lips move over my delicate skin. "Ethan…"

"Come on. Haven't you ever wanted to have sex on your couch? I feel like that's almost a required therapist fantasy."

"I mean…maybe."

"Fuck. We're doing it then." He pulls me by the hand to the back room in my office, shutting the door behind us.

"The front door isn't locked, Ethan."

"Yes it is. I locked it when I walked in."

"This was your plan all along, wasn't it?" I tease him as I push him back over to my couch, his hard body landing with a thump on the leather.

"All I've been thinking about since Friday night was having you again."

I straddle his lap, pulling up the sides of my dress as I settle over his hard length straining against his slacks. "I've been thinking about that too."

"And seeing this smile." He traces over my lips with one finger. "Every time you smile, and I'm the one responsible for it, it makes me feel ten feet tall."

Running my hands through his hair, I lean down and press my lips to his softly. "You make me happy, Ethan. A little crazy and frustrated too, but happy nonetheless. And alive."

He chuckles. "I'm gonna make mistakes, Amelia. I haven't done the relationship thing in a long time, and even then, my marriage was a joke. It wasn't like how I feel about you."

I slowly rub myself over him as he lets out a groan. "And how are you feeling?"

"Like if I could spend all day with my dick buried inside you, I'd be the happiest man on earth."

"Is that it?"

He laughs as he grips my waist. "No. You make me feel hopeful, and awake—like I was sleepwalking, just going through the motions, accepting the idea of being alone for the rest of my life. But you've woken me up from my slumber, pulled me from the unmarked path I was on, and drew me to you. And I look forward to every time we see each other more than I ever imagined I could."

Smiling and reeling from his words, I reach down and begin to unbutton his slacks. "I'm glad I can make you feel that way, Ethan. We don't have all day, but we do have about twenty minutes together now. Care to use them wisely?"

"Fuck yes."

As my lips hover over his while I remove his cock from his pants, I ask, "Do you have a condom?"

"Uh-huh." Ethan and I maneuver ourselves so he can reach his wallet in the back of his pants. After he covers himself and slides his pants to the floor, he reaches between my legs and moves my thong to the side before lining himself up to me. "Ride me, Amelia."

Without wasting another second, I slide down his length slowly, memorizing how it feels as he fills me completely. We moan simultaneously as I adjust to him and then find a rhythm. I flick my hips, lift up and down, and use every inch of his cock for my pleasure.

"God, I can't get enough of you," he mutters, pulling me down to him by the back of my head again so our lips meet and we can kiss as our bodies move. He thrusts up from under me, holding me to his chest and squeezing my ass with his other hand.

"So good..."

"Fuck yeah, we are."

Goosebumps spread over my skin as the promise of my orgasm

begins to build, and I can feel Ethan grow harder inside of me as I begin to race to get there.

"Are you getting close, baby?"

"Yes," I whisper in his ear and then lean back so I can stare into his eyes. And as we hold each other's gazes, my orgasm detonates.

Moaning out in ecstasy, Ethan and I find our release together, clutching to one another as the pleasure rolls through us. My body snaps like a rubber band, and my lungs fight for oxygen as I slowly come down from the high, feeling every tremor down to the tips of my toes.

Slinking against his chest, we sit there for a minute with nothing but the sounds of our ragged breaths filling the room.

"Are you okay?" he asks, running his fingers over my back.

"Yes. You?"

"Never better."

When I sit up and look at him again, his smile holds me captive. "Thank you…for earlier."

"You're welcome. And thank you—for just now."

The corner of my mouth lifts. "The pleasure was all mine."

We clean ourselves up, and then Ethan gives me one hell of a kiss before he leaves. "I'll call you later."

"Okay."

"Have a good day, babe."

And little does he know, he just turned my horrible day into one of the best I've had in a long time—with the possibility of something more with him.

Chapter 12

Ethan

"Go, Oliver!" I clap my hands while cheering on my kid. It's his second soccer game since the season started, and I never thought I'd feel so much pride watching my son chase and kick a ball around. But damn, is this one of the best things ever.

The entire sideline screams when Oliver scores a goal, and the teams return to their sides of the field for a kickoff.

"Nice job, buddy!"

"Can we get ice cream after this now?" he yells across the field to me, entirely serious.

I laugh as well as some of the other parents around me. "Absolutely, bud!"

Before the game today, I told Oliver we would get ice cream from the gelato shop by my office whether his team won or lost as long as he tried his best. Well, after scoring a goal, I think I might have to let him have two scoops.

"That kid is going to break your bank account if you hold up that promise each week," one of the other parents jokes with me.

"Apparently so."

But before I can say another word, a flash of blond hair catches my eye across the park. Wild curls, the color of sunshine, bounce as the woman who has turned my life upside down in the last two weeks walks briskly around the perimeter of the sports complex, getting in her morning exercise.

Amelia and I have been seeing each other as more than friends with benefits for two weeks now. After that day in her office, I had no choice but to jump in with her. Even though I've had many talks with myself about remaining calm and taking things slow, my heart can't deny how enamored I am with her.

We've eaten lunch with each other as long as work allows, talking about anything and everything. I've shared stories with her about Oliver, she's told me more about her childhood and how she was a perfectionist in school, and we spent entirely too much time one day taking a picture of her gnomes guarding treasure so that I could show Oliver after school that day.

She listened intently when I told her about my fantasy football league, how I planned on fixing my mother's porch as soon as the summer heat died down, and how Oliver read an entire book to me the other night before bed, and I cried afterward.

And yesterday, on our lunch break, I bent her over the arm of her couch and spanked her ass so hard while I pounded into her that I left a handprint. The sight of the red mark on her skin shouldn't have turned me on even more, but it did. I made sure she was okay afterward, of course. But she and I both liked it a little too much, and just thinking about it now is making me hard.

I reach down to slyly adjust myself as I focus back on the game.

But my eyes do double the work, alternating between watching Oliver and watching Amelia. Wanting to catch her attention, I decide to send her a text.

Me: *What do you think you're doing wearing shorts that tight and short in public? That ass is reserved just for me, Dr. St. Clair.*

I watch her to see if she is aware of my message. And almost instantly, she's pulling her phone from her pocket and reading the screen, freezing in her steps as she looks around. I wave in her direction, and when she sees me, our smiles build at the same time.

She shoves her phone into her pocket, pulls out her earbuds, and makes her way toward me as Oliver's game continues.

"Hey, you," she says when she arrives next to me, playfully nudging me with her shoulder as she stands by my side and watches the game with me. I imagined she would kiss me with the look that was on her face, but I guess she's trying to be discreet.

"Good morning. You didn't answer my question."

With a peek at me over her shoulder, she shrugs. "These are my workout shorts, Ethan. I have smaller ones I wear to my pole dancing class that I could wear instead if that makes you happier."

Wrapping my arm around her shoulders, I draw her into my side, pressing a kiss to her temple. And with my voice low, I let her know how her sass is making me feel. "Is there still a handprint on your ass from yesterday?"

She chuckles. "No."

"Shame. Guess I'll have to spank you a bit harder next time for that sass you're giving me right now."

Her head slowly turns in my direction. "Maybe you're the one that needs to be punished."

Nuzzling my nose into her hair, I breathe her in. "The only thing that feels like a punishment right now is not being alone with you."

"Aw, I missed you too."

I smile down at her. "What are you doing here?"

"I walk around the park sometimes on Saturday mornings for a little exercise. As soon as I saw all of the cars, I figured you'd be here. I didn't want to interrupt you though. I mean, I know this is your time with Oliver, so…"

"Hi, Amelia." My mother comes back from the snack bar with two breakfast burritos, interrupting us.

"Oh, hi." She wipes her hand on her shorts and then reaches out to shake my mother's. "It's nice to see you again…"

"Lisa," she finishes for her.

"Lisa."

"Ethan didn't tell me you were coming." My mother glances up at me with an arch of her brow as she hands me my breakfast burrito.

"Oh, this wasn't planned. I was just here walking around the complex getting some exercise in, and he actually saw me."

"I see. Well, I hope you'll stay and watch with us."

Amelia looks to me for guidance because this wasn't something we had planned.

After we agreed we were dating, I told Amelia I would be more comfortable waiting a while until she came around Oliver. And I know they've already met, but now that we're dating, the stakes are higher. It's not that I don't trust her with him or think they wouldn't get along. It's the exact opposite. I know he already loves her, wants to ask her a million questions, and would probably have her move in with us tomorrow. But until I'm more confident in how I'm feeling, I wanted to prevent him from growing too attached too quickly.

Him, or you, Ethan?

"I'd better go before Oliver sees me, Ethan." She begins to walk away, but I grab her hand before she gets too far.

"No, stay."

"Are you sure?"

The whistle blows before I can answer her, and Oliver comes running over to us. "Daddy! We won!"

"I know, buddy! You did so great!" I bend down and hug him, soaking up the dirt on his cheeks and the smelliness that makes him a little boy. But then he looks up and sees Amelia.

"Amelia! Did you see me play soccer?"

"I did! You did such a fantastic job, Oliver. You worked so well with your team."

"Daddy is gonna buy me ice cream 'cause I scored a goal. You wanna get ice cream with us?"

"I think that's a great idea," my mother interjects. And I know exactly what she's doing right now.

Amelia's eyes flick to mine, questioning me with her gaze.

"I mean, we're going to the gelato place by the office, and I know you love it there."

"I do." She smiles softly. "But I don't want to intrude on your time together."

"You're not," I interrupt her. "We're inviting you."

"Yes!" Oliver shouts. "You have to come with us! We can both get the lemon kind since that's our favorite!"

Amelia laughs and tucks a loose curl behind her ear. "Okay. I'm there."

My mother bends down to hug Oliver. "You three have a good time." And then she pats me on the shoulder. "It was lovely to see you again, Amelia. I hope we see more of each other soon."

"Nice to see you too."

"Let's go, Daddy!" Oliver tries to run toward the car, but I have to remind him that there are things to do at the end of the game with his coach before we can leave.

Once the kids have high fived each other and all the after-game snacks have been passed out, the three of us walk over to my car.

"I wanna walk with you, Amelia." Oliver grabs Amelia's hand with his free one, the other holding his Capri Sun.

"Oh, okay." She hesitantly wraps her hand around his and then peers back at me, asking me for permission with her eyes.

The sight of the two of them together squeezes my chest and cracks open the vault I keep tight under lock and key—the place where I stored images of Monica doing the same thing with him, something she chose to walk away from.

My heart lurches at the possibility of pain, but I can't keep them apart any longer—Oliver is the biggest part of my world, and Amelia is quickly becoming the second.

And in that moment, I know I'm taking a huge risk here—with my son and my heart. I just hope it's worth it.

"Lemon and strawberry today?"

Oliver nods his head since his mouth is full. "Daddy said I got two scoops since I scored a goal."

Amelia smiles around her spoon as she talks with my son. We're seated on the outdoor patio of the gelato shop, enjoying our treats in the shade. The September weather is still quite warm, but the gelato is definitely helping us cool off.

"That is very impressive, Oliver. Congratulations."

"Daddy and my coach say I'm a natural."

"Well, you must have gotten some of your talent from your dad then." She turns to me. "Did you play soccer?"

"Nope. Football guy, remember?" I point my thumb to my chest. "But he wanted to play soccer, so I'm learning about it as I go. We watched YouTube videos this summer to prepare and learn."

"That was smart. I grew up playing soccer though," she says, turning back to Oliver.

"You did?"

"Yup. I played defense and goalie."

"I don't like goalie. I played that in practice one night, and people scored on me. It made me feel bad."

"Yeah, that part was never fun. But it happens. That's how you win the game, though, by scoring goals."

"Yeah."

"I also swam in high school."

"Really?" I ask, taking note that this isn't something Amelia and I have discussed yet.

"Yeah, I only did it my junior year, but I was actually pretty good."

"I bet you looked good doing it too," I tease, bouncing my eyebrows at her.

"I love to swim!" Oliver exclaims, inserting himself back into the conversation.

"You do? Well, guess what? I have a pool at my house…"

"Really?"

"Yup. Maybe if it's okay with your dad, you two can come over and go swimming with me next weekend after your soccer game?" She turns to me, lifting a brow.

And my first inclination is to say it's too soon, but that's not how I really feel.

"Can we, Daddy? Please!" Oliver juts out his lip and everything, laying it on thick. And Amelia smirks when she sees his manipulation tactics.

"I think we could make that happen."

"Yes!" Oliver throws his fist in the air. "Do you have pool toys? And rafts? Or a slide?" His mouth starts moving one hundred miles an hour. "Oh! And do you have gnomes at your house too?"

Amelia's eyes go wide. "I do. And do you know what? I think all the gnomes have been talking because the ones at my house started moving the other day after the ones at my office did. Something must be happening, and they're all trying to protect their treasure."

Oliver's eyes bug out. "I bet it's gold. Gold is shiny and worth a lot of money!"

"I think you're right."

"Do you have a grumpy gnome at your house too? Like the one that looks like my dad?"

"I do. Every place needs a grumpy gnome because they are the best ones at protecting the treasure."

"Why?"

"Because when something they care about feels threatened, their protective instincts kick in, and they make sure to keep whatever they care about safe."

Oliver smiles. "Yeah, that makes sense. My daddy is grumpy, but he always protects me."

God, is there something in my eye? Seriously, can you see it? Help me get it out, please.

"Your dad is the best at protecting you." Amelia winks over at me and goes to reach for my hand but stops before we touch.

"I wanna do that for Harper," Oliver says before I can react to Amelia's hesitance to touch me.

I turn back to my son. "Who's Harper?"

Oliver sighs. "She's a girl in my class. She's really nice and pretty, and she has the coolest backpack."

Amelia and I choke back laughter. "The coolest backpack, huh?"

Oliver nods slowly. "It has all the girl superheroes on it."

I mean, I guess you can't deny the girl has sophisticated taste for a kindergartener, but I make a mental note to dive more into his little crush later. "Okay, well, here's the deal, Oliver. If you want to go swimming at Amelia's house next weekend, you have to be on your best behavior this week for Grandma, me, and your teacher. I don't want to hear about any talking back, refusing to eat your vegetables, none of that." I know my kid well enough to know that I'm going to use this little playdate to my advantage and get the best behavior possible out of him.

"Okay, Daddy."

"I really want you to come over, Oliver, so don't let me down, okay?" Amelia backs me up.

"I promise." He draws a cross over his heart.

"All right, now let's finish our ice cream so we can get home and you can take a shower. You stink, little man." I reach over and ruffle his hair.

"You're stinky, Daddy!"

Amelia giggles as she takes another bite of her ice cream, watching us tease each other. It feels so normal, the three of us together, laughing and talking.

And I'm surprised by how much I like it.

When we're finished with our ice cream, we head back to the cars, and I buckle Oliver inside, turning on the air conditioning and the soundtrack to *Encanto* to keep him occupied while I say goodbye to Amelia.

"See you for swimming next weekend, Amelia!" he shouts from behind his window.

She goes over to the door and opens it to give him a high five. "I'm so excited for it. Remember to be on your best behavior."

"I will."

She gently shuts the door and then turns to me. "I hope I wasn't overstepping with that invitation."

"I know I said we needed to take things slowly with him, but he really likes you, so I think a little time here and there can't hurt."

"I really like him too. And his dad." She places her hand on my chest, staring up at me from behind her glasses, her hair still pulled back in her ponytail high on her head. The sun is making her skin glow, and her lips look shiny from where she just licked them.

"His dad kind of likes you too." I press a quick peck to her lips and then rear back. If I do more than that, I'll maul her in front of my kid.

She takes a deep breath and then speaks. "So, I'll see you tomorrow, right?"

"I'll be there."

Last week Amelia asked me if I'd like to join her family for dinner this Sunday. Nick is bringing Elena to introduce her, so she figured this would be the perfect opportunity to introduce me too.

I'm not going to lie, I'm a little nervous about it. Monica's parents weren't involved much in our relationship since they lived hours away. I met them a handful of times before she got pregnant with Oliver, but we didn't see them often. However, based on what Amelia has told me and what I know of Nick, she's very close with her parents.

So the pressure is on.

Not to mention, I need to speak with Nick and let him know that

I'm dating his sister, and that she was my friend I was just seeing casually, the one we spoke of before.

I grab her by the waist and hold her in place. "You seem nervous about it."

She nods, staring down at the ground. "I am. It's been a long time since I've introduced someone to them."

"Then I'm glad I get to be the lucky guy this time."

That has her smiling. "Me too."

"And I'll make sure to speak with Nick first so he knows I'm serious about you."

Her eyes bug out. "You haven't talked to him yet?"

"No. Was I supposed to?"

"I just thought you would have by now."

"We don't talk all the time, babe. Guys aren't like girls and their friends where they text each other a hundred times a day. Plus, I've been busy." I nuzzle her neck. "There's this woman I'm seeing who's keeping me preoccupied."

She moans as I kiss that spot where her neck meets her collarbone, that spot I know makes her instantly wet. "You're lucky that you're hot, or I'd be more mad at you."

"Thank God for good looks." I lift my head and kiss the tip of her nose. "It will be fine. Trust me."

"Okay. If you say so. I'll text you the address tomorrow."

"See you then." With one more kiss on her lips, I watch her get into her car and drive off before I do the same, wondering when this woman started to become more to me than any other woman I've met.

~

"Ethan? What the hell are you doing here?"

As soon as the door to Amelia's parents' house opens, I'm face-to-face with Nick. Nothing like ripping the Band-Aid off to get this evening going. "I'm here for your sister."

"Amelia?" he asks before his eyes dip down to the flowers in my hands, his brow drawing together. And in a few seconds, I watch the lightbulb turn on. "Wait? Are you telling me you're the guy she's seeing?"

"I am." I blow out a harsh breath and then take a step back. "Look, can we talk for a minute?"

"Yeah, I think we need to." Nick shuts the door behind him as we stand across from each other on the porch. "Explain, please, because the last time we had beers, you told me you were seeing a woman casually, and you had found someone to release your tension," he says, using finger quotes.

"You used those words, not me. But to clarify, your sister and I have been seeing each other for a while now."

He arches a brow at me. "What do you mean by seeing each other?"

"I'm not going to go into details with you, man. But we're dating, seeing where this goes, and I'm sorry I didn't talk to you about it first, but I wasn't sure if I wanted it to go anywhere, honestly."

Nick crosses his arms over his chest, uncertain about my intentions by the look on his face. "I'm confused. The last I heard from her, she wasn't happy about you being in her complex. Then, you tell me you're not looking for anything serious, hence why you found a friend to help you out, if you catch my drift." I nod. "But now, you two are dating?"

"I know. It's complicated and took us both by surprise, but I'm invested in her, man. She's incredible, and Oliver loves her. I know I should have said something sooner, but I'm telling you now, and I hope you'll be supportive of us. I'm serious about her…"

His face softens. "She's met Oliver?"

"Yeah. And you know I don't take that shit lightly."

"Fuck, you're right." He drops his arms and exhales in acceptance. "Okay, fine. Just promise me something, Ethan?"

"What's up?"

He points a finger at my chest, jostling the bouquet of flowers in my arm. "Don't fuck around with her, all right? My sister is one of the best people on the planet. She has a heart of pure fucking gold, and she deserves to be happy with someone who will put her first."

"I know that, Nick. I do. She's changed my world in just the few months I've known her. I'm serious about her, and I'm sorry I wasn't honest with you before."

He drops his hand. "I get it. You've been through some shit, but Amelia is my sister, and even though you and I are friends, I will always take her side."

"Got it."

"Unless she nags on you for something stupid. Then it's bros before…" He pauses, contorting his face in thought.

"Hos?" I finish for him.

"I…I don't feel comfortable calling my sister a ho, man."

Laughing, I slap him on the back as he reaches for the door. "Yeah, let's not go there."

"Agreed. Come on in and meet the fam."

I follow Nick inside, and the first person I see on the other side of the door is Amelia, standing there in a light-blue sundress looking radiant, but nervous.

"You two okay?" she asks, fiddling with her thumbs but faking confidence.

"Yeah, we're good, babe." I wrap my arm around her shoulders and kiss her cheek. "Hi."

"Hi," she says, staring up at me with reverence in her eyes. And that look—it makes my chest swell. She's looking at me like I've just made her day, and I definitely know that seeing her has made mine.

Nick clears his throat, drawing our attention to him. "Care to explain something to me, Sis?"

She purses her lips and then crosses her arms over her chest. "Ethan and I are dating, Nick, as I'm sure you've gathered by now. And I know you take your protective-older-brother role seriously, but I'm thirty-one years old and a grown woman. And I'm happy, so deal with it."

Nick's eyes bounce back and forth between Amelia and me. "You sure you're willing to put up with this attitude?" He juts his thumb in Amelia's direction just as she reaches out to punch his arm.

"Shut up, Nick. Come on, Ethan, let me introduce you to my parents." She grabs me by the hand and drags me away from her brother just as a woman comes around the corner, leaning into Nick. I'm assuming this is Elena.

"You're lucky Elena is here, or else you'd be sorry."

"Yeah, yeah," she mutters as I laugh behind her. But before we get into the kitchen, she pulls me down a hallway away from the open space we were just in. "Seriously, is everything okay with you two?"

"Yes, it's fine. He was surprised and threatened me a bit…you know, the typical big-brother warning." She laughs. "But when I told him that you and Oliver have spent time together, he understood that I'm serious about this."

She runs her hands up my chest and then around my neck, pulling me down to her lips. "Thank you. It feels really good hearing you say that."

"It's the truth."

"I'm serious about you too, you know. Like I said, it's been a long time since I've introduced anyone to my parents, which feels odd given my age. But dating nowadays seems so hit or miss. I figure it's not worth bringing anyone around until I know I see potential with them."

"Potential for what?"

She looks up at me under her dark lashes and through her glasses, biting her lip. "Everything."

"I like the sound of that." We meet each other in a soft kiss that neither of us allows to get out of hand.

And it's just as well because Nick breaks up our moment anyway. "Mom! Dad! Amelia is making out with her boyfriend in the hallway!"

Amelia spins around and swings for her brother. "Nick!"

He pulls away before she can connect with his arm, laughing at his outburst. "Damn. It's been a long time since I've been able to tattle on you about something like that."

The woman standing beside him just shakes her head. "Typical brother behavior. I have four of them, so I feel for you, Amelia." She steps forward and reaches for Amelia's hand. "I'm Elena, and it's so nice to meet you. I've heard a lot about you."

Amelia brushes her hair from her face and pushes her glasses up her nose as she shakes Elena's hand. "It's nice to meet you too. And this is Ethan, my boyfriend."

"Pleasure to meet you." I shake Elena's hand as my new title rolls around in my brain, not making me as uneasy as I thought it might.

"What is going on out here?" A woman who looks just like an older version of Amelia rounds the corner, wiping her hands on a dish towel.

"Mom. We were just about to head into the kitchen…" Amelia explains.

"Yeah, but Amelia was practically naked when I caught them, Mom. It was a good thing I interfered when I did."

Elena smacks Nick upside the head. "Jesus, leave your sister alone."

Amelia's mom points a finger at Elena. "I like you already."

Nick rubs his head. "I'm being ganged up on."

"You asked for it, buddy. Even I know not to mess with the women, especially when you're related to them." Stepping forward, I hand Amelia's mom the bouquet of flowers I brought. "It's lovely to meet you, Mrs. St. Clair. I'm Ethan."

She accepts the flowers and smiles up at me and then at her daughter. "I like you already too." Smelling the flowers, she closes her eyes and then pops them back open. "These are lovely. Thank you. Now everyone get in the kitchen, and Nick, I'm sure your father needs reminding to stop watching the game and check the grill."

"The game's on?" My ears perk up. I knew I'd be missing out on Sunday night football by being here, but I mean, if Amelia's dad is already watching it…

"Ethan's a bit of a football fan," Amelia explains as the four of us follow her mother into the kitchen, where the smells of something fresh and bright waft up to my nose.

"Then he and your father should get along just fine. Now go on, boys, head outside and leave us ladies to chat."

"But Mom, I didn't even get to properly introduce Elena to you," Nick says.

"Her slapping you upside the head was all the introduction I needed. She's a keeper. Now scram."

I follow Nick outside, giving Amelia a quick peck on the cheek before leaving, hoping that winning over her father will be as easy as it was with her mom.

"So, Ethan, what is it that you do?" Sarah, Amelia's mother, asks me from across the table as we all sit down to eat. The sun is beginning to slide down toward the horizon, granting a reprieve from the hot September day, so we are eating outside on the patio, enjoying the cooler weather.

"Ethan's a divorce lawyer," Amelia answers for me, placing her hand over mine as I gather my composure. I don't know how much she's told her parents about me or how we interacted with each other when we first met, so I'm glad she felt the need to interject.

"Really?"

"Yes."

"And how did you get into that?"

Wiping my mouth with my napkin, I set my fork down. "Well, I knew I wanted to practice law and just kind of fell into that area after my own divorce."

"You're divorced?" George, her father, now asks.

"Yes, sir. And I have a son." There's no point in trying to make excuses.

"Really? How old is he?"

Amelia answers for me. "He's five, almost six, and just the cutest little guy. Oliver is a great kid, a testament to Ethan and how well he's raised him."

"Where is he tonight?"

"With my mom. I moved back to L.A. to be closer to her. She helps me a lot with him, and she loves being a grandmother, so…"

Sarah nods. "Understandable. I mean, I personally can't wait to be a grandmother, too, you know."

Nick pipes up. "Jesus, Mom. Don't scare Elena and Ethan away already, all right?"

Everyone chuckles. "All in due time, but that begs the question, do you ever want more children, Ethan?"

Suddenly that cool summer air feels a thousand degrees hotter in a flash. "Uh, well, never say never, but I guess it just depends on the situation. After my divorce, I never thought I'd date again either, but then I met Amelia."

"Ethan's practice is in the same complex as mine. That's how we met."

"Oh. I figured you met through Nick," her mother explains.

"Not exactly, but Nick is the reason we both ended up with offices there."

"You're welcome, you two." Nick smirks from across the table.

"And before the question is asked, no, Amelia and I did not see eye to eye at first," I declare, inserting myself back into the conversation. "I was a bit of a jerk. A divorce attorney right across the courtyard from a marriage counselor wasn't exactly ideal for either of us. But we eventually started to get along, and I apologized for being an idiot, because I was."

Her father raises his beer. "As all men are at some point." Everyone laughs. "At least you owned up to it. I can respect that."

"Obviously, Amelia has the capacity to see the best in people, so she gave me the opportunity to show her that, and I couldn't be more grateful. She definitely showed me that she wasn't backing down, though, before we called a truce."

"It doesn't surprise me that Amelia would hold her ground when someone threatens her job."

I turn to her. "That she definitely did."

"You know, Amelia got into therapy because of us," her mother explains.

"Mom…"

"Is that right?" I look between Amelia and her mother, eager to hear more about this. Deep down, I always wondered how and why she chose the area she did. We decided not to discuss our jobs so long ago that it doesn't seem valid at this point, given that now we're actually dating.

"Yes. George and I almost divorced when she was sixteen." Suddenly my stomach begins to twist as I watch Amelia stare across the table at her mom, whose eyes crinkle at the corners as she smiles softly. "She begged us to see a therapist, to try to save our marriage. And even though George and I weren't sure there was anything to be saved, we did it for our kids." She looks at Nick now, whose arm is around Elena's shoulders. "It was tough, and things didn't magically get fixed overnight. Relationships, and marriages, are complicated, which you'll find out as you experience them yourself. But eventually, we realized how much we truly loved each other and all that we had to fight for, and now we're better than we ever were." George leans over and kisses his wife, and my heart twists a bit.

I don't see happy couples much in my line of work, so it's

comforting to know there are people who are happily married and fight for that.

"After watching what they went through and how much therapy helped them—and Nick and I because we talked to someone too—I realized that I wanted to be able to help people like Dr. Collins helped us. So, I majored in psychology and never looked back."

Looking at Amelia next to me, so many things about her start to click into place. I already knew she was passionate about her work, but now the amount of pride she takes in it makes even more sense, and the connection she feels to her clients. The woman has an emotional connection and investment in what she does, which I can relate to completely—because I can connect to what I do too.

"Now, I'm not saying every marriage can be saved because, believe me, we're not naive," Sarah continues. "But I'm proud of our girl for helping as many people as she has."

"And now she's been nominated for best marriage counselor by the *Los Angeles Times*," Nick adds, reaching across the table to clink his glass with Amelia's.

"Oh, now you're going to be nice?" she teases him back as they touch glasses.

"My brotherly love has various levels, Sis. But you know how freaking proud I am of you."

"Thank you."

"That's incredible, Amelia. I wish you would have told me," I say as a twinge of irritation sparks in my chest.

"We can talk about it later." She clears her throat and then changes the subject, avoiding my gaze. And I know it's not the time to press her, but something about the way she dismisses me doesn't sit right in my gut. "So, Elena? Is Nick more or less mature than the high school students you teach?"

She laughs while Nick rolls his eyes. "Honestly? They're about the same."

"Hey, I take offense to that," he admonishes as everyone laughs.

"Don't, baby. I enjoy being with someone who makes things fun. It reminds me not to be so serious all the time." Nick leans over and kisses her as the attention shifts to them.

And for the rest of the meal, everyone talks about work and life. I share stories about Oliver, Amelia and Nick trade embarrassing stories about each other, and even their parents get in on the action. And for just a second, I catch a glimpse of the type of family that I've never been a part of—two parents who love each other so much that they were willing to go to therapy to save their marriage and their family, two kids who had the example of a healthy relationship in the sense that their parents took the good with the bad and worked past it, and a woman who deserves to have the same one day.

And that's when it hits me. Perhaps I was foolish about how strongly I would feel for Amelia and what that means for us moving forward. Because no matter how much I care for her or can see her fitting into my life, there's one detail I can't get past: I don't ever want to be married again, and I'm pretty sure that's something she wants down the line, something I may not be able to give her.

Chapter 13

Ethan

"Do you need to pick up Oliver soon?" Amelia asks as we leave her parents' house, and I walk her to her car. Darkness has descended around us as the evening progressed as well as cooler temperatures, so I pull Amelia to my side and rub the chill off her arm.

"No. He's actually staying the night with my mom since I'd just be returning him to her in the morning before school anyway. It's easier this way."

"Makes sense. So the rest of your evening is free?" Spinning to face me, she leans against her car door with a sly smile on her lips.

"It is. What did you have in mind?"

"Wanna go back to my place?"

I toy with her a bit. "Uh, I don't know. The dinner was kind of a lot to handle."

Her face falls, and suddenly I feel like a dick. "Really?"

"Fuck, no, Amelia. I was joking. Shit."

"Oh." Nervous laughter leaves her lips.

"Sorry. I was just trying to mess around with you." I crowd her against her car now. "I had a great time actually. Your parents are great. Nick is…well, Nick. And you…"

"What?" She stares up at me, blinking as she waits for my answer.

"You're the kind of woman who makes me wonder if I can ever be the type of man who deserves you."

She croons, "Ethan…"

But I use this as an opportunity to press about something from earlier. "Why didn't you tell me about your nomination with the *Los Angeles Times*?"

She rears back. "Because right after I found out, you showed up in my life and not in a good way." I cringe. "And honestly, I kind of pushed it to the back of my mind. There's a dinner in November that I have to attend where the nominees are celebrated. It's just incredible to be nominated for something like that, but I wasn't sure I should share that stuff with you."

Gripping her chin, I tip her head up so her eyes meet mine. "Don't do that. Don't diminish your accomplishments. You should be proud of what you've done. And now that I know a little bit more about how you got into therapy, I understand and respect you even more."

"Really?"

"Absolutely."

"And did you go into family law because of your experience?"

"I did. I got pretty lucky with Monica because she didn't want anything to do with Oliver and me, so our divorce wasn't messy. But others aren't so lucky, and I wanted to be able to help people get out of marriages that don't suit them anymore."

She reaches up and brushes a few errant hairs from my face. "Well, I guess I can respect that too. But now, I just want you to disrespect me." She waggles her eyebrows.

And my dick grows rock hard in a flash. "Is that so?"

"Yes. And I have a little surprise for you if you're interested."

"I'm not usually a big fan of surprises, but a surprise from you that involves you naked might just make me change my mind."

"Then I'll see you at my house." She playfully pushes me away as she opens her car door.

"See you there. Drive safe."

"You too."

After following Amelia to her house, we step inside, and she leads me upstairs to her room. My eyes trail her as she grabs a single chair from the vanity in the corner and places it at the foot of her bed, facing the stripper pole that caught my eye the first time I was here.

"Sit."

"I thought you wanted me to disrespect you?" I tease as I take a seat on the chair, adjusting my cock as I sit down.

"You'll have your chance in a minute. But first, I want to do something I've been dying to do for you for a while now." She walks over to her nightstand and takes out a rather sizable box, sturdy considering its size, walking back over to me and placing it on the bed behind me. I watch her pull a black silk sash from the box and run it through her fingers.

"You're going to blind fold me?"

"Just until I'm ready for you to see what I have planned for you."

"Amelia…fuck, I'm already hard, baby. I don't think I can take this."

She leans forward, giving me a glimpse of the cleavage peeking out of the top of her sundress. "You can and you will."

"I knew you had a kinky side. The straight-laced marriage counselor had to be a little mischievous behind closed doors." Smirking, I watch her eyes dilate, which only makes me harder.

With a soft press of her lips to mine, she stares into my eyes as I feel her hands reach behind me and place my wrists together, tying the sash around them. "Honestly, Ethan? You make me feel confident enough to do things like this."

"Really?"

"Yes. That day in my office with the dildo was the only time I've ever let a man have that kind of control over me, and I barely knew you at that point. And every time we're together, I feel like I can let go with you." She trails her lips up my neck until she reaches my ear. "The look of desire in your eyes when we're together is enough to make any woman feel wanted and beautiful, but you reserve that look for me. And now, I want to take another risk with you, try something that only you make me safe enough to do."

"Fuck, Amelia. When you say things like that…"

"You want to make love to me and defile me all at the same time, don't you?"

"God, yes."

"Well, now you know how I feel." She stands up again and grabs another black sash from the box, placing it over my eyes this time.

"What else do you have in that box?" I ask once I can see nothing but black.

"Toys, and lots of them. Remember, I work with companies and supply things to my clients. Perks of the job require me to test them out. Maybe I'll let you test some out on me too."

"Fuck me. Hurry up so I can make you scream, baby."

Her soft chuckle moves away from me. "Patience, Ethan. Good things come to those who wait."

After what feels like an eternity but is only five minutes or so, I hear movement heading toward me before soft lips meet mine. "You ready for your surprise?"

"Amelia, I'm going to fuck you so hard when this is over."

"I'm counting on it."

Her fingers graze my neck, and then she drags her nails through my hair before untying the sash on my eyes, revealing herself to me. She leaves my wrists bound behind me—which, let's be honest, I could easily break out of, but I don't because she's obviously put a lot of thought into this little show tonight.

And what a show it's turning out to be.

Dressed in a bright-yellow lace bodysuit, Amelia backs up and gives me the full view of her body encased in see-through lace. Delicate straps hold up a corset bodice, and as she spins around, I get the perfect view of her ass exposed by the thong attached to the bottom of it.

"Fuck. Me."

"You like?"

"Hell yeah, baby. Jesus." I wish I could lift my hand to wipe the drool from my mouth right now, but unfortunately, that's not possible.

"I'm glad." She walks toward the pole in front of me and then spins around so I can see her face again. "So remember when you were here that first night and said you wanted to see me dance for you?"

"Yes."

"Well, you're about to get your own private show, Mr. Fuller." She reaches for her phone on the bathroom counter, presses a few buttons, and then music starts to fill the air. She takes off her glasses, throws her hair in a ponytail, and then spins around to face me. And fuck me, it's "Pour Some Sugar on Me" by Def Leppard, only the hottest fucking stripper song known to mankind.

But let me preface something—I've never been a huge fan of strip clubs or women stripping in general. It's not how I would choose to spend an evening with the guys if I had the choice, nor do I enjoy watching a woman I don't know dance erotically. But the idea of a woman—one who you are being intimate with—dancing and tearing her clothes off for you to this particular song is enough to have me wishing I could pinch the tip of my dick since I already feel like I'm about to come.

"Jesus Christ." I spread my legs wider and try to get comfortable, keeping my eyes locked on Amelia as she reaches up and grabs the pole behind her, bending her knees as she slowly begins to slide down toward the ground. The curves of her body roll and sway as she stands back up, faces the pole, and then jumps up and wraps her legs around it, climbing toward the ceiling.

I'm fucking mesmerized watching her—how she holds on with one leg, trusting her body to keep her up, how she swings her body around and upside down, keeping her eyes on me as she teases me with the way she's moving. Even her sexy little smirk is enough for me to know that I will undoubtedly be spanking this woman so fucking hard when she's done because this is the best and worst tease of my life.

I remain frozen in place, watching her and trying not to choke on my tongue as she mesmerizes me through the end of the song.

"I want you to know something, Ethan," she says as she continues to spin on the pole.

"What?"

With some witchcraft move, she flips around and lands on the carpet flawlessly, catching her balance before letting go of the pole and walking over to me. "You are the only man I've ever danced for."

"I'm fucking glad because if I knew any other man has seen you like this, I'd fucking rip their eyes out."

She giggles. "Someone is possessive."

"Only of you, Amelia."

Kneeling before me, I watch her reach up and unbutton my shorts, sliding them off my legs as I lift my ass from the chair and grant her access to rip them off me. My dick stands tall and proud, hard as stone, and eager to pound into her for all the teasing she's been doing. But something tells me she's not done yet.

With her this close, I can see her dark nipples through the fabric of her bodysuit, the delicate straps sliding off her shoulders as she moves. And as she wraps her hand around my cock, stroking it a few times for good measure, I groan and throw my head back just long enough to bring me back to reality when her mouth finds the head of my dick, and her tongue swirls around it in a perfect stroke. "Fuck, baby."

"I love your cock, Ethan."

"I love your mouth, your tongue, and your ass."

"Hmmm," she moans as she draws me back toward her throat, sucking my length hard as she starts to work me in and out of her mouth. I'd love nothing more than to be able to bury my hands in her hair and encourage her right along, but alas, my hands are still tied behind my back, and I promised myself I would play along with this.

"God damn, you're blowing my mind, Amelia."

She releases me from her mouth with a pop. "Mission accomplished." Slowly, she stands and begins to slide the straps of her bodysuit completely off her shoulders. It basically looks like a bathing suit, but one I would never let her wear in public.

As she pushes the fabric down her body, keeping her eyes locked on mine the entire time, I feel my breathing pick up. I'm growing impatient. I want to touch her and ravage her, yet I'm still under her mercy—and it's so fucking hot.

Once the suit has left her body, she stands before me, completely naked. "You ready to play?"

"I'm ready to fuck you into next week, Amelia. Now untie me."

"I don't know." She bites her lip coyly. "I'm still having a little too much fun. Maybe I need to show you a few more things."

"I swear to God…" The groan I let out could probably be heard by her neighbors.

She walks toward me, straddling me as she lowers herself and rubs her soaked pussy over my cock. "You feel so good."

"I'd feel better inside of you, sweetheart. Now untie me…"

"That's not how you ask for something, Ethan, and you know it." She reaches behind me to the box of toys and grabs something, but then moves her hand quickly behind her so I can't see it. The sounds of vibrations echo as she turns it on, and before I can say anything, I feel her press the vibrator to my balls.

"Oh fuck."

She holds it there while sliding her wetness up and down my cock again, never letting me inside her but rubbing her clit over my shaft and sliding the vibrator up and down my balls. "Spread your legs."

"Baby, I'm begging you…please untie me and let me fuck you."

"Not yet. Spread your legs, Ethan."

I do as I'm told, feeling her growing wetter as she keeps moving, including moving the vibrator closer to my ass. She doesn't insert it but teases the pressure point between my balls and asshole, and I swear to God, I'm about to lose my shit.

And then I do.

I rip the sash in half—which, let's face it, was more decoration and an exercise in trust than an actual restraint—and lift Amelia from my lap so quickly she screams. Tossing her on the bed, I dip my head down and suck on her nipples, giving myself a few moments to calm down so I don't blow my load all over her stomach this soon.

"You didn't listen," she mewls as my hands move all over her, making up for the lost time when I couldn't touch her.

"You were fucking torturing me, Amelia."

She giggles as I move my hand between her legs and run my fingers up and down her slit before pushing two fingers inside her effortlessly, sliding them in and out. "I know. Oh God, Ethan. Fuck me, please."

"Oh, I plan on it. Believe me." I release her nipple from my mouth and grab my shorts, locating a condom from my wallet and putting it on at record speed. But then my eyes drift over to the box of toys, and I decide to take a peek inside.

Fuck me sideways. Amelia has a smorgasbord of pleasure in here, things I've seen but never used myself. It's hard to feel comfortable enough to explore things with a wife who didn't want you. But now, I want to do anything and everything with Amelia if she'll let me.

I pull out an anal plug, studying it in the soft light. "You ever used this?"

"Not with anyone."

"Just by yourself?"

She shrugs, pushing herself up off the bed. "Yeah. I told you, I test everything out."

"I wanna see this in your ass while I fuck you, baby. You okay with that?"

She bites her lips and nods. "Yes."

Amelia gets on all fours, and I grab a bottle of lube from the box, spreading it around her asshole and all over the plug so she's as comfortable as possible when I put it in. "You ready?"

"Yes. God, Ethan, hurry. I want to feel you so bad."

"Same, Amelia. But you started this, remember?"

"Well, you'd better plan on finishing it," she counters with a glance at me over her shoulder.

I give her ass cheek a little smack and then move the toy toward her ass, pressing gently against her hole, letting her body adjust as I slowly push the plug inside. I feel her clench as I work the toy in and out. "Just breathe."

"Keep going."

It takes a few more minutes of patience, but when the plug is finally in, she lets out a sigh that goes straight to my dick. "You okay?"

"Yes."

"Good. Now hold on, Amelia." I place my cock at her entrance and fight my way inside. She's so fucking tight from the plug in her ass that it takes more control than I have left to slide in—but when I do, we groan in unison. "Holy fuck."

"Oh my God. Move, Ethan, please."

Carefully, I pull out and thrust in again, giving her and me time to adjust to how intense this is, this unexplainable high of feeling her wrapped this tight around me. But once her moans become borderline wild, I flip the switch and pound into her.

"Yes, oh God, yes…"

"Jesus Christ, Amelia. You feel incredible."

"Don't stop, please."

"If I could last, I'd fuck you all night. But I'm not gonna last, baby." The sound of my hips smacking her ass as I pound into her almost makes it hard to hear her words.

"Grab me a vibrator," she cries as I keep up a punishing pace.

Without losing focus, I reach over and locate a vibrating wand, handing it to her and watching her turn it on and place it between her legs, moaning out in appreciation when it hits her clit.

"God, I'm going to come so hard."

"Me too. Oh God, Ethan!" In a matter of seconds, she's fucking screaming, burying her face in the comforter and pulling me over with her. I spill myself into the condom, squeezing her hips so tight as we finish together that I leave marks when we're through.

And Amelia leaves a puddle on the bed.

After I slowly pull out of her, we both collapse and fight for normal breaths.

"I don't think I've ever come that hard in my life," she whispers and then laughs beside me, trailing her fingernails through my short chest hair.

"You came so hard, you made a mess on the sheets, babe."

"Really?" She lifts her head and stares down at the wet spot on the sheets. "Yikes."

Reaching over, I roll her into my chest and line my body up with hers, pressing kisses to her neck and the back of her head. "That was, by far, the hottest fucking sex of my life." And then I place a kiss on her orchid tattoo on her shoulder, a detail that I love to put my lips on. Last week after a round of sex in her office, she told me the story of how she and the girls each got their favorite flowers tattooed on their shoulders together. And I find it kind of kismet that I gave her orchids before I ever knew that detail about her.

"Me too." She looks back at me, her face relaxed and content. And then she kisses me. "Thanks for letting me torture you."

"If that was torture, I'd let you do that to me every day."

She rolls over so we're facing each other now. "I meant what I said, Ethan. You make me feel comfortable enough to let go with you." Her fingernails drag through the scruff on my jaw as she studies my face. "The intimacy we share? It's what I encourage and try to help my clients find. I just…sometimes it scares me that I found it with you, but I love it too."

"I've never felt this way with a woman either, Amelia." I press a kiss to her nose and then one to her lips, lingering on her mouth for a few moments as we say things with our lips that I don't think either one of us is ready to say out loud.

"I'm glad. Now, can you take this plug out of my ass, please?"

Laughing, I sit up and roll her back over, smacking her ass cheek for good measure. "Next time, it's gonna be my cock in your ass, babe."

"Don't get too cocky, Ethan, or that vibrator just might find its way into yours."

"Amelia! Your gnomes moved!" Oliver doesn't even wait one second after Amelia opens the door to her house to tell her about his discovery.

"They did? Show me!" She follows him out the door, smirking at me as she passes, indicating that she knows exactly how and why the gnomes moved. Since the gnome escapades started, we now take bi-weekly pictures of the ones in front of her office and the ones at her house. To say Oliver is obsessed would be an understatement.

"Here!" He points to where they are in the flower bed, a good five feet away from where they were before and on the other side of her sidewalk.

"Oh my gosh. I didn't even notice. They must have been protecting the flowers from something last night."

"Maybe it was a raccoon. My grandma says raccoons like to cause all kinds of trouble."

"Your grandma is right. So, are you excited to go swimming today, Oliver?"

"Yes!" he shouts again. "I have my floaties, and Dad brought lots of sunblock so I don't get burned, even though I hate the way it smells." He scrunches up his face.

Amelia laughs. "I don't like the way it smells either, but it's important to wear it to protect your skin." She bops him on the nose and then leads us into the house. Closing the door after me, she finally pauses and makes eye contact with me. "Hi, Ethan."

"Hey, babe. Long time no see," I joke. Amelia joined me at Oliver's soccer game earlier, and then we followed her to her house afterward. "Thanks again for inviting us over. Oliver has been talking about this non-stop all week. My mom said he had a count-down on the refrigerator at her house."

She smiles, tucking one of her blond curls behind her ear. "That is so sweet. And it's my pleasure. I paid a lot of money for that pool, so I feel better knowing it's being enjoyed."

"Dad! Can I jump in?" Oliver calls from the backyard at the edge of the pool, where he must have slipped to while I was busy admiring Amelia in a yellow cover-up over her suit. She must have quickly changed before we got here.

"Jesus, Oliver!" I run out the backdoor, yanking him away from the edge before he falls in. "You know you have to have your floaties and sunscreen on before you get in the water."

"Then do it, Daddy. Fast!" He holds out his arms to the side, staring up at me with his brows raised high.

"I didn't hear your manners, young man."

"Please." He juts out his lip as he stares up at me, and Amelia chuckles from the door.

"He's good," she says.

"Don't I know it." I reach into the small backpack I brought with us and begin to slather sunscreen on him as he squirms to get away from me. "Hold still."

"It's so smelly." His face scrunches up again as he wiggles in my hands, making me practically chase him to rub him down.

Amelia steps up to us. "Here, Oliver. Why don't you put sunscreen on my back while your dad puts it on you, so it will help you stay still?"

"Okay!" He holds out his hands to me as I squeeze a few drops in his palm. Momentarily, I wonder if I gave him too much because lord knows he's going to get it everywhere, but I only have a few seconds to ponder that decision before I'm frozen in place, watching

Amelia lift her cover-up over her head, revealing a matching yellow bikini on her body—her incredible, curvy, silky, and tan body—a body that has my dick tenting my trunks in seconds. Maybe swimming with her with my kid around wasn't a bright idea after all. And it's not like I haven't seen the woman naked, but that pathetic excuse for a bikini she's wearing is such a fucking tease.

Amelia has the body of a woman, curves accentuated by the dip in her waist that leads to the flare of her hips, a thick and luscious ass that is held up by toned legs and voluptuous thighs, and her breasts are the perfect handful for her body, keeping up the proportion of her hourglass figure.

She drives me crazy and makes me feel at peace all at the same time.

Because it's not just her body that I love, but the way she is with my kid. I was so nervous about letting Oliver spend time with her, but the more they interact, the more I see how loving and nurturing she is with him. This week she even let him hang out with her in her office while I finished up a call in mine before we left for his soccer practice. They played tic-tac-toe, and he helped her stack the business cards neatly again on the table by her door. All Oliver did was talk about her in the car once we left, and part of me wished he'd had more to say.

I crouch down, bending my knees not only to reach Oliver better but to help conceal the physical reaction my body is having to her. And as I stare up at her from my new position, she gathers her wild hair into a ponytail and secures it on the top of her head, exposing the long column of her neck that I instantly want to kiss and lick every inch of.

"There." Twisting around, she drops to her knees in front of Oliver as he smears the sunscreen on her back, the expanse of her skin barely covered by two thin strings of fabric holding up her top. "Make sure to cover all of my back, Oliver, so I don't get sunburned."

"Okay." As he concentrates harder than I've ever seen him, determined to accomplish a task, I finish covering him from head to toe in sunblock and then move to blow up his new floaties.

"Is it all rubbed in?" Amelia asks, glancing over her shoulder at him, catching my eyes in the process as she flashes me a smile.

"Yup!" Oliver proudly exclaims as I peek at her back, noticing a few spots of white still lingering—and by a few spots, I mean her entire back is still pasty.

"Here, Oliver." I help him slide his arms into his floaties before he combusts from anticipation.

"Can I jump in now, Daddy?"

"Yup! Go ahead."

"Yay! Cannonball!" he screams, running toward the pool at full speed and then stopping right at the edge just before jumping as high as he can, splashing the concrete when he hits the water.

"He'll be doing that over and over again until we make him stop to eat or take a drink of water," I say, turning toward Amelia, who I catch glancing at my ass. With an arch of my brow, I catch her attention. "Like what you see?"

"Always." She clears her throat and then smiles.

"Um, you might want to turn around for a second."

"Why?"

"Because my son still needs to work on his sunscreen application skills."

She chuckles. "Oh." Twisting away from me, I take a few seconds to admire her backside again before pressing my fingers to her skin, rubbing the white cream in the spots he missed. A faint moan rings out, but I can't tell if it came from my mouth or hers. Eager to touch her more and use this as an excuse, I use both hands now, massaging her shoulders as her head falls back.

"That feels nice," she whispers breathlessly.

"God, I wish we were alone right now. I'd be fucking you on that lounger under the gondola over there, and then we'd be skinny dipping so I could feel your naked, wet body all over mine."

"Ethan, you can't say things like that to me in front of your son."

"He's occupied." I run my hands down her back and then grip her hips. "Fuck, you're so sexy, Amelia." And then I press my cock against her ass so she can feel how close I am to losing my composure.

"Dad! Watch this!" I turn around just in time to see and hear the sound of Oliver jumping into the pool again, bringing me back to reality.

"Nice, bud," I tell him when his head bobs up from under the water." Then I turn back to Amelia. "To be continued. And there you go. All rubbed in."

"Thank you." She spins to face me again, her cheeks slightly pink as she glances over at Oliver paddling to the steps again. "I love when we're alone, but I'm glad Oliver is here. He's a part of your life, and I want to spend time with him too."

"I can't tell you what that means to me, babe." I lift her hand and press a kiss to her wrist as Oliver screams out in delight.

"I'm glad he's happy and having fun. I'm going to go inside and grab us some drinks. Do you want anything in particular? I made lemonade…"

"That sounds great. Thanks." I watch her walk back into the house before turning again to the pool, observing Oliver climb out via the steps and then race back over to where he jumped before. "No running on the concrete, Oliver. You'll slip and fall."

"I know, Daddy. Now watch!" He plugs his nose and jumps into the water again, alerting me to the fact that I'm going to be watching this same routine repeatedly all afternoon. But I can't help but smile watching him, knowing he's prospering and accepting Amelia into our lives too. I truly did miss my little sidekick this week while he was at school and I was working long days to catch up on work. A day of swimming sounds like a good way to make up for lost time.

"Here we go." Amelia walks out of the house with a tray in her hands, strutting toward me before depositing it on the small table between the two chairs under the gondola she has in the corner of her yard behind the pool.

"Damn. This is some fancy lemonade." The tray contains a pitcher, three glasses, and a tray of sliced fruit.

"I thought Oliver would like being able to add fruit to his drink. I made popsicles for later too, but I remember you saying that he liked to help cook, so for lunch, I bought stuff for a charcuterie board." She shrugs. "I thought he'd like to help me fill it up with what we can snack on, give him a little say over what we're eating." She stares down at the ground, and if I didn't know any better, I'd say she's questioning her idea.

"Hey." Her head pops back up, her eyes locking onto mine. "That's a great idea. I really appreciate you thinking about that. You didn't have to, but I know Oliver will love it."

"Well, I invited you two over, so I planned on feeding you both and wanted to be accommodating." Reaching for the pitcher, she pours me a glass and then one for herself, picking up a few slices of raspberries and strawberries, gently dropping them inside. "I don't spend much time with kids, but I wanted to do my best to make you feel welcome."

"Dad!" Oliver screams from the pool, breaking our conversation before I can praise Amelia for her thoughtfulness.

"What's up, bud?"

"Are you gonna come swimming?"

I turn to Amelia, who's smiling across the yard at Oliver, holding her glass of lemonade.

"Duty calls. You don't mind, do you?"

"Oh, no. Of course not. Go. I'm right behind you."

With a nod, I stand and reach behind me to peel off my shirt, tossing it on the lounger. And when I look back at Amelia, her eyes are heated as they drift down my chest.

"You okay?" I ask her, pulling her from her perusal of my body.

"Yup. Seems today won't be easy for either of us." With a wink, she stands, sets her drink down, and walks around me, casting me a glance over her shoulder. And then she turns to Oliver. "This is how you cannonball, Ollie!" Jumping from the ledge, she tucks her knees into her chest and splashes both him and me a bit, laughing when she breaks through the surface of the water.

"Dad! You have to beat Amelia's splash now!"

"That's too easy!" Racing to the pool, I make sure to avoid them both as I jump in to join them, reeling with how effortless this all feels. These moments with the three of us remind me of the memories we've missed out on without Monica around. But as I glance at my son, I realize his happiness isn't dependent on his mother being present—just that people who truly care about him are, and Amelia is quickly becoming one of those people.

～

"So what do you think, Oliver? What should we put on the tray to take outside for lunch?"

"Sour gummy worms and olives!"

Amelia laughs and begins filling up the small bowls she placed on the large wooden cutting board. "Okay, those are two of my favorites too, but we need some vegetables as well."

"I don't like vegetables."

"Not even with ranch dressing?"

"I like carrots and ranch."

Amelia nods. "I'll tell you a little secret, Oliver." She kneels down to whisper in his ear. "That's the only way I'll eat them too."

His eyes go wide. "Really?"

"Yup. I don't like carrots by themselves, but with ranch, I can eat them all day."

"Then we need to have ranch for the carrots," he agrees with a bob of his head.

"I think so too."

I watch Amelia offer up so many choices to my kid that I wonder if she cleared out the deli and snack aisles at the grocery store just to appease him. But watching her and Oliver together makes my chest do that funny twinge again. Having someone who makes me feel alive and accepts my son is filling a void in my chest I didn't realize was empty until I started watching the two of them interact, and it gets better each time.

Before we came in for lunch, Amelia was playing with Oliver in the pool. She was trying to teach him how to do a flip underwater, which I didn't mind at all every time her ass peeked out from under the surface as she spun. Oliver was growing restless when he couldn't get it, so she switched to throwing diving rings into the shallow end of the pool so he could retrieve them while wearing his goggles, working on holding his breath underwater.

She's a natural with him, and it has me daydreaming of all of the things the three of us could do together, experiences to share, and memories to make as this thing progresses between us. But deep down, I know there's a limit to how far I can let it go.

"Okay, I think we have a good combination of everything, so let's go sit under the shade and eat, then we can swim some more."

"Okay!" Oliver races out to the patio table under her gondola as I take the tray from her hands.

"I've got it."

"Thank you. I'm just going to use the bathroom really quick, and then I'll be right out."

"See you out there." I head over to Oliver, who is sipping on his second glass of lemonade. "After that one, you're drinking water for the rest of the day."

"Okay, Daddy."

"Are you having fun, buddy?" I ask him as I take my seat.

"So much fun! I like Amelia. She has a pool and gnomes and makes yummy lunches for us that have sour gummy worms."

I laugh at how black and white my kid can be. Oh, to be that age again where all you can see are the rights and wrongs, the things you like and the things you don't.

"Yeah, that's not something I would offer you, that's for sure."

"Nope." He sticks a worm in his mouth and rips it in half with his teeth. "But she also makes you smile and less grumpy, so I like her for that reason too."

"Is that so?"

He nods. "You kiss her too, and Grandma says that when grown-ups like each other, they kiss sometimes. And I'm okay with it, just so you know."

"You're okay with it?"

"Yup. Grandma said I should tell you that too so we can keep being friends with her."

Jesus, Mom…really?

"But she said I can't kiss Harper yet because we're too little, and I think kissing sounds gross even though I know that's what you're supposed to do when you like someone."Running a hand down my face, I make a mental note to talk to my mother the next time I see her about the things she's telling my son.

"How is lunch?" Amelia asks as she walks back out to us with her cover-up back on over her suit. And at that moment, I realize that everything I feel toward her is the complete opposite of black and white—it's actually quite gray.

I value her friendship and company, but I also love the way she tastes and the sounds she makes when I'm buried inside of her. She's honest and hardworking but also has a vulnerable side to her when it comes to her work. She's thoughtful, beautiful, and funny, and she makes me want to be a saint—the type of man that she deserves who knows what he has when he has her—even though sinning with her is incredible too. She's the type of woman you look for in a wife but I've been down that road and know I don't want to do it again.

The further this thing between us gets, the more I realize I need to be upfront with her about where my heart lies. I want her in my life and Oliver's; that much is becoming crystal clear. But is that enough for her? And do I say something now so she's aware? Or do I wait because I'm afraid of what she might say when I tell her how I feel about her and a possible future with her, a future I didn't think I'd ever have to contemplate again?

"What are we trying first, Oliver?" She takes her seat between the two of us, peering over at my son.

"I already had a sour gummy worm, but now I want a pepperoni," he answers as he reaches forward and grabs a slice from the board.

"Good choice. I'm going to have pepperoni too, but I'm going to make a cracker sandwich with mine." She grabs the meat, a slice of mozzarella cheese, an olive, and a cracker, stacking them together before she takes a bite.

"I wanna try that!"

"Here, I'll help you. Why don't you come sit on my lap?"

"But I don't want to squish your Veronica."

I lean forward because I'm not sure I just heard my son correctly. "What did you say, Oliver?"

"If I sit on Amelia's lap, I'm gonna squish her Veronica."

Amelia snorts, turning her head to the side in laughter. But my mouth just drops open. "Her Veronica?"

"Yeah. You know…" He points between his legs.

I'm done.

"Where did you hear that?"

"From Harper. She said she has a Veronica, and I have a Peter."

"Oh my God," Amelia breathes out, shaking from her giggles. And I'm not going to lie, it's getting harder to keep a straight face as this conversation goes on.

"But you said I have a penis, Daddy, so it made me kind of confused."

I run a hand down my face. "Yeah, you and me both, kid."

Amelia finally chimes in once her laughter is under control. "It's okay, Oliver. You don't have to sit on my lap. I can just help you make a cracker sandwich from here." She winks in my direction and then directs my son to gather his ingredients, giving me a chance to process the conversation that just took place.

We spend the next fifteen minutes trying different combinations of foods, and Amelia even gets my kid to eat carrots and ranch dressing more than once.

"Can I have more sour gummy worms now?" Oliver asks, practically salivating.

"A few."

"Yay!" He grabs three and then shoves one in his mouth. "Amelia, did Daddy tell you about the play I'm in at school?"

Amelia casts her eyes in my direction while popping an olive in her mouth. "No, he did not. Why don't you tell me about it?"

Oliver sits up on his knees while reaching for another carrot. "It's about all of the helpers in the world, like policemen, firefighters, and teachers."

"Oh, nice."

"I get to be a doctor because doctors help people when they're sick or have boo-boos."

She nods. "They do. Although I'm a doctor too."

Oliver tips his head to the side. "You are? But you don't work at a hospital…"

Amelia smiles. "No. I'm the kind of doctor that helps people talk about their feelings."

"Like when you're sad?"

"Exactly. Or angry, or scared." She looks over at me for a minute to gauge my reaction, but I nod, urging her to continue. "I help people realize that talking about their feelings can help solve a lot of problems in their lives and heal the boo-boos we have on the inside."

"Like what?"

"Like a broken heart," she answers honestly. "Or when someone doesn't feel brave or had something bad happen to them that makes them scared to try something again."

Oliver's eyes light up. "Oh! Like when I fell off my bike and scraped my knee and was scared to get back on it, huh, Dad?"

"Yeah, exactly like that, bud."

"Yup. There are all kinds of doctors, Oliver."

"I'm gonna tell my teacher that when I go back to school." He grabs another piece of cheese and pops it in his mouth before he leaps from his chair. "Will you come see my play, Amelia?"

Amelia looks surprised before she smiles at him, ruffling his hair. "I would love to."

"Yay!"

"Where are you going?" I ask him as he walks away from us.

"I have to go to the bathroom!" he announces as he runs inside, leaving Amelia and me alone.

"This was a great idea, Amelia," I say, gesturing to the board in front of us full of food. "I'll have to steal it. I can't remember the last time I saw my kid eat a carrot without me threatening to take away something." She laughs. "Thank you again for today."

"You're welcome. It's been nice to have company. Oliver is so sweet. And I know that things between us are new…" I wait for her to keep speaking. "But seriously, if you ever need help with Oliver, I'd be more than happy to be there for you."

"I appreciate that. Thank you."

Silence descends between us, so I try to switch gears, going back to the food. "Perhaps I'll try packing him lunches like this for school. He'd probably love it."

"He's in Kindergarten already…how does that make you feel?"

I scoff. "Old, like it's not possible he's already headed to school when I feel like it was just yesterday that I was still changing his diapers."

"I can see that. I've always heard that raising a child goes by fast."

"It does, faster than you realize. The days are long, but the years are short."

Amelia smiles. "My mother used to say that to us."

"Mine says it too. She always reminds me to soak up every moment with him and make decisions with his best interests at heart. But there are days when I feel like I'm barely surviving this parenting gig. It's a lot, which is why I haven't dated much, if at all." I reach across the table and place my hand over hers. "Letting him meet you is a big step for me. I want you to know that."

"I know. But I like where this is going. I see a future with you, Ethan," she says, her eyes bouncing back and forth between mine, looking for some agreement on my part, I'm sure. And this would be the perfect time to tell her my reservations and let her know that I want her in my life too, but there are limitations to that as well.

"And I know it might be soon to tell you that, but I want you to know how I'm feeling. I want you to know how serious I am about you and Oliver, that I don't take this lightly. I've never dated anyone with a kid before, Ethan, but I know the stakes are a lot higher. So when I told him I would be at his play, I meant it. If I tell him something, I will follow through with my words. I don't want him to feel like he can't trust me, and I don't want you to feel that way either."

Jesus, this woman is too good to be true. "Amelia…" But before I can finish, a loud bang from the house has me bolting from my seat. "Fuck!" Racing across the yard, I struggle to open the screen door.

"Daddy!" I hear Oliver yell from upstairs once I get inside the house.

"Oliver? Are you okay?" Another bang rings out as I hear Amelia behind me, trailing me up the stairs. But when I get to her room and see my son, nothing could have prepared me for what my eyes would take in.

Lying on the ground beneath a stripper pole is my kid, groaning.

"Oh my God!" I spin to find Amelia with both hands over her mouth, her eyes wide with shock and a twinge of fear in her vision as her eyes bounce back and forth between my son and me.

"Oliver," I say, moving the few steps toward him. "Are you okay?"

"Yeah, I think so. I was looking for the bathroom and found this room with this pole in it, Daddy. And it looked like the ones at the fire station. Do you remember when we saw the one at the fire station?" he says, looking up at me from the ground.

"Yeah, buddy, I remember that." I reach forward and brush the hair from his face, nervously searching him for signs of serious injury, but he looks fine, and he's talking, which is a good sign.

"I found that pole in here, Daddy, so I tried to climb it." Glancing over my shoulder, I see Amelia's face completely obscured by her hands now. "But it started spinning."

"Is that right?"

"Yes. So I started spinning around and around, jumping up and down. I wanted to get higher, so I found that box and used it to climb up the pole."

That's when my eyes take in the sturdy box sitting just on the other side of the pole, a box I recognize from a few weeks ago—a box full of items my son has no business seeing at his age. I can only hope and pray he didn't open it and only used it as a ladder of sorts.

Jesus Christ. No one prepares you for this shit when you have kids.

"Why does that pole spin, Daddy?"

I have no words. Nothing I can say right now will make this experience any less horrifying. "Um…"

"It was fun until I fell down," he says next, luckily moving the conversation forward and helping me avoid trying to find an answer to any of his questions. I help him sit up now, leaning back against the pole.

"Really?"

"It spins too fast."

I bite my lip, keeping my smile and laughter at bay just as Amelia finally chimes in. "Oh my God, Ethan. I am so sorry," she whispers.

"It's okay. My son shouldn't have been up here in the first place or going through your things." I turn back to him to see him starting to stand up. "Are you sure you're okay, Oliver? Does anything hurt?"

He rubs the side of his head. "Just my head. But I'm okay, Daddy."

"I think you owe Amelia an apology for going into her room and touching her things without asking."

"Sorry, Amelia."

"It's okay, Oliver. I'm just glad you didn't get hurt badly."

He rubs the side of his head. "I just bonked my head. Daddy says it happens sometimes."

"It does," she replies.

"Can I still go swimming, Dad?"

"Um, I don't know. Listen, why don't you go sit on the couch for a minute while I talk to Amelia, and then we can decide if swimming is still a good idea."

He stands from his spot on the ground. "Okay. I like your room, Amelia," he says as he walks past her, hobbling down the stairs slowly as Amelia watches him descend.

Standing from the ground, I run a hand through my hair until I realize the box is still on the ground. Reaching down, I pick it up and hand it to her. "My son is going to need your doctor's services after this experience," I tease her. "And I may need them as well."

She nervously grabs it from me, shaking her head through broken chuckles. "Oh my God, Ethan. I am mortified. Do you think he opened this up?"

"Well, I'd be lying if I said I wasn't either. Freaking kids, man. And to answer your question, no, I don't think he did—because if he had, there would be many more questions to answer."

She takes the box back over to her nightstand and puts it in the bottom drawer. "Apparently, my home isn't very kid friendly. The next item for purchase on my list will be a safe for all of my sex toys." She puts her face in her hands again as she walks back over to me.

"Well, my son shouldn't have been up here in your room, to begin with," I counter. "And don't worry, we'll have a long talk about it later." Sighing, I pull her into my chest and kiss the top of her head. "It's okay. He'll be fine. But I should probably check on him and make sure he doesn't have a concussion."

"Are you guys leaving now?" she asks, looking up at me.

"Do you want us to?"

Her eyes bounce back and forth between mine. "I mean, I still have popsicles for us to eat…"

"You're sure?"

"Yeah, I'm not ready for you two to leave just yet."

"I'm not ready to leave either." I grab her hand, kiss her lips, and lead her out of her room. "Let's go eat some popsicles, Amelia." And with a smirk over my shoulder, we traipse down the stairs and back to my kid, knowing that the questions over what just happened will plague me all night, especially those from Oliver.

But here's the thing—with any other woman, I'd be running out the door. Hell, I never would have let Oliver get to know another woman like I've let him get to know Amelia. And as Amelia brings out the popsicles for us to eat and cues up a movie for us to watch, I make sure Oliver's head is okay. We settle into the couch, just the three of us, spending the rest of the day laughing and being together —that should be enough for me to know that things with her could never be the same as they were with anyone else because she's not just anyone else.

She's the woman making me question every notion about love I've ever had. And even though I'm terrified, I want to believe that things happen for a reason too.

But deep down, I'm afraid that something or someone will fuck this up—and that someone might just be me.

Chapter 14

Amelia

"He did what?" Noelle leans across the table to make sure she heard me correctly.

"He fell off my stripper pole. And used my box of sex toys as a stool."

Penelope about falls out of her chair from laughing. "Oh my God, Amelia Be Delia! This kind of shit would only happen to you."

"Thanks for making me feel worse about it." I drain the rest of my mimosa and then gesture for Charlotte to fill my glass back up, which she does without question.

"The first time your boyfriend's kid goes to your house, and this is what happens?" Noelle continues. "Jesus."

"I know. He was fine, just bumped his head and not bad, but it was definitely a wake-up call."

"For what?"

"That I need to change a few things around the house if Oliver is going to be there more."

Charlotte sits back and smiles at me. "Do you see that happening?"

I can't fight the grin that comes over my lips. "I do. Things are going really well with us. Ethan is…"

"Oh, I know that look! I had that look!" Charlotte practically shrieks. "You're falling for him, aren't you?"

Sighing, I nod my head. "I am. I know it's soon but being with him is so different from any other relationship I've had. Our chemistry is so hot when we're together, but I enjoy the small moments with him too. And Oliver…" I shake my head as my heart beats faster. "I've never dated a man with a kid before, but I seriously can't imagine my life without him in it. He asked me to go to his play at school in November, and going to watch his soccer games on Saturdays has become my new favorite thing to look forward to. I think I'm just as attached to him as I am to his dad."

"I mean, there is something incredibly sexy about a hot, single dad. Why do you think it's such a profitable trope in romance novels?" Noelle explains. "And what about Oliver's mom?"

"She's not in the picture." I spend a few moments explaining the situation surrounding Ethan's divorce to the girls, something I realize I hadn't up until now.

"Okay, so are you two on the same page then about where this is headed?" Noelle continues to dig.

"I think so. I was very open with him yesterday about my intentions. I didn't want him to doubt that I took this seriously, especially because I know he had reservations about dating again and letting Oliver and I get to know each other. I mean, he met my parents. Nick knows we're seeing each other now, and what started as hate toward one another has blossomed into a relationship that I never saw coming. I feel like everything fell into place the way it was supposed to. We were both on our own paths and kind of found our way to each other."

Charlotte raises her glass. "Then welcome to the club, Amelia." She clinks her glass with mine. "Looks like you've found your guy."

"I really think I did," I say, holding back the tears of happiness that I can feel building. But I am happy. I feel like this is exactly where I'm supposed to be right now—with Ethan and Oliver.

Penelope sighs and then looks over at Noelle. "Looks like it's just you and me left in the single's club then, Noelle."

"Well, I won't be single for much longer. I won't be bringing a man around, but I will be part of a package deal soon. I'm going to move forward with finding a sperm donor."

Penelope sets her glass down. "Seriously?"

Noelle nods. "Yes. I'm tired of dating. I'm tired of waiting on the right man. I mean, look at Charlotte and Amelia now." She gestures toward Charlotte and me. "They found their guys, but it wasn't like they were necessarily looking for them. I've been looking. I've been searching, and I'm tired. I want children, and I want to be pregnant. So I can start my family and not waste any more time—mine or someone else's."

"What is the timeline like for this?" I ask.

"I have an appointment in two weeks at the clinic to start the preliminary process. Essentially, it can take up to a month to choose a donor and get ready for the transfer of sperm. They have to run a bunch of tests on me, check my cycle for when I'm ovulating, etc. It's gonna take a few months before I can be inseminated, so I want to start the process."

Charlotte reaches over and grabs Noelle's hand. "You're sure this is what you want?"

Noelle bobs her head up and down confidently. "Yes."

"Then let us know what you need, and we will be there."

Penelope and I also reach over and place our hands on theirs, showing our support.

"It takes a lot of courage to take control of your life, Noelle, and go after what you want. I'm proud of you."

"Thank you, Amelia. I'm not gonna lie, I'm nervous, more about telling my parents than anything. But I know this is what I want. I don't need a man in my life to be a mom. Being a mother is something I've wanted since I was a little girl, and I'm ready to make that dream a reality."

"It's time to choose Noelle's baby daddy, girls. I feel like I've been training for this my entire life," Penelope says assertively.

We share a laugh, and then Frankie comes by with our food as we ask Noelle more questions about her life-changing decision. And as we talk with her, I realize that the dynamic of our friend group is changing. Charlotte is happy and in love, I'm building my own little blended family with Ethan and Oliver, Noelle could have a baby sitting here at brunch with us this time next year, and Penelope, well, I'm sure something will tackle her out of left field and knock her on her ass too.

That just seems to be the way of the world for us right now, and I can't wait to see what happens next.

"Thank you for agreeing to see me again." Anne Lyle stands in front of my office early Wednesday morning.

"I was actually grateful that you called." She steps through the door and then turns to face me. "What happened in your office a few weeks ago was mortifying, and I want to apologize."

"Nonsense. That wasn't on you."

"But it is," she says, sinking down into the couch right by my front door as tears begin streaming down her face. "My husband is not the man I married anymore, and I begged him to talk to someone with me. But the more I think about it, the more I realize that perhaps I don't want to save a relationship he's no longer willing to put any effort into."

My heart sinks because my goal is always to help save relationships, to encourage communication and invest energy into the person you chose to spend your life with once upon a time. But looking at Anne and knowing how her husband is from the brief encounter I had with him, all I can see on her face is defeat.

"The entire reason I wanted to speak with you alone today was to gauge how you were feeling and make sure that you're okay. Sometimes therapy on your own can help you solve problems in your relationship as well," I offer, thinking back to several clients of mine who came to see me without their spouses. Their relationships improved anyway because they could finally communicate effectively about what they needed.

"There's not much of a relationship to salvage, Dr. St. Clair," she concedes. "Coming to see you was more of a last-ditch effort on my part. But after that day, Thomas made it clear to me that he would not be attending any sort of therapy, regardless of whether the therapist was married or not. And I'm so sorry he said those things to you, by the way."

"You do not have to apologize for him, Anne. That's not your cross to bear."

"Neither is his lack of respect for me anymore." She clears her throat. "Look, I know this is probably the opposite of what you do, but I was wondering if you could point me in the right direction…"

"Toward?"

"Leaving my husband, Dr. St. Clair. I can't stay in my marriage anymore. I've thought about this a lot over the past year, and now I know that it's the right decision for me."

Swallowing down my pride, I stare at the woman across from me and realize that leaving her husband is the best choice for her because it's what she wants. Internally, I feel frustrated that I couldn't help her the best way I know how, but then I realize I still can help her, and someone else I know can too.

"I actually have someone I would recommend."

Leading Anne across the courtyard of the complex, we enter Ethan's office and are greeted by Yvonne as soon as we get inside.

"Hi, Dr. St. Clair. How can I help you?"

"I was wondering if Mr. Fuller had a moment to speak with me and my client? I know he's busy, and we didn't have an appointment…"

She cuts me off. "Nonsense. He's in between meetings right now. Let me see if he's on the phone." Standing from her desk, she walks down the hall toward Ethan's office as I direct Anne to take a seat in the waiting area.

"Thank you for doing this," Anne says, reaching for my hand and squeezing it.

"My goal is always to help in the best way I can."

"Amelia?" Ethan questions, pulling my attention to him as he comes around the corner.

I look to Anne as we stand in unison. "Mr. Fuller, this is a client of mine, Anne Lyle."

"Nice to meet you," she says, extending her hand to shake Ethan's.

"Likewise." Curiosity blankets his features as he looks between Anne and me. "Is everything okay?"

"I was hoping you had a moment to speak with Anne. She… she's in need of your services."

Ethan's eyebrows pop up. "Oh. Well, yes, of course. I have a little bit of time right now, actually." He spins toward Yvonne. "Yvonne, can you set us up in the conference room, please?"

"Absolutely."

I watch Yvonne gather some papers and then lead Anne to the room off to our left. I then turn back toward Ethan. "I appreciate you doing this on such short notice. She and I have spoken, and I know this is what's best for her."

"Amelia, are you sure?"

"Yes. We can talk later." Afraid I might lose my composure, I spin on my heels and exit his office without another word, walking back to mine and shifting my mind to my next client, a couple that I know I can help—but that's because it's what they both want.

And even though my chest hurts for Anne, I know she's doing what she wants and needs to, so I have to accept that.

Just before lunch, there's a knock on my door. Ethan texted me earlier and told me he was bringing me lunch so we could talk, so I know it has to be him.

"Hey, babe." He walks through the door and sets the food down on the table before he pulls me into his chest. "You okay?"

"Yeah, I'm fine."

He rears back so his eyes can meet mine. "Are you sure? I'm not gonna lie, Amelia…earlier with Anne? You took me completely by surprise."

"Well, the entire thing surprised me too, but I know it was the best thing for her."

"She's planning on filing for divorce." He lets me go and grabs the food as we settle into the couch and begin eating.

"I know. We talked about it, and it's her decision. And you know what? I don't blame her."

"Really?"

"Her husband is the one that went off on me a few weeks ago, Ethan. He was controlling and just plain mean. And Anne said seeing me was a last resort for her to save the relationship anyway. But why fight for something they both don't want? Why invest any more of your time into someone that doesn't want the same things you do?"

My mind has been reeling with thoughts of Anne all morning, and I know it's not going to stop there.

"Well, you know I have no problem helping her get out." He avoids my gaze while we speak. "But I'm just more worried about how this might affect you."

"Me?"

"Yeah. I mean, I know her husband had you questioning things that day, and now she's choosing divorce."

I stand from the couch, staring down at him. "I'm not against divorce, Ethan. And I know that not all of my clients are going to stay together, as I've had plenty that have separated," I assure him. "Ultimately, I just want to know that she's happy. That's what matters to me."

"Well, she left my office feeling relieved and strong about her decision. I told her to follow up with you, though, if she needs someone to talk to." Ethan stands now and closes the distance between us. "You're sure you're okay?" Wrapping his arms around my waist, he encases me in his embrace, and I feel like I can breathe again.

"Yes, I'm okay."

And then the corner of his mouth lifts up. "Do you realize that we just worked together?"

"You mean combined forces?"

"Yeah, used our superpowers for good."

His metaphor has me laughing. "We did. Look at how far we've come, Ethan." Running my hands through his hair, I stare up into his eyes. "We went from competing and trying to piss each other off to having lunch together in my office and you consoling me out of concern."

With a light press of his lips to mine, he says, "I never thought I'd get this far with another woman again, Amelia. I…my feelings for you…" He takes a deep breath. "They're really fucking strong. Seriously, it scares me how much I enjoy being with you."

"I feel the same way," I reply, rising on my tiptoes and pressing my mouth to his, knowing that he can't say those things and not see a future with me. And as we kiss, I relinquish that last little bit of restraint I was holding onto for my feelings for him.

The past two months of dating Ethan have made me realize everything I was missing before in other relationships. Even though Ethan and I are opposites in many ways, we balance each other out. I can make him smile and relax when I know he struggles with that. He really is an incredible father to his son, which makes him even sexier to me, and I love being able to spend time with him and Oliver together. Our physical connection is unreal as well, something that is extremely important to me because I feel safe and confident with him.

And I know it's early to think this way, but after last weekend when they swam at my house and how Ethan makes me feel every time we're together, all I see is my future with these two guys—they are who I want in my life. It's like those daydreams I had as a little girl are finally becoming a reality, and the man in those visions, whose face was always blurry, is starting to look like Ethan.

"So, do you want to hear something funny that will hopefully turn your day around?" Ethan asks when we part.

"Okay…"

"Now, I just want to preface this story with the notion that what my son did is not your fault."

Now I'm taking a step back from him. "Oh my God, Ethan. What did Oliver do?"

He runs a hand through his hair as we stand there. "I swear to God, nothing can prepare you for the choices that children make sometimes. No parent is equipped to handle this shit, no matter how together you think you have it."

"You're scaring me. Is he okay?" I shriek, borderline manic now, afraid I did something to hurt his kid.

"Calm down. He's fine. I just…" He bites his lip, fighting his laughter. "I got a phone call from Oliver's teacher this morning regarding the story and picture he created the other day in class. Each Monday morning, they share what they did over the weekend, and Oliver recalled how he fell off a spinning pole and hit his head last weekend."

I freeze, my eyes bugging out of my head as my mouth drops open. "No…"

"Yup. My son basically drew a picture of himself looking like a stripper and wrote a sentence or two to back it up."

I fall forward, bracing my hands on my knees as laughter bubbles out of me. "Oh. My. God."

Ethan holds his stomach as he joins me, laughing so hard we can barely breathe. "I swear, I didn't even know what to say. And then I had to explain to her what had happened. I told his teacher that it happened on a jungle gym, not in your house, and I think she bought it. But holy shit…"

"I've traumatized your son, Ethan!"

"No." He shakes his head, still laughing. "He's five, Amelia. He's going to talk about weird shit and tell stories. This isn't the first time he's done something like that. I remember the first time I cussed in front of him in the car. I told some fucker to get out of my way. Then a few days later, we were in the grocery store, and some lady had her cart blocking the aisle, so Oliver said to her, 'Hey, fucker. Get out of the way!'"

"I'm…I don't even know what to say to that." My cheeks hurt from smiling and laughing.

"Same. He was three. But this whole conversation made you laugh, didn't it?"

Nodding, I walk back over to him and throw my arms around his neck. "It did. You have this uncanny ability to make me smile after I feel pretty sad. It's one of my favorite things about you."

"You're welcome. By the way, I was wondering if you'd like to take Oliver to the zoo with me on Sunday? They have—"

"I'll be there."

His eyebrows pop up. "Wow. Just like that, you agree? I thought for sure I'd have to convince you a little more."

I shake my head at him. "Nope. I told you, I'm in this. Plus, it's been years since I've been to the zoo, and the last time I went, it was with the girls. Penelope was drunk by one o'clock, and we were kindly asked to leave when she tried to get the gorilla to hump the glass."

"She's special, isn't she?"

"You have no idea."

Ethan glances over at the clock on my wall. "We have fifteen minutes of lunch left. Care to let me take care of you in another way before I have to get back to work?"

"What did you have in mind?"

He backs me up to my desk, lifting me up and setting me on top of it. "Well, I am still hungry. Perhaps I'll find something to satisfy my appetite down here." And then he slowly lowers himself to the ground, lifts my dress, and makes me come on his tongue, turning my entire day around yet again.

"**A**re you ready to cook dinner for Amelia?" Ethan turns to Oliver as he adjusts his chef's hat on his head.

"Yes, Daddy. Let's make spaghetti."

My cheeks hurt from smiling so much watching the two of them together. It's a Thursday night, and instead of going out, Ethan invited me over to his house so Oliver and he could make me dinner.

How is a woman supposed to say no to that?

Over the past few weeks, we've settled into a routine that I love. On the nights when I don't have my pole dancing classes, we take turns having dinner together at each other's houses or out at a restaurant. I go to Oliver's soccer games each Saturday with Ethan, and then we get gelato afterward. Last weekend we went to the zoo, and I got to experience it through the eyes of a child, which made it ten times better.

I've barely seen the girls except for brunch because any spare moment I have, I just want to be with these boys—*my boys*.

"Have you made spaghetti before, Oliver?" I ask, snapping a picture of the two of them on my phone before placing it upside down on the counter. Reaching for my wine glass, I relax into the back of the stool and admire the sight before me while trying not to cry because I'm just so damn happy.

"Yup. We make spaghetti a lot."

"Hey, it's easy and cheap. Plus, I know you'll eat it, little man."

Oliver nods. "I really like spaghetti."

"Well, it's a good thing because I really like spaghetti too."

"We like a lot of the same things, Amelia," Oliver says as he helps Ethan dump the pasta into the boiling water.

"Yes we do."

"We both like the lemon gelato," he says, and I nod. "We both like the lions at the zoo," he continues as my smile grows. "And now we both like spaghetti."

"That's right. And I bet there's so much more that we both like that we haven't even discovered yet." Oliver hops down from his stool and runs over to me, wrapping his arms around my waist since that's as high as he can reach because I'm on the stool. "Hey, what's this for?"

"I am really happy you're my daddy's girlfriend, Amelia," he mumbles into my side, bringing tears to my eyes instantly.

I lean down and press a kiss to his head. "Me too, buddy."

"And I hope you get to be my new mommy someday." He kisses my stomach and then rushes back over to Ethan, who's standing by the stove, completely stoic.

And I don't even know what to say right now because how are you supposed to respond to that when deep down, you hope the same thing? But Ethan and I haven't spoken about those things yet, and I know better than to offer any glimmer of hope to a kid when I don't have a clear answer to his question.

However, by the look on Ethan's face, I'm guessing that conversation may happen later.

"Okay, Oliver, it's time to start the sauce." Ethan clears his throat and starts to shake the jar of pasta sauce before twisting the lid off. And then I settle back into my chair, sipping my wine and focusing back on the sight before me, one that I hope never gets old.

I watch them finish cooking our meal, and then we all settle around the table to eat like a family. Oliver eats two full plates of spaghetti and only manages to spill noodles on the floor once.

"Dinner was fantastic, boys." I stand from the table and begin to clear the dishes, bringing them over to the sink. "You are incredible chefs."

"I want to be a chef when I grow up," Oliver says. "And a lawyer like Daddy, and a doctor of feelings like you, Amelia. And a firefighter..."

"You are gonna be really busy if that's the case," I reply through a chuckle.

"Oliver, it's time for your bath. And then Daddy is gonna try to catch the second half of the game."

"Okay." Oliver runs down the hallway, and then I hear the bathwater start to run.

"Who's playing tonight?" I ask Ethan as I turn on the sink faucet and begin rinsing dishes.

"New Orleans and Tampa Bay."

"Nice."

Ethan smirks at me. "You don't know who that is, do you?"

"Yes, I do. Remember, I grew up with a father and older brother who love the game. I would watch here and there. I know some stuff, but I'm definitely not a diehard fan." I point a soapy fork at him. "Don't assume things about me, remember, Mr. Fuller?"

Ethan leans over and kisses me on the cheek. "You're just full of surprises, aren't you? And don't worry, I plan on changing your fandom status, for sure…just for the Dallas Cowboys." He moves behind me, wrapping his arms around my waist. "You okay with cleaning up while I supervise Oliver's bath?"

"Absolutely. Go, I've got this."

I feel his lips move up the column of my neck to right under my ear, sparks of energy from his touch racing down my spine as his lips nip at my skin. "I don't know what I did to deserve you."

"I don't know either. Given how much of an ass you were at first, I should have run in the other direction and never turned back."

"I'm glad you didn't though."

"Yeah, me too." I peer at him over my shoulder. "I think you're stuck with me now, Mr. Fuller."

"I think I'm okay with that." Our lips meet again in a chaste peck. "I'll be back out in a few."

"Okay, I'll be here."

As I finish up the dishes, I listen to Ethan and Oliver talking in the bathroom; their random conversations and all of the observations that Oliver makes in a day have me laughing. But as we settle into the couch later with Oliver on the floor below us playing with Legos, I get even more comfortable in this world.

"Sorry the place is a mess, by the way."

My eyes veer around the room. "Nonsense. Don't apologize. There's a life being lived here, Ethan. It's everywhere I turn—the toys on the ground, shoes by the door, drawings on the fridge—they are all details of the child you're raising and a life that I only wish to have one day."

"You want this life?"

I cup the side of his face just as cheering echoes out of the television. But he doesn't turn toward the noise. His eyes stay locked on me. "I do. I want you and Oliver."

He blows out a breath that sounds like relief, but then his eyebrows draw together. "I want that too."

I lean forward and press my lips to his, restraining myself from showing him how I truly feel.

"We can talk more…after Oliver goes to bed."

"Sounds good." Nerves spike in my veins instantly, even though the adrenaline coursing through me is the good kind.

For the next hour, I watch Ethan shout at the television every time there's a bad call made, and he and Oliver jump up and down and cheer when a touchdown is scored. I laugh at their shenanigans as Ethan shows him how to properly celebrate a touchdown with a signature move—Oliver's is roaring like a lion since that seems to be his obsession since the zoo—and Ethan's is a little dance on his tiptoes.

By the time the game is over, it's slightly past Oliver's bedtime, but he insists on one bedtime story instead of his usual three.

"I want Amelia to read to me," he says.

I glance back at Ethan to make sure he's okay with it, and he gives me a nod in return.

"I would love to read to you, Oliver."

We settle into his bed, and I read *Love You Forever*, fighting back tears as I say the words of the story out loud. I've never read this book before, but it should definitely come with a warning that its message will send you into emotional turmoil, especially if you're about to start your period.

When I finish, I close the book as Oliver leans up against me. "I love you forever, Amelia," he whispers as his eyes shut, and then more tears begin to fall.

Closing my eyes, I pull him in closer. "I love you too, Oliver." Kissing him on the head, I slowly slide out of the bed and tuck him under the blankets, just in time to see Ethan standing in the doorway, watching me.

As he closes the door behind us, he leads me to the couch and hands me a tissue. "Are you all right?"

"Um, yeah. I think so. Damn, your kid can lay it on thick."

Ethan laughs, but it's reserved. "Yes, he can." And then he runs a hand through his hair. "He really loves you. He talks about you all the time. I swear, he likes you more than me."

"I love him too, Ethan. I hope it was okay that I said it back… but seriously, he means so much to me. You both do."

"Yes, it's okay." Ethan stands from the couch and then crouches down in front of me, his eyes bouncing back and forth between mine as he smiles. "I'm falling in love with you too, babe…"

"Really?"

"Yeah. I don't know why I keep fighting it. You being here with us just feels right. I should have known you would be the woman to put me in my place in more ways than one."

Laughter leaves my lips, but all I care about in that moment is making sure that Ethan knows I feel the same way. "I love you too, Ethan."

He rises from the couch and climbs over me as I lay down. "I don't deserve you."

"You keep saying that, but yes, you do. You deserve to be happy…and that's what you make me too—happy. My entire world feels more meaningful with you two in it."

Our lips meet in a reverent kiss that I feel in my soul, and in a matter of minutes, our clothes are gone and our bodies are connected.

"Amelia," he groans as we move in sync. Our bodies say so much more than any words we've spoken tonight. "I want to feel you, baby."

"I want that too."

Ethan wastes no time sliding into me without a condom this time, and we both moan as we absorb the new sensation.

He makes love to me on the couch—slow, intense, all-consuming love. Our hands grip and squeeze, our lips move over delicate skin and over each other's mouths, and Ethan builds us both up slowly before we find our release together.

This man has turned my world around in the past four months, him and his son. He's given me the possibility of forever with someone that I feel is my person, the man I'm meant to be with and his child that I'm meant to love—which is why the bomb I discover two days later completely takes me by surprise and threatens all of our happiness, even though I should have seen the warning signs coming from a mile away.

Chapter 15

Amelia

"Amelia, I'm so glad you're here." Ethan's mom, Lisa, greets me when she answers the door.

"Thank you for having me."

"Nonsense. I had to threaten Ethan with bodily harm just so he would invite you over."

"That's not true!" Ethan calls from behind her, walking up to the door, wiping his hands on a dish towel. "Don't listen to her. She'd never harm me. I'm her pride and joy."

"No, Oliver is now," Lisa teases as she takes the bottle of wine from my hands. "Thank you for bringing this."

"Well, Ethan said you're a big wine drinker, and I happen to love a good glass of white wine myself, so I thought I'd bring you one of my favorites."

"That was very thoughtful. Come in. Let's crack this open."

"Perfect. Where's Oliver?"

"Amelia!" Oliver screams as he runs into the house from outside, slamming into my legs as he reaches me. "You're here!"

"I am, buddy. I just saw you earlier though. Did you miss me?"

He peers up at me. "I did," he answers softly and then grabs my hand. "Did the gnomes move at your house?"

"They did. Look!" I crouch down and open up my phone to the newest picture I snapped of them.

"The raccoon must be back."

"I think you're right."

"Wanna come see my playground?" he asks, pulling on my hand again as I stand back up.

"Absolutely."

"You can come swing with me. I know you love the swings." Last night after the three of us went to dinner, we took Oliver to the park to run off some energy, and Oliver and I competed to see who could swing the highest. I let him win, of course, but laughing with him and watching him pump his little legs with determination was the highlight of my week, besides him and his dad telling me that they love me.

"I do. Let's go."

"Wait." Ethan reaches for my hand, preventing me from moving further away from him. He cups my face and leans down to kiss me. "Hey, babe."

"Hey."

"Thanks for coming."

"I'm happy to be here. I missed you."

"It's only been a few hours."

"I know, but it felt like longer."

"I'll be out there in a few, okay? I'm just going to help my mom finish up a few things in the kitchen."

"No worries. Take your time."

"Come on, Amelia," Oliver whines as Ethan places one more kiss on my lips.

"Oliver, you can wait a few minutes for me to say hello to my girlfriend."

"Amelia is my friend too, Daddy."

I ruffle his hair. "Yes I am. Now let me see your playground, Oliver."

The little boy who has stolen my heart leads me out to his swing set, the wooden structure centered in the rather sizable yard. "Did your grandma buy this for you?"

"Yes. She said I needed somewhere to play, and now my friends come over, and we play together." Oliver runs to the swings and situates himself in one as I take a seat next to him.

"Well, she's right, and that was very nice of her."

"My grandma is the best."

"I have a pretty great grandma too."

We spend a good fifteen minutes swinging as Oliver tells me about school, and we recall details from his soccer game earlier.

"I told my teacher about what kind of doctor you are," he says, referencing his play.

"You did?"

"Yup. And she said that I could talk about it during my part if I wanted to."

Pride soars through me. "I can't wait to see it."

"What's going on, you two?" Ethan stalks toward us, looking calm and collected. His hair wafts in the wind a bit, but his smile spreads from ear to ear as he approaches me.

"We were just talking about school and soccer. He played a great game today."

"Yeah, you did, Oliver."

"I should practice some more right now," he declares, jumping from the swing and running over to his soccer ball on the small patch of grass.

"Does he ever stop moving?" I jokingly ask as Ethan comes up behind me and places his hands on my shoulders, massaging me.

"Nope."

"Do you and your mom need any help in the kitchen?"

"Everything should be good now, but I do know that she was waiting for you to crack open the bottle of wine."

I take a deep breath and then stand from the swing. "Well, I guess there's no time like the present."

"Don't worry. Just be yourself, babe. She's not gonna drill you. That's not her style. She just wants to know you better."

"That's understandable. I know we've met a handful of times, but we haven't really been able to talk."

He kisses me on the lips and then smacks my ass. "We'll be out here when you two are done."

"Did you just smack my ass at your mom's house?"

"Yeah, I did. What are you gonna do about it?"

I narrow my eyes at him as I walk backward toward the house. "I don't know yet, but don't worry…I'm sure I can think of something."

"Looking forward to seeing what you come up with," he challenges as I shake my head at him and walk back up to the house.

"Lisa?" I ask as I step inside.

"Hi, Amelia." I turn to my right to find her in the kitchen, chopping up some vegetables for a salad. "I poured you a glass of that wine."

"Thank you." I take a seat at the counter across from where she's working and intercept the glass. "And thank you for having me here."

"It's my pleasure, truly." She sets down the knife and reaches for her glass of wine as well. "Amelia, my son and Oliver are my entire world."

"I understand."

"And I just want them to be happy."

"I want that too."

She smiles. "I can tell. I worried about Ethan after Monica left. He closed himself off so much, became jaded, and only focused on work and his son. But you've changed that."

"He's changed my life too."

"He smiles, and he laughs again. He talks about you and makes plans…"

"We've come a long way since we first met."

She laughs. "Yes, he's told me a little about that. And Oliver loves you. Seriously, he talks about you all the time."

"I think I fell for him before I fell for Ethan."

"Are you in love with my son, Amelia?"

Swallowing down the emotion I feel, I nod. "I am."

"I think he's in love with you too."

"He told me so the other night." She holds her wine close to her chest as she listens. "He knows how serious I am about them, and I know that being a part of their lives comes with expectations, and the last thing I want to do is let them down, Lisa. I see my future with them."

She licks her lips and nods at me. "Then I hope this is the start of many dinners with all of us together." Raising her glass toward me, we knock them together lightly before taking a sip of the crisp liquid. "Now, tell me more about yourself…"

After we eat dinner, I insist on cleaning the dishes. It's the least I can do after Lisa made an incredible meal. The spinach and artichoke chicken was so good that I overate because I didn't want to waste a bite. And then I begged her for the recipe.

"I really love her," Lisa's voice echoes out from the hallway.

Eavesdropping on their conversation wasn't on my list of things to do, but of course, my curiosity wins. And knowing that Lisa accepts me makes me feel even more content with where I'm at in my life at this moment.

"I love her too. She's amazing, Mom."

"I'm so happy you get a second chance, honey. And not later in life like I did, but right now when the three of you can be a family. That woman is the one you marry, Ethan."

There's a pause in his voice, which has my heart rate picking up. "I'm—I'm not getting married again, Mom."

And then my stomach drops.

"What? Why?"

"I think of all people you would understand why."

"Because of what happened with Monica? Ethan, you and Monica were doomed from the start, honey. And she's the one who chose to walk away, not you."

"I know. But I have no desire to go through another divorce again, Mom. I mean, look at what I see on a daily basis. Besides, Amelia and I don't have to be married in order to be happy. We can be one-hundred percent committed to each other without that piece of paper."

I feel like someone just stabbed me in my gut and then twisted the knife around.

Is this really how he feels? I mean, I'm hearing the words he's saying, but his actions speak so differently. And he told me he loves me...why would he say that if he didn't see us together down the line?

Part of me shouldn't be shocked by this revelation, but another part feels like someone just took my future from me and ripped it to shreds.

"She's incredible with Oliver. I seriously couldn't have asked for anyone better to accept my son. But I just can't go through that again—the dividing of assets, the cost, the stress, and feelings of failure."

"Maybe you'll change your mind. That woman is one in a million, Ethan, and she told me she sees a future with you. Does she know how you feel?"

"Not exactly," he answers honestly, but I feel completely blind-sided right now, followed by irritation building in my chest. This is something he should have brought up a long time ago if it's really how he feels.

I see clients in second and third marriages still trying to make their relationships work. I know it can be done, and people can find happiness and true love the second time around.

But apparently, Ethan doesn't believe that can happen to him, or with me.

"Well, you need to tell her if this is what you want. But I don't think you're being honest with yourself about how you feel about her. Not all marriages end in divorce, honey. There's a reason why some last for a lifetime, and that's because two people found the right person to make it work. Monica was not your person. But I truly think Amelia is."

"It's not just about that, Mom. It's about the fact that divorce is messy. And when shit hits the fan, love can't save you. In fact, I've seen it turn so ugly that people question why they ever married the other person in the first place, even after twenty or thirty years. I don't want to ever feel that way about her."

"Sounds like you've given this a lot of thought."

"I have. I care about her. I love her. But I don't want to be married again."

"Then you need to tell her because it's not fair to lead her on if you're not going to give her what she wants out of life."

"I will, I just haven't had the chance."

Haven't had the chance? Wouldn't a few nights ago been the perfect time to tell me this before you told me that you loved me? Or before you agreed to date me in the first place?

Rage and hurt run through me as my mind spins with this revelation.

"This isn't something to put off, Ethan. That woman deserves to know…unless you think you might change your mind down the road."

"I…I honestly don't know if I will. I want to, but after my divorce was final, I made the decision that I would never marry again, and it's hard to move back on a decision like that."

Before I realize it, my hand is frozen in mid-air, and I'm staring out the window above the sink, looking intently at the patio lights blinking outside as I come back to reality.

What the hell do I do now? Do I say something and let him know I overheard him, running the risk of having a conversation that may not end the way I want it to? Or do I bank on the fact that he might change his mind one day, keyword being might?

Instantly my mind veers into therapist mode as if I'm handling a crisis. What would I tell my client in this position?

You would tell her to have the tough conversation because then there's nothing left to ponder. It's better to know where you stand with someone than waste time in your life hoping for them to change their mind and then regret not walking away and finding someone who wants the same things you do. You would tell her that part of taking control of your life is not letting people use you and then wonder why you let them go down that road. You would tell her to consider the alternative if you didn't speak up and ask yourself if you're willing to live with those consequences.

Taking a deep breath, I place the rag back in the sink of hot water and wipe my hands on a towel, knowing what I need to do.

"I can't believe you're willing to gamble your chance at a life with her," Lisa says as I turn the corner, tucking a curl behind my ear.

"Ethan?" Both of their eyes flash to me, wide with alarm. "I think we need to talk."

"Oh, shit," Lisa says, frantic within a second. "Amelia, I'm sorry if you overheard that…"

I hold up my hand. "No, it's probably better that I did. I think it's time for me to go. I'm just going to say goodbye to Oliver really quick."

I grab my purse and hold back my tears as I enter the backyard to find Oliver swinging again, talking to the neighbor kid over the fence. "Oliver, I have to leave."

He jumps from the swing and runs over to me. "But we haven't had dessert yet."

"I know," I say, brushing his hair from his face. "But I have something to do that I forgot about."

"Will I see you tomorrow?" he asks, his eyes begging for answers that I can't give him right now.

"I don't know. But I promise we'll see each other soon." *Don't make promises you can't keep, Amelia.*

Wrapping his arms around my legs, he gives me a hug. "Okay. Bye, Amelia. I love you."

Choking back a sob, I say, "I love you too."

I re-enter the house and make eye contact with Ethan long enough for him to see me head for the front door. "Thank you again, Lisa, for the invitation."

"It was a pleasure, Amelia. I hope to see you again soon. And I'm sorry…"

"Yeah, me too."

Walking down to the sidewalk where my car is parked, I place my purse inside and turn to find Ethan standing right behind me. We don't say anything for a while, searching each other's eyes as I ponder what to say before I finally speak up, anger fueling my words now to mask my hurt. "So, are we going to talk about what I overheard?"

"What did you hear exactly?"

"Everything. Particularly how you never want to get married again."

Ethan shrugs, acting angry right back at me. "Well, what do you want me to say? That's how I feel. Although right now, I'm fucking pissed that my mother brought this up, and I wasn't able to talk to you alone about it."

"Yeah, me too." I point a finger at my chest. "I feel blindsided right now, Ethan, and really fucking confused. Why on earth would you tell me you love me before telling me that you don't ever want to be married again?"

"Because I do love you. You've become someone I want in my

life long-term. But you can't tell me that you're actually surprised by this fact, can you?"

"Well, you shouldn't be surprised that marriage is something that I want. When I said I see my future with you and Oliver, I meant as your wife someday."

"Look at what I do for a living, Amelia," he says, raising his voice and fanning his arms out to the side. "I watch people fight and get nasty with each other, with the people they vowed to love forever. And my own wife and the mother of my kid walked out on him and me. Why on earth would I ever want to do that again?"

"So why even date me then?"

He takes a step closer, but I retreat slightly, making him pause. "Because I do care about you. I do love you. I couldn't help but fall for you, and I want you in my life. I just can't risk going through a divorce again. And I can't do that to Oliver either. He's already had one woman walk out on him..."

"So, we're not worth the risk? Do you honestly think I would do that to you and Oliver? That I wouldn't do everything in my power to make our relationship work after what I witness on a daily basis?"

"You've never been married, Amelia, or had a child of your own. You can't possibly understand what's going through my mind right now or why I feel this way."

He might as well have slapped me across the face. "How dare you," I grate out between clenched teeth. "I don't have to have experienced the same things as you in order to be compassionate or to support you. All I'm asking is for you to pause for a moment before you throw away something really good because you're scared."

"I'm not throwing you away. I still want you. You're just thinking too far into the future. Believe me, a piece of paper isn't going to change how I feel about you. And I think over time, you'll see that."

"No. I *want* to think about my future, Ethan. I want to know that I'm investing time with someone who wants the same things I do. I want a family of my own, my own children to love and care for, and a husband that I promise to love until we take our last breaths. And you don't want that, so what the hell are we doing?"

"We're spending time together…"

"And I love the times when we're together, I do." I place my hands over my heart, trying to guard it against what's happening. "But I want more eventually. I want a commitment. And I shouldn't have to sacrifice that to be with you, Ethan. Is that what you're asking me to do?"

"I'm committed to you. That's not going to change." He reaches up and pulls on his hair. "Can we just…can we talk about this later? This is…this isn't how I envisioned this night going. You were supposed to come home with Oliver and me. I wanted to lie down next to you in my bed…" he says, his voice almost pleading now. And then he closes the distance between us, grabbing my hands and holding them over his heart. "You'll see. Nothing will be different between us if we don't get married one day. You might change your mind about needing that title."

"Well, are you going to change yours?" I can literally feel my heart start to break as he stands there silently and doesn't say a word. So I lower my voice, fighting back emotions threatening to bubble over right now. "I've done everything in my life to make others happy, Ethan, even helped other people repair their marriages, and I deserve to have one of my own. I want that, and I believe that people can be happily married for the rest of their lives. But if you can't see that taking that risk with me is worth it, then I don't want to waste any more of my time." I pull my hands from his as he steps back, his entire demeanor shifting from pleading to resolute.

"This is what I can give you, Amelia," he says coldly, flicking a switch right in front of me.

"Well, it's not enough. I'm sorry. It's not fair that you're punishing me for Monica's choices or using your experiences as an excuse not to want more for your life and Oliver's. I would do anything for you two, and I've done nothing but show you that. But until you can see that and accept it, I don't think we should see each other anymore."

"Amelia," he whispers as I round the hood of my car and hop inside. But I don't say another word, giving him only one last glance before driving away, breaking down the second I pull into my drive-way, wishing I had never let him in.

I should have known better than to fall for the divorce lawyer across the complex, the one who doesn't believe in marriage. But the worst part is, I fell in love with his son, too, and now the future I thought I saw has vanished just as quickly as it appeared.

Chapter 16

Amelia

Charlotte: *Are you coming to brunch?*

I toss my phone on the coffee table and pick up the tube of cookie dough again, gnawing on the end as another tear falls from my eye.

It's Sunday morning, and I should be at Frankie's right now drowning my sorrow in mimosas and commiserating with my best friends about the bomb that Ethan dropped on me last night. But I haven't left my couch since I ran through my door and threw myself down on it as soon as I got home—well, except to retrieve the tube of cookie dough from the fridge to drown my sorrows in about five minutes ago.

Staring up at the ceiling, I replay the last few weeks on repeat in my mind, torturing myself with how happy I was just a few days ago to how I ended up here now, alone and miserable, missing the boy and the man that had me thinking I had found my future.

But look at how wrong I was...

On the outside, everyone would assume I have a handle on my life. I feel like I'm on solid ground in every facet, except for when it comes to love. Hell, I even advised my best friend to put boundaries in place when she decided to enter into a fake relationship because I know that's what you should do. But when it came time for me to do the same, I threw caution to the wind and did whatever I felt like doing in the moment as soon as Ethan entered my life. I acted impulsively. I sacrificed who I was and who I knew he was for the chance to be with him, hoping at the same time that I could change his mind and we could create something unique and powerful.

Being with him was unlike any other relationship I'd been in. He was addicting, even in the worst ways, with his commanding and irrational persona. But then, those were the same qualities that made me feel wanted and desired by him, a feeling any woman can relate to. But when I found out he was divorced and had a child, it seemed like all the versions he showed me of himself made sense. And when he opened up to me, I saw how beautiful of a man he truly was—until he shattered my heart last night.

Throughout my twenties, I prided myself on using a list of criteria for how I would pick my men—not too loud, agreeable and not argumentative, good-looking but not hot—and I rarely ended up hurt, while many of my friends, including the girls, would nurse indescribable heartbreak.

I always picked the safe guy, the one with very few red flags, or any flags, that made him addicting or gave him the power to destroy me.

Now I realize that Ethan was the exception to all of my rules. He was the type of man I had been avoiding my entire life because I knew the devastation he could render if I let him. And boy, did he do one hell of a job breaking me apart.

I lose track of how long I stare up at the ceiling before I hear a knock on my door.

"Amelia! Open up!" More banging. "I swear, you'd better have a good excuse for missing brunch!" Charlotte shouts as I groan, roll off the couch, and head for the door. "You'd better be sick or…" Her words stop as soon as I open the door and she sees me, Noelle and Penelope standing right behind her. "Oh hell…"

I take another bite out of the tube of cookie dough, and then my lips start to tremble. "I'm sorry I missed brunch, okay? I just…"

Charlotte rushes toward me, encasing me in her arms as pieces of cookie dough fall out of my mouth while I sob. I don't know what I was thinking, not letting my friends be there for me, but I just couldn't leave my house today. Not today…

"Amelia?" Penelope asks beside me, rubbing my back. "My little Be Delia, what's wrong?"

"I…Ethan…Oliver…"

"I think she's trying to tell us something," Penelope says mockingly as Noelle reaches for the tube of cookie dough from my hand, removing it slowly.

"Ya think?" Charlotte moves us further into my house, and I hear the front door shut, but I cling to her for dear life while we continue to stand there, avoiding lifting my head to look at them. My friends let me have my moment, the same way I would do for them because sometimes you just need to cry out everything you're feeling.

When I finally feel like I've gained some composure, I raise my head and breathe in a shaky breath. "Ethan and I broke up last night."

"What?" they all say in unison as we move to the couch, and I take the tube of cookie dough back from Noelle.

"Start from the beginning, babe," Charlotte suggests, continuing to rub my back from the side where's she's sitting next to me.

I spend the next several minutes filling them in on the last week since, as of last Sunday at brunch, I was boasting about how in love with Ethan I was and all the things we had planned together in the coming weeks.

"You heard him actually say he never wants to get married again?" Noelle confirms.

"Yes. And we both told each other where we stand, so what was I supposed to do?"

"I mean, I get what you're saying, and hell, I even agree with what you did. You stood up for yourself and what you want. But do you honestly think you two can't work this out?" Charlotte asks.

"How do you work this out? He doesn't want to get married ever again, and I do." I shake my head, letting a few tears run again. "The thing is, deep down, I knew he might feel this way. It would only make sense, but I didn't want to believe it. I wanted to have faith that things would be different between him and me, that the way he felt about me would be stronger than his fear and disdain toward marriage. But I was wrong, and now I just feel…" Taking a deep breath, I admit what's causing me the most heartache right now, "Stupid."

"Look, you convinced yourself that you would be the woman to make him change. Any woman can tell you that they've been there a time or two with a guy," Penelope says, and the other two girls nod in agreement.

Hell, I've had many clients think the same, so I know I'm not alone, but it doesn't make me feel better at the moment.

"Letting yourself get wrapped up in Ethan doesn't make you a failure, Amelia. It doesn't make you any less of a professional or a woman. It just makes you human."

"Yeah, well, this side of being human sucks." I chomp the tube of cookie dough again as Noelle winces.

"You know there's actual edible cookie dough you can eat now, right? The kind that doesn't come with the risk of contracting salmonella?"

"Newsflash, Noelle. We've all been eating raw cookie dough our entire lives, and only a rare few have died from it. I take the risk." I gnaw at the end of the tube again, crunching down on the chocolate chips as they hit my teeth, trying to find solace in the sugar but having no such luck.

"Sorry. I'm just trying to look out for you."

And then something internally snaps. "I wish I had been looking out for myself!" I shout, flinging my arms to the side as a chocolate chip goes flying across the room. "I should have known better. I should have listened to my gut when it told me that getting involved with him would only lead to heartbreak."

"Even though you're scaring me a bit right now, Amelia, like you might be on the verge of a nervous breakdown, I support you, girl," Penelope declares. "Let it out, sister."

"I should have never said sorry to Ethan for walking away." I grow more emotional again within seconds, the emotional roller-coaster I'm on sending me up and down hills of feelings. "He's the one that drew a line in the sand. He's the one that put the limit on what we could be. And because I want more, I'm supposed to apologize? Fuck that."

"Oh, Amelia's cussing! I love it!" Penelope claps her hands as she bounces up and down in her seat.

"I'm just so angry and mad, and..." Here come the sobs again. "Sad, you guys. I'm really freaking sad. I...I love him. I love his son. I thought I found the one, and now..."

Charlotte pulls me into her chest as chocolate drool falls out of my mouth, and Noelle grabs the cookie dough again. "Shhhh. It's okay, Amelia. It's okay. We're here. Cry it out, honey. It's gonna be okay..."

And that's the last thing I remember before I fall asleep on my friend.

Monday morning comes, and even though I want nothing to do with going to work, it's too late to reschedule any of my clients. Besides, I think the distraction might be good and get my mind off things.

The girls stayed until seven last night, making sure I took a shower, putting eye patches under my eyes to help with the swelling from crying, and making sure I ate something besides cookie dough for dinner, even though I really didn't have that much of an appetite.

Nonetheless, without their encouragement and support, I don't know that I would be standing today, even though I'm barely coherent if I'm being honest.

And the worst part is, I know I might see Ethan at some point, and I'm not sure how I'm going to handle it.

I make it through the morning without crossing paths with him and, like I thought, having my client sessions helps keep my mind off the situation. Even though I'm sitting here helping people repair their marriages when I know my relationship can't be repaired and that still freaking stings. But it's my job, so I'm going to use work as a distraction as best I can for as long as it helps.

However, right before noon, there's a knock on my door that has my heart rate jump starting.

Slowly rising from my desk, I walk to the door and peek through the curtains to see Ethan standing there. I don't move or make a sound because I don't want to talk to him. Seeing him, hearing what he has to say, is only going to confuse me, even though knowing he's out there has me missing him even more.

How am I going to get through this?

I know I made the right decision by standing up for myself and what I want out of my life. I never considered myself to be someone to sacrifice my dreams for a man, and I'm not going to start being that woman now, no matter how much I love the man and his son.

"Amelia? I know you're in there." He knocks lightly again. "Can we talk, please?"

I hold my breath as I contemplate a reply. "I don't think that's a good idea, Ethan. We said what we needed the other night."

"I won't take much of your time, I swear. It's about Oliver."

Fuck, really? He wants to use his son as bait? Would he really do that?

Deep down I know the answer is no.

Inhaling a breath of courage, I unlock my door and open it up to find Ethan looking about as haggard as I feel. His tie is gone, his shirt wrinkled, and the bags under his eyes are just as bad as mine.

"Amelia…" he breathes out, swallowing hard. "You look…"

I hold my hand up, cutting him off. "Don't. What did you need to speak with me about, Ethan? About your son?"

"Oliver wanted to know if you would be at his last game this

Saturday, and I…" He shoves his hands in his pockets. "I didn't know what to say to him."

"I'll be there," I reply soundly.

"You will?"

"Yes, Ethan. I told you that I would never lie to him. I promised I would attend his games and his play, so I plan to make good on those promises. Oliver doesn't deserve being let down just because you and I aren't together anymore."

He takes a step toward me, but I take one back. "Please, can we talk about the other night?"

I hold up a shaky hand. "No. We said all that we needed to say. You were very clear…"

"I love you, Amelia," he says, pleading with his voice.

"People that love you care about how they make you feel, Ethan. The end. You made me feel disposable like you were using me for what you wanted but weren't ever willing to let me in completely. And I don't deserve that."

"I wasn't using you. I just…"

"I'll be at Oliver's game, Ethan. Tell him to look for me. But please don't come by here again. I need space from you so I can move on."

"Move on?"

"Yes, someday. Not now because it's going to take me a long time to get over you. But one day, I want to find someone who wants the same things I do, and I can't do that if you keep inserting yourself into my life." I reach for the door and start to close it slowly.

"Amelia, don't do this."

"I didn't end this, Ethan. You did." Clicking the door in place, I inhale a shaky breath and then cover my mouth as a sob runs through me. And I let myself feel everything at that moment—the disappointment, the anger, the sadness, and the love I still feel for him. It's going to take me a long time to be ready to find that with someone else, but I have faith that I can. I have to believe that—otherwise, I don't want to think about the alternative.

L eaning up against a tree, I remain far enough from the sideline that I'm not in close proximity to Ethan but close enough that Oliver can see me standing there at his game, cheering him on.

It's been a hell of a week, a very long week of avoiding Ethan around the complex and dodging his calls. I'm not sure what he thought would happen if I picked up the phone the two times he felt brave enough to dial my number. Nothing has changed as far as I know, and one week isn't enough time to come to that sort of epiphany anyway.

"Go Oliver!" I shout as he races down the field with the ball, taking a shot at the goal but missing it narrowly. Seriously, the kid has skills, and I'm going to miss watching him play and seeing him progress as he gets older, something I didn't realize until just now. I'm going to miss out on his entire life.

"Amelia." A familiar voice to my left has me twisting my head to find Lisa, Ethan's mom, standing there fumbling with her hands in front of her.

"Hi, Lisa."

"Hi, sweetie. How are you?" she asks with a tilt of her head.

"Oh, I've been better. But I'm still standing."

She sucks in her bottom lip. "You're not the only one suffering, honey. First, I want you to know how sorry I am for having that conversation with my son while you were in the house…"

"You don't have to apologize to me for speaking with him in your home, Lisa. And you actually did me a favor. It's better that I found out how he feels now than years down the line."

"But that's the thing, Amelia, I don't think my son feels that way at all. I know he's just scared. And believe me, he's hurting too. He misses you, and so does Oliver."

I choke back tears. "I miss them too, Lisa, but it doesn't change anything. Ethan was clear about what he wants, and I can't settle."

She nods. "I understand that more than you know. It's partly my fault, really."

"Why do you say that?"

"Because Ethan is a product of divorce. His father and I separated when he was just two, and then Monica left just after Oliver turned three. He's never seen an example of a healthy relationship, of two people who fight for one another and genuinely love each other. I have a man in my life now, but it's too late for that to help change the way he feels."

"I'm sorry that you've experienced divorce as well, Lisa. But Ethan has decided not to try again even with the right person, and that's his choice. I think if he really considered what's at stake, he would find that being alone is worse than the probability of committing to someone again who would do everything in their power not to hurt him, especially someone who isn't his ex-wife."

"You're right. And I know I have no business saying this," she says, reaching for my hand and squeezing it. "But please don't write him off. I know my son, and I know what he feels for you. He just needs to figure it out, and once he does, he will be the most loyal man, the way he is as a father to his son. I know he wants to take the chance with you, he just needs to come to that realization on his own."

Her words offer me a sliver of hope, one I haven't felt this entire week apart from him. But would I be stupid to believe in that possibility when I'm still so fragile from the hurt he caused?

"Don't say anything. I know I'm asking a lot. But just promise me you'll think about it, and please accept my apology again."

"I'll miss you, Lisa." Pulling her in for a hug, I hold her close for a few moments before releasing her, not wanting to give her false hope, but hopefully some closure.

"This isn't the last you'll be seeing of me, Amelia." And with a knowing smile, she returns to the sideline next to her son, who casts me yet another glance over his shoulder.

Ethan has looked in my direction five times since I arrived at the game earlier, and each time the length of his stare gets longer. But I can't get a read on what he's thinking, even though it shouldn't matter. I'm not here for him. I'm here for Oliver.

"Amelia!" Oliver runs up to me as soon as the game ends, plowing into my legs.

"Hey, buddy." Tears well in my eyes as I bend down and hug him tightly. "God, I've missed you."

"I miss you too! Where have you been?" he asks as we part. "You haven't been over for dinner, and Daddy hasn't shown me any pictures of your gnomes."

"I've been busy, kiddo," I grate out against the emotion clogging my throat. "But I do have a picture to show you." Reaching behind me, I grab my phone from the back pocket of my jean shorts and open it up to the picture I snapped yesterday in anticipation of his question.

"Why are they apart?" Oliver asks as we stare at the picture of the gnomes that are separated on either side of my office door now.

"I don't know. Maybe they decided to spread out from each other, take a break and protect themselves for a while."

Oliver's face scrunches up. "That doesn't make sense though. They would work better as a team if they were together."

"Yeah, they would." Ethan's deep voice above me interrupts our conversation as I stand to take him in. He's so handsome, it literally makes my heart hurt. Under the bill of his ball cap, his eyes burn a hole through me, almost as if he's mad that I'm here or that he wants me just as badly as I want him.

My body hasn't quite gotten the memo yet that there will be no more physical interaction with this man, but I'm working on it—slowly.

"You played such a great game, though, Oliver. I can't believe the season is over."

"I'm gonna miss my teammates," he says. "But I do see some of them at school, so we can still play together. It's nice that I get to see them every day." And then his thoughts switch gears like the flick of a switch. "The play is this week. Are you still coming?"

"Yes, I'll be there. I wouldn't miss it."

"See? I told you she'd be there, Oliver," Ethan confirms.

"Are you coming to get gelato with us too?" Oliver looks up at me, his eyes wide with anticipation. I cast a glance in Ethan's direction to gauge his reaction, but he doesn't give me any direction.

"Not today, buddy. I have somewhere I have to be, but I wouldn't have missed your game. I'm so proud of you." Giving him one more hug, I stand and then prepare to leave. Lisa takes Oliver back to his team, and I begin to walk away, but I feel someone grab my hand before I get too far.

"Amelia, wait."

"Please don't do this here, Ethan."

"I just wanted to say thank you… for showing up."

"I told you I would. I don't break my promises, especially to your son."

"I appreciate that, truly. But how much longer are you going to show up?"

"What do you mean?"

"I mean, today it was his game, next week it's the play, but after that?"

"Well, I guess it just depends on what he asks me to go to. I love your kid, so if he wants me there for anything, I'll be there."

"Amelia, how can you not see that we're supposed to be together?" he whispers, running his thumb over the top of my hand.

"I could ask you the same question, Ethan," I reply, retracting my hand from his grip. And then I walk away, leaving another piece of my heart behind with him.

"Okay. Her hair is brushed, she's wearing something besides sweatpants, and she's on time. Those are all good signs."

I take my seat at our table at Frankie's as Penelope assesses my appearance out loud. Reaching for my mimosa, I take a large drink before I reply. "I'm here, and yes, I may look all right on the outside, but I am far from okay, you guys." The threat of tears comes forward, which shouldn't surprise me since I basically feel like I could cry all day right now.

Charlotte rubs my back with her hand since she's sitting next to me. "Talk to us. Tell us what's going on."

I blow out a breath. "I went to Oliver's soccer game yesterday because I promised him that I would go to all of his games, and you know how I feel about keeping my word," I explain to my girls as they all nod. "Well, Ethan's mom came up and talked to me, asked me not to give up on him. But it's easier just to be mad at him than keep a sliver of hope alive inside." I reach up and rub my chest right over my heart as the tears cloud my vision. "My heart just aches, you guys. Constantly. Every time I see him at work, or he pleads with me to reconsider. I just want to scream and cry."

"He asked you to reconsider what?" Noelle asks.

"Yesterday, he grabbed my arm before I could walk away completely and asked me why I couldn't see that we belonged together."

"And what did you say back?"

"I told him that I could ask him the same question."

Penelope claps her hands. "Nice comeback."

"I thought so too, because it's true. If he would only get past his fear, we could work through it."

"Men and their freaking fear," Noelle speaks with a roll of her eyes. "I've read so many books where men do stupid shit out of fear, and you just want to slap them upside the head, shake them by the shoulders, and tell them to stop letting their lives pass them up because they're freaking scared. And the reality is, men in real life do the same shit."

"Believe me, I want to. But I don't want him to change his mind because I convince him to. He has to arrive at that realization on his own. And his mother seems to think he will."

"Well, she knows him better than anyone. Do you think she's right?"

"I don't know. I want to believe it, but a part of me won't let myself. The thing is, I have to be near him again this Friday at Oliver's play." I told the girls about his play once Oliver told me about it and how he's so excited to be a doctor.

"That's this week? Isn't the newspaper dinner this week too?" Penelope asks, opening her phone and looking at her calendar. "You girls and all of your dinners…I can't keep up."

Last week was Charlotte's awards dinner, where she was recognized as a Mover and Shaker in Los Angeles by the mayor. Naturally, we all attended, but I was in such a daze, and I feel bad that I wasn't more mentally present.

"No, it's next Tuesday."

Penelope nods. "Okay, that's what I have. Forgive me, but there's a lot going on at work right now, and I'm having a hard time keeping everything straight. You should see the number of emails waiting in my inbox when this brunch is over."

"You girls will still be there, right?"

Charlotte scoffs. "Um, duh. As if we would miss it."

I smile, but it doesn't reach my eyes. Nothing seems to bring me an insurmountable amount of joy lately, not like Oliver and Ethan did. "Okay."

Penelope winces. "God, Amelia. You're like oozing sadness and depression right now, and I don't like it."

"Well, this is the Amelia you get right now," I reply, fanning my hand down my body.

"Your sunshine is gone. You're the one always looking for the bright side in everything, the voice of reason for the rest of us. It's like a piece of my friend is missing."

Her words bring on more tears. "Well, it does feel like a piece of me is missing. I can't even laugh right now, guys. I tried watching a comedy special last night on Netflix to take my mind off things, and

I barely laughed. Although, the comedian was talking about all of her horrible dating stories, and all it did was remind me that my life will be back to that point one day again—going on terrible first dates, wondering if I'll ever find a man that I feel as strongly about as I felt about Ethan."

Noelle grabs my hand. "Maybe you and I can take a stand together—no more bad dating. Come to the sperm bank with me, go shopping for a man without ever having to talk to him, and let's have babies together." Her eyes light up with excitement.

"I'm not quite at that point yet, but I will definitely keep it in mind."

Penelope interjects. "Are you still doing your pole dancing classes?"

Shaking my head, I reach for my drink again. "I haven't been in two weeks. I should go because exercise is a natural antidepressant and helps regulate anxiety, which I have a ton of at the moment. But all it does is remind me of the dance I did for Ethan a few weeks ago, which just makes me cry again."

Her brows lift. "You stripped for him? Spun around on a pole, ripped off your clothes, and he still won't marry you?" She shakes her head. "What the fuck is wrong with him?" And her surprise turns to irritation almost instantly. "Shit like that makes me want to send him three hundred of something again. What could I send?" She taps her chin in thought before opening up her phone to search for ideas. "Stink bombs? Spring-loaded glitter bombs? Penis gummies?" She keeps scrolling through her phone as I let out a small chuckle.

"I know. Even the ability to spin on a stripper pole isn't enough to make a man fall in love and want to marry you anymore, ladies. And if that's the case, then I guess we're doomed from the start."

We share a laugh, and then Charlotte clears her throat. "Well, I have some news, but I'm kind of scared to share it right now."

"Why?" Noelle asks.

"I don't want to upset Amelia." She turns to me.

"Why would you upset me?"

"Well, I know you're mending a broken heart right now, but my love life is taking off, and the last thing I want is to make you feel worse."

I grab her hand. "You should know me better than to think I could possibly be mad at you for being happy, Charlotte. I know what you've gone through to get where you are, and even though I'm not where I want to be, that doesn't mean I can't celebrate moments in your life."

She fights back a few tears. "Okay. I just wanted to make sure." She releases my hand and digs through her purse, pulling out a massive diamond ring and sliding it onto her finger. "Damien asked me to marry him after the Movers and Shakers dinner Thursday night, and I said yes."

"Oh my God!" Noelle screams as Penelope yanks her hand toward her to inspect the ring. And my tears flow harder as a slice of jealousy races through me, but I still feel overwhelming happiness for my friend.

"Two-and-a-half carats, easy." Penelope squints down at the diamond. "Fourteen-karat white gold. He did good, my dear." She releases Charlotte's hand and grabs her mimosa, taking a sip with a smile on her face.

"Let me see!" Noelle inspects the ring this time as Charlotte turns to me.

"I'm so happy for you, Char. I mean it."

She reaches up and wipes a tear from my cheek, holding her

palm there. "Thank you. And I know you feel like your future was ripped away from you right now, but I'm telling you—my gut tells me this thing with Ethan isn't over yet, babe. Just give it time."

"I appreciate that, but right now, let's focus on the fact that at least one of us is getting our happily ever after." I reach for my mimosa as the other girls follow suit. "To Charlotte and Damien. May you two know long-lasting love and happiness. And if you need a marriage counselor at any point, I know someone." We all laugh in unison.

"To childhood enemies turned fake relationship turned lovers. What a romance novel in the making!" Noelle continues.

And, of course, in true Penelope fashion, she gets the last word. "To what every woman deserves: her king, a ring, and a good ding-a-ling."

"**W**here's Ethan?"

It's Sunday night, and after brunch this morning and a nap this afternoon, that means I'm at my parents' house for our monthly family dinner, minus my boyfriend because I haven't told them that Ethan and I are no longer together.

"Um, he won't be coming."

"Did something happen with Oliver?" my mother asks, genuinely concerned.

"No. Something happened with us."

She turns around and stares at me—and like the good mother she is, it doesn't take her long to cross the kitchen and pull me into her arms once she realizes the meaning of my words. "I'm so sorry, Amelia."

It's been a few hours since I've cried, but the tears still flow pretty easily. "It's okay. It's better this way."

"What happened?"

I fill her in on the conversation that led to our breakup, and all she does is nod her head along as I speak. "Well, you did the right thing. There's no sense in wasting your life with someone that doesn't want the same things as you."

"I know."

"In all honesty, I was scared this might happen once he told us he was divorced. You have to remember that not everyone has the same desire as you to work on the relationships in their lives. There are some people that never figure that out either, Amelia. And if I'm being honest, if it weren't for your push when you were younger, I don't know what would have become of your father and me."

"Mom..."

She holds up her hand, cutting me off. "You deserve someone who will fight for you and with you for your relationship, sweetie. And I'm sad for you that he wasn't it. It breaks my heart to know that you're hurting."

"I am, but I'll be okay." At least, I hope so, although that doesn't feel very promising at the moment.

"Yes, you will because you are Amelia St. Clair, and only the right man will realize what a treasure you are when he has you. Unfortunately, Ethan wasn't that guy. Or apparently he's not ready to be him." She sighs. "That was what I went through with your father when we separated, remember?"

"Yes."

"I was so convinced he wouldn't listen to what I had to say that we both just let our relationship dissolve. But ultimately, he also needed things that he was too scared to vocalize. There are so many facets to a marriage, Amelia…"

"I know, Mom."

"You do, but you don't. Counseling couples and being part of one are two different things, my dear." She cups the side of my face. "But the reason I'm telling you this is that perhaps the timing just isn't right. Your father and I experienced that, and once we agreed to talk—through a little convincing from you, that is—we figured it out. Maybe you two will too. I'd hate to see you throw away this relationship with Ethan that has clearly made you happy because you won't communicate…"

"What about Ethan?" Nick walks into the kitchen from outside, draining the last of his beer.

And now I have to tell my brother too. "Um, Ethan and I broke up."

"What?" He freezes in his steps. "Why? When?"

"It's personal, Nick. I really don't want to talk about it anymore…"

"He didn't hurt you, did he?" His vision narrows from his accusations.

"God, no. Emotionally, yes. But not physically. You know him better than that."

Exhaling, he breathes out harshly. "Fuck. Yeah, I do. But I swear, I'll kick his ass if you want me to."

Smiling, I walk over to him and give him a hug. "That's not necessary. We just wanted different things, Nick. His divorce is apparently something he's not willing to work past, and if he can't see that what we have is different, then I didn't want to be strung along."

"Shit." Nick runs a hand through his hair. "I haven't spoken to him in a while, but maybe I should give him a call, talk some sense into him. Would you be okay with that?"

"I know you're friends, but I would appreciate it if you didn't interfere. I don't want him convinced that he should want a future with me. I want him to realize it on his own, if he ever does, that is."

He studies me for a second. "You fell in love with him, didn't you?"

Another tear trails down my cheek. "Yeah, I did. But he made it clear we didn't have a future that included marriage, so…"

"Fuck. Come here." He pulls me into his chest again, inhaling deeply as he holds me tight. "I'm sorry, Sis. He's a moron if he doesn't want to marry you one day."

"Thank you."

"Is there anything I can do to make this easier?"

"You can come with me to the *L.A. Times* dinner next week for that award. The girls will be there, but I'd love for you and Elena to come too."

"I already planned on being there whether you wanted me to or not."

"Then that's all I need. I'll add your name to my list."

And with my family still by my side, I feel just an ounce better that everything is going to work out for me because of the people I have in my life, even though I wish one of them was the man I'm in love with too.

Chapter 17

Ethan

"Does that guy have a GoPro?" I slide my head around the person sitting in front of me, trying to get a better look at one of the dads in the front row.

"What's a GoPro?" my mother asks beside me, following my line of sight.

Shaking my head, I crinkle the program in my hands again, fighting off my anxiousness. "A camera made for action shots. People strap them to their bike helmets while riding or surfboards while surfing, for example, so they can record themselves in action. I just never thought I'd see a parent using one at a kindergarten play."

My mother snickers beside me. "Well, maybe his kid has a rather physical role and wanted to catch him or her in action."

I look over at her as she grins. "You do know what this play is about, don't you?"

"Yes." She rolls her eyes at me. "Will you relax, Ethan? I'm going to find another seat if you can't get yourself together."

"I'm fine," I lie as I glance back to the door of the auditorium for the hundredth time. Amelia hasn't arrived yet, and even though I know she wouldn't miss this, a part of me wishes she would so she could give me a reason to justify why we can't be together—a reason other than the fact that I'm a miserable human being that is using my past experiences as an excuse for avoiding moving on with my life in a productive and healthy manner.

No, you don't. You want her to show up for Oliver. You want her to prove that she'll keep her word. You want her to continue to be the woman that she's already proven herself to be.

But then, if she does, that still makes you look like an idiotic ass, which is the real problem, right?

"You are far from fine, son, but I'm banking on the fact that you'll figure that out sooner rather than later." She pats my leg. "By the way, Amelia is already here."

"What?" My head spins so fast on my neck that I almost fall out of my chair. But sure enough, tucked in the back corner is a mane of curly blond hair that I'm surprised I missed.

"She walked in about ten minutes ago, but I was having too much fun watching you squirm."

"You wonder why I parent the way I do," I retort before glancing back at Amelia. And then the ache in my chest magnifies like the size of an earthquake on the Richter scale.

With glasses pushed up her nose, Amelia studies the pamphlet in her lap, smiling as she reads through the information. She's wearing a tan sweater under a black jacket, far more of her covered up than I'm used to seeing since the weather has finally turned in Southern

California. But she looks stunning nonetheless—the most beautiful woman I've ever seen, and I let her walk away from me.

The past two weeks have been torture, my mood shifting worse than it did after Monica left, which should tell me something. But I've been too fucking stubborn to accept what I already know deep down—I never should have let Amelia go.

The thing is, she's the one that walked away, and I can be as pissed about it as much as I want, but she made the decision based on what was best for her; something that's taken me this long to realize.

However, I know it wasn't what's best for Oliver or me because we've both been miserable without her around.

My son has been acting out, screaming and crying when he asks for her, and I tell him that she won't be coming over or that we can't go to her house. I hate the fact that he's hurting too, and that's exactly what I was trying to avoid by introducing him to another woman in the first place.

But can I really say that I regret it? No. I don't regret one moment of our time with Amelia, except for the fact that I can't give her everything that she wants and deserves.

The lights dim, signaling the start of the play as my mother pats my shoulder to get my attention.

"You can talk to her later."

"And what do I say that I already haven't said?" I whisper back to her.

"You can thank her for showing up for your son, Ethan, because honestly, isn't that the most important part about tonight? Her being here for him because she said she would. Lord knows Monica would never do that…" She arches a brow at me and then faces forward as the curtains draw back and reveal Oliver's entire kindergarten class on stage.

I take a deep breath, smile at the sight of my kid dressed as a doctor, and settle into my chair as pride and irritation emanate from my gut—pride for my kid, but also irritation with myself that Amelia isn't sitting next to me as we watch him together.

About twenty minutes pass before Oliver finally gets to say his part. I lean forward in my chair, lift my phone up to record, and hold my breath when he starts to speak.

"Doctors are helpers in our community who help us feel better when we are sick or if we get hurt. Doctors wear scrubs or lab coats so they can move quickly and to hold their tools." He opens up the lab coat he's wearing and points to the thermometer in his pocket and stethoscope around his neck. "Doctors will examine you on a bed or table and give you medicine to help you feel better if your body hurts. But not all doctors fix broken bones or colds. Some doctors help you fix your feelings."

He takes off the coat, grabs a pair of fake glasses out of his pocket and puts them on, and then grabs a notepad and a pen from the table to his right. "A doctor called a therapist helps you talk about your feelings and fix problems we have on the inside, like a broken heart or when you're scared about something in your life. I know a doctor of feelings, and she's the best." He waves to Amelia in the corner of the room, and I take that moment to look back at her, finding her recording him as well as she dabs her eye with a tissue.

The entire audience follows his line of sight and chuckles lightly as she waves back at him.

And I swear, I have something in my eye again. I think I need to get that checked out.

Choking back my emotions, I stare forward again just in

time to see Oliver pick up his lab coat and scurry off the stage so the next group of kids can come up and sing a song about doctors.

"Now that was enough to make any father proud," my mother says next to me.

"Yeah. The kid has a heart of gold…"

"And a soft spot for Amelia."

"Well, he's not the only one…"

"There's my kiddo!"

Oliver comes racing down the hallway after his play, flinging himself into my arms. "My teacher said I did a great job, Daddy!"

"You did, bud. So good…" But before I can get another word in, Oliver pushes himself out of my arms and runs down the hall, straight into Amelia's legs.

"Amelia. You're here!"

She crouches down and pulls him into her arms. "I am. I told you I would be."

He leans back and stares into her eyes. "Did you see me talk about doctors of feelings?"

She nods proudly. "I did, Oliver. You did so great. And you made me cry." Her eyes are still wet with tears.

His face falls. "Don't cry, Amelia. Are you sad?"

"A little, but not because of you."

"I miss you. You never come over anymore," he whines, growing more emotional by the second. "Did I do something wrong?"

Fuck. There's the exact moment you were trying to avoid all along, Ethan. And look whose fault it is—not Amelia's.

"Oh, buddy. No, you didn't do anything wrong. It's just… grown-ups sometimes change their minds about things, and your dad and I changed our minds about our feelings. It happens."

"Oliver," I say, pulling his attention from Amelia as she stands again and meets my eyes. "We talked about this."

"Why did you change your feelings, Daddy?" he asks, looking up at me, anger in his eyes.

Both of us remain silent, not sure what to say that will make this any better. Other families are gathered around us, and the last thing I want is for there to be a scene.

Luckily, my mother senses the predicament and intercepts my son. "Oliver, let's go backstage and get your things so we can leave and get ice cream before we go home like I promised." She begins to steer him away, but he runs back to Amelia, wrapping his arms around her legs.

"I miss you, Amelia."

"I miss you too, Oliver."

"Maybe you and Daddy need to talk about your feelings so you can get ice cream with us again." He releases her and waves his hand as my mother leads him backstage.

I watch them go, kicking myself for being the one responsible for my son feeling abandoned and not knowing what else to do. But when I turn around to say something to Amelia, I find she has already left, her hair bouncing as she retreats through the auditorium and back out to the parking lot.

Without a second thought, I chase after her, weaving between families without knocking anyone over, trying to catch her before she gets in her car.

"Amelia, wait!"

"I have to go, Ethan. I have a long day tomorrow."

I reach her just as she arrives at her car, grabbing her wrist and spinning her around, crowding her against the door. "Don't go yet." Staring down into her eyes, I find so much emotion swirling through them.

"You can't keep doing this to me. It hurts too much." She shakes her head, her body shaking from her stifled sobs.

"Come on. I miss you. I'm fucking miserable without you, but I don't know what else to do."

"I miss you too, but that doesn't change things. I gave you all of me, Ethan—my mind, my body, my heart. I want a future with you, but I'm not getting that from you in return. So why should I listen to what you have to say? I can't do this back and forth. I deserve more. And what hurts the most is we were so close to having something real…"

"What we had was real, Amelia. My kid fucking loves you. I love you. Why can't that be enough?"

"Because it's not. I'm not going to sacrifice who I am and what I want for a man. I refuse." She pushes me away. "Don't worry. You won't have to worry about me showing up anymore after tonight. I held up my promises, but this was the last one as far as I know."

"So that's it? We just won't see you again?"

"What would be the reason?"

My mind goes blank except for the words, *"because we belong together."*

And then she scoffs, wiping tears from under her eyes. "Yeah, I thought so too. Take care of that little boy, Ethan. He's incredible. I wish I could be around to see the man he turns into. Hopefully, he'll be more open to love than his father."

And after delivering those words like an icepick straight through my heart, she opens her car door, hops inside, and drives off, leaving me standing there listening to my heart thump in my ears.

This can't be the end…

"Are you sure this is a good idea?" Damien whispers next to me outside of the Morgan Hotel in downtown Los Angeles, huddled around the corner from the main entrance.

"No, but I have to be here, Damien. I have to send her a message."

After being irritated with myself and my choices all weekend—and maybe a few too many beers at night—I realized that actions were going to speak far louder than words with Amelia. I still don't have a solid decision made up in my mind about whether I can give her everything that she wants, but I know that I can't just let her slip out of my and Oliver's life.

She's the only woman that has ever made me want to change. And tonight is the first step in that direction.

"Okay, but I'm just telling you right now…if Charlotte asks me if I knew anything about you being here, I'm not going to lie to her."

"I'm not asking you to. I just need you to help me get in."

"There's a list, man. How on earth am I supposed to do that?"

"I don't know. Use your charm. Use…"

"Ethan? Is that you?" Jeffrey walks up to us, reaching out to shake my hand.

"Last time I checked, yeah."

He laughs and then winces. "Fuck, are you supposed to be here?"

"I'm guessing you heard about Amelia and me too, huh?"

"Well, yeah. I mean, I'm around the girls a little because of Damien, who also filled me in on you two splitting. But honestly, it was Nick who told me first."

Fuck. I didn't even think about Nick being here too. And why wouldn't he be? He's her fucking brother.

"Damn it. Maybe this isn't a good idea. Is he mad? He and I haven't spoken in weeks."

Jeffrey teeters his head from side to side. "I don't know if mad would be the appropriate word to use. But he definitely is pretty protective of Amelia right now."

"He always has been. Look, I just need to get inside. I won't say a word to anyone. I just need Amelia to know I was here."

"Why?" Damien asks. "Why is it so fucking important? I mean, I know why you two split and the last thing I want is for Charlotte to chop off my dick because I had a part in letting you back into Amelia's life. I've seen heartbreak, man, on many a woman, including my own mother. It's not pretty, and Amelia has not been herself in the past three weeks. She's hurting, but she's trying to stay strong."

Running a hand through my hair, I stare down at the ground. "I know, all right? It's my fucking fault that we're in this mess. But honestly, Damien, can you blame me for never wanting to go down that path again?"

"Marriage?" he clarifies, and I nod. "Yeah, I do blame you. I think you're fucking stupid."

His candidness actually shocks me a bit. "Really?"

"Hell yes. Amelia is fucking amazing. Women like her are not a dime a dozen, and she loves your fucking kid. What else could you want, man?"

Jeffrey chimes in. "I've had many a naughty librarian fantasy about her, and I'm insanely jealous that she chose you. I mean, I don't see us together long-term, but if I had a shot at tapping that…"

I step up in his face. "Stop talking while you're ahead."

His face lights up with a mischievous smile. "You know I'm not the only man who will ever have those thoughts of her, Ethan."

"Don't fucking talk about her like that, Jeffrey, or I swear to God…"

Jeffrey laughs and then takes a step back. "I was joking, man, but I think you just clarified how strongly you feel about her."

"I've never contested my feelings for her. I just know that she deserves someone who wants the same things she does, and I don't know that I can give them to her."

"But do you want to?" Damien asks.

And for the first time in three weeks, I begin to break down that wall I put up around the idea of ever getting married again. "I do. I don't know if I can, but I want to try."

Jeffrey slaps me on the back. "Well then, I want to be a part of this reconciliation. When you two get married, I want credit in a speech or something. Hell, maybe on the invitations!" He turns to Damien and nods enthusiastically.

"Shut up, Jeffrey. Jesus."

"Or, better yet—if you have a son, name him Jeffrey. That is the ultimate honor."

I turn to Damien, tossing my thumb at Jeffrey. "Does he ever shut up?"

"Nope. But don't worry, you get used to him. He's like a puppy dog that's always under your feet. It's annoying, but you'd ultimately miss him if he wasn't there."

Jeffrey narrows his eyes and purses his lips in Damien's direction. "I take offense to that."

"Don't. It's our love language, remember?"

And then his face softens. "I love you too, man." Jeffrey rushes Damien and hugs him fiercely.

"While I'm all for bromances, gentlemen, I have a romance with an incredible woman to save, so can we focus on that right now, please?"

Damien and Jeffrey part, straightening their jackets. "Right. Let's do this."

I follow the two of them through the automatic sliding glass doors, across the hotel lobby, and up to a hostess stand in front of conference room B.

"Hello, beautiful." Jeffrey greets the woman standing behind the podium, checking the list of names in front of her, not bothering to look up at him.

"Name?"

"Jeffrey Davis. And this here is Damien Shaw and Ethan Fuller."

She looks through the list, checking off both Damien and Jeffrey's names, but searches for a few minutes before she finally looks up at us, her eyes widening as she does. I'm going to interpret her reaction as surprise because we're three fairly good-looking men and we're not actually scaring her.

"Um, there's no Ethan Fuller on the list."

"No, there won't be. But he's actually here to surprise one of the award recipients—his girlfriend." Jeffrey leans on the podium. "Isn't that romantic?"

She smiles softly but then leans forward, leaving only a few inches between her face and his. "It is. But sadly, since his name is not on the list, I can't let him in."

"Not even for me?" He winks at her.

"Not even for you."

"Do you know who we are?" he asks, pointing between himself and Damien.

"Am I supposed to?"

"You ever heard of Remedy feminine products?"

Her brow furrows, and her mouth drops open slightly. "Um, yes…"

"Well, we sell them."

Damien slaps himself on the forehead. "Dear Lord, help us."

The hostess's face contorts with more confusion as I glance over at Damien with wide eyes, pleading with him to take control of this conversation because, as of right now, my shot of getting in here is dwindling fast.

"You sell tampons?"

"We do. We just created an ad that is sweeping the country. Maybe you've seen it? The mother and her daughter in the aisle full of period products…"

And then the woman's face completely changes from one of utter disgust and confusion to fandom and glee. "Oh my God! Yes! I've seen it! It's amazing!"

Jeffrey stands tall again, buttoning up his jacket. "My man Damien and I came up with that."

She shakes her head, clutching her hands to her chest. "You've got to be kidding me…"

"Nope."

"I love it! I even told my girlfriends, why can't there be men out there like that who aren't afraid of buying feminine products for their girlfriends and then running through the store, buying her everything that she wants?"

"Well, there are. You're looking at three of them right here." He points his thumb at Damien and me.

And hey, I haven't actually done that for a woman I've been with, but I would for Amelia in a heartbeat, so I'll let him include me on principle. "So, let's get back to the problem here. My man, Ethan, needs to get inside this event to surprise his girlfriend. He wasn't supposed to be here in time but took an earlier flight." Nice, Jeffrey. Okay, maybe I was wrong about him…

But the girl winces. "I understand and really find that romantic, but we have a limited number of seats and meals paid for."

"I can stand. I don't need to sit," I interject. "And I'm not even hungry."

"I'm sorry…"

"Has someone canceled?" Damien chimes in.

"Not that I know of." She looks back down at her list, scouring the pages, but then pauses when she goes back to the first page. "Oh, wait! One of the names is on here twice!"

"Well, there you go."

"Brayden Anderson," she says, and my adrenaline instantly spikes. *Why on earth is he here?* "He doesn't need two meals." She crosses off his name once on the paper as she laughs to herself and then writes mine instead. "There you go."

Clearing my throat and tamping down my pulse, I button my jacket up and step forward. I can deal with Brayden later. "Thank you. Truly. You've helped me out so much tonight."

"You're welcome. And you," she says, leaning forward again toward Jeffrey. "I'd love to hear how you came up with the idea for that commercial."

His eyebrows lift. "Is that so?"

She bites her bottom lip, moving her eyes up and down his body. "Uh-huh."

"Well then, after the event, I'll be sure to come back out here and tell you."

"Or you could just ask for my number now so we can hang out later?"

Jeffrey almost falls down as he tries to locate his phone at record speed. But I don't stand around to watch if he falls or not. I'm on a mission, and I can't fail.

"Thank you, man." I pat Jeffrey on the shoulder and then Damien follows me as we enter the space, observing the crowd as the packed room overwhelms me.

Round tables covered in black tablecloths are spread out throughout the room. A stage is standing at the furthest wall from the entrance, covered in chairs with a gold and silver backdrop and the *Los Angeles Times* logo splayed across the fabric. Gold and silver accents are sprinkled throughout—in place settings, center-pieces with white roses, and serving trays held up by waiters.

The event is top-notch, but I don't care about any of that. All I care about is making sure that Amelia can see me, that she knows I showed up for her.

"Our table is upfront. You might not want to sit there with the girls because they're not your biggest fans right now, but instead find a spot where Amelia can still see you," Damien explains as we walk further into the room, and I see Penelope, Noelle, and Charlotte standing together near the bar. But I don't see Amelia anywhere.

"Okay. I'm going to keep a low profile and stay out of the way until Amelia goes up on stage. Thanks again for your help."

"I'd better be able to still have kids after this, Ethan," he jokes. "But in all honesty, work through your shit, man, if you love her and can't imagine your life without her. Nothing else is as scary as living without her, knowing it was your decision that made you both miserable. Remember that." And with a nod of his head, he walks away toward the girls.

Internalizing his words, I glide around the perimeter of the room, taking in familiar faces and strangers that I'm sure have some part in this evening's festivities. When I found out about Amelia's nomination during that dinner with her parents, my gut reaction was to want to be here to support her, even though, at first, I didn't agree with her job. That right there should have been an indication that my feelings for her were unparalleled. And obviously, my thoughts about her career have changed in the last three and a half months. Now I have nothing but pride in what she does and how seriously she takes it.

I actually went online and researched the process of this event after that dinner and now know that every nominee gets an award. Amelia doesn't have to make a speech, but she will receive a plaque to hang in her office, her name will be published in the *Los Angeles Times*, and of course, this event is held to honor all the businesses that have been nominated by citizens of L.A.

Before I get too far into the room, those blond curls that drive me insane catch my eye as Amelia heads for her friends. She's wearing an emerald-green dress that has a slight shimmer to it and tall black heels. Her glasses are missing, which means she must have opted for her contacts, and she looks far more composed than she did the last time I saw her.

But then I see that Brayden is trailing her, close on her heels.

What the fuck? Is she here with him?

Straightening my spine, I slide into an alcove so I can spy from afar, trying not to be seen. Brayden stands next to her with his hand on her lower back, and my stomach begins to twist while rage rushes through me. He's touching her, claiming her in a room full of people when she's not his to begin with.

But she's not exactly yours at the moment either, is she, Ethan?

Amelia smiles up at him before looking back at her friends, and suddenly, I wonder if coming here was a mistake. If she's already moving on, does that mean I'm too late? Was my stupidity the straw that broke the camel's back, and now I have to live with the fact that Brayden will be around the complex, picking her up for dates, bringing her lunch, and possibly fucking her in her office like I did?

The urge to throw up comes on hard.

I know deep down she'll never experience the passion with him that we had. I know that being with him will mean she's settling since she admitted the lack of chemistry with him to begin with. And I know that watching her fall for him will be like someone showing me one of my worst nightmares, the one where I lose the love of my life.

But can you offer her something different, Ethan? Along with everything else that she wants too?

I take a deep breath, ready to march across the room and draw my sword for battle, but a man comes over the speaker, asking everyone to take their seats so the ceremony can begin.

Taking the interruption as a sign not to do anything stupid and impulsive, I find a seat at a table in the back, smiling at the people sitting with me while I stew with rage and impatience. I know going over to their table and saying something will not produce the results I wanted to achieve this evening, so even though it's killing me to sit here, I wait until the nominees are brought up on stage and use that as my cue to move to a position where Amelia can see me as she walks off the stage after accepting her award.

"What are you doing here?" I freeze in my steps and twist back to look at Nick, standing behind me with his arms crossed over his chest. He must have seen me and headed toward the back of the room when I wasn't paying attention.

Names are still being called, and I haven't heard Amelia's yet, so I know I have time.

"I'm here for your sister," I answer honestly, standing tall across from him as we stare each other down.

"I thought you didn't want her, Ethan." I go to reply, but he holds up his hand in front of my face. "Before you start spouting off excuses, let me say a few things." Nodding, I swallow down my rebuttal and wait for him to continue. "I warned you not to hurt her. I told you how incredible she is and that you shouldn't take her for granted, but you did anyway."

"You're right," I interrupt him, "which is why I'm here. I want to support her through this, Nick. I wanted to show up for her like she's done for Oliver and me so many times."

He eyes me cautiously. "Why should I believe you?"

"Because you were the one that said it so eloquently—the best things in life are a good woman, a home, and a family. And when I was with your sister, I had all three. I fucked up, man, and it probably won't be the last time, but I'm trying to show Amelia that I want to change—for her."

He sighs, staring across the room. "I'm torn. She's my sister, Ethan, and she's been a mess for weeks. But you're my friend, and man-to-man, I know it's not easy to admit when we're wrong, when we've fucked up royally. My gut is telling me to protect my sister, but on the flip side, I know that being with you will make her happy too. So…"

"So…"

"I'm gonna pretend I didn't see you here and let you do what you came here to do. But if I hear another word about you fucking with her mind, our next conversation won't be so pleasant."

I release the breath I was holding. "I promise, man. I'm going to do everything to get her back."

"Good luck. She's fucking stubborn and really fucking hurt right now."

"I know, but I can't fix things if I don't try."

"Then try…really fucking hard." He pats me on the shoulder and walks off just in time for Amelia's name to be called over the sound system.

Blowing out the oxygen I was holding in, I focus back on my mission and move around the room again.

A round of applause and cheering rings out from the front, where I see Penelope, Noelle, Charlotte, Damien, Jeffrey, Nick, and Amelia's parents clapping and whistling for her. And Brayden—fucking Brayden—smiling from ear to ear in a way that makes me feel all murdery inside.

Because I should be there, cheering her on as well. And I can't, through no one's fault but my own.

Instead, I move as quickly as I can around the perimeter of the room to a spot on the side of the stage where Amelia will descend the stairs in a few moments.

After what feels like an eternity, the nominees are asked to exit the stage, and as Amelia holds the railing while taking slow steps down, I take a few steps toward her.

"Congratulations, beautiful."

She gasps, freezing at the bottom of the stairs, holding her plaque in one hand while the other rests over her rapidly beating heart. At least, I'm assuming hers is beating just as fast as mine is at this moment.

"Ethan? What are you doing here? Your name wasn't on the list."

"I have my ways."

People coming off the stage behind her clear their throats, alerting her that she's blocking the path, one of which is Brayden. I notice the plaque in his hand as well, which means he was also a nominee tonight.

"Is everything okay, Amelia?" he asks, stepping around her as we move out of the way.

"Yes, I'm fine."

"Do you want me to stay with you?"

She looks over her shoulder at him, furrowing her brow. "No. You can go back to your seat."

"Are you sure?"

"She said no, dipshit," I mutter under my breath, but he hears it.

With a glare, he takes off toward their table as I grab Amelia's hand and pull her to the side, out of sight of the rest of the venue and in a small hallway where we can talk.

"Why are you here, Ethan?" she asks me again once we're alone.

"I showed up for you. I wanted to be here to support you."

"Why?" She takes her hand back and holds her plaque to her chest.

"Because showing up for the people you love is something you should always do."

She closes her eyes. "Ethan…"

I press a finger to her lips as her eyes pop back open. "Don't say anything else. I just wanted you to know that I was here, that I clapped for you, cheered you on, and supported you in your career, despite how I felt at first. That your success means just as much if not more to me than my own. That I want to be here cheering you on every day for the rest of our lives, Amelia."

Her eyes move back and forth between mine for a few seconds before she finally says, "Thank you."

"You're welcome." I close the distance between us and press a kiss to her forehead. "And remember what I said. If I have to see Brayden put his hands on you, I'll chop them off myself."

With a few steps back, I take in her face—eyes bugged out, flushed cheeks, and a little 'o' formed by her lips.

"See you Monday, Amelia. Have a good night."

And then I leave, not bothering to look back because I've done what I set out to do tonight. And now, it's about coming up with my next move.

Chapter 18

Ethan

"Good afternoon, Mr. Fuller."

I take a seat in one of the miniature chairs in Oliver's kindergarten classroom right after I walk through the door, and my knees instantly hit my chin. "Hello. Uh, do you have regular-sized seats?" I look around the room as the teacher chuckles.

"Yes. I was about to tell you I have a table set up for us over here, but you seemed eager to sit."

Standing, I follow Miss Turner's lead over to the table suitable for adults. "Sorry. I guess I'm just nervous. I've never done this before."

She laughs, taking the seat across from me and then reaching for a folder full of papers. "No worries. There's nothing to be nervous about though. Parent-teacher conferences are supposed to be a memorable experience, and based on how Oliver's doing in class, I think you'll be quite pleased at what you learn today."

His teacher spends the next ten minutes going through his reading and writing scores, emphasizing where he's excelling and where he still needs to show improvement. "Don't worry though. At this age and this point in the school year, all kids have things to improve on. Remember, kindergarten is about developing the skills he will use throughout school as he gets older."

"Okay."

"He's doing very well in math as well." She pulls out a few more papers. "His number sense is inherent, but he likes to race through his work so he can finish and move on to something else, which means he will often make silly mistakes."

"The kid has very little patience. He gets that from me, unfortunately."

She smiles across the table at me. "It's not necessarily a bad thing, but perhaps you can remind him to take his time on his work so he doesn't make mistakes because I know he has the knowledge. He just gets problems wrong because he's rushing."

"Noted. I will talk to him about it."

"Excellent. Now, let's move on to his artwork." She slides a picture out of the folder and spins it around so that it's facing me. "This was our family project that he completed last week."

As I stare down at the paper, my heart lurches. Oliver's depiction of our family only serves as a reminder that I need to do what I can to convince Amelia that I've changed my mind—and I think this picture will definitely help with that.

Standing side-by-side are drawings of three people—me, Oliver, and a girl I'm assuming is Amelia, based on the yellow curls all around the person's head. We're all smiling and holding hands, and we look like the perfect family.

And damn it, we were.

Despite how quickly it happened, the three of us did become a family. Despite how fast my feelings developed, I think deep down, I knew I was powerless to stop them anyway. And despite the fact that things right now aren't fixed yet, I know that I have to do everything in my power to change that.

"When did he draw this?" I ask, clearing the emotion from my throat.

"About three weeks ago. He wrote a story to go along with it last week though. We had to break up the project into parts since we were finalizing the play last week—which by the way, Oliver was outstanding in." She slides another paper in front of me, where I attempt to piece together the broken and misspelled words. But it's far easier than I thought.

"My family is me, my dad, and Amelia, my daddy's girlfriend. We all go to my soccer games together and get gelato after. Amelia lets me swim at her house and she shows me pictures of her gnomes, and she has a spinning pole in her house. My daddy always smiles when we're together. I hope Amelia gets to be my new mommy because mine left. But she hasn't been spending time with us anymore and it makes me sad. I miss Amelia. I love her and I want my family back."

"Fuck," I mutter, dragging my hand down my face before lifting my eyes to see Miss Turner staring at me with wide eyes. "Sorry."

She laughs. "It's okay. Oliver talks about Amelia all the time. You can tell he feels very strongly for her, but he has mentioned that she hasn't been around much lately."

"That's my fault."

"Well, for the sake of you both, I hope you find some solace soon." I watch her put all the papers she's shown me back in the folder. "His drawings are very detailed, and his writing is fairly advanced for this point in the year, so with my help, we were able to put into words what he was trying to say." She pushes the folder toward me, and I intercept it. "Despite the obvious emotional hurdles you and him are facing, I want you to know that he is doing very well, and I look forward to seeing how much progress he makes by the end of the year."

"Thank you, Miss Turner."

"My pleasure, Mr. Fuller. And I hope you three can get your family back together soon."

"Please let me know if his feelings about the matter become an issue in your classroom," I offer as I stand, and she follows my lead.

"He's had a few moments here or there, but nothing I couldn't steer him around relatively quickly. It's just obvious that he feels very strongly for her."

"He and I both."

I leave the conference feeling even shittier than I did before, considering that I was feeling confident after the awards dinner the other night. I haven't seen Amelia since, but perhaps showing her Oliver's drawing is the perfect excuse to catch a glimpse of her honey-colored eyes and that smile I miss more than I care to admit —and a way to convince her to give me another chance.

When I get back to the office, though, I see something I wasn't anticipating—yet another obstacle that I instantly want to smash.

Standing outside her office door are her and Brayden. She has her purse slung over her shoulder, and he has his hands in his pockets, staring down at her with a gleeful smile on his fucking face.

As I walk up to the complex, Amelia's eyes shift in my direction and then widen as they take me in.

"Good afternoon," I say even though on the inside I want to

curse and start a fight with this guy. But that's not going to get me very far, so I refrain.

"Mr. Fuller," Amelia replies.

"Ethan," Brayden answers with a smug lift of his lips. "How's it going?"

"Oh, it's been better. One hell of a day, and people just seem to continue to irritate me more as the day goes on."

Brayden huffs out a laugh. "Well, sometimes it's our own fault when that happens, isn't that right?"

I stop walking, pausing right in front of my office door. "I like to think of it as people getting in my way that should know better at this point. But sadly, some people are just too delusional to realize they won't ever be able to compete."

"Well, maybe—" Brayden goes to reply, taking a step toward me, but Amelia reaches out to grasp his arm, holding him back.

"Brayden. Let's go."

He swallows and then straightens his jacket. "Yeah. We have a reservation to get to."

Fuck. They're going on a date?

"Have a good afternoon, Mr. Fuller," Amelia says to me as they begin to walk away.

And my heart aches as I watch them move toward the parking lot, kicking myself for the unfortunate timing and wondering if she'll be back later today so I can talk to her in private.

For the rest of the afternoon, I'm extremely unproductive. I can't concentrate, wondering where Amelia went with Brayden or what they're doing. I can't stop looking out of my blinds to see if she's returned. And I can't stop thinking that I'm too late to try to win her back.

I thought after I left the awards dinner the other night that slipping back into her good graces would be easier than it's proving to be, and that has me approaching my boiling point.

The click of heels outside my window has me peering through the blinds once again just in time to see Amelia approaching her office alone.

I spin around so fast that I slam my leg into the corner of my desk, crying out in agony. "Fuck!" Rubbing the spot, I reach for the folder with Oliver's papers and walk toward my door. "That's going to leave a bruise."

At a punishing pace, I exit my office and glide across the courtyard to Amelia's door, knocking softly before checking to see if the door is unlocked, which it is. So instead of waiting for her to answer, I let myself in and find her back to me as she places something in her filing cabinet.

"Amelia."

She doesn't bother turning around to face me. "What do you want, Ethan?" I guess she was expecting this visit, which could be a good or a bad thing.

"I came here to show you something."

"Oh really? You're not here to ask me questions about why I was leaving with Brayden earlier?" Finally, she turns and shows me her face, the pain and irritation in her features prevalent. And I hate that her face is beginning to look like that every time I see her.

Anger flashes through me just from the mention of that dickhead's name, but I tamp it down. "Not unless you want to share with me. But honestly, I don't even like hearing his name coming off your lips, so hearing about why he was here would be enough to make my ears bleed."

"Jealousy isn't a good look on you, Ethan, especially when you have no one to blame but yourself for him being around."

"You're right."

Her face falls with shock, but she quickly recovers. "What do you need to show me? I don't have a lot of time. I have somewhere else I need to be tonight."

Walking toward her, I open the folder and bring out the drawing Oliver made of the three of us. "I thought you'd want to see this."

Her eyes well with tears as she takes in his artwork. "Why are you showing this to me? This isn't going to fix anything."

"I know, but I want you to see that this is what I intend to fight for."

Her head lifts. "Fight for what?"

"The three of us together."

She sighs and hands the paper back to me. "Nothing has changed."

"Yes, it has."

"We still want different things."

"What if I changed my mind?"

Crossing her arms over her chest, she narrows her eyes at me. "Just like that? You've changed your mind? This doesn't have to do with Brayden, does it?"

I toss the folder on her desk and close the distance between us. "I don't give a shit about that fuckface. You are all that matters to me. You and Oliver and the three of us together." I reach up and frame her face with my hands. "The longer we're apart, the more I realize what an idiot I've been. You're the woman I can't live without. You're the one I want in my life forever, and I'm willing to do anything to show you that."

Tears stream down her face. "All I hear are words, Ethan. And words are great, but they aren't actions. There's so much more that has to happen before this can be resolved."

"I know. I just…"

The bell above her door rings, distracting us. And the visitor that walks through is even more of a reason to put this conversation on pause.

"Oliver?"

"Amelia!" He races toward her as she intercepts his hug around her waist.

"Hi, buddy. What are you doing here?"

A few seconds later, my mother comes barreling through the door, breathing heavily. "I'm so sorry. He took off from the gelato shop, and I couldn't keep up with him. He was insistent about coming to see you." And then her eyes flick between Amelia and me. "I hope we weren't interrupting anything."

I immediately want to tell them to leave, but Amelia drops down to Oliver's level and covers up our turmoil. "No, it's fine. I'm happy to see you too, Oliver. How was school?"

"It was fun. Today was my parent-teacher conference, so I got out early. Grandma picked me up, and we've been running errands before she brought me back to Daddy."

"And you got gelato?"

"Yes. I got strawberry today."

"That's a good choice."

"Your gnomes haven't moved, Amelia," he says. "Does that mean the treasure is safe?"

"For now. But something could happen at any moment, and they might have to protect it."

"Can you make sure you take a picture if they move and have Daddy show it to me?"

She brushes his hair from his face. "I promise."

"Oliver, can you wait with grandma outside, please?"

"But Daddy, I wanna spend time with Amelia."

"She's busy, bud."

"I'll make sure to come say goodbye to you before I leave, okay? Your dad and I just need to finish talking."

His ears perk up. "Are you talking about your feelings?"

"Something like that," I reply. "Now go, please."

"Bye, Amelia!" He waves, and then my mother flashes us a small smile before they exit her office.

"Ethan, I have to go." She walks away from me, gathering some files and her purse.

"This isn't over, Amelia. We're going to talk about this. I want to have lunch tomorrow."

She pauses, staring up at me. "I don't think that's a good idea. And even though I don't feel you deserve to know, Brayden and I are just friends, nothing more."

A small wave of relief rushes through me, but then I focus back on why I'm here. "I don't care. I want you to hear me out. That's the least you can do for me…and for Oliver."

She sighs, closing her eyes. "Fine. But I really have to go. I'll see you tomorrow."

I leave her office first, holding the door for her. Locking the door behind us, she fulfills her promise as she bends down to hug my son goodbye.

"Bye, Amelia!" He waves at her and then turns to me once she walks out to the parking lot. "Did you talk about your feelings, Daddy?"

"Not yet, bud. But soon."

"You'd better do it fast, Daddy. I want Amelia back in our family."

Nothing like pressure from your kid to man up fast.

J ust before noon the next day, with Chinese food in hand, I knock on the door of Amelia's office. Waiting on pins and needles, I anticipate hearing some movement from behind the door, but silence is all I can detect.

I knock again, wondering if she changed her mind, if she thought long and hard last night about what I said, and she realized I wasn't worth the effort. And if she did, what can I do about it?

I mean, it's my fault we've been apart for nearly a month now. And if she decided that it was best for us to really part ways, there's nothing I would be able to do but accept that.

But I honestly don't think that's what she wants because I sure as hell know I don't, and every time we talk, I can see the same longing I feel for her reflected back at me in her eyes.

"Amelia!" I knock harder, wondering if she's in the back room of her office and didn't hear me the first time. But more time passes without any acknowledgment from inside. I step up to the glass door and attempt to see inside through the curtains, but that's when I notice there are no lights on.

That's strange. Amelia should be here. Did she have to step out? Was there an emergency of some sort?

Just then, footsteps behind me pull my attention to my left, and that's when I see Nick striding toward me, his face sullen and his hair in disarray.

"Nick?"

He stops dead in his tracks. "Ethan."

"What are you doing here, man?"

"Fuck, you haven't heard?"

"Heard what?" My stomach drops as I take in his face. He has bags under his eyes, his eyelids are swollen, and his clothes are askew. My gut tells me something happened, and I'm not going to like what comes out of his mouth next.

"Amelia…was in a car accident last night. She's…she's in the hospital."

I drop the bag of food to the ground and rush toward him, but he holds me away from him at arm's length, pushing against my chest. "Is she okay? Fuck, tell me she's okay, Nick!"

"She's banged up pretty bad. A few broken ribs, a humerus fracture, and cuts all over her face from the glass. But she's going to be okay."

I let out a shaky breath as tears build in my eyes. "Fuck, Nick. I—" I choke back my desire to crumble right now. I can feel my legs starting to give out, so we walk over to the fountain while Nick holds me up before we sit on the edge.

"I know, man. It's been a long night. I've been at the hospital with my family and the girls since seven. I haven't slept. I came by her office to grab a few things for her, but then I'm headed right back."

"I need to see her."

Nick pushes a hand through his hair. "I don't know if that's a good idea right now."

"Why not?"

"Because you upset her, man. Seeing you sends her into a tailspin. And she's sleeping. They've had her on morphine to help with the pain, and she just got out of surgery to fix her arm."

"I have to see her, Nick. She could have died, and I never got a chance to…" Fuck, I could have lost her. She could have died, and I would never have had the opportunity to tell her that I want to spend the rest of my life with her.

And like the flick of a switch, it all becomes so clear to me—I want Amelia to be my everything. I always have, and I always will.

He shakes his head, staring down at the ground. "I know, but she's alive, man. She's going to pull through this. I just—I'd feel better if I asked her how she feels about it first, okay?"

Even though it's not what I want to hear, I have to respect his hesitation. However, I also know that I could just override him. "I could just show up, you know?"

And that's when he scoffs. "You could, but you're not family, so they won't let you in." And with an arch of his brow, he stands. "Bet you wish you were married now, huh?"

And with one last parting look, he unlocks the door to her office and steps inside, shutting the door behind him.

"Fuck!" I shout, pulling on my hair just as my eyes land on the gnomes in the flower beds by her door. And without thinking, I step toward them, crouch down and pick them up, and then send them sailing across the courtyard, shattering as they hit the ground.

"God damn it!" Huffing in frustration, I stare at the remnants of the gnomes and then spin and race toward my office. I don't give a shit what Nick says. I'm going to that hospital. I'm going to see the woman I love and make sure she's okay with my own two eyes.

"Cancel all of my meetings for the rest of the day, Yvonne!" I bark out at her as I run back to my office, grabbing my wallet and keys from my desk.

"Is everything okay?" she asks as she pops her head in the door, taking in my frantic state.

"No. Amelia was in a car accident last night, and I have to go see her."

Her hands cover her mouth. "Oh my God. Is she okay?"

"She's pretty banged up, but apparently, she's going to be fine. But I'm not. I have to see her. I have to talk to her."

She shakes her head at me. "It's about damn time, Ethan."

"Yeah, I know."

My eyes run all over my office, making sure I didn't forget anything. But then I remember that my phone is in my desk drawer.

"Good luck. I'll hold down the fort as long as I need to."

"Thank you, Yvonne."

I watch her leave with a smile on her face before I open the drawer where I always place my phone. But it's not there. Pulling open another drawer, I see that I put it in a different place this morning for some reason, but another object in the drawer catches my eye next.

Lifting the pamphlet from beneath my phone, I stare down at Amelia's writing, and that's when it hits me. I know exactly how to show her that I've had a change of heart. I know exactly what I need to do to move forward in my life with her. And I just hope she gives me the opportunity to prove it to her.

Chapter 19

Amelia

"Easy, Amelia." A familiar voice pulls me out of the deep sleep I was just under, and as I slowly blink my eyes, I take in the fluorescent lights above me.

"Where am I?"

"You're at the hospital, honey."

"Mom?" I go to turn my head in the direction of her voice, but a flash of pain shoots through my body.

"Don't move, sweetie. You've been in an accident."

Like a movie reel, flashes of the past twenty-four hours play out in my mind—Ethan showing me the picture that Oliver drew, Oliver coming into my office and breaking my heart with his words and love, running out of my office just to get away from them, the crunch of metal as someone ran a red light and plowed into the driver's side of my car, and then the doctors telling me I would need surgery to repair my arm—it all hits me like a ton of bricks that no amount of drugs can abate.

"The surgery?" I croak out as more faces come into view.

"You did good, Amelia Be Delia," Penelope says as she hovers over me. "Doc said you have a bionic arm now, so you'll be back to spinning on the pole in no time."

Laughter bubbles out of me but at the price of pain. "Don't make me laugh."

"I'm going to go get the nurse," Noelle declares, and then I hear the door to my room opening and closing.

"Is there anything I can get you, baby?" my mom asks, smoothing my hair from my face.

"I'd like some water, please. And to sit up if that's possible."

"You've got it."

A nurse comes in at that moment and checks my vitals before using the switch on the side of my bed to incline the top half so I can see. My left arm is in a cast that I struggle to lift, but all I care about right now is clearing the fuzziness from my mind. "The doctor will be in shortly. I'm going to increase the pain meds, which may make her sleepy again, so don't be alarmed if she starts going in and out of consciousness," she explains to my friends.

Like ice traveling through my veins, I feel the medication enter my body and bring reprieve from the aches, both physical and emotional. It's the first time I've felt numb in weeks, and I'm going to enjoy it, at least while it lasts.

"I don't give a fuck what anyone thinks. I need to see her. I need to tell her so many things, and no one is going to stop me!" A voice from outside has my mother and my friends all turning their heads toward the door.

"You're sure you've figured out your shit?" my brother asks the man outside.

"I've never been more sure about anything, man. I love her. Now let me in before you regret standing in my way."

Ethan.

"Is that Ethan?" I turn to my mom, asking for clarification.

"I think so. Your brother said he ran into him at your office when he went by to collect some things for you and insisted on coming by to see you, but Nick told him no."

"He did?"

She smooths her hand down my face again. "He wanted to make sure you were okay with seeing him first. What should I tell him?"

I look between the eyes of my friends and my mom, who have now gathered around me. "I don't know…" My mind begins to feel woolly, but my heart begins to ache again. Even the pain medication can't make that go away when it comes to him.

Before I can answer, Nick opens the door and closes it behind him. "Hey, look who's up."

"Is that Ethan out there?"

"Yes. I got him to sit down and take a few breaths while I came in here to check on you. How are you feeling?"

"Well, they gave me more drugs, so that's helping." Everyone laughs. "What does he want?"

Nick walks over to my bed and sits softly on the edge by my legs, reaching for my hand. "Look, I know things between the two of you are broken. But the man has been blowing up my phone for the past three hours, begging to see you. I kept him away for as long as I could, but I think it's time you two talk. You didn't see his face when I told him about your accident, Amelia. I thought his knees were going to buckle, and he stopped breathing for a good minute.

He loves you, and he planned on telling you how much before your lunch plans were derailed."

Our lunch. We were supposed to meet up for lunch today. He must have been waiting for me and then realized I wasn't there.

I forgot that I agreed to those plans today as I ran away from him the night before. Turns out, running from him has become my M.O., and that's not something I'm proud of. But every time we talk, his pleading grows more desperate with nothing closer to concrete evidence that he's reevaluated a possibility of our future. And even though he said he changed his mind yesterday afternoon before my accident, I'm reluctant to believe him—because believing him would mean putting myself in a position to be hurt again, to be even more disappointed because I allowed myself to hold onto hope with the potential to be shattered once more.

And I don't know that I can handle any more pain.

"I appreciate you trying to advocate for him, Nick, I do…but I was actually going to ask you for your help with something before the accident happened." I blow out a breath and then speak. "I was thinking you could help me find another office once I get out of here."

"What?" Noelle and Charlotte say simultaneously.

Everyone stares at me as I find the words. "I…I can't work there anymore. It's too hard. The last few weeks have been the hardest of my life, and seeing him and Oliver around the complex is preventing me from moving on. I can't try to move forward knowing he's across the courtyard and watching my every move. I can't ask him to leave, so that only leaves one option. For me to do it."

"Amelia, I don't think this is what you want," Noelle declares.

"Me neither, Amelia Be Delia," Penelope chimes in. "Which is why I'm going to let Ethan in here in about five minutes, and there will be no more talking about moving offices." She looks down at her phone and then back up to me, smiling.

"Are you joking?"

Noelle chimes in. "Nope. We were actually talking about this before your accident and had planned an intervention. You need to talk to him. Ethan has been blowing up our phones too." My three best friends share a look.

"Damien even told me he's been calling him, trying to get updates on your condition. The man is in knots, and the least you can do is hear him out. If, after you talk, you decide you want nothing to do with him, then we will stand by your side and support you. But we're your best friends, and we know what's best for you even if you can't see it. So shut up and let the man say what he needs to say. Then if you decide you're really done, we will guard you like soldiers outside of a castle until the end of time, and we won't let him through. Nick will help you find another office, and Noelle will even venture out into the dating world again to help you back on the saddle when you're ready." Charlotte reaches for my good hand and gives it a squeeze.

"But my gut tells me you're letting your fear rule your decisions right now, and I might know a thing or two about that," my mother adds softly before leaning down so only I can hear her. "Remember how scared I was when your father and I separated, how terrifying it was that I had to tell him what I wanted, that so many aspects of our marriage had fallen by the wayside, and it was no one's fault but our own? We grew complacent, Amelia—our sex life, our friendship—it all became so stagnant that one day we didn't realize how far apart we'd grown. And if we had just talked about what we needed and were feeling years before that point, we never would have separated in the first place." I stare up at her as my bottom lip starts to tremble.

"But Ethan is here. He wants to talk to you, he wants to resolve your issues, and that's something you shouldn't ignore. So, take a piece of advice from me and hear him out. Wouldn't you advise your clients to do the same?"

Everyone grows fuzzy as moisture builds in my eyes, and I feel my eyelids grow heavy. "Okay." And then a collective sigh fills the room. "I do feel like I'm about to pass out again though."

"That's okay. I'll let him in, and then everyone can go grab something to eat since I just heard your brother's stomach rumbling," my mother teases.

Nick throws his hands up in defense. "I'm starving, which is making me more angry, but I can use that aggression to rough Ethan up a little bit more if you want me to before I leave?"

Chuckling, I close my eyes and then shake my head. "No. That's okay. You can let him in. Thank you, you guys."

My friends take turns kissing my forehead.

"Anything for you, Amelia Be Delia. You are one strong fucking woman, and I love you for it, but this has gone on long enough."

If you're lucky in life, really lucky, you get blessed with friends like these girls. I heard a metaphor once that sums up our friendship perfectly, and it comes rushing back to me at this moment.

Be the type of friend that's like the roots on a tree.

Don't be a leaf that blows away when a strong breeze passes through, the type of friend that is only there when it's suitable for you and then leaves when the seasons change.

Don't be the branch that snaps when you least expect it, catching the person off guard when, all of a sudden, you're no longer there.

Be the roots. Be the reason that tree survives, the reason why that tree stands and can live and thrive and have the strength to withstand every season and storm in its life.

My girls are my roots, and I know that I would not have survived the past month without them.

Penelope winks at me when I open my eyes long enough to see her open the door and motion for Ethan to come in.

And when he appears in the doorway, the crack in my heart bursts wide open.

His demeanor is almost manic—hair sticking up in every direction, bloodshot eyes, shirt sleeves rolled up, his shirt untucked, and every line in his face etched with worry.

"Fucking hell." He sets down a plastic bag on a chair and rushes toward the bed, leaning over me and pressing his lips to my forehead, and I can feel his body shaking as he reaches out to touch me. "Jesus Christ, Amelia. Are you okay?" His hands tremble as he cups the side of my face.

"I'm a little broken, but it's nothing that can't heal."

"I'm broken too, baby. Fuck, you have no idea how shattered I feel right now."

"We're going to leave you guys alone," my mother whispers as she's the last one out of the room.

"I'm tired, Ethan. They gave me drugs." My eyes fall closed again, and then the drugs begin to pull me back under. I vaguely hear the screech of a chair as Ethan pulls one close to the bed and takes a seat, reaching for my hands and holding them in his own close to his lips.

"Sleep, baby. I'm not going anywhere."

"I love you," I whisper as everything goes black. And even though I know we're not in a place to say that again, it's the truth. I can't deny it, and having him here only reminds me of how strongly I feel for him and how fragile life is.

My friends and family were right. I do want him in my life, and it's time to stop fighting it. If I were a client, I would ask myself point blank what I wanted, and my answer would be him and Oliver, irrevocably. So it's time to start fighting for what I want. It's not going to be easy, but I know in my gut that it will be worth it.

"I love you too, Amelia. So fucking much," he chokes out on a sob, and the shaking of his body as he lays his head on my hands and cries is the last thing I remember before I fall asleep again.

When I open my eyes after an unknown length of time, the entire hospital room is dark except for the lamp on the table next to my bed illuminating the space.

I blink a few times and then turn my head to see Ethan still holding my hands with one of his, staring up at me as if he were waiting for me to wake up, his chin resting in his other palm.

"Hi."

"Hey, beautiful." He presses a kiss to my hands and then sits up taller in his chair. "Do you want some water?"

"Sure."

He reaches for the cup and brings the straw to my mouth. I take down a few large gulps, welcoming the liquid as it edges off the scratchiness of my throat. "How long was I asleep?"

Reaching into his pocket, he checks his phone. "About an hour and a half."

"And where is everybody?"

"They went to eat dinner. The girls said they might stop by to say goodnight, but if not, they would for sure be back in the morning. But your mother and Nick insisted they'd return tonight with your dad."

"Oh. Okay."

"How are you feeling?"

As soon as he asks, my eyes cloud with tears. "I'm feeling a lot right now, so I can't give you a clear-cut answer to that question."

"Fuck. I understand that completely." He kisses my hand again. "Amelia, baby, I love you so much, and there's so much I need to say to you."

"I love you too, Ethan. But…"

He presses a finger to my lips. "Let me talk, okay?"

I nod, and then he removes his finger. "Okay."

He takes a deep breath and then sits up again. "Knowing you were hurt, that something could have happened to you, and I would never have had the chance to tell you what you mean to me, made me realize even more that I don't want to live a life without you in it. I'm not saying I won't mess this up. I'm not saying things between us will be perfect. But what I am saying is that I want a life with you. I want everything with you. I would be willing to put my heart on the line again as long as you're the one I'm giving it to."

"It took my accident for you to realize that?"

He shakes his head. "No. I actually realized it when you showed up to Oliver's play after you promised you would. I was just too stubborn to admit it. You showed up for us because you love us, and that's something no one has ever done for my son and me before besides my mom."

I swallow roughly. "And what about marriage?"

"After watching mine disintegrate, I lost faith in the idea. I swore I'd never go down that path again. But mostly over the past few weeks, I realized that Monica and I shouldn't have gotten married in the first place." He blows out a breath. "We were young, I was fresh out of college, and we had only been dating about six months before she wound up pregnant. I wanted to do right by her, to have our family together, unlike how I grew up without my father, so I married her without a thought about the commitment we were entering into. I thought I was doing the right thing, but ultimately, we both were naive about what marriage entailed, and she was the one who made the decision to leave. And part of me is glad that she did."

"Really?"

"Yes. Even though Oliver doesn't have his mom in his life, I would go through all the shit with my ex ten times over as long as it meant I get to have you on the other side of it—as long as he gets to have you too—because you have been more of a mother to him than his biological one, and that's what he deserves. And one day, you'll be the wife I know I deserve too. And I want to be the husband you deserve in your life, Amelia. I want to build a family with you. The entire path I've been on was the one that I had to travel on to get to you."

"So why are you telling me this now?" I ask as my heart pounds, his words blowing up that balloon of hope in my chest with each passing second.

"Because I'm scared, but I'm ready to work past it." He reaches into his pocket and pulls out one of the pamphlets I left in his office back when we were fighting. But it's not just any pamphlet; it's the one I signed for 20 percent off a therapy session with me. "I'd like to schedule an appointment with you. I think I need to process my divorce so I can move on."

His gesture has me smiling and tears moving down my cheeks. "You're willing to attend therapy?"

"I am. I'm tired of living in the past. I want a future, and I want it with you. But I'm scared, Amelia."

"What are you scared of?"

"I'm scared of getting things wrong with you, that you and I'll end up like my first marriage did. If we ever divorced, it would destroy me."

"I'm scared too," I reply honestly. But this time, I offer him some of my wisdom as I see his walls start to crumble. "You see, that's what you're overlooking though. The fact that we're both scared of getting things wrong is what will ensure we get things right, Ethan. That means we're both invested in fighting for each other every day, through the highs and the lows. That means taking our vows seriously. But I want to be clear about something…"

"What?"

I reach out and cup his jaw. "I never said we had to get married right now. I just wanted to know that it was a possibility, that somewhere down the line, I would get to be Mrs. Ethan Fuller."

His smile is instant. "Damn, I sure like the sound of that."

"Me too."

But then he releases my hand and reaches for the plastic bag on the chair behind him as a wave of relief rolls through me.

This man. He's breaking down his walls and striving to be a better person for his son, me, and himself. What more could I ask for? And why on earth have I been fighting our connection this entire time instead of reassuring him of it?

Because most men need to come to realizations on their own before they can accept something—and it seems to me that Ethan is coming to terms with what he really wants.

"I bought you something." He takes three garden gnomes out of the bag and places them on the bed in front of us—a man that looks like him, a woman that looks like me, and a little boy that looks just like Oliver.

"Why do you have those?"

"I bought you new ones. I kind of broke the other ones."

"You broke my gnomes?"

He winces. "I kind of threw them against the concrete after Nick told me I couldn't come see you…"

"So you broke my gnomes?" I ask in clarification with a smirk on my lips.

"Look, I'm not proud of it, okay? But fuck, I bought you new ones. Call it a peace offering, a way for us to start over again, but this time all three of us will be together."

"What are you saying, Ethan?"

"Sunshine and Grumpy belong together," he says, gesturing to the gnomes. "I realized you're my second chance, and all I want is the chance to love you forever. I can't control what happens later down the road, but I can do everything in my power to show you what you mean to me—and to Oliver."

Tears stream down my face.

"I promise to choose you, show you every day how much you have changed my life, how you made my world feel hopeful again instead of a place where I swore never to love again, even though I didn't stand a chance the moment I saw you. And the way you love my son?" He shakes his head as a tear of his own falls. "There's nothing more I could have asked for in the woman that I want to let in, the one I want to take the risk with. I want to build a life with you, a marriage with you that others want, and I want to have more babies with you. You're the only person I can see myself doing that with. No one else. So, what do you say? Will you let me love you? Will you be a family with me and Oliver?"

I can barely make out Ethan's face because my eyes are so

clouded with moisture. And before I can reply, the door to my room opens.

Noelle pokes her head in through the crack. "If you don't say yes to that, we can no longer be friends. That speech is romance novel gold, my friend, and you're hearing it from a real-life man! Kiss him already!"

Ethan and I both break out in laughter as she shuts the door, and he turns back to me. "What do you say, baby? Are you willing to take the risk? To take a chance on me?"

I pull on his arm so he stands and hovers over me since I can't really move toward him. "You were always worth the risk, Ethan. You and Oliver. I was just waiting for you to realize it."

He stares down at me, framing my face with his hands. "I love you, Amelia. So fucking much."

"I love you too. So, yes. Let's do it."

Ethan's entire body relaxes as he leans forward and kisses me. And as our lips touch, so much pain I've been carrying around melts away. There's still an ache in my arm and in my ribs, and the sting of the scratches on my face. But that ache in my heart? It's instantly gone, and now I know my future is standing right before me—and there's no other man I'd want to share it with.

Ethan is my person, and finding him feels like finding a treasure, the kind that garden gnomes protect from thieves.

But the only thieves left are the two boys who stole my heart, and now I'll never let them go.

Chapter 20

Amelia

Two-and-a-half months later

"Do you need any more help, babe?" Ethan comes up behind me as I finish squeezing sour cream across potato skins to make them look like footballs, wrapping his arms around my waist and burying his face in my hair.

"No, I think I've got it."

He breathes in deeply before mumbling in my ear. "God, I love how you always smell like lemons. And you look so hot in this little apron, especially since my team's logo is splayed across your tits."

"Well, maybe later I'll wear nothing but this after the game, and we can check that fantasy off your list."

"Sounds like a plan."

"Dear God, please don't say that shit with other people in your house," my brother Nick whines as he walks into the kitchen to get another beer.

"I do believe it was your meddling and suggestion that helped us get to this blissful state, big brother, so you have no one to blame but yourself," I toss over my shoulder at him.

"You're right. But I still don't like hearing about it."

"Then go back into the living room."

He holds up his beer as he closes the refrigerator door. "On my way."

It's Super Bowl Sunday, and even though the Dallas Cowboys aren't in the running, Ethan and I decided to have everyone over for a party at my house, which will soon be our house. Ethan is in the process of selling the home he purchased for him and Oliver with the assistance of my brother, and we've been slowly moving things over in the meantime. A lot has changed since Ethan came to the hospital after my accident but in all the best ways.

When Ethan brought up the idea of us living together, I was against it at first. I didn't want him to suggest something so pivotal in our relationship so soon just to prove to me that he'd changed his mind about our future.

"That's not what this is about, Amelia. Sure, I want you to accept that I meant what I said about building a life with you. But ultimately, my reasons for us living together are about moving forward and knowing that you're safe and we're together as much as we can be. Almost losing you was one of the scariest fucking things I've ever experienced, so I want each and every day of our future to start with you next to me when the sun rises and right beside me as we drift off to sleep."

With a declaration like that, it was hard to argue with him, and we talked about multiple details pertaining to the move before beginning the process. And much to Oliver's delight, it only made sense to live at my house because I had the pool.

Other than that, the past two-and-a-half months have been both blissful and challenging. My scarred man has made leaps and bounds where our relationship is concerned. Ethan has been seeing a therapist I recommended to him once a week since, obviously, we have a personal relationship, which would be a conflict of interest if he actually cashed in on the coupon I gave him. But I'm just proud of him for wanting to move forward in this way.

He's been processing the fear and doubt his marriage evoked in him and also working on how to combat that fear with me as it arises. We've had our fair share of arguments and challenges as his overbearing behavior after my accident got to be too much. He still has trouble communicating his frustrations and feelings when we disagree. But no human is perfect, so why is it that we demand that of our loved ones sometimes?

No matter what we battle, though, I know that fighting through it with him is worth it.

And that's the truth. I am hopelessly in love with this man. Not because he's perfect, not because he's without fault and stubborn and impatient at times. No. I love him because he loves with his whole heart, he's fiercely protective of his son and me, and he is willing to better himself to be the man I deserve.

We should never expect someone to change for us, but if someone is willing to change for themselves and it allows us room in their lives, that's a rare action that should be valued.

And Ethan has shown me that growth in him more than I could have ever imagined.

For me, though, nothing makes me happier than the idea of being in the same home as my boys—two men that have completely changed my life. And with each passing day, I'm stepping deeper into the role of a motherly figure for Oliver, something that has come with its own challenges as well, especially as I was healing from the accident. But it's also come with so much love I feel like my heart is gonna burst multiple times throughout the day.

"Let me finish these for you. Your hand has to be killing you. And I need you to save your strength for later." Ethan takes the bag of sour cream from my hand while bouncing his eyebrows, pulling me back to the present, and squeezing the remaining white substance on the last two potato skins as I move out of his way.

My cast is finally off my left arm, which hasn't inhibited me too much since I'm right-handed. But not having another hand to use for months definitely made some tasks harder than others. However, two-and-a-half months later, I'm finally starting to feel normal again, but physical therapy is on the horizon to get my entire strength back so I can eventually do the things I did before, like pole dancing. God, I've missed those classes.

Noelle comes over at that moment and grabs a carrot from the veggie tray, dips it in ranch, and pops it in her mouth. "Might want to lower your voice with the dirty talk, Ethan."

Ethan stands up straight and looks her dead in the eye. "I have no shame in anyone knowing how much I love and want this woman. And if you guys can't handle it, then don't listen."

And then Noelle shakes her head at him. "At least someone is getting laid." She crunches down on the orange stick. "And why is it that two of my best friends can find men that teeter that line of asshole and softy, but I couldn't?"

"I thought you swore off men?" Ethan counters as he takes one of the potato skins off the plate and inhales half of it.

"Well, while I'm trying to get pregnant, I kind of have to."

"Who's getting pregnant?" Jeffrey walks up to us, holding a beer.

"Me," Noelle answers. "First implantation starts next month. Fingers crossed it takes, and I'll have a baby before Christmas."

"If you have a baby on Christmas Eve, we will share a birthday!" Oliver shouts as he runs past us and down the hall. Noelle giggles at him.

Jeffrey's eyes bug out of his head. "Implantation? Like with a turkey baster?" He gestures squeezing the bulb on such a device with his free hand. "What's wrong with the good old-fashioned way? Or is that out of style now?" He looks between the three of us. "Have I been out of the game for so long that people aren't even having sex anymore to make babies?" he asks, panicked.

Damien walks up behind him and smacks him on the back of the head. "Jesus, Jeffrey. This is why you don't get invited places."

Noelle chuckles, and Jeffrey rubs the spot on his skull that just took a beating. "It's okay. Sort of. I'm choosing to have a child via sperm donor, so no actual sex will be taking place, sadly."

Jeffrey frowns. "Well, damn. It sounds to me like you just took the fun out of the baby-making process."

"Yeah, it's so fun trying to find a man who is normal, good in bed, isn't afraid of commitment, and wants children right away." Noelle rolls her eyes. "I'm tired of that nonsense."

"Well, I will gladly step in and volunteer as tribute," Jeffrey says, holding his hand in the air. "I can make this guy down here go from six to noon in a heartbeat." He points to his crotch.

Damien smacks his head again. "What is with you, man?"

"Jesus, will you stop doing that?"

Noelle reaches over and places her hand on Jeffrey's shoulder. "I appreciate the offer, Jeffrey, but I found the father of my child, and I didn't even have to endure a date from hell to get his swimmers." With a smirk, she grabs a potato skin and walks off.

"You can't just go up to people talking about your dick, man," Damien chastises Jeffrey as Ethan and I watch, his arms back around my waist as he pulls me into his chest.

"Noelle's the one who brought up sperm," he counters. "But don't worry, I won't whip it out or anything, even though it's been a while since the little guy has seen any action."

"Perhaps the problem is that you're referring to him as 'the little guy,'" Ethan mutters from behind me, making us laugh.

"My dick is not little, okay? He's average, more than enough to get the job done."

"What ever happened with that girl from the *Los Angeles Times* dinner, the hostess you were flirting with?" Ethan asks.

"We went out a couple of times. It was nice. I swear, I never knew that being a creator of an advertisement for period products would help me with the ladies, but it didn't go very far."

"You didn't…you know…get any action with her?" Ethan asks while rubbing my hip with his finger, making my body heat up.

Jeffrey drops his head, rubbing the back of his neck. "Nope. When we went out, I told her I wanted to take things slow, but she just wanted in my pants." He holds his hands up in defense again. "And I know, I'm here complaining about not getting any action, but in all honesty, I'm looking for a connection too. I don't want to just sleep with a bunch of women. I want what you guys have," he says, gesturing to Ethan and me and Damien just as Charlotte walks up.

"Jeffrey, you're a good guy, honey," Charlotte says, wrapping her arm around his shoulder. "You'll find the right woman for you. Just be patient. But honestly, none of us were looking for the other person when it happened. Hell, I never thought in a million years I'd be engaged to Damien at this point in my life."

"Yeah, stop looking for the person. I've heard that before. But that's easy for you to say. You're in love. You snagged this guy right here, and now you're happy. You're so far past the point of remembering what it's like to be single that your perception of the dating world is fuzzy."

"It was more like I snagged her, but whatever." Damien reaches over and hauls Charlotte into his chest, kissing her lips and then bringing her hand where her engagement ring lies up to his mouth and kissing that finger as well. "But in four months, she's going to be Mrs. Damien Shaw, and I can't fucking wait."

"Me neither, babe," Charlotte replies before they kiss. Nick found them a house they moved into last month, and now it's just the countdown to their wedding.

Jeffrey rolls his eyes before draining the rest of his beer and walking toward the fridge. "I need another drink if I have to endure all the happy couples for the rest of the afternoon."

Suddenly the door slams open, and Penelope appears with two bottles of champagne held high up in the air. "The party is here, bitches!"

"Aunt Penelope, you said a bad word!" Oliver rushes over to her.

Penelope drops her arms and looks down at him. "You're right. I'm sorry, Ollie. But one day, when you're an adult, you'll understand why we say bad words all the time."

"Why?"

"Because life fucking sucks." She winks at him and then heads toward us in the kitchen. "I brought the champagne, ladies."

Charlotte claps her hands. "Good thinking. We didn't get to have brunch this morning because someone was too busy preparing for a Super Bowl party," she says with a side glance in my direction.

Ethan releases me as I move toward the cupboard to fetch champagne glasses. "Hey, this was Ethan's idea, so if you want to blame anyone, blame him."

"I'll take the blame," he says, kissing me on the cheek. "Besides, that just means I got to enjoy her this morning instead of her running out the door to meet you girls."

"That'd better mean you got laid, Amelia," Penelope interjects. "Otherwise, that's just a waste of a Sunday morning without brunch."

"Don't worry. Ethan made sure staying home was worth it." I smirk in his direction as he grabs a beer and the boys head toward the couch.

"So, how are things going? Are he and Oliver officially moved in yet?" Charlotte asks once Ethan is on the couch, just as Noelle comes into the kitchen from the bathroom.

"Almost. Next weekend should be the last move with a bunch of little stuff. Oliver's room is already set up, Ethan donated a bunch of their furniture since most of my stuff was newer and was already here anyway, and they've pretty much been sleeping here for the past week, so I'd say everything is almost official."

"We're so happy for you, Amelia." Noelle gestures to Charlotte and Penelope, who nod their heads.

"Thank you. I'm insanely happy."

"Good. And if he ever messes up again, just let me know. I can deliver three hundred tubes of hemorrhoid cream to his office with the click of a button," Penelope declares just as her cell phone rings. "Jesus, why on earth is my boss calling me on a Sunday like this?"

"Does he not usually call on Sundays?" I ask.

"Every once in a while because PR never stops, you know? But this is like the fifth time he's called."

"Should you call him back then?"

"Ugh, I really don't want to think about work right now. I just wanted to get champagne drunk with my girls and watch hot men run around in tight pants," she groans. "But I'd better see what he wants before I get too drunk to have a normal conversation with him."

Noelle chimes in. "Do you even know how to have a normal conversation?"

"Hardy, har har." Penelope grabs a potato skin and then saunters off toward the stairs to go somewhere quieter.

"Amelia." Oliver runs up to me, pulling on my apron.

"Yes, buddy?"

"Can I have sour gummy worms now?"

I gesture to the charcuterie board that we made earlier together, complete with sour gummy worms, of course. But I made Oliver wait until the party started before he was allowed to eat any. Okay, maybe I let him have one earlier. "Just a few. But you'd better have a carrot afterward."

"Okay." He hugs my legs. "Thanks for letting Daddy and me come live with you and having this party. I love you," he says, and then he runs off.

Charlotte and Noelle both look at me as I watch him grab three sour gummy worms and a carrot.

"Yup. I totally get it. I'd fall in love with him too," Noelle says, sniffling. "This is why I don't want to wait to have kids, you guys."

"I know. And don't get me wrong, he is still a kid. He has breakdowns and argues with us, but then he says something like that, and you just can't help but melt. This week I get to help him make Valentine's Day cards for his entire class, and I'm legitimately looking forward to it. I've been on Pinterest for weeks looking at ideas. Six months ago, this was all a dream; this thought about the future that I hoped one day would come true. And now it has, albeit, in an unorthodox way. But it's seriously the best. I get to be a mom…" I trail off in a whisper as I fight tears from forming.

"Yes, you do. Seems as though your life has changed quite a bit, but in a good way," Charlotte says on a smile and then turns to Noelle. "Are you crying?" Charlotte asks her as she sniffles again and wipes under her eye.

"It's the damn hormones, Charlotte. We've been through this. You girls are just going to have to get used to mood swings from me until I have this baby." She grabs a potato skin and walks into the living room, where the men are already yelling at the television.

"I love her, but we might have to give her a tranquilizer at some point," Charlotte mutters just as the boys shout at the television. I pour three glasses of champagne since Noelle isn't drinking alcohol at the moment and then make my way into the living room with Charlotte so we can watch the game.

A few minutes later, Penelope returns to the room after grabbing the glass of champagne that I left on the kitchen counter for her.

"Damn! Come on, Kansas City!" Ethan shouts. "This game better not be like this the entire time."

"Like it would be any different if Dallas were playing," Nick mutters under his breath.

"You're just pissed that New Orleans didn't make it so you could drool at Maddox Taylor on the screen the entire time."

Nick puts a finger in the air. "As a heterosexual man in a very loving relationship, I have no problem admitting that Maddox Taylor is a fine male specimen. But didn't you hear? Maddox's contract is up this year, and rumor is that New Orleans is gonna let him go."

"What?" Damien, Ethan, and Jeffrey all turn their heads in Nick's direction.

"Yeah. Don't you guys keep up with this shit?"

They all give Nick a deadpan gaze.

"No, man. Sorry, I'm not reading the gossip magazines. I've been kinda busy," Ethan mutters as Nick shakes his head.

"And you call yourself a football fan."

A commotion rings out from the television, pulling everyone's heads back to the game.

"Touchdown!" Oliver shouts before breaking into his victory dance.

And everyone laughs as the boys take turns showing off their best touchdown celebrations.

It's so normal, so us. My friends, my family—and I can't believe this is my life now.

Four months later

"Shit. Hold on!" My phone is vibrating across my desk, and I know it's Ethan, but I just don't have time to stop and pick up his call. I'm already running late to pick up Oliver from Ethan's mom, and then we're supposed to be taking him to the circus tonight. He's been talking about it all week.

Oliver has been on summer vacation for a few weeks now, so he's been with Lisa during the day while Ethan and I are working. It's a Friday night, though, so we always try to plan something fun for the three of us to do together after a long week of work, and the activity this week was chosen once we saw an advertisement that the circus would be in town. I'm sure if Charlotte and Damien weren't on their honeymoon right now, they'd be joining us.

My best friend and her fiancé got married last weekend at a beautiful hotel in Dana Point, The Waldorf Astoria Monarch Beach Resort & Club. It was an elegant black-tie affair that was everything a fairytale wedding should be, courtesy of Charlotte's parents' bank account.

Charlotte and her mother have made considerable strides to reconcile their relationship, but I can't help but think that offering to pay for an extravagant wedding was a way for her mother to try to apologize even further. Things aren't perfect there, but they're improving. But nonetheless, one of my best friends married the man she never thought she would at sunset with the ocean in the background last weekend, and it was stunning, beautiful, and perfect.

A reminder that love can conquer all.

Except for a nagging boyfriend who knows that I'm probably trying to leave my office at this moment and that's why I can't answer the phone. He was in court all day, so I know he's probably on a tight timeline right now as well.

The phone stops making noise, allowing me to breathe out a sigh of relief as I tuck my last client file into my cabinet, grab my computer bag and purse, and then push through my office door, locking it from the outside before I trot to my car.

Once inside, I buckle up, pull out of the parking lot, and then connect my Bluetooth to call Ethan back.

"Hey. Where are you?" he asks as I come up to a red light.

"I'm on my way. I was trying to leave when you called so I couldn't pick up."

"Well, there's been a change of plans."

My head rears back. "What? Why?"

"I need you to come home instead."

"Ethan? I thought we were going to the circus…" The light turns green, so I continue going straight, mentally making a note not to turn up ahead toward Ethan's mom's house anymore.

"We were never going to the circus with Oliver tonight."

Disappointment makes my chest cave in. "Why?"

"Because I have other plans for us."

"Where are we going?"

"Just get your ass home, Amelia. You'll see soon enough." He hangs up, leaving me confused and intrigued.

"What the heck?" I mutter as I take a deep breath and wonder what on earth Ethan has up his sleeve. I wanted to go to the circus, damn it, and now I feel deflated and irritated. If he had never planned on going there tonight, why did he make such a big deal about it with Oliver?

By the time I pull into the driveway of our house, I'm ready to give the man a piece of my mind. It's been a long week after an even longer weekend, and I wanted some quality family time with just the three of us.

But once I open the door and look inside our living room, my jaw drops open, and I almost drop my bags on the floor.

Orchids of every color fill the room, covering every surface, including the carpet and tile. My eyes are so overwhelmed by the array of colors and the massive amount of flowers in our home that I barely register Ethan coming down the stairs, pulling my attention in his direction.

"What is this?" I ask as I gently set my bags on the tile floor of the entryway. He lands on the bottom step and walks toward me, dressed in a white button-down that's rolled up to his elbows and plain black slacks. His hair is styled, and his jaw has that day-old scruff that I love to run my fingernails through.

"This is what three hundred orchids look like."

"Three hundred?" I gasp. "Why on earth would you order this many?"

He takes my hand and rubs the top of it with his thumb. "Because once upon a time, someone ordered three hundred of something and had them delivered to my office. And back then, I had every intention of retaliating in some way. But then, I fell in love with you, so I knew I'd have to save my three hundred of something for a moment that was much grander than that."

"Wow."

Chuckling, Ethan leans in and plants a kiss on my lips. "Do you know what today is?"

Searching my mind for the significance of today has me puzzled and looking at him for answers. "I honestly don't know."

Shaking his head at me in disappointment, he smirks. "Damn. I thought for sure you'd remember."

"I'm sorry. I'm just a little overwhelmed right now. Where is Oliver?"

"Staying with my mom for the evening and the next seven days, actually."

"What?"

"After we talk, we're going on a vacation to celebrate."

"Celebrate what?" I ask. "I wanted to go to the circus."

Ethan laughs. "Come here, babe." He takes me by the hand and leads me over to the couch, the only surface in our home not covered with orchids. We both take a seat as he still holds my hand. "Today is the first day we met last year."

Like a flash of a movie scene, the vision of running into him at the complex right before I left for Hawaii comes back to me with full force. "Oh my God, is it really?"

He nods. "Yes. It was also the day my life changed forever because you came into it."

"I mean, I see where you're going with this, but we didn't start off on the greatest foot there, Ethan."

He smiles. "I know. But even on that day, I recognized how beautiful you are, the underlying passion you possessed, and little did I know it wouldn't take very long for me to fall in love with every part of you once I got to know you." He takes a deep breath and then stands from the couch, dropping to one knee in front of me.

And I swear all of the air in my lungs freezes. "Oh my God."

"Amelia…I know there was a time when I never thought I'd do this again. And I was hell-bent on keeping that promise to myself. But then you came into my life and Oliver's and changed everything I thought I wanted for our future. And luckily, it didn't take long for me to realize that my marriage to you would be nothing like my first marriage. Because being married to you would mean I'd have an actual partner in my life—someone who wants my son and me, someone who pushes me to be the man I know you deserve, someone who never realized that sunshine in the form of a person truly can brighten your darkest days."

Tears begin to stream down my face.

"I told you right after your accident that I would do everything in my power to prove to you that you are who I wanted, that you are the person I'm meant to be with, that I would love you unconditionally, and that I want to build a future with you, Amelia—no one else. Well, baby, I think it's time we take the next step and make it official." He reaches into his pocket and pulls out a yellow diamond on a platinum gold band, shimmering as the sunlight hits it and stealing my breath. "Amelia St. Clair, will you marry me? Will you be my wife and Oliver's mother for the rest of our lives? Will you adopt my son and continue to love him like your own? And will you let us love you through all the ups and downs and continue to push me to be the man you chose several months ago and for the rest of your life?"

"Yes." I nod, unable to say much more because I'm thoroughly shocked. I knew that Ethan meant what he said about getting to this point someday, but I just never expected it to be now.

Staring down at the ring he just placed on my finger, I lift my eyes back up to him. "I don't even know what to say."

"I hope I said everything you needed to hear," he replies, tears building in his eyes.

I reach forward and cup the sides of his face. "All I need is you, Ethan. No one else. By continuing to show up, stand up, and be here for me every day. That's all I've ever wanted."

"I love you so fucking much, Amelia," he mutters as a tear rolls down his cheek, and then we both lean forward at the same time, so our lips meet.

And as I breathe in the scent of orchids and the man in front of me, my entire future comes together. Falling for this man was a risk I wasn't sure I should take, but there was no stopping my heart from jumping in with both feet, from pulling me toward him even when I was fighting it. And now I know that the chance we took—the chance we took to find love with someone we were least expecting —was a risk that paid off for us both.

And now we get to reap the rewards and love for the rest of our lives.

THE END

Thank you for reading Amelia and Ethan's story! And if you're interested in a sneak peek into Amelia and Ethan's future, read the extended epilogue here.

BUT WAIT!

I think we need one more brunch scene to see where our ladies will lead us next 😉

One Week Later

"Where is she?" Noelle glances at her phone for the hundredth time since we sat down for brunch this Sunday morning.

Ethan and I got home from Cabo yesterday afternoon, and even though I'm tired, I was eager to see the girls after my vacation celebrating our engagement.

Charlotte was also eager to see us since she and Damien returned from their honeymoon just a few days before Ethan and I got home. It's been weeks since the four of us have been together, but one leg of our group is late—and not just a few minutes late, almost an hour with no response to any of our calls or text messages.

Noelle rubs her belly as her eyelids droop closed. "Good thing we didn't wait for her to order food; otherwise, I'd probably be passed out from starvation right now." She covers up her mouth as she yawns. "And if she doesn't hurry up, I'm going to pass out at the table from my food coma."

After a failed round of insemination, Noelle saw two pink lines on her second try and is expecting a baby in early January. She's only two months along, but pretty soon, you'll definitely know she's growing a human. Lucky for us, we get to live vicariously through her experience with the many conversations surrounding pregnancy side effects in the first trimester. Pregnancy just sounds like such a pleasant experience.

Did you sense the sarcasm there?

Charlotte darts her eyes between Noelle and me. "You guys, I'm genuinely worried. It's not like Penelope to not answer her phone. I mean, I know it's a Sunday, but she never misses brunch."

"I agree. I don't want to think the worst, but perhaps we should get the authorities involved. Has it been more than twenty-four hours since anyone has spoken to her?" I ask as I look between my friends.

Noelle shakes her head. "No. She and I texted a few times last night. So we'd have to wait until…" She checks her text message thread with Penelope. "At least seven tonight to file a missing person's report."

Charlotte shakes her head. "She'd better have a good reason for standing us up though. You know she'd be the first to say something if any of us weren't here."

Just as Charlotte finishes her thought, Penelope comes bursting through the door of Frankie's, her hair and eyes wild, her face contorted with anger. Wearing a barely-there purple dress and heels, that clearly had to be her outfit from the night before, she stomps across the restaurant toward us and plops herself down into her seat, seething.

"Uh, hello? Where have you been?" Noelle asks, clearly not taking in Penelope's demeanor correctly. And even though I feel I should correct her, I kind of want to hear Penelope's answer.

"I'm going to kill him," Penelope grates out.

"Who?" Charlotte asks.

"Maddox Taylor."

All of us shoot wide-eyed looks in Penelope's direction.

"I'm sorry?" I ask. "Did you just say, Maddox Taylor? The football player?"

Penelope takes a deep breath through her nose and blows it out of her mouth harshly. "Yup."

"And why are we planning to murder Maddox Taylor?" Charlotte interrogates further. "I mean, I'm all for trying to get away with murder. I've actually always wondered if I could get away with it. I think I could, that I'm smart enough. I've watched enough murder documentaries and listened to one too many murder podcasts…but my hair is always getting everywhere, girls. Even Damien complains about it…"

Noelle cuts her off. "Jesus, Charlotte. Let her speak." She turns to Penelope. "Honey, what's going on? Don't get me wrong, I'm glad you're okay and that we don't have to file a missing person's report for you anymore. But why on earth are you pissed off at Maddox Taylor?"

She reaches into her purse and pulls out a pair of handcuffs, slapping them on the table, the loud clash of metal hitting the surface, drawing the attention of people around us.

"Did you get arrested?" Noelle asks.

Charlotte rolls her eyes. "Jesus, Noelle. Really? Do you think if she got arrested, they would have let her go and taken the handcuffs with her?"

Noelle scoffs. "Jeez. Sorry. Pregnancy brain is a real thing, all right?"

I decide this is the appropriate time to chime in. "Penelope, why do you have handcuffs in your purse, and what does this have to do with Maddox Taylor?"

She huffs, crossing her arms over her chest. "Because that dickhead fucked me within an inch of my life last night and several times all week, then handcuffed me to his bed this morning and left me there as a punishment."

All of our mouths drop open.

"He handcuffed you to the bed? And just left you there? How did you get out?" I ask, thoroughly interested. I mean, doesn't everybody contemplate what they would do in such a situation at least once in their life?

Wait? Is it just me that's thought that?

Ugh. Never mind.

She shakes her head, popping her tongue against her cheek. "His cleaning lady came in and found me butt-ass naked on his bed. The keys were right on the nightstand, so she was able to unlock me, but not before she saw my snatch."

And now we all laugh under our breaths.

"Jesus, Penelope. What are you going to do now? And you and Maddox Taylor? When the hell did this happen?"

She reaches for her mimosa and drains half of it before replying. "Buckle up for one hell of a story, ladies, especially because this one is just getting started."

To Be Continued....

Penelope and Maddox's story will be told this Fall and you can pre-order/read here!

And don't forget to grab Amelia and Ethan's bonus epilogue here!

Acknowledgments

Another book in the series is complete, and right now, I am inching my way closer to finishing Penelope's story, who I know everyone is excited for.

A book about marriage and the ups and downs it can bring was fulfilling to write in so many ways. It allowed me to look at my own relationship with my husband, those marriages I watch from afar, and think about what would life be like without the man I chose. I know marriage isn't for everyone, but with the right person—someone who is willing to foster that growing relationship day in and out—it can be a beautiful thing.

These women have been so fun to write, and my hope is that through this series, every reader can find of hint of themselves in one of them and their stories.

I saw a Tik Tok the other day where a woman was comparing being female to being mother nature—an ever-evolving, changing, living entity—and it hit home for me.

We *are* constantly changing, constantly growing, and the roller coaster of emotions we experience on a daily basis is something a man will never understand.

So like Amelia said in this book, thank God for champagne and good friends, because I don't know how else we would survive!

I truly am loving this series and writing it, and I hope to entertain and make you proud while I do it.

Amelia and Ethan were a rollercoaster couple, but their story isn't over. You'll get more of them in the next two books in the series. And if you haven't already, make sure to download that extended epilogue to give yourself a little sneak peek into their future.

To my husband: Thank you for cheering me on and celebrating my success with me as I release each book. Thank you for understanding how much joy this hobby brings me. And thank you for being my real life book husband and giving me my own true love story to brag about.

To Liz: You are my right-hand woman. Thank you for answering every phone call when I get excited about a new idea. Thank you for cheering me on and listening to me vent. I couldn't do this without you. Who would have thought we'd be plotting 17 books and counting when this started?

To Jeanine: It has been a pleasure working with you as the editor on this book, and your reaction to it was amazing. Thank you for your dedication to my stories.

To Melanie: As always, your expertise and friendship had made this author journey even more rewarding. I'm so grateful for our connection and honest discussions about this author gig. So thankful to have you in my corner.

And to my beta readers, ARC readers, and every reader (both old and new): Thank you for taking a chance on a self-published author. Thank you for sharing my books with others. Thank you for allowing me to share my creativity with people who love the romance genre as much as I do.

And thank you for supporting a wife and mom who found a hobby that she loves.

About the Author

Harlow James is a wife and mom who fell in love with romance novels, so she decided to write her own.

Her books are the perfect blend of emotional, addictive, and steamy romance. If you love stories with a guaranteed Happily Ever After, then Harlow is your new best friend.

When she's not writing, she can be found working her day job, reading every romance novel she can find time for, laughing with her husband and kids, watching re-runs of FRIENDS, and spending time cooking for her friends and family while drinking White Claws and Margaritas.

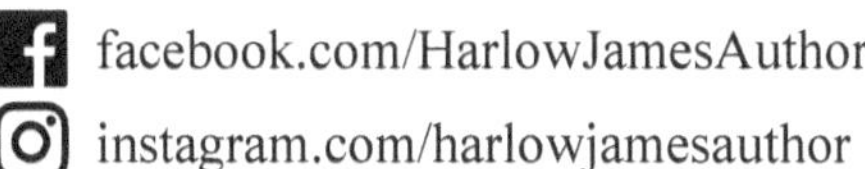

facebook.com/HarlowJamesAuthor

instagram.com/harlowjamesauthor

More Books by Harlow James

One Look, A Baseball Romance Standalone

Guilty as Charged

An intense enemies to lovers standalone that will melt your kindle.

McKenzie's Turn to Fall

A holiday romance where a romance author falls for her neighborhood butcher.

The Emerson Falls Series

Tangled (Kane & Olivia)

Enticed (Cooper & Clara)

Captivated (Cash and Piper)

Revived (Luke and Rachel)

Devoted (Brooks and Jess)

The California Billionaires Series

My Unexpected Serenity (Wes and Shayla)

My Unexpected Vow (Hayes and Waverly)

My Unexpected Family (Silas and Chloe)

Lost and Found in Copper Ridge

A holiday romance in which two people book a stay in a cabin for the same amount of time thanks to a serendipitous $5 bill

<u>The Ladies Who Brunch</u>

<u>Never Say Never (Charlotte and Damien)</u>

<u>No One Else (Amelia and Ethan)</u>

<u>Now's The Time (Penelope and Maddox)</u>